PUFFIN BOOKS

UNCLES, AUNTS AND ELEPHANTS

Born in Kasauli (Himachal Pradesh) in 1934, Ruskin Bond grew up in Jamnagar (Gujarat), Dehradun, New Delhi and Simla.

His first novel, *The Room on the Roof*, written when he was seventeen, received the John Llewellyn Rhys Memorial Prize in 1957. Since then he has written over five hundred short stories, essays and novellas (some included in the collections *Dust on the Mountains* and *Classic Ruskin Bond*) and more than forty books for children. He received the Sahitya Akademi Award for English writing in India in 1993, the Padma Shri in 1999, and the Delhi government's Lifetime Achievement Award in 2012. He was awarded the Sahitya Akademi's Bal Sahitya Puraskar for his 'total contribution to children's literature' in 2013 and honoured with the Padma Bhushan in 2014.

Ruskin Bond lives in Landour, Mussoorie, with his extended family.

Also in Puffin by Ruskin Bond

Tales from
your Favourite
Storyteller

RUSKIN BOND

Uncles, Aunts & Elephants

ILLUSTRATIONS BY
ARCHANA SREENIVASAN

PUFFIN BOOKS

PUFFIN BOOKS
Published by the Penguin Group
Penguin Books India Pvt. Ltd, 7th Floor, Infinity Tower C, DLF Cyber City,
Gurgaon 122 002, Haryana, India
Penguin Group (USA) Inc., 375 Hudson Street, New York, New York 10014, USA
Penguin Group (Canada), 90 Eglinton Avenue East, Suite 700, Toronto,
Ontario, M4P 2Y3, Canada
Penguin Books Ltd, 80 Strand, London WC2R 0RL, England
Penguin Ireland, 25 St Stephen's Green, Dublin 2, Ireland (a division of
Penguin Books Ltd)
Penguin Group (Australia), 707 Collins Street, Melbourne, Victoria 3008, Australia
Penguin Group (NZ), 67 Apollo Drive, Rosedale, Auckland 0632, New Zealand
Penguin Books (South Africa) (Pty) Ltd, Block D, Rosebank Office Park,
181 Jan Smuts Avenue, Parktown North, Johannesburg 2193, South Africa

Penguin Books Ltd, Registered Offices: 80 Strand, London WC2R 0RL, England

First published in Puffin by Penguin Books India 2014

ISBN 9780143332626

Typeset in Cochin by R. Ajith Kumar, New Delhi
Printed at Thomson Press India Ltd, New Delhi

A PENGUIN RANDOM HOUSE COMPANY

Contents

Contents

Contents

Foreword

Since my first Puffin Treasury came out, five years ago, there has been a steady flow of tales to tell. The desk near my window is overflowing with notebooks and manuscripts. My cat ('Fat Cat') does her utmost to knock everything to the ground, but I am a patient soul and I do my best to restore order where confusion reigns. Uncle Ken keeps popping up with new escapades; Mr Oliver endeavours to control a bunch of high-spirited students; talking parrots and playful elephants take the stage; I make friends with a mouse (Fat Cat would disapprove); recall the scenes of my childhood; and look out of my window at the mountains striding away into the distance and know that more friends and memories will come my way.

My thanks to Mimi Basu, a kind Puffin editor, who has done all the hard work in making this selection. I have written over fifty books for the Penguin and Puffin list, so she had a busy time choosing stories that would please our readers.

And to make Fat Cat happy, there is a cat poem too.

Ruskin Bond
At my window
Landour, 12 March 2014

Fiction

Flip Flap

A Little Friend

When I first arrived in London I knew no one. I was eighteen and on my own, looking for a room, looking for a job. I spent a week in a students' hostel, a noisy place full of foreign students talking in every tongue except English. Then I saw an ad for a room to let, for just a pound a week. I was on the dole, getting just three pounds a week, so I took the room without even looking at it.

It turned out to be a tiny attic at the top of the building. Nothing above me but a low ceiling and a slanting tiled roof. There was a bed, a small dressing table, and a gas fire in the corner of the room. You had to shove several pennies into a slot before you could light the fire. It was November, very cold, and I kept running out of pennies. The toilet was about two floors below me. Above the potty was a notice which said 'Do not throw your tea leaves in here.' As I did not have anything to cook on, I had no tea leaves to deposit in the loo. I supposed that the other tenants (whom I rarely saw) were given to flushing away their tea leaves.

My landlady was Jewish, and I did not see much of her either, except when the rent was due. She was a Polish refugee, and I think she'd had a hard time in Europe during the War. It was seldom that she emerged from her room.

There was no bath in the building. I had to use the public baths some way down Belsize Road. I took my meals, the cheapest I could get, at a snack bar near the underground station. Some evenings I would bring home a loaf of bread and a tin of sardines; *this* was luxury.

Was I lonely? You can bet I was . . . terribly lonely. I had no friends in that great city. Even the city looked lonely, all grey and fogbound. Every day I visited the employment exchange, and after two weeks I landed a job as a ledger clerk in a large grocery store. The pay was five pounds a week.

I was rich! For once I could have a proper lunch instead of the usual beans on toast. I bought ham and cheese and celebrated with sandwiches and a bottle of cheap sherry. Soon there were crumbs all over the floor of my room. My landlady wouldn't like that. I was about to get up to sweep them away when there was a squeak and a little mouse ran across the floor with a bit of cheese that it had found. He darted across the room and disappeared behind the dressing table.

I decided not to clear away the crumbs; let the mouse

have them. 'Waste not, want not,' as my grandmother used to say.

I did not see the mouse again, but after I'd put the light out and gone to bed, I could hear him scurrying about the room, collecting titbits. Now and then he emitted a little squeak, possibly of satisfaction.

'Well, at least I did not have to celebrate alone,' I said to myself, 'a mouse for company is better than no company at all.'

I was off to work early next morning, and in my absence the landlady had my room cleaned. I came back to find a note on the dressing table which said: 'Please do not scatter food on the floor.'

She was right, of course. My room-mate deserved better than a scattering of crumbs. So I provided him with an empty soap dish, which I placed near the dressing table, and I filled it with an assortment of biscuit crumbs. But for some reason he wouldn't go near the soap dish. I stayed up quite late, waiting for him to appear, and when he did, he explored all corners of the room and even approached my bed, but stayed well away from the soap dish. Perhaps he didn't like the colour, a bright pink. I've been told by a scientist that mice are colour-blind and wouldn't be able to distinguish a pink soap dish from a blue one. But I think the scientist got it wrong. Quite often, they do.

I couldn't tell if my mouse was a male or a female, but

for some indefinable reason I felt that he was a bachelor, like me. Surely a female mouse would be living with her family. This one was very much a loner.

I threw the soap dish away, and the following evening, on my way home from work, I bought a pretty little saucer, and this I placed near his residence, with a piece of cheese in the middle. He came to it almost instantly, nibbled at the cheese, approved of it, and carried the rest of it back to his hole behind the dressing table.

A fussy mouse! No soap dish for him. He had to have a saucer with a Chinese willow-pattern design.

After some time we become protective of our own. Summer came to London early in May, and finding the room stuffier than usual, I opened the small window that looked out upon a sea of rooftops, all similar to ours and to each other. But I could not leave it open for long. Suddenly I heard an agitated squeak from below my bed, and the mouse scurried across the room to the safety of the dressing table. Looking up, I saw a large tabby cat framed in the open window, looking in with a speculative air. I think he had seen, or sensed, that there was a free lunch in the offing if he was patient enough.

'No free lunches for cats,' I said. I closed the window and kept it shut.

On weekends I roamed the city, occasionally visiting suburban cinemas where the seats were cheap; but on weekdays I'd stay at home in the evenings, working on my novel, my romance of India, and occasionally reading aloud from my manuscript.

The mouse wasn't a very good listener, he was never long in one place, but he was now trusting enough to take a piece of cheese or bread from my fingers, and if I spent too much time on my book, he would remind me of his presence by giving several little squeaks—scolding me for not paying attention to his needs.

Alas, the time came when I had to consider parting from the 'Lone Ranger', as I had come to call my fellow lodger. A slight increase in salary, and a cheque from BBC radio for a couple of stories, meant I could move to bigger and better lodgings in a more congenial area of London. My landlady was sorry to see me go, for, in spite of my untidy ways, I had been regular with the rent. And the little mouse—would he too be sorry to see me go? He would have to forage further afield for his meals. And the next tenant might prefer cats to mice!

This was my worry, not his. Unlike humans, mice don't worry about the future—their own or the world's.

The problem was partly resolved by the arrival of another tenant—not a human tenant, but another mouse, presumably a female, because she was a little smaller and a little prettier than my room-mate. Two or three days before I was to leave, I came home to find them chasing each other about the room with a great deal of squeaking and acrobatic play. Was this romance?

I felt a twinge of envy. My little friend had found a companion, and I was still without one. But when the time came for me to leave, I made sure they were well supplied with an assortment of crackers and rusks — enough to last well over a month, provided our landlady did not find them first.

I packed my battered, old suitcase and left that small attic behind. As we journey through life, old friends and new friends are often left behind, never to be met with again. There are times when we are on our own, lonely, in need of a friendly presence. Just someone to be there when we return to that empty, joyless room. And at such times, even a little mouse, can make a big difference.

Boy Scouts Forever!

I was a Boy Scout once, although I couldn't tell a slip knot from a granny knot, or a reef knot from a thief knot, except that a thief knot was supposed to be used to tie up a thief, should you happen to catch one. I have never caught a thief, and wouldn't know what to do with one since I can't tie a knot. Just let him go with a warning, I suppose. Tell him to become a Boy Scout.

'Be prepared!' That's the Boy Scout motto. And a good one, too. But I never seem to be well prepared for anything, be it an exam or a journey or the roof blowing off my room. I get halfway through a speech and then forget what I have to say next. Or I make a new suit to attend a friend's wedding, and then turn up in my pyjamas.

So how did I, the most impractical of boys, become a Boy Scout? I was at boarding school in Simla when it happened.

Well, it seems a rumour had gone around the junior school (I was still a junior then) that I was a good cook. I had never cooked anything in my life, but of course I had spent a lot of time in the tuck shop making suggestions and advising Chippu, who ran the tuck shop, and encouraging him to make more and better samosas, jalebis, tikkees and pakoras. For my unwanted advice he would favour me with an occasional free samosa, so naturally I looked upon him as a friend and benefactor. With this qualification I was given a cookery badge and put in charge of our troop's supply of rations.

There were about twenty of us in our troop, and during the summer break our Scoutmaster, Mr Oliver, took us on a camping expedition to Tara Devi, a temple-crowned mountain a few miles outside Simla. That first night we were put to work, peeling potatoes, skinning onions, shelling peas and pounding masalas. These various ingredients being ready, I was asked—as the troop's cookery expert—what should be done with them.

'Put everything in that big *degchi*,' I ordered. 'Pour half a tin of ghee over the lot. Add some nettle leaves and cook for half an hour.'

When this was done, everyone had a taste, but the general opinion was that the dish lacked something.

'More salt,' I suggested.

More salt was added. It still lacked something.

'Add a cup of sugar,' I ordered.

Sugar was added to the concoction. But still it lacked something.

'We forgot to add tomatoes,' said Bimal, one of the Scouts.

'Never mind,' I said. 'We have tomato sauce. Add a bottle of tomato sauce!'

'How about some vinegar?' asked another boy.

'Just the thing,' I agreed. 'A cup of vinegar!'

'Now it's too sour,' said one of the tasters.

'What jam did we bring?' I asked.

'Gooseberry jam.'

'Just the thing. Empty the bottle!'

The dish was a great success. Everyone enjoyed it, including Mr Oliver, who had no idea what went into it.

'What's this called?' he asked.

'It's an all-Indian sweet-and-sour jam-potato curry,' I ventured.

'For short, just call it a Bond-bhujji,' said Bimal.

I had earned my cookery badge!

*

Poor Mr Oliver! He wasn't really cut out to be a Scoutmaster, any more than I was meant to be a Scout. The following day he announced that he would give us a lesson in tracking. He would take a half-hour start and walk into the forest, leaving behind him a trail of broken twigs, chicken feathers, pine cones and chestnuts, and we were to follow the trail until we found him.

Unfortunately, we were not very good trackers. We did follow Mr Oliver's trail some way into the forest, but were distracted by a pool of clear water which looked very inviting. Abandoning our uniforms, we jumped into the pool and had a great time romping around or just lying on the grassy banks and enjoying the sunshine. A couple of hours later, feeling hungry, we returned to our campsite and set about preparing the evening meal. Bond-bhujji again, but with further variations.

It was growing dark, and we were beginning to worry about Mr Oliver's whereabouts when he limped into camp, assisted by a couple of local villagers. Having waited for us at the far end of the forest for a couple of hours, he had decided to return by following his own trail, but in the gathering gloom he was soon lost. Some locals returning from the temple took charge of him and escorted him back to camp. He was very angry and made us return all our good-conduct and other badges, which he stuffed into his haversack. I had to give up my cookery badge, too.

An hour later, when we were all preparing to get into our sleeping bags for the night, Mr Oliver called out: 'Where's dinner?'

'We've had ours,' said Bimal. 'Everything is finished, sir.'

'Where's Bond? He's supposed to be the cook. Bond, get up and make me an omelette.'

'Can't, sir.'

'Why not?'

'You have my badge. Not allowed to cook without it. Scout rule, sir.'

'Never heard of such a rule. But you can have your badges back, all of you. We return to school tomorrow.'

Mr Oliver returned to his tent in a huff. But I relented and made him an elaborate omelette, garnishing it with dandelion leaves and an extra chilli.

'Never had such an omelette before,' confessed Mr Oliver, blowing out his cheeks. 'A little too hot, but otherwise quite interesting.'

'Would you like another, sir?'

'Tomorrow, Bond, tomorrow. We'll breakfast early tomorrow.'

But we had to break up our camp very early the next day. In the early hours, a bear had strayed into our camp, entered the tent where our stores were kept, and created havoc with all our provisions, even rolling our biggest *degchi* down the hillside.

In the confusion and uproar that followed, the bear entered Mr Oliver's tent (he was already outside, fortunately) and came out entangled in Mr Oliver's dressing gown. It then made off in the direction of the forest.

A bear in a dressing gown? It was a comical sight. And though we were a troop of brave little Scouts, we thought it better to let the bear keep the gown.

Bitter Gooseberries

As a young man, Grandfather had spent a few years in Burma, and this was one of the stories he liked to tell us . . .

This is the story of the snake and the gooseberries and much else besides, so be still, don't interrupt, and don't ask questions. Are you listening? Well, then. There was once a snake and he lived in a gooseberry bush, and every night he turned into a handsome prince. Now there is nothing extraordinary about this; it happens all the time, especially in Burma where everyone is handsome anyway . . . But a story can't succeed unless there's a woman in it, so there was also a woman who lived in a little bamboo house with orchids hanging in the veranda, and she had three daughters called Ma Gyi, Ma Lat and Ma Nge. And Ma Nge was the youngest and the nicest and the most beautiful, because a story can't succeed unless she is all these things.

Well, one day the mother of Ma Nge had to go out to fetch gooseberries from the forest. They were bitter gooseberries: Burmese ladies call them *zi-byu-thi,* and prefer them to sweet gooseberries. The woman took her basket along, and just as she was starting to pick gooseberries, the snake who lived in the gooseberry bush hissed at her, as much as to say: 'Be off.' This was the snake who was a prince by night, but now of course it was broad daylight, and anyway Burmese women aren't afraid of snakes. Moreover, the snake recalled that this was the mother of three daughters, and he had a fondness for daughters, so he changed his mind about sending the woman away, and waited for her to speak first, because she was a woman, and women are remarkable for their business capacity.

The woman said, 'Please give me a gooseberry.' Women are always wanting something; it's a part of their business philosophy.

But the snake said no. He had remembered that he was a prince and that princes aren't supposed to say yes to anything; not at first, anyway. It was a matter of principle.

Then the woman said, 'If you like my eldest daughter, Ma Gyi, give me a gooseberry.' The snake didn't care for Ma Gyi, because he knew she had a terrible temper (or perhaps it was a distemper), but he gave the woman a gooseberry as a matter of policy. 'One gooseberry is about all that Ma Gyi is worth,' he said to himself.

But women all over the world, from Burma to

Bermuda and beyond, are never satisfied with only *one* of anything, and so she said, 'If you like my second daughter, Ma Lat, give me another gooseberry.'

The prince knew that Ma Lat had a squint, but he didn't want to hurt anyone's feelings, so he gave the woman another gooseberry; and thus encouraged, she continued, 'And if you like my youngest daughter, Ma Nge, give me another gooseberry.'

At that, the snake trembled so violently from tip to tail that every gooseberry fell off the bush; for the snake prince knew that Ma Nge was the youngest and nicest and most beautiful of them all. And the woman gathered up all the gooseberries, put them in her basket, and took them home because they were bitter (*zi-byu-thi*), and because she was a woman of remarkable business capacity.

On the way she met a signpost and gave it a gooseberry, saying, 'If a snake comes enquiring which way I have gone, don't tell him, but point in the opposite direction.' She said this because she knew the signpost would do just the opposite.

Then she went on and said the same thing to two more signposts (everything has to be done three times in the best stories), and the posts all did the same thing, which was to show the snake the proper road, because that is what signposts are supposed to do.

The snake had little difficulty in following the woman to her house. He hid in a large jar, and when she came to get something, he slid out and coiled round her arm in the manner of a prospective son in-law.

'If you love my daughter Ma Gyi, let go,' cried the woman, pretending to be frightened. (She knew quite well that the snake was a prince.)

But the snake hung on, because he didn't love Ma Gyi, who had a bad temper and probably distemper, too.

'If you love Ma Lat, let go!'

But the snake hung on. Although he personally had nothing against squinty-eyed women, he did not relish the prospect of being stared at by one all his life.

And then (because everything must be done three times) the woman cried, 'If you love my daughter Ma Nge, let go!'

The snake fell swooning to the ground. And as night had come on quite suddenly, in the snake's place the mother found the supplicant prince, smitten with love for her youngest daughter. And she wasted no time in getting him married to Ma Nge.

That ought to be the end of the story. But in Burma stories don't end, they just go on and on forever, so that sometimes it is difficult to print them. But the prince had to do something to break the spell, because after some time Ma Nge found it rather irritating being married to a prince who was her husband by night and a snake by day. She said she preferred a man about the place even during the day. It was she who managed to break the spell because, like her mother, she too had this remarkable business capacity. All she did was to find her husband a job, and the shock was so great that it broke the spell. It was the first time in his life that the prince had been expected to do any work, and he was so shaken that he completely forgot how to turn himself back into a snake.

But the prince stuck to his job, and worked so hard that sometimes his wife felt quite lonely; she didn't know that his employers had provided him with a beautiful secretary, and that this was encouraging him to work overtime. And so, when he came home late and went straight to bed after dinner, she began to scold him and complain of his indifference. One morning he became so disgusted with her constant nagging that he found he could remember the magic spell and immediately turned himself into an enormous snake.

He started by trying to swallow his wife's feet. Ma Nge called out to her mother, but her mother said that was quite all right.

'He has swallowed my knees,' wailed poor Ma Nge.

'Never mind, dear,' replied her mother, who was cooking in the next room. 'You never can tell what an amorous husband will do.'

'He has swallowed my neck.'

The mother thought this was going too far; and when no further calls came from her daughter, she burst into

19

the room and remonstrated with the snake, who had entirely swallowed Ma Nge.

'Give her up at once,' cried the indignant mother.

'Not unless you agree to my terms,' said the snake. 'First, I'm to be a snake whenever I feel like it. Second, I'm to be a real prince and go to work only when I feel like it. How can your daughter love me if I come home tired from the office like any other man? You wanted a prince for a son-in-law. You got one. Now you must let me live like a prince.'

The mother agreed to his terms, and he un-swallowed his wife, and from that day onwards the two women did all the work while the prince sat in the veranda under the hanging orchids and drank a wonderful beer made from bitter gooseberries.

❁

'Can you make gooseberry beer?' I asked Grandfather when he had finished his story.

'Certainly,' said Grandfather. 'The day your grandmother allows it, I'll make gooseberry beer and plum wine and apple cider and a gin tonic, too!'

But Grandmother did not allow it. Strong drink had been banned ever since Uncle Ken had taken too much and fallen into a ditch.

Uncle Ken's Feathered Foes

Uncle Ken looked smug and pleased with life. He had just taken a large bite out of a currant bun (well-buttered inside, with strawberry jam as a stuffing) and was about to take a second bite when, out of a clear blue sky, a hawk swooped down, snatched the bun out of Uncle Ken's hands and flew away with its trophy.

It was a bad time for Uncle Ken. He was being persecuted—not by his sisters or the world at large, but by the birds in our compound.

It all began when he fired his airgun at a noisy bunch of crows, and one of them fell dead on the veranda steps.

The crows never forgave him.

He had only to emerge from the house for a few minutes, and they would fling themselves at him, a noisy gang of ten to fifteen crows, swooping down with flapping wings and extended beaks, knocking off his hat and clawing at his flailing arms. If Uncle Ken wanted to leave the compound, he would have to sneak out of the back veranda, make a dash for his bicycle, and pedal furiously down the driveway until he was out of the gate and on the main road. Even then, he would be pursued by two or three outraged crows until he was well outside their territory.

This persecution continued for two or three weeks, until, in desperation, Uncle Ken adopted a disguise. He put on a false beard, a deer-stalker cap (in the manner of Sherlock Holmes), a long, black cloak (in the manner of Count Dracula) and a pair of Grandfather's old riding boots. And so attired, he marched up and down the driveway, frightening away two elderly ladies who had come to see Grandmother. The crows were suitably baffled and kept at a distance. But Grandmother's pet mongrel, Crazy, began barking furiously, caught hold of Uncle Ken's cloak and wouldn't let go until I came to his rescue.

❉

The mango season was approaching, and we were all looking forward to feasting on our mangoes that summer.

There were three or four mango trees in our compound, and Uncle Ken was particularly anxious to protect them from monkeys, parrots, flying foxes and other fruit-eating creatures. He had his own favourite mango tree, and every afternoon he would place a cot beneath it, and whenever he spotted winged or furred intruders in the tree, he would put a small bugle to his lips and produce a shrill bugle call—loud enough to startle everyone in the house as well as the denizens of the trees.

However, after a few shattering bugle calls Uncle Ken would doze off, only to wake up an hour later bespattered with the droppings of parrots, pigeons, squirrels and other inhabitants of the mango tree. After two or three days of blessings from the birds, Uncle Ken came out with a large garden umbrella which protected him from aerial bombardment.

While he was fast asleep one afternoon (after spoiling Grandfather's siesta with his horn blowing), Grandmother caught me by the hand and said, 'Be a good boy; go out and fetch that bugle.'

I did as I was told, slipping the bugle out of Uncle Ken's hands as he snored, and handing it over to Grandmother. I'm not sure what she did with it, but a few weeks later, as a wedding band came down the road, drums beating and trumpets blaring, I thought I recognized Uncle Ken's old bugle. A dark, good-looking youth blew vigorously upon it, quite out of tune with everyone else. It looked and sounded like Uncle Ken's bugle.

✳

Summer came and went, and so did the mangoes. And then the monsoon arrived, and the pond behind the house overflowed, and there were frogs hopping about all over the veranda.

One morning Grandfather called me over to the back garden and led me down to the pond where he pointed to a couple of new arrivals—a pair of colourful storks who were wading about on their long legs and using their huge bills to snap up fish, frogs, or anything else they fancied. They paid no attention to us, and we were quite content to watch them going about their business.

Uncle Ken, of course, had to go and make a nuisance of himself. Armed with his Kodak 'Baby Brownie' camera (all the rage at the time), he waded into the pond (wearing Grandfather's boots) and proceeded to take pictures of the visiting birds.

Now, certain storks and cranes—especially those who move about in pairs—grow very attached to each other, and generally resent any overtures of friendship from clumsy humans.

Mr Stork, seeing Uncle Ken approaching through the lily-covered waters, assumed that my uncle's intentions were of an amorous nature. Uncle Ken in hat and cloak might well have been mistaken for a huge bird of prey— or a member of the ostrich family.

Mr Stork wasn't going to stand for any rivals, and leaving Mrs Stork to do the fishing, advanced upon Uncle Ken with surprising speed, lunged at him, and knocked the camera from his hands.

Leaving his camera to the tadpoles, Uncle Ken fled from the lily pond, hotly pursued by an irate stork, who even got in a couple of kung fu kicks before Uncle Ken reached the safety of the veranda.

Mourning the loss of his dignity and his camera, Uncle Ken sulked for a couple of days, and then announced that he was going to far-off Pondicherry to stay with an aunt who had settled there.

Everyone heaved a sigh of relief, and Grandfather and I saw Uncle Ken off at the station, just to make sure he didn't change his mind and return home in time for dinner.

Later, we heard that Uncle Ken's holiday in Pondicherry went smoothly for a couple of days, there being no trees around his aunt's seafront flat. On the beach he consumed innumerable ice creams and platters full of French fries, without being bothered by crows, parrots, monkeys or small boys.

And then, one morning, he decided to treat himself to breakfast at on open-air café near the beach, and ordered bacon and eggs, sausages, three toasts, cheese and marmalade.

He had barely taken a bite out of his buttered toast when, out of a blind blue sky, a seagull swooped down and carried off a sausage.

Uncle Ken was still in shock when another seagull shot past him, taking with it a rasher of bacon.

Seconds later a third gull descended and removed the remaining sausage, splattering toast and fried egg all over Uncle Ken's trousers.

He was left with half a toast and a small pot of marmalade.

When he got back to the flat and told his aunt what had happened, she felt sorry for him and gave him a glass of milk and a peanut butter sandwich.

Uncle Ken hated milk. And he detested peanut butter. But when hungry he would eat almost anything.

'Can't trust those seagulls,' said his aunt. 'They are all non-veg. Stick to spinach and lettuce, and they'll leave you alone.'

'Ugh,' said Uncle Ken in disgust. 'I'd rather be a seagull.'

Escape from Java

It all happened within the space of a few days. The cassia tree had barely come into flower when the first bombs fell on Batavia (now called Jakarta) and the bright pink blossoms lay scattered over the wreckage in the streets.

News had reached us that Singapore had fallen to the Japanese. My father said, 'I expect it won't be long before they take Java. With the British defeated, how can the Dutch be expected to win!' He did not mean to be critical of the Dutch; he knew they did not have the backing of the Empire that Britain had. Singapore had been called the Gibraltar of the East. After its surrender there could only be retreat, a vast exodus of Europeans from South-East Asia.

It was the Second World War. What the Javanese thought about the war is now hard for me to say, because I was only nine at the time and knew very little of worldly matters. Most people knew they would be exchanging their Dutch rulers for Japanese rulers; but there were also many who spoke in terms of freedom for Java when the war was over.

Our neighbour, Mr Hartono, was one of those who looked ahead to a time when Java, Sumatra and the other islands would make up one independent nation. He was a college professor and spoke Dutch, Chinese, Javanese and a little English. His son, Sono, was about my age. He was the only boy I knew who could talk to me in English, and as a result we spent a lot of time together. Our favourite pastime was flying kites in the park.

The bombing soon put an end to kite flying. Air raid alerts sounded at all hours of the day and night, and although in the beginning most of the bombs fell near the docks, a couple of miles from where we lived, we had to stay indoors. If the planes sounded very near, we dived under beds or tables. I don't remember if there were any trenches. Probably there hadn't been time for trench digging, and now there was time only for digging graves. Events had moved all too swiftly, and everyone (except, of course, the Javanese) was anxious to get away from Java.

'When are you going?' asked Sono, as we sat on the veranda steps in a pause between air raids.

'I don't know,' I said. 'It all depends on my father.'

'My father says the Japs will be here in a week. And if you're still here then, they'll put you to work building a railway.'

'I wouldn't mind building a railway,' I protested.

'But they won't give you enough to eat. Just rice with worms in it. And if you don't work properly, they'll shoot you.'

'They do that to soldiers,' I said. 'We're civilians.'

'They do it to civilians, too,' said Sono.

What were my father and I doing in Batavia, when our home had been first in India and then in Singapore? He worked for a firm dealing in rubber, and six months earlier he had been sent to Batavia to open a new office in partnership with a Dutch business house. Although I was so young, I accompanied my father almost everywhere. My mother left when I was very small, and my father had always looked after me. After the war was over he was going to take me to England.

'Are we going to win the war?' I asked.

'It doesn't look it from here,' he said.

No, it didn't look as though we were winning. Standing at the docks with my father, I watched the ships arrive from Singapore crowded with refugees— men, women and children, all living on the decks in the hot tropical sun; they looked pale and worn out and worried. They were on their way to Colombo or Bombay. No one came ashore at Batavia. It wasn't British territory; it was Dutch, and everyone knew it wouldn't be Dutch for long.

'Aren't we going too?' I asked. 'Sono's father says the Japs will be here any day.'

'We've still got a few days,' said my father. He was a short, stocky man who seldom got excited. If he was worried, he didn't show it. 'I've got to wind up a few business matters, and then we'll be off.'

'How will we go? There's no room for us on those ships.'

'There certainly isn't. But we'll find a way, lad, don't worry.'

I didn't worry. I had complete confidence in my father's ability to find a way out of difficulties. He used to say, 'Every problem has a solution hidden away somewhere, and if only you look hard enough you will find it.'

There were British soldiers in the streets but they did not make it feel much safer. They were just waiting for troop ships to come and take them away. No one, it seemed, was interested in defending Java, only in getting out as fast as possible.

Although the Dutch were unpopular with the Javanese people, there was no ill feeling against individual Europeans. I could walk safely through the streets. Occasionally small boys in the crowded Chinese quarter would point at me and shout, 'Orang Balandi!' (Dutchman!) but they did so in good humour, and I didn't know the language well enough to stop and explain that the English weren't Dutch. For them, all white people were the same, and understandably so.

My father's office was in the commercial area, along the canal banks. Our two-storeyed house, about a mile away, was an old building with a roof of red tiles and a broad balcony which had stone dragons at either end. There were flowers in the garden almost all the year round. If there was anything in Batavia more regular than the bombing, it was the rain, which came pattering down on the roof and on the banana fronds almost every afternoon. In the hot and steamy atmosphere of Java, the rain was always welcome.

There were no anti-aircraft guns in Batavia — at least we never heard any — and the Jap bombers came over at will, dropping their bombs by daylight. Sometimes bombs fell in the town. One day the building next to my father's office received a direct hit and tumbled into the river. A number of office workers were killed.

The schools closed, and Sono and I had nothing to do all day except sit in the house, playing darts or carrom, wrestling on the carpets, or playing the gramophone. We had records by Gracie Fields, Harry Lauder, George Formby and Arthur Askey, all popular British artists of the early 1940s. One song by Arthur Askey made fun of Adolph Hitler, with the words, *Adolph, we're gonna hang up your washing on the Siegfried Line, if the Siegfried Line's still there!* It made us feel quite cheerful to know that back in Britain people were confident of winning the war!

One day Sono said, 'The bombs are falling on Batavia, not in the countryside. Why don't we get cycles and ride out of town?'

I fell in with the idea at once. After the morning all-clear had sounded, we mounted our cycles and rode out of town. Mine was a hired cycle, but Sono's was his own. He'd had it since the age of five, and it was constantly in need of repair. 'The soul has gone out of it,' he used to say.

Our fathers were at work; Sono's mother had gone out to do her shopping (during air raids she took shelter under the most convenient shop counter) and wouldn't be back for at least an hour. We expected to be back before lunch.

We were soon out of town, on a road that passed through rice fields, pineapple orchards and cinchona plantations. On our right lay dark green hills; on our left, groves of coconut palms and, beyond them, the sea. Men and women were working in the rice fields, knee-deep in mud, their broad-brimmed hats protecting them from the fierce sun. Here and there a buffalo wallowed in a pool of brown water, while a naked boy lay stretched out on the animal's broad back.

We took a bumpy track through the palms. They grew right down to the edge of the sea. Leaving our cycles on the shingle, we ran down a smooth, sandy beach and into the shallow water.

'Don't go too far in,' warned Sono. 'There may be sharks about.'

Wading in amongst the rocks, we searched for interesting shells, then sat down on a large rock and looked out to sea, where a sailing ship moved placidly on the crisp, blue waters. It was difficult to imagine that half the world was at war, and that Batavia, two or three miles away, was right in the middle of it.

On our way home we decided to take a shortcut through the rice fields, but soon found that our tyres got bogged down in the soft mud. This delayed our return; and to make things worse, we got the roads mixed up and reached an area of the town that seemed unfamiliar. We had barely entered the outskirts when the siren sounded, followed soon after by the drone of approaching aircraft.

'Should we get off our cycles and take shelter somewhere?' I called out.

'No, let's race home!' shouted Sono. 'The bombs won't fall here.'

But he was wrong. The planes flew in very low. Looking up for a moment, I saw the sun blotted out by the sinister shape of a Jap fighter-bomber. We pedalled furiously; but we had barely covered fifty yards when there was a terrific explosion on our right, behind some houses. The shock sent us spinning across the road. We were flung from our cycles. And the cycles, still propelled by the blast, crashed into a wall.

I felt a stinging sensation in my hands and legs, as though scores of little insects had bitten me. Tiny droplets of blood appeared here and there on my flesh. Sono was on all fours, crawling beside me, and I saw that he too had the same small scratches on his hands and forehead, made by tiny shards of flying glass.

We were quickly on our feet, and then we began running in the general direction of our homes. The twisted cycles lay forgotten on the road.

'Get off the street, you two!' shouted someone from a window; but we weren't going to stop running until we got home. And we ran faster than we'd ever run in our lives.

My father and Sono's parents were themselves running about the street, calling for us, when we came rushing around the corner and tumbled into their arms.

'Where have you been?'

'What happened to you?'

'How did you get those cuts?'

All superfluous questions but before we could recover our breath and start explaining, we were bundled into our respective homes. My father washed my cuts and scratches, dabbed at my face and legs with iodine — ignoring my yelps — and then stuck plaster all over my face.

Sono and I had had a fright, and we did not venture far from the house again.

That night my father said, 'I think we'll be able to leave in a day or two.'

'Has another ship come in?'

'No.'

'Then how are we going? By plane?'

'Wait and see, lad. It isn't settled yet. But we won't be able to take much with us—just enough to fill a couple of travelling bags.'

'What about the stamp collection?' I asked.

My father's stamp collection was quite valuable and filled several volumes.

'I'm afraid we'll have to leave most of it behind,' he said. 'Perhaps Mr Hartono will keep it for me, and when the war is over—if it's over—we'll come back for it.'

'But we can take one or two albums with us, can't we?'

'I'll take one. There'll be room for one. Then if we're short of money in Bombay, we can sell the stamps.'

'Bombay? That's in India. I thought we were going back to England.'

'First we must go to India.'

The following morning I found Sono in the garden, patched up like me, and with one foot in a bandage. But he was as cheerful as ever and gave me his usual wide grin.

'We're leaving tomorrow,' I said.

The grin left his face.

'I will be sad when you go,' Sonu said. 'But I will be glad too, because then you will be able to escape from the Japs.'

'After the war, I'll come back.'

'Yes, you must come back. And then, when we are big, we will go round the world together. I want to see England and America and Africa and India and Japan. I want to go everywhere.'

'We can't go everywhere.'

'Yes, we can. No one can stop us!'

We had to be up very early the next morning. Our bags had been packed late at night. We were taking a few clothes, some of my father's business papers, a pair of binoculars, one stamp album and several bars of chocolate. I was pleased about the stamp album and the chocolates, but I had to give up several of my treasures — favourite books, the gramophone and records, an old Samurai sword, a train set and a dartboard. The only consolation was that Sono, and not a stranger, would have them.

In the first faint light of dawn a truck drew up in front of the house. It was driven by a Dutch businessman, Mr Hookens, who worked with my father. Sono was already at the gate, waiting to say goodbye.

'I have a present for you,' he said.

He took me by the hand and pressed a smooth, hard object into my palm. I grasped it and then held it up against the light. It was a beautiful little seahorse, carved out of pale blue jade.

'It will bring you luck,' said Sono.

'Thank you,' I said. 'I will keep it forever.'

And I slipped the little seahorse into my pocket.

'In you get, lad,' said my father, and I got up on the front seat between him and Mr Hookens.

As the truck started up, I turned to wave to Sono. He was sitting on his garden wall, grinning at me. He called out: 'We will go everywhere, and no one can stop us!'

He was still waving when the truck took us round the bend at the end of the road.

We drove through the still, quiet streets of Batavia, occasionally passing burnt-out trucks and shattered buildings. Then we left the sleeping city far behind and were climbing into the forested hills. It had rained during the night, and when the sun came up over the green hills, it twinkled and glittered on the broad, wet leaves. The light in the forest changed from dark green to greenish gold, broken here and there by the flaming red or orange of a trumpet-shaped blossom. It was impossible to know the names of all those fantastic plants! The road had been cut through a dense tropical forest, and on either side the trees jostled each other, hungry for the sun; but they were chained together by the liana creepers and vines that fed upon the struggling trees.

Occasionally a *jelarang*, a large Javan squirrel, frightened by the passing of the truck, leapt through the trees before disappearing into the depths of the forest. We saw many birds: peacocks, junglefowl, and once, standing majestically at the side of the road, a crowned pigeon, its great size and splendid crest making it a striking object even at a distance. Mr Hookens slowed down so that we could look at the bird. It bowed its head so that its crest swept the ground; then it emitted a low, hollow boom rather than the call of a turkey.

When we came to a small clearing, we stopped for breakfast. Butterflies, black, green and gold, flitted across the clearing. The silence of the forest was broken only by the drone of airplanes. Japanese Zeros heading for Batavia on another raid. I thought about Sono, and wondered what he would be doing at home: probably trying out the gramophone!

We ate boiled eggs and drank tea from a thermos, then got back into the truck and resumed our journey.

I must have dozed off soon after, because the next thing I remember is that we were going quite fast down a steep, winding road, and in the distance I could see a calm blue lagoon.

'We've reached the sea again,' I said.

'That's right,' said my father. 'But we're now nearly

a hundred miles from Batavia, in another part of the island. You're looking out over the Sunda Straits.'

Then he pointed towards a shimmering white object resting on the waters of the lagoon.

'There's our plane,' he said.

'A seaplane!' I exclaimed. 'I never guessed. Where will it take us?'

'To Bombay, I hope. There aren't many other places left to go to!'

It was a very old seaplane, and no one, not even the captain—the pilot was called the captain—could promise that it would take off. Mr Hookens wasn't coming with us; he said the plane would be back for him the next day. Besides my father and me, there were four other passengers, and all but one were Dutch. The odd man out was a Londoner, a motor mechanic who'd been left behind in Java when his unit was evacuated. (He told us later that he'd fallen asleep at a bar in the Chinese quarter, waking up some hours after his regiment had moved off!) He looked rather scruffy. He'd lost the top button of his shirt, but instead of leaving his collar open as we did, he'd kept it together with a large safety pin, which thrust itself out from behind a bright pink tie.

'It's a relief to find you here, guvnor,' he said, shaking my father by the hand. 'Knew you for a Yorkshireman the minute I set eyes on you. It's the songfried that does it, if you know what I mean.' (He meant sangfroid,

French for a 'cool look'.) 'And here I was, with all these flippin' forriners, and me not knowing a word of what they've been yattering about. Do you think this old tub will get us back to Blighty?'

'It does look a bit shaky,' said my father. 'One of the first flying boats, from the looks of it. If it gets us to Bombay, that's far enough.'

'Anywhere out of Java's good enough for me,' said our new companion. 'The name's Muggeridge.'

'Pleased to know you, Mr Muggeridge,' said my father. 'I'm Bond. This is my son.'

Mr Muggeridge rumpled my hair and favoured me with a large wink.

The captain of the seaplane was beckoning to us to join him in a small skiff which was about to take us across a short stretch of water to the seaplane.

'Here we go,' said Mr Muggeridge. 'Say your prayers and keep your fingers crossed.'

The seaplane was a long time getting airborne. It had to make several runs before it finally took off. Then, lurching drunkenly, it rose into the clear blue sky.

'For a moment I thought we were going to end up in the briny,' said Mr Muggeridge, untying his seat belt. 'And talkin' of fish, I'd give a week's wages for a plate of fish an' chips and a pint of beer.'

'I'll buy you a beer in Bombay,' said my father.

'Have an egg,' I offered, remembering we still had some boiled eggs in one of the travelling bags.

'Thanks, mate,' said Mr Muggeridge, accepting an egg with alacrity. 'A real egg, too! I've been livin' on egg powder these last six months. That's what they give you in the army. And it ain't hens' eggs they make it from, let me tell you. It's either gulls' or turtles' eggs!'

'No,' said my father with a straight face. 'Snakes' eggs.'

Mr Muggeridge turned a delicate shade of green; but he soon recovered his poise, and for about an hour kept talking about almost everything under the sun, including Churchill, Hitler, Roosevelt, Mahatma Gandhi, and Betty Grable. (The last-named was famous for her beautiful legs.) He would have gone on talking all the way to Bombay had he been given a chance, but suddenly a shudder passed through the old plane, and it began lurching again.

'I think an engine is giving trouble,' said my father.

When I looked through the small glassed-in window, it seemed as though the sea was rushing up to meet us.

The co-pilot entered the passenger cabin and said something in Dutch. The passengers looked dismayed, and immediately began fastening their seat belts.

'Well, what did the blighter say?' asked Mr Muggeridge.

'I think he's going to have to ditch the plane,' said my father, who knew enough Dutch to get the gist of anything that was said.

'Down in the drink!' exclaimed Mr Muggeridge.

'Gawd 'elp us! And how far are we from Bombay, guv?'

'A few hundred miles,' said my father.

'Can you swim, mate?' asked Mr Muggeridge looking at me.

'Yes,' I said. 'But not all the way to Bombay. How far can you swim?'

'The length of a bathtub,' he answered.

'Don't worry,' said my father. 'Just make sure your life jacket's properly tied.'

We looked to our life jackets; my father checked mine twice, making sure that it was properly fastened.

The pilot had now cut both engines, and was bringing the plane down in a circling movement. But he couldn't control the speed, and it was tilting heavily to one side. Instead of landing smoothly on its belly, it came down on a wing tip, and this caused the plane to swivel violently around in the choppy sea. There was a terrific jolt when the plane hit the water, and if it hadn't been for the seat belts we'd have been flung from our seats. Even so, Mr Muggeridge struck his head against the seat in front, and he was now holding a bleeding nose and using some shocking language.

As soon as the plane came to a standstill, my father undid my seat belt. There was no time to lose. Water was already filling the cabin, and all the passengers — except one, who was dead in his seat with a broken neck — were scrambling for the exit hatch. The co-pilot pulled a lever and the door fell away to reveal high waves slapping against the sides of the stricken plane.

Holding me by the hand, my father was leading me towards the exit.

'Quick, lad,' he said. 'We won't stay afloat for long.'

'Give us a hand!' shouted Mr Muggeridge, still struggling with his life jacket. 'First this bloody bleedin' nose, and now something's gone and stuck.'

My father helped him fix the life jacket, then pushed him out of the door ahead of us.

As we swam away from the seaplane (Mr Muggeridge splashing fiercely alongside us), we were aware of the other passengers in the water. One of them shouted to us in Dutch to follow him.

We swam after him towards the dinghy, which had been released the moment we hit the water. That yellow dinghy, bobbing about on the waves, was as welcome as land.

All who had left the plane managed to climb into the dinghy. We were seven altogether — a tight fit. We had hardly settled down in the well of the dinghy when Mr Muggeridge, still holding his nose, exclaimed, 'There she goes!' And as we looked on helplessly, the seaplane sank swiftly and silently beneath the waves.

The dinghy had shipped a lot of water, and soon everyone was busy bailing it out with mugs (there were a couple in the dinghy), hats, and bare hands. There was a light swell, and every now and then water would roll in again and half fill the dinghy. But within half an hour we had most of the water out, and then it was possible to take turns, two men doing the bailing while the others rested. No one expected me to do this work, but I gave a hand anyway, using my father's sola topee for the purpose.

'Where are we?' asked one of the passengers.

'A long way from anywhere,' said another.

'There must be a few islands in the Indian Ocean.'

'But we may be at sea for days before we come to one of them.'

'Days or even weeks,' said the captain. 'Let us look at our supplies.'

The dinghy appeared to be fairly well provided with emergency rations: biscuits, raisins, chocolates (we'd lost our own) and enough water to last a week. There was also a first-aid box, which was put to immediate use, as Mr Muggeridge's nose needed attention. A few others had cuts and bruises. One of the passengers had received a hard knock on the head and appeared to be suffering from a loss of memory. He had no idea how we happened to be drifting about in the middle of the Indian Ocean; he was convinced that we were on a pleasure cruise a few miles off Batavia.

The unfamiliar motion of the dinghy, as it rose and fell in the troughs between the waves, resulted in almost everyone getting seasick. As no one could eat anything, a day's rations were saved.

The sun was very hot, and my father covered my head with a large spotted handkerchief. He'd always had a fancy for bandana handkerchiefs with yellow spots, and seldom carried fewer than two on his person; so he had one for himself too. The sola topee, well soaked in sea water, was being used by Mr Muggeridge.

It was only when I had recovered to some extent from my seasickness that I remembered the valuable stamp album, and sat up, exclaiming, 'The stamps! Did you bring the stamp album, Dad?'

He shook his head ruefully. 'It must be at the bottom of the sea by now,' he said. 'But don't worry, I kept a few rare stamps in my wallet.' And looking pleased with himself, he tapped the pocket of his bush shirt.

The dinghy drifted all day, with no one having the least idea where it might be taking us.

'Probably going round in circles,' said Mr Muggeridge pessimistically.

There was no compass and no sail, and paddling wouldn't have got us far even if we'd had paddles; we could only resign ourselves to the whims of the current and hope it would take us towards land or at least to within hailing distance of some passing ship.

The sun went down like an overripe tomato dissolving slowly in the sea. The darkness pressed down on us. It was a moonless night, and all we could see was the white foam on the crests of the waves. I lay with my head on my father's shoulder, and looked up at the stars which glittered in the remote heavens.

'Perhaps your friend Sono will look up at the sky tonight and see those same stars,' said my father. 'The world isn't so big after all.'

'All the same, there's a lot of sea around us,' said Mr Muggeridge from out of the darkness.

Remembering Sono, I put my hand in my pocket and was reassured to feel the smooth outline of the jade seahorse.

'I've still got Sono's seahorse,' I said, showing it to my father.

'Keep it carefully,' he said. 'It may bring us luck.'

'Are seahorses lucky?'

'Who knows? But he gave it to you with love, and love is like a prayer. So keep it carefully.'

I didn't sleep much that night. I don't think anyone slept. No one spoke much either, except, of course, Mr Muggeridge, who kept muttering something about cold beer and salami.

I didn't feel so sick the next day. By ten o'clock I was quite hungry; but breakfast consisted of two biscuits, a piece of chocolate and a little drinking water. It was another hot day, and we were soon very thirsty, but everyone agreed that we should ration ourselves strictly.

Two or three still felt ill, but the others, including Mr Muggeridge, had recovered their appetites and normal spirits, and there was some discussion about the prospects of being picked up.

'Are there any distress rockets in the dinghy?' asked my father. 'If we see a ship or a plane, we can fire a rocket and hope to be spotted. Otherwise there's not much chance of our being seen from a distance.'

A thorough search was made in the dinghy, but there were no rockets.

'Someone must have used them last Guy Fawkes Day,' commented Mr Muggeridge.

'They don't celebrate Guy Fawkes Day in Holland,' said my father. 'Guy Fawkes was an Englishman.'

'Ah,' said Mr Muggeridge, not in the least put out. 'I've always said, most great men are Englishmen. And what did this chap Guy Fawkes do?'

'Tried to blow up Parliament,' said my father.

That afternoon we saw our first sharks. They were enormous creatures, and as they glided backward and forward under the boat it seemed they might hit and capsize us. They went away for some time, but returned in the evening.

At night, as I lay half asleep beside my father, I felt a few drops of water strike my face. At first I thought it was the sea spray; but when the sprinkling continued, I realized that it was raining lightly.

'Rain!' I shouted, sitting up. 'It's raining!'

Everyone woke up and did his best to collect water in mugs, hats or other containers. Mr Muggeridge lay back with his mouth open, drinking the rain as it fell.

'This is more like it,' he said.

'You can have all the sun an' sand in the world. Give me a rainy day in England!'

But by early morning the clouds had passed, and the day turned out to be even hotter than the previous one. Soon we were all red and raw from sunburn. By midday even Mr Muggeridge was silent. No one had the energy to talk.

Then my father whispered, 'Can you hear a plane, lad?'

I listened carefully, and above the hiss of the waves I heard what sounded like the distant drone of a plane; it must have been very far away, because we could not see it. Perhaps it was flying into the sun, and the glare was too much for our sore eyes; or perhaps we'd just imagined the sound.

Then the Dutchman who'd lost his memory thought

he saw land, and kept pointing towards the horizon and saying, 'That's Batavia, I told you we were close to shore!' No one else saw anything. So my father and I weren't the only ones imagining things.

My father said, 'It only goes to show that a man can see what he wants to see, even if there's nothing to be seen!'

The sharks were still with us. Mr Muggeridge began to resent them. He took off one of his shoes and hurled it at the nearest shark; but the big fish ignored the shoe and swam on after us.

'Now, if your leg had been in that shoe, Mr Muggeridge, the shark might have accepted it,' observed my father.

'Don't throw your shoes away,' said the captain. 'We might land on a deserted coastline and have to walk hundreds of miles!'

A light breeze sprang up that evening, and the dinghy moved more swiftly on the choppy water.

'At last we're moving forward,' announced the captain.

'In circles,' said Mr Muggeridge.

But the breeze was refreshing; it cooled our burning limbs, and helped us to get some sleep. In the middle of the night I woke up feeling very hungry.

'Are you all right?' asked my father, who had been awake all the time.

'Just hungry,' I said.

'And what would you like to eat?'

49

'Oranges!'

He laughed. 'No oranges on board. But I kept a piece of my chocolate for you. And there's a little water, if you're thirsty.' I kept the chocolate in my mouth for a long time, trying to make it last. Then I sipped a little water.

'Aren't you hungry?' I asked.

'Ravenous! I could eat a whole turkey. When we get to Bombay or Madras or Colombo, or wherever it is we get to, we'll go to the best restaurant in town and eat like—like—'

'Like shipwrecked sailors!' I said.

'Exactly.'

'Do you think we'll ever get to land, Dad?'

'I'm sure we will. You're not afraid, are you?'

'No. Not as long as you're with me.'

Next morning, to everyone's delight, we saw seagulls. This was a sure sign that land couldn't be far away; but a dinghy could take days to drift a distance of thirty or forty miles. The birds wheeled noisily above the dinghy. Their cries were the first familiar sounds we had heard for three days and three nights, apart from the wind and the sea and our own weary voices.

The sharks had disappeared, and that too was an encouraging sign. They didn't like the oil slicks that were appearing in the water.

But presently the gulls left us, and we feared we were drifting away from land.

'Circles,' repeated Mr Muggeridge. 'Circles.'

We had sufficient food and water for one more week at sea; but no one even wanted to think about spending another week at sea.

The sun was a ball of fire. Our water ration wasn't sufficient to quench our thirst. By noon, we were without much hope or energy.

My father had his pipe in his mouth. He didn't have any tobacco, but he liked holding the pipe between his teeth. He said it prevented his mouth from getting too dry.

The sharks had come back.

Mr Muggeridge removed his other shoe and threw it at them.

'Nothing like a lovely wet English summer,' he mumbled.

I fell asleep in the well of the dinghy, my father's large handkerchief spread over my face. The yellow spots on the cloth seemed to grow into enormous revolving suns.

When I woke up, I found a huge shadow hanging over us. At first I thought it was a cloud. But it was a shifting shadow. My father took the handkerchief from my face and said, 'You can wake up now, lad. We'll be home and dry soon.'

A fishing boat was beside us, and the shadow came from its wide, flapping sail. A number of bronzed, smiling, chattering fishermen—Burmese, as we discovered later—were gazing down at us from the deck of their boat.

A few days later my father and I were in Bombay. My father sold his rare stamps for over a thousand rupees, and we were able to live in a comfortable hotel. Mr Muggeridge was flown back to England. Later we got a postcard from him saying the English rain was awful!

'And what about us?' I asked. 'Aren't we going back to England?'

'Not yet,' said my father. 'You'll be going to a boarding school in Simla, until the war's over.'

'But why should I leave you?' I asked.

'Because I've joined the RAF,' he said. Then he added, 'Don't worry, I'm being posted to Delhi. I'll be able to come up to see you sometimes.'

A week later I was on a small train which went chugging up the steep mountain track to Simla. Several Indian, Anglo-Indian and English children tumbled around in the compartment. I felt quite out of place among them, as though I had grown out of their pranks. But I wasn't unhappy. I knew my father would be coming to see me soon. He'd promised me some books, a pair of roller skates and a cricket bat, just as soon as he got his first month's pay.

Meanwhile, I had the jade seahorse which Sono had given me.

And I have it with me today.

The Black Cat

Before the cat came, of course, there had to be a broomstick.

In the bazaar of one of our hill stations is an old junk shop—dirty, dingy and dark—in which I often potter about looking for old books or Victorian bric-a-brac. Sometimes one comes across useful household items, but I do not usually notice these. I was, however, attracted to an old but well-preserved broom standing in a corner of the shop. A long-handled broom was just what I needed. I had no servant to sweep out the rooms of my cottage, and I did not enjoy bending over double when using the common short-handled *jharoo*.

The old broom was priced at ten rupees. I haggled with the shopkeeper and got it for five. It was a strong broom, full of character, and I used it to good effect almost every morning. And there this story might have ended—or would never have begun—if I had not found the large black cat sitting on the garden wall.

The black cat had bright yellow eyes, and it gave me a

long, penetrating look, as though it were summing up my possibilities as an exploitable human. Though it miaowed once or twice, I paid no attention. I did not care much for cats. But when I went indoors, I found that the cat had followed and begun scratching at the pantry door.

It must be hungry, I thought, and gave it some milk.

The cat lapped up the milk, purring deeply all the while, then sprang up on a cupboard and made itself comfortable.

Well, for several days there was no getting rid of that cat. It seemed completely at home, and merely tolerated my presence in the house. It was more interested in my broom than me, and would dance and skittle around the broom whenever I was sweeping the rooms. And when the broom was resting against the wall, the cat would sidle up to it, rubbing itself against the handle and purring loudly.

A cat and a broomstick — the combination was suggestive, full of possibilities . . . The cottage was old, almost a hundred years old, and I wondered about the kind of tenants it might have had during these long years. I had been in the cottage only for a year. And though it stood alone in the midst of a forest of Himalayan oaks, I had never encountered any ghosts or spirits.

Miss Bellows came to see me in the middle of July. I heard the tapping of a walking stick on the rocky path outside the cottage, a tapping which stopped near the gate.

'Mr Bond!' called an imperious voice. 'Are you at home?'

I had been doing some gardening, and looked up to find an elderly straight-backed Englishwoman peering at me over the gate.

'Good evening,' I said, dropping my hoe.

'I believe you have my cat,' said Miss Bellows.

Though I had not met the lady before, I knew her by name and reputation. She was the oldest resident in the hill station.

'I do have a cat,' I said, 'though it's probably more correct to say that the cat has me. If it's your cat, you're welcome to it. Why don't you come in while I look for her?'

Miss Bellows stepped in. She wore a rather old-fashioned black dress, and her ancient but strong walnut stick had two or three curves in it and a knob instead of a handle.

She made herself comfortable in an armchair while I went in search of the cat. But the cat was on one of her mysterious absences, and though I called for her in my most persuasive manner, she did not respond. I knew she was probably quite near. But cats are like that—perverse, obstinate creatures.

When finally I returned to the sitting room, there was the cat, curled up on Miss Bellows' lap.

'Well, you've got her, I see. Would you like some tea before you go?'

'No, thank you,' said Miss Bellows. 'I don't drink tea.'

'Something stronger, perhaps. A little brandy?' She looked up at me rather sharply. Disconcerted, I hastened to add, 'Not that I drink much, you know. I keep a little in the house for emergencies. It helps ward off colds and things. It's particularly good for—er—well, for colds,' I finished lamely.

'I see your kettle's boiling,' she said. 'Can I have some hot water?'

'Hot water? Certainly.' I was a little puzzled, but I did not want to antagonize Miss Bellows at our first meeting.

'Thank you. And a glass.'

She took the glass and I went to get the kettle. From the pocket of her voluminous dress, she extracted two small packets, similar to those containing chemists' powders. Opening both packets, she poured first a purple powder and then a crimson powder into the glass. Nothing happened.

'Now the water, please,' she said.

'It's boiling hot!'

'Never mind.'

I poured boiling water into her glass, and there was a terrific fizzing and bubbling as the frothy stuff rose to the rim. It gave off a horrible stench. The potion was so hot that I thought it would crack the glass; but before this could happen, Miss Bellows put it to her lips and drained the contents.

'I think I'll be going now,' she said, putting the glass

down and smacking her lips. The cat, tail in the air, voiced its agreement. Said Miss Bellows said, 'I'm much obliged to you, young man.'

'Don't mention it,' I said humbly. 'Always at your service.'

She gave me her thin, bony hand, and held mine in an icy grip.

I saw Miss Bellows and the black cat to the gate, and returned pensively to my sitting room. Living alone was beginning to tell on my nerves and imagination. I made a half-hearted attempt to laugh at my fancies, but the laugh stuck in my throat. I couldn't help noticing that the broom was missing from its corner.

I dashed out of the cottage and looked up and down the path. There was no one to be seen. In the gathering darkness I could hear Miss Bellows' laughter, followed by a snatch of song:

With the darkness round me growing,
And the moon behind my hat,
You will soon have trouble knowing
Which is witch and witch's cat.

Something whirred overhead like a Diwali rocket.

I looked up and saw them silhouetted against the rising moon. Miss Bellows and her cat were riding away on my broomstick.

Grandfather's Many Faces

Grandfather had many gifts, but perhaps the most unusual—and at times startling—was his ability to disguise himself and take on the persona of another person, often a street vendor or carpenter or washerman: someone he had seen around for some time, and whose habits and characteristics he had studied.

His normal attire was that of the average Anglo-Indian or Englishman—bush shirt, khaki shorts, occasionally a sola topee or sun helmet—but if you rummaged through his cupboards you would find a strange assortment of garments: dhotis, lungis, pyjamas, embroidered shirts, colourful turbans . . . He could be a maharaja one day, a beggar the next. Yes, he even had a brass begging bowl, but he used it only once, just to see if he could pass himself off as a bent-double beggar hobbling through the bazaar. He wasn't recognized but he had to admit that begging was a most difficult art.

'You have to be on the street all day and in all weather,' he told me that evening. 'You have to be polite to everyone—no beggar succeeds by being rude! You have to be alert at all times. It's a hard work, believe me. I wouldn't advise anyone to take up begging as a profession.'

Grandfather really liked to get the 'feel' of someone else's occupation or lifestyle. And he enjoyed playing tricks on his friends and relatives.

Grandmother loved bargaining with shopkeepers and vendors of all kinds. She would boast that she could get the better of most men when it came to haggling over the price of onions or cloth or baskets or buttons . . . Until one day the sabziwala, a wandering vegetable-seller who carried a basket of fruit and vegetables on his head, spent an hour on the veranda arguing with Granny over the price of various items before finally selling her what she wanted.

Later that day, Grandfather confronted Grandmother and insisted on knowing why she had paid extra for tomatoes and green chillies. 'Far more than you'd have paid in the bazaar,' he said.

'How do you know what I paid him?' asked Granny.

'Because here's the ten-rupee note you gave me,' said Grandfather, handing back her money. 'I changed into something suitable and borrowed the sabziwala's basket for an hour!'

Grandfather never used makeup. He had a healthy tan, and with the help of a false moustache or beard, and a change of hairstyle, could become anyone he wanted to be.

For my amusement, he became a tongawala; that is, the driver of a pony-drawn buggy, a common form of conveyance in the days of my boyhood.

Grandfather borrowed a tonga from one of his cronies, and took me for a brisk and eventful ride around the town. On our way we picked up the odd customer and earned a few rupees which were dutifully handed over to the tonga-owner at the end of the day. We picked up Dr Bisht, our local physician, who failed to recognize him. But of course I was the giveaway. 'And what are you doing here?' asked the good doctor. 'Shouldn't you be in school?'

'I'm just helping Grandfather,' I replied. 'It's part of my science project.' Dr Bisht then took a second look at Grandfather and burst out laughing; he also insisted on a free ride.

On one occasion Grandfather drove Grandmother to the bank without her recognizing him. And that too in a tonga with a white pony. Granny was superstitious about white ponies and avoided them as far as possible. But Grandfather, in his tonga-driver's disguise, persuaded her that his white pony was the best-behaved little pony in the world; and so it was, under his artful guidance. As a result, Granny lost her fear of white ponies.

One winter the Gemini Circus came to our small

north Indian town, and set up its tents on the old parade ground. Grandfather, who liked circuses and circus people, soon made friends with all the show folk—the owner, the ringmaster, the lion tamer, the pony-riders, clowns, trapeze-artistes and acrobats. He told me that as a boy he'd always wanted to join a circus, preferably as an animal trainer or ringmaster, but his parents had persuaded him to become an engine driver instead.

'Driving an engine must be fun,' I said.

'Yes, but lions are safer,' said Grandfather.

And he used his friendship with the circus folk to get free passes for me, my cousin Melanie and my little friend Gautam who lived next door.

'Aren't you coming with us?' I asked Grandfather.

'I'll be there,' he answered. 'I'll be with my friends. See if you can spot me!'

We were convinced that Grandfather was going to adopt one of his disguises and take part in the evening's entertainment. So for Melanie, Gautam and me the evening turned out to be a guessing game.

We were enthralled by the show's highlights—the tigers going through their drill, the beautiful young men and women on the flying trapeze, the daring motor-cyclist bursting through a hoop of fire, the jugglers and clowns—but we kept trying to see if we could recognize Grandfather among the performers. We couldn't make too much of a noise because in the row behind us sat some of the town's senior citizens—the mayor, a turbaned maharaja, a formally dressed Englishman with a military bearing, a couple of nuns, and Gautam's class teacher—but we kept up our chatter for most of the show.

'Is your Grandfather the lion tamer?' asked Gautam.

'I don't think so,' I said. 'He hasn't had any practice with lions. He's better with tigers!' But there was someone else in charge of the tigers.

'He could be one of the jugglers,' suggested Melanie.

'He's taller than the jugglers,' I said.

Gautam made an inspired guess: 'Maybe he's the bearded lady!'

We looked hard and long at the bearded lady when she came to our side of the ring. She waved to us in a friendly manner, and Gautam called out, 'Excuse me, are you Ruskin's grandfather?'

'No, dear,' she replied with a deep laugh. 'I'm his girlfriend!' And she skipped away to another part of the ring.

A clown came up to us and made funny faces.

'Are you Grandfather?' asked Melanie.

But the clown just grinned, somersaulted backwards, and went about his funny business.

'I give up,' said Melanie. 'Unless he's the dancing bear.'

'It's a real bear,' said Gautam. 'Just look at those claws!'

The bear looked real enough. So did the lion, though a trifle mangy. And the tigers looked tigerish.

We went home convinced that Grandfather hadn't been there at all.

'So did you enjoy the circus?' he asked, when he sat down to dinner late that evening.

'Yes, but you weren't there,' I complained. 'And we took a close look at everyone—including the bearded lady!'

'Oh, I was there all right,' said Grandfather. 'I was sitting just behind you. But you were too absorbed in the circus and the performers to notice the audience. I was that smart-looking Englishman in the suit and tie, sitting between the maharaja and the nuns. I thought I'd just be myself for a change!'

He Said It with Arsenic

Is there such a person as a born murderer — in the sense that there are born writers and musicians, born winners and losers?

One can't be sure. The urge to do away with troublesome people is common to most of us, but only a few succumb to it. If ever there was a born murderer, he must surely have been William Jones. The thing came so naturally to him. No extreme violence, no messy shootings or hackings or throttling — just the right amount of poison, administered with skill and discretion.

A gentle, civilized sort of person was Mr Jones. He collected butterflies and arranged them systematically in glass cases. His ether bottle was quick and painless. He never stuck pins into the beautiful creatures.

Have you ever heard of the Agra Double Murder?

It happened, of course, a great many years ago, when Agra was a far-flung outpost of the British Empire. In those days, William Jones was a male nurse in one of the city's hospitals. The patients — specially terminal cases—spoke highly of the care and consideration he showed them. While most nurses, both male and female, preferred to attend to the more hopeful cases, Nurse William was always prepared to stand duty over a dying patient.

He felt a certain empathy for the dying; he liked to see them on their way. It was just his good nature, of course.

On a visit to nearby Meerut, he met and fell in love with Mrs Browning, the wife of the local stationmaster. Impassioned love letters were soon putting a strain on the Agra-Meerut postal service. The envelopes grew heavier—not so much because the letters were growing longer but because they contained little packets of a powdery, white substance, accompanied by detailed instructions as to its correct administration.

Mr Browning, an unassuming and trustful man—one of the world's born losers—was not the sort to read his wife's correspondence. Even when he was seized by frequent attacks of colic, he put them down to an impure water supply. He recovered from one bout of vomiting and diarrhoea only to be racked by another.

He was hospitalized on a diagnosis of gastroenteritis, and, thus freed from his wife's ministrations, soon got better. But on returning home and drinking a glass of nimbu pani brought to him by the solicitous Mrs Browning, he had a relapse from which he did not recover.

Those were the days when deaths from cholera and related diseases were only too common in India, and death certificates were easier to obtain than dog licences.

After a short interval of mourning (it was the hot weather and you couldn't wear black for long), Mrs Browning moved to Agra, where she rented a house next door to William Jones.

I forgot to mention that Mr Jones was also married. His wife was an insignificant creature, no match for a genius like William. Before the hot weather was over, the dreaded cholera had taken her too. The way was clear for the lovers to unite in holy matrimony.

But Dame Gossip lived in Agra too, and it was not long before tongues were wagging and anonymous letters were being received by the superintendent of police. Inquiries were instituted. Like most infatuated lovers, Mrs Browning had hung on to her beloved's letters and billet-doux, and these soon came to light. The silly woman had kept them in a box beneath her bed.

Exhumations were ordered in both Agra and Meerut.

Arsenic keeps well, even in the hottest of weather, and there was no dearth of it in the remains of both victims.

Mr Jones and Mrs Browning were arrested and charged with murder.

'Is Uncle Bill really a murderer?' I asked from the drawing-room sofa in my grandmother's house in Dehra.

(It's time that I told you that William Jones was my uncle, my mother's half-brother.)

I was eight or nine at the time. Uncle Bill had spent the previous summer with us in Dehra and had stuffed me with bazaar sweets and pastries, all of which I had consumed without suffering any ill effects.

'Who told you that about Uncle Bill?' asked Grandmother.

'I heard it in school. All the boys were asking me the same question, "Is your uncle a murderer?" They say he poisoned both his wives.'

'He had only one wife,' snapped Aunt Mabel.

'Did he poison her?'

'No, of course not. How can you say such a thing!'

'Then why is Uncle Bill in jail?'

'Who says he's in jail?'

'The boys at school. They heard it from their parents. Uncle Bill is to go on trial in the Agra fort.'

There was a pregnant silence in the drawing room, then Aunt Mabel burst out, 'It was all that awful woman's fault.'

'Do you mean Mrs Browning?' asked Grandmother.

'Yes, of course. She must have put him up to it. Bill couldn't have thought of anything so — so diabolical!'

'But he sent her the powders, dear. And don't forget — Mrs Browning has since . . .'

Grandmother stopped in mid-sentence, and both she

and Aunt Mabel glanced surreptitiously at me.

'Committed suicide,' I filled in. 'There were still some powders with her.'

Aunt Mabel's eyes rolled heavenwards. 'This boy is impossible. I don't know what he will be like when he grows up.'

'At least I won't be like Uncle Bill,' I said. 'Fancy poisoning people! If I kill anyone, it will be in a fair fight. I suppose they'll hang Uncle?'

'Oh, I hope not!'

Grandmother was silent. Uncle Bill was her stepson but she did have a soft spot for him. Aunt Mabel, his sister, thought he was wonderful. I had always considered him to be a bit soft but had to admit that he was generous. I tried to imagine him dangling at the end of a hangman's rope, but somehow he didn't fit the picture.

As things turned out, he didn't hang. During the Raj, white people in India seldom got the death sentence, although the hangman was pretty busy disposing of dacoits and political terrorists. Uncle Bill was given a life sentence and settled down to a sedentary job in the prison library at Naini, near Allahabad. His gifts as a male nurse went unappreciated; they did not trust him in the hospital.

He was released after seven or eight years, shortly after the country became an independent republic. He came out of jail to find that the British were leaving, either for England or the remaining colonies. Grandmother was dead. Aunt Mabel and her husband had settled in South Africa. Uncle Bill realized that there was little future for him in India and followed his sister out to Johannesburg. I was in my last year at boarding school. After my father's death, my mother had married an Indian, and now my future lay in India.

I did not see Uncle Bill after his release from prison, and no one dreamt that he would ever turn up again in India.

In fact, fifteen years were to pass before he came back, and by then I was in my early thirties, the author of a book that had become something of a bestseller. The previous fifteen years had been a struggle—the sort of struggle that every young freelance writer experiences—but at last the hard work was paying off and the royalties were beginning to come in.

I was living in a small cottage on the outskirts of the hill station of Fosterganj, working on another book, when I received an unexpected visitor.

He was a thin, stooped, grey-haired man in his late fifties, with a straggling moustache and discoloured teeth. He looked feeble and harmless but for his eyes which were pale cold blue. There was something slightly familiar about him.

'Don't you remember me?' he asked. 'Not that I really expect you to, after all these years . . .'

'Wait a minute. Did you teach me at school?'

'No—but you're getting warm.' He put his suitcase down and I glimpsed his name on the airlines label. I looked up in astonishment. 'You're not—you couldn't be ...'

'Your Uncle Bill,' he said with a grin and extended his hand. 'None other!' And he sauntered into the house.

I must admit that I had mixed feelings about his arrival. While I had never felt any dislike for him, I hadn't exactly approved of what he had done. Poisoning, I felt, was a particularly reprehensible way of getting rid of inconvenient people; not that I could think of any commendable ways of getting rid of them! Still, it had happened a long time ago; he'd been punished, and presumably he was a reformed character.

'And what have you been doing all these years?' he asked me, easing himself into the only comfortable chair in the room.

'Oh just writing,' I said.

'Yes, I heard about your last book. It's quite a success, isn't it?'

'It's doing quite well. Have you read it?'

'I don't do much reading.'

'And what have you been doing all these years, Uncle Bill?'

'Oh, knocking about here and there. Worked for a

71

soft drink company for some time. And then with a drug firm. My knowledge of chemicals was useful.'

'Weren't you with Aunt Mabel in South Africa?'

'I saw quite a lot of her, until she died a couple of years ago. Didn't you know?'

'No. I've been out of touch with relatives.' I hoped he'd take that as a hint. 'And what about her husband?'

'Died too, not long after. Not many of us left, my boy. That's why, when I saw something about you in the papers, I thought why not go and see my only nephew again?'

'You're welcome to stay a few days,' I said quickly. 'Then I have to go to Bombay.' (This was a lie, but I did not relish the prospect of looking after Uncle Bill for the rest of his days.)

'Oh, I won't be staying long,' he said. 'I've got a bit of money put by in Johannesburg. It's just that so far as I know you're my only living relative, and I thought it would be nice to see you again.'

Feeling relieved, I set about trying to make Uncle Bill as comfortable as possible. I gave him my bedroom and turned the window seat into a bed for myself. I was a hopeless cook but, using all my ingenuity, I scrambled some eggs for supper. He waved aside my apologies; he'd always been a frugal eater, he said. Eight years in jail had given him a cast-iron stomach.

He did not get in my way but left me to my writing and my lonely walks. He seemed content to sit in the spring sunshine and smoke his pipe.

It was during our third evening together that he said, 'Oh, I almost forgot. There's a bottle of sherry in my suitcase. I brought it specially for you.'

'That was very thoughtful of you, Uncle Bill. How did you know I was fond of sherry?'

'Just my intuition. You do like it, don't you?'

'There's nothing like a good sherry.'

He went to his bedroom and came back with an unopened bottle of South African sherry.

'Now you just relax near the fire,' he said agreeably. 'I'll open the bottle and fetch glasses.'

He went to the kitchen while I remained near the electric fire, flipping through some journals. It seemed to me that Uncle Bill was taking rather a long time. Intuition must be a family trait, because it came to me quite suddenly—the thought that Uncle Bill might be intending to poison me.

After all, I thought, here he is after nearly fifteen years, apparently for purely sentimental reasons. But I had just published a bestseller. And I was his nearest relative. If I were to die, Uncle Bill could lay claim to my estate and probably live comfortably on my royalties for the next five or six years!

What had really happened to Aunt Mabel and her

husband, I wondered. And where did Uncle Bill get the money for an air ticket to India?

Before I could ask myself any more questions, he reappeared with the glasses on a tray. He set the tray on a small table that stood between us. The glasses had been filled. The sherry sparkled.

I stared at the glass nearest me, trying to make out if the liquid in it was cloudier than that in the other glass. But there appeared to be no difference.

I decided I would not take any chances. It was a round tray, made of smooth Kashmiri walnut wood. I turned it round with my index finger, so that the glasses changed places.

'Why did you do that?' asked Uncle Bill.

'It's a custom in these parts. You turn the tray with the sun, a complete revolution. It brings good luck.'

Uncle Bill looked thoughtful for a few moments, then said, 'Well, let's have some more luck,' and turned the tray around again.

'Now you've spoilt it,' I said. 'You're not supposed to keep revolving it! That's bad luck. I'll have to turn it about again to cancel out the bad luck.'

The tray swung round once more, and Uncle Bill had the glass that was meant for me.

'Cheers!' I said, and drank from my glass.

It was good sherry. Uncle Bill hesitated. Then he shrugged, said 'Cheers', and drained his glass quickly.

But he did not offer to fill the glasses again.

Early next morning he was taken violently ill. I heard him retching in his room, and I got up and went to see if there was anything I could do. He was groaning, his head hanging over the side of the bed. I brought him a basin and a jug of water.

'Would you like me to fetch a doctor?' I asked.

He shook his head. 'No, I'll be all right. It must be something I ate.'

'It's probably the water. It's not too good at this time of the year. Many people come down with gastric trouble during their first few days in Fosterganj.'

'Ah, that must be it,' he said, and doubled up as a fresh spasm of pain and nausea swept over him.

He was better by the evening — whatever had gone into the glass must have been by way of the preliminary dose, and a day later he was well enough to pack his suitcase and announce his departure. The climate of Fosterganj did not agree with him, he told me.

Just before he left, I said, 'Tell me, Uncle, why did you drink it?'

'Drink what? The water?'

'No, the glass of sherry into which you'd slipped one of your famous powders.'

He gaped at me, then gave a nervous, whinnying laugh. 'You will have your little joke, won't you?'

'No, I mean it,' I said. 'Why did you drink the stuff? It was meant for me, of course.'

He looked down at his shoes, then gave a little shrug and turned away.

'In the circumstances,' he said, 'it seemed the only decent thing to do.'

I'll say this for Uncle Bill: he was always the perfect gentleman.

Here Comes Mr Oliver

Apart from being our Scoutmaster, Mr Oliver was also our maths teacher, a subject in which I had some difficulty in obtaining pass marks. Sometimes I scraped through; usually I got something like twenty or thirty out of a hundred.

'Failed again, Bond,' Mr Oliver would say. 'What will you do when you grow up?'

'Become a Scoutmaster, sir.'

'Scoutmasters don't get paid. It's an honorary job. But you could become a cook. That would suit you.' He hadn't forgotten our Scout camp, when I had been the camp's cook.

If Mr Oliver was in a good mood, he'd give me grace marks, passing me by a mark or two. He wasn't a hard man, but he seldom smiled. He was very dark, thin, stooped (from a distance he looked like a question mark) and balding. He was about forty, still a bachelor, and it was said that he had been unlucky in love—that the girl he was going to marry had jilted him at the last moment, had run away with a sailor while he was waiting at the church, ready for the wedding ceremony. No wonder he always had such a sorrowful look.

Mr Oliver did have one inseparable companion—a Dachshund, a snappy little 'sausage' of a dog, who looked upon the human race and especially small boys with a certain disdain and frequent hostility. We called the dog Hitler. He was impervious to overtures of friendship, and if you tried to pat or stroke him, he would do his best to bite your fingers—or your shin or ankle. However, he was devoted to Mr Oliver and followed him everywhere, except into the classroom; this our Headmaster would not allow.

You remember that old nursery rhyme:

Mary had a little lamb,
Its fleece was white as snow,
And everywhere that Mary went
The lamb was sure to go.

Well, we made up our own version of the rhyme, and I must confess to having had a hand in its composition. It went like this:

Olly had a little dog,
'Twas never out of sight,
And everyone that Olly met
The dog was sure to bite!

It followed him about the school grounds. It followed him when he took a walk through the pines, to the Brockhurst tennis courts. It followed him into town and home again. Mr Oliver had no other friend, no other companion. The dog slept at the foot of Mr Oliver's bed. It did not sit at the breakfast table, but it had buttered toast for breakfast and soup and crackers for dinner. Mr Oliver had to take his lunch in the dining hall with the staff and boys, but he had an arrangement with one of the bearers whereby a plate of dal, rice and chapattis made its way to Mr Oliver's quarters and his well-fed pet.

And then tragedy struck.

Mr Oliver and Hitler were returning to school after their evening walk through the pines. It was dusk, and the light was fading fast. Out of the shadows of the trees emerged a lean and hungry panther. It pounced on the hapless dog, flung it across the road, seized it between its powerful jaws, and made off with its victim into the darkness of the forest.

Mr Oliver, untouched, was frozen into immobility for at least a minute. Then he began calling for help. Some bystanders who had witnessed the incident began shouting, too. Mr Oliver ran into the forest, but there was no sign of dog or panther.

Mr Oliver appeared to be a broken man. He went about his duties with a poker face, but we could all tell that he was grieving for his lost companion. In the classroom he was listless, indifferent to whether or not we followed his calculations on the blackboard. In times of personal loss, the Highest Common Factor made no sense.

Mr Oliver was not to be seen on his evening walk. He stayed in his room, playing cards with himself. He played with his food, pushing most of it aside; there were no chapattis to send home.

'Olly needs another pet,' said Bimal, wise in the ways of adults.

'Or a wife,' suggested Tata, who thought on those lines.

'He's too old. Over forty.'

'A pet is best,' I decided. 'What about a parrot?'

'You can't take a parrot for a walk,' said Bimal. 'Olly wants someone to walk beside him.'

'A cat, maybe . . .'

'Hitler hated cats. A cat would be an insult to Hitler's memory.'

'He needs another Dachshund. But there aren't any around here.'

'Any dog will do. We'll ask Chippu to get us a pup.'

Chippu ran the tuck shop. He lived in the Chotta Simla bazaar, and occasionally we would ask him to bring us tops or marbles or comics or little things that we couldn't get in school. Five of us Boy Scouts contributed a rupee each, and we gave Chippu five rupees and asked him to get us a pup. 'A good breed,' we told him. 'Not a mongrel.'

The next evening Chippu turned up with a pup that seemed to be a combination of at least five different breeds—all good ones, no doubt. One ear lay flat, the other stood upright. It was spotted like a Dalmatian, but it had the legs of a Spaniel and the tail of a Pomeranian. It was quite fluffy and playful, and the tail wagged a lot, which was more than Hitler's ever did.

'It's quite pretty,' said Tata. 'Must be a female.'

'He may not want a female,' put in Bimal.

'Let's give it a try,' I said.

During our play hour, before the bell rang for supper, we left the pup on the steps outside Mr Oliver's front door. Then we knocked, and sped into the hibiscus bushes that lined the pathway.

Mr Oliver opened the door. He looked down at the pup with an expressionless face. The pup began to paw at Mr Oliver's shoes, loosening one of his laces in the process.

'Away with you!' muttered Mr Oliver. 'Buzz off!' And he pushed the pup away, gently but firmly.

After a break of ten minutes we tried again, but the result was much the same. We now had a playful pup on our hands, and Chippu had gone home for the night. We would have to conceal it in the dormitory.

At first we hid the pup in Bimal's locker, but it began yapping and struggling to get out. Tata took it into the shower room, but it wouldn't stay there either. It began running around the dormitory, playing with socks, shoes, slippers, and anything else it could get hold of.

'Watch out!' hissed one of the boys. 'Here's Ma Fisher!'

Mrs Fisher, the Headmaster's wife, was on her nightly rounds, checking to make sure we were all in bed and not up to some mischief.

I grabbed the pup and hid it under my blankets. It was quiet there, happy to nibble at my toes. When Ma Fisher had gone, I let the pup loose again, and for the rest of the night it had the freedom of the dormitory.

At the crack of dawn, before first light, Bimal and I sped out of the dormitory in our pyjamas, taking the pup with us. We banged hard on Mr Oliver's door, and kept knocking until we heard footsteps approaching. As soon as the door opened just a bit (for Mr Oliver, being a cautious man, did not open it all at once) we pushed the pup inside and ran for our lives.

Mr Oliver came to class as usual, but there was no pup with him. Three or four days passed, and still no sign of the pup! Had he passed it on to someone else, or simply let it wander off on its own?

'Here comes Olly!' called Bimal, from our vantage point near the school bell.

Mr Oliver was setting out for his evening walk. He was carrying a stout walnut-wood walking stick—to keep panthers at bay, no doubt. He looked neither left nor right, and if he noticed us watching him, he gave no sign of it. But then, scurrying behind him, came the pup! The creature of various good breeds was accompanying Mr Oliver on his walk. It had been well brushed and was wearing a bright red collar. Like Mr Oliver it took no notice of us, but scampered along beside its new master.

Mr Oliver and the pup were soon inseparable companions, and my friends and I were quite pleased with ourselves. Mr Oliver gave absolutely no indication that he knew where the pup had come from, but when the end-of-term exams were over, and Bimal and I were sure we had failed our maths paper, we were surprised to find that we had passed after all—with grace marks!

'Good old Olly!' said Bimal. 'So he knew all the time.'

Tata, of course, did not need grace marks; he was a whiz at maths. But Bimal and I decided we would thank Mr Oliver for his kindness.

'Nothing to thank me for,' said Mr Oliver brusquely. 'I've seen enough of you two in junior school. It's high time you went up to the senior school—and God help you there!'

Mr Oliver's Diary

Mr Oliver, our maths teacher and Scoutmaster, kept a diary. Here is an extract.

25 April

We have a sleepwalker in the junior dormitory.

Last night Basu, who is prefect in the junior dorm, comes knocking on my door at around 11 p.m. with the startling information that the Chopra boy has walked out of the dormitory and is presently wandering about on the playing field.

Putting on my dressing gown and slippers, I follow the pyjama-clad Basu on to the field where, true enough, young Chopra is walking around in some kind of trance.

'Chopra!' I call out. 'What do you think you're up to? Get back to your dormitory at once!'

No response. He keeps walking away from us.

We follow at a discreet distance. Don't want to startle

him. Sleepwalkers should be woken gently, or so we are told.

Chopra picks up speed. I have a hard time keeping up with him.

'Shall I catch him, sir?' asked Basu.

'No, let's see where he goes?'

Chopra left the field and walked out of the school gate!

'He is going to town, sir!' exclaimed Basu.

'He can't sleepwalk all the way to town.'

I was right. He walked about 100 metres up the road, then turned, and walked straight back straight past us!

'His eyes are open, but he doesn't see us,' observed Basu.

'Definitely sleepwalking.'

Chopra next made a round of H.M.'s vegetable garden, disturbing a couple of porcupines who were rooting around for potatoes; then returned to the main building (with Basu and I in hot pursuit), passed through the dining room and took the stairs to his dormitory. We were in time to see him climb into his bed and nestle down under the blankets. After leading us a merry chase, he was sleeping peacefully, unaware of what had happened.

Basu returned to his bed, and I returned to my room, disturbing Tota in the process, who greeted me with a squawk and a 'bottom's up'.

Made this diary entry in the morning. Looking over

it, I see that I have got my tenses all mixed up. Must have been the excitement.

4 May

Someone has disfigured our Founder's portrait, and H.M. is furious.

The portrait hangs at one end of our assembly hall—a portrait in oils of Rev Constant Endover, who started our schools a century ago. His other achievement was translating the gospels into Pashtu. Later, he was murdered by one of his retainers. His grave (near Peshawar) bears the inscription: 'Well done, thou good and faithful servant.'

But let me not digress.

The Rev Endover was a clean-shaven man, but the desecrator had given him a large handlebar moustache, a bright red clown's nose, a yellow paper hat and a pair of earrings!

We were all ordered in the Assembly Hall, where H.M. harangued us for half an hour, describing the unknown perpetrator as a fiendish and sinister creature who would grow up to be a terrorist. To make matters worse, a closer scrutiny of the portrait's inscription revealed that the lettering of the Founder's name had been altered, so that it read 'Rev Constant Bendover'!

When this was discovered, some of us couldn't help

laughing; this was infectious, and ripples of laughter spread through the hall.

'Silence!' bellowed H.M. 'I want to know who committed this outrage!'

There was an absolute silence, and no one attempted to break it by confessing to the crime.

'Unless the culprit comes forward there will be no exits this weekend.'

A murmur of protest, but no one spoke out.

'And the tuck shop will be closed for a week!' added H.M. Groans all around. This is the unkindest cut of all.

Suddenly a squeaky voice from the front row (Class 1) piped up, 'It was me, sir!'

Popat, the smallest boy in the school, had confessed to the greatest of crimes!

Although taken aback, H.M. was always fussy about grammar.

'It was *I*, Popat!' corrected H.M., his passion for correct usage strong even in a crisis.

'No, sir, it wasn't!' cried Popat, under the impression that H.M. was taking the blame. 'It was *me*!'

'It was *I*!'

'It was *me*!'

At this exchange, everyone in the hall broke down in fits of laughter, and eventually H.M. couldn't help smiling as well.

Popat promised to clean up the portrait in his spare

time, and Miss Ramola promised to help him. Weekend exits restored, tuck shop closure postponed, and Popat a hero for a day.

20 June

Conducted the school marathon. Everyone ran, but hardly anyone crossed the finishing line.

I accompanied the boys to the starting point, near the Governor's mansion, and flagged them off, then followed at a slow jog.

The first to drop out was Chopra, our sleepwalker. I found him on the parapet, holding his sides.

'Exhausted, sir,' he said. 'The distance is too much for me.'

'You cover enough distance in your sleep,' I remarked. 'You've led us a merry chase on several occasions.'

'Maybe that's why I'm so tired, sir. All that sleepwalking. But I don't remember any of it.'

'Well, if you finish the marathon perhaps you'll be too tired to sleepwalk, so get a move on !'

Chopra groaned, got up, and trundled down the road.

The next dropout was Gautam.

'I've got a stich in my side, sir. Not used to so much running.'

'Well, here's your chance to get used to it. Exits next Saturday for the first three to cross the finishing line. You're a good sprinter, always first to reach the tuck shop, so try your luck at a longer distance.' And I prodded him into action.

Rounded a corner and found Tata, Mirchi and Basu standing around a small fire on which corn cobs were being roasted.

'Have a bhutta, sir,' said Tata, always hospitable.

'They're good with a little salt,' added Mirchi.

'But best with butter,' said Basu,' except we don't have any butter.'

'I'll butter the three of you if you don't get a move on,' I said. And they collected their roasted corn and sped down the road. But I've no idea where they went next, because they did not finish the race.

Caught up with Rudra who was strolling along, talking to someone on his cell phone.

'You know cell phones are not allowed in school,' I said, taking it from him.

'But we're outside the school, sir. And I was only listening to music.'

'You can collect the phone at the end of the term. Now make music with your feet. Let's see you tap dance down the school.'

Rudra grinned and started dancing on the road.

'That's not a tap dance,' I said.

'No sir, it's Kathakali. Didn't you know I'm from the South?'

'Well, Kathakali down to the school, then. Maybe you'll get a prize from Mrs Tonk.'

Mrs Tonk, principal of the girls' school, was waiting to give away the first prize—a hamper of chocolates, biscuits, buns, and laddoos. And who should come in first but 'Fatty' Prakash, huffing and puffing, but pounding down the road with grim determination. He must have had prior information as to the nature of the first prize. If you have an object in life, you will attain it with a little extra effort.

Uncle Ken's Rumble in the Jungle

Uncle Ken drove Grandfather's old Fiat along the forest road at an incredible 30 mph, scattering pheasants, partridges and junglefowl as he clattered along. He had come in search of the disappearing red junglefowl, and I could see why the bird had disappeared. Too many noisy human beings had invaded its habitat.

By the time we reached the forest rest house, one of the car doors had fallen off its hinges, and a large lantana bush had got entwined in the bumper.

'Never mind,' said Uncle Ken. 'It's all part of the adventure!'

The rest house had been reserved for Uncle Ken, thanks to Grandfather's good relations with the forest department. But I was the only other person in the car. No one else would trust himself or herself to Uncle Ken's driving. He treated a car as though it were a low-flying aircraft having some difficulty in getting off the runway.

As we arrived at the rest house, a number of hens made a dash for safety.

'Look, junglefowl!' exclaimed Uncle Ken.

'Domestic fowl,' I said. 'They must belong to the forest guards.'

I was right, of course. One of the hens was destined to be served up as chicken curry later that day. The jungle birds avoided the neighbourhood of the rest house, just in case they were mistaken for poultry and went into the cooking pot.

Uncle Ken was all for starting his search right away, and after a brief interval during which we were served with tea and pakoras (prepared by a forest guard, who it turned out was also a good cook) we set off on foot into the jungle in search of the elusive red junglefowl.

'No tigers around here, are there?' asked Uncle Ken, just to be on the safe side.

'No tigers on this range,' said the guard. 'Just elephants.'

Uncle Ken wasn't afraid of elephants. He'd been for numerous elephant rides at the Lucknow zoo. He'd also seen Sabu in *Elephant Boy*.

A small wooden bridge took us across a little river, and then we were in thick jungle, following the forest guard who led us along a path that was frequently blocked by broken tree branches and pieces of bamboo.

'Why all these broken branches?' asked Uncle Ken.

'The elephants, sir,' replied our guard. 'They passed through last night. They like certain leaves, as well as young bamboo shoots.'

We saw a number of spotted deer and several pheasants, but no red junglefowl. That evening we sat out on the veranda of the rest house. All was silent, except for the distant trumpeting of elephants. Then, from the stream, came the chanting of hundreds of frogs.

There were tenors and baritones, sopranos and contraltos, and occasionally a bass deep enough to have pleased the great Chaliapin. They sang duets and quartets from *La Boheme* and other Italian operas, drowning out all other jungle sounds except for the occasional cry of a jackal doing his best to join in.

'We might as well sing,' said Uncle Ken, and began singing the 'Indian Love Call' in his best Nelson Eddy manner.

The frogs fell silent, obviously awestruck; but instead of receiving an answering love call, Uncle Ken was answered by even more strident jackal calls—not one, but several—with the result that all self-respecting denizens of the forest fled from the vicinity, and we saw no wildlife that night apart from a frightened rabbit that sped across the clearing and vanished into the darkness.

Early next morning we renewed our efforts to track down the red junglefowl, but it remained elusive. Returning to the rest house dusty and weary, Uncle Ken exclaimed: 'There it is—a red junglefowl!'

But it turned out to be the caretaker's cock-bird, a handsome fellow all red and gold, but not the jungle variety.

Disappointed, Uncle Ken decided to return to civilization. Another night in the rest house did not appeal to him. He had run out of songs to sing.

In any case, the weather had changed overnight and a light drizzle was falling as we started out. This had turned to a steady downpour by the time we reached the bridge across the Suswa river. And standing in the middle of the bridge was an elephant.

He was a lone tusker and didn't look too friendly.

Uncle Ken blew his horn, and that was a mistake.

It was a strident, penetrating horn, highly effective on city roads but out of place in the forest. The elephant took it as a challenge, and returned the blast of the horn with a shrill trumpeting of its own. It took a few steps forward. Uncle Ken put the car into reverse.

'Is there another way out of here?' he asked.

'There's a side road,' I said recalling an earlier trip with Grandfather. 'It will take us to the Kansrao railway station.'

'What ho!' cried Uncle Ken. 'To the station we go!'

And he turned the car and drove back until we came to the turning.

The narrow road was now a rushing torrent of rain

water and all Uncle Ken's driving skills were put to the test. He had on one occasion driven through a brick wall, so he knew all about obstacles; but they were normally stationary ones.

'More elephants,' I said, as two large pachyderms loomed out of the rain-drenched forest.

'Elephants to the right of us, elephants to the left of us!' chanted Uncle Ken, misquoting Tennysons's *Charge of the Light Brigade*. 'Into the valley of death rode the six hundred!'

'There are now three of them,' I observed.

'Not my lucky number,' said Uncle Ken and pressed hard on the accelerator. We lurched forward, almost running over a terrified barking deer.

'Is four your lucky number, Uncle Ken?'

'Why do you ask?'

'Well, there are now four of them behind us. And they are catching up quite fast!'

'I see the station ahead,' cried Uncle Ken, as we drove into a clearing where a tiny railway station stood like a beacon of safety in the wilderness.

The car came to a grinding halt. We abandoned it and ran for the building.

The stationmaster, seeing our predicament, beckoned to us to enter the station building, which was little more than a two-room shed and platform. He took us inside his tiny control room and shut the steel gate behind us.

'The elephants won't bother you here,' he said. 'But say goodbye to your car.'

We looked out of the window and were horrified to see Grandfather's Fiat overturned by one of the elephants, while another proceeded to trample it underfoot. The other elephants joined in the mayhem and soon the car was a flattened piece of junk.

'I'm Stationmaster Abdul Rauf,' the friendly stationmaster introduced himself. 'I know a good scrap dealer in Doiwala. I'll give you his address.'

'But how do we get out of here?' asked Uncle Ken.

'Well, it's only an hour's walk to Doiwala,' said our benefactor. 'But I wouldn't advise walking, not with those elephants around. Stay and have a cup of tea. The Dehra Express will pass through shortly. It stops for a few minutes. And it's only half an hour to Dehra from here.'

He punched out a couple of rail tickets. 'Here you are, my friends. Just two rupees each. The cheapest rail journey in India. And those tickets carry an insurance value of two lakh rupees each, should an accident befall you between here and Dehradun.'

Uncle Ken's eyes lit up. 'You mean, if one of us falls out of the train?' he asked.

'Out of the moving train,' clarified the stationmaster. 'There will be an enquiry, of course. Some people try to fake an accident.'

But Uncle Ken decided against falling out of the train and making a fortune. He'd had enough excitement for the day. We got home safely enough, taking a pony-cart from the Dehra station to our house.

'Where's my car?' asked Grandfather, as we staggered up the veranda steps.

'It had a small accident,' said Uncle Ken. 'We left it outside the Kansrao railway station. I'll collect it later.'

'I'm starving,' I said. 'Haven't eaten since morning.'

'Well, come and have your dinner,' said Granny. 'I've made something special for you. One of your Grandfather's hunting friends sent us a junglefowl. I've made a nice roast. Try it with apple sauce.'

Uncle Ken did not ask if the junglefowl was red, grey or technicoloured. He was first to the dining table.

Granny had anticipated this, and served me with a chicken leg, giving the other leg to Grandfather.

'I rather fancy the breast myself,' she said, and this left Uncle Ken with a long and scrawny neck—which was rather like his own neck, and definitely more than he deserved.

Monkey Trouble

Grandfather bought Tutu from a street entertainer for the sum of ten rupees. The man had three monkeys. Tutu was the smallest but the most mischievous. She was tied up most of the time. The little monkey looked so miserable with a collar and chain that Grandfather decided she would be much happier in our home. He had a weakness for keeping unusual pets. It was a habit that I, at the age of eight or nine, used to encourage.

Grandmother at first objected to having a monkey in the house. 'You have enough pets as it is,' she said, referring to Grandfather's goat, several white mice and a small tortoise.

'But I don't have any,' I said.

'You're wicked enough for two monkeys. One boy in the house is all I can take.'

'Ah, but Tutu isn't a boy,' said Grandfather triumphantly. 'This is a little girl monkey!'

Grandmother gave in. She had always wanted a little girl in the house. She believed girls were less troublesome than boys. Tutu was to prove her wrong.

Tutu was a pretty little monkey. Her bright eyes sparkled with mischief beneath deep-set eyebrows. And her teeth, which were a pearly white, were often revealed in a grin that frightened the wits out of Aunt Ruby, whose nerves had already suffered from the presence of Grandfather's pet python in the house at Lucknow. But this was Dehra, my grandparents' house, and aunts and uncles had to put up with our pets.

Tutu's hands had a dried-up look, as though they had been pickled in the sun for many years. One of the first things I taught her was to shake hands, and this she insisted on doing with all who visited the house. Peppery Major Malik would have to stoop and shake hands with Tutu before he could enter the drawing room, otherwise Tutu would climb on his shoulder and stay there, roughing up his hair and playing with his moustache.

Uncle Ken couldn't stand any of our pets and took a particular dislike to Tutu, who was always making faces at him. But as Uncle Ken was never in a job for long, and depended on Grandfather's good-natured generosity, he had to shake hands with Tutu like everyone else.

Tutu's fingers were quick and wicked. And her tail, while adding to her good looks (Grandfather believed a tail would add to anyone's good looks), also served as a third hand. She could use it to hang from a branch, and it was capable of scooping up any delicacy that might be out of reach of her hands.

Aunt Ruby had not been informed of Tutu's arrival. Loud shrieks from her bedroom brought us running to see what was wrong. It was only Tutu trying on Aunt Ruby's petticoats! They were much too large, of course, and when Aunt Ruby entered the room all she saw was a faceless, white blob jumping up and down on the bed.

We disentangled Tutu and soothed Aunt Ruby. I gave Tutu a bunch of sweet peas to make her happy. Granny didn't like anyone plucking her sweet peas, so I took some from Major Malik's garden while he was having his afternoon siesta.

Then Uncle Ken complained that his hairbrush was missing. We found Tutu sunning herself on the back verandah, using the hairbrush to scratch her armpits. I took it from her and handed it back to Uncle Ken with an apology; but he flung the brush away with an oath.

'Such a fuss about nothing,' I said. 'Tutu doesn't have fleas!'

'No, and she bathes more often than Ken,' said Grandfather, who had borrowed Aunt Ruby's shampoo for giving Tutu a bath.

All the same, Grandmother objected to Tutu being given the run of the house. Tutu had to spend her nights in the outhouse, in the company of the goat. They got on quite well, and it was not long before Tutu was seen sitting comfortably on the back of the goat, while the goat roamed the back garden in search of its favourite grass.

The day Grandfather had to visit Meerut to collect his railway pension, he decided to take Tutu and me along—to keep us both out of mischief, he said. To prevent Tutu from wandering about on the train, causing inconvenience to passengers, she was provided with a large, black travelling bag. This, with some straw at the bottom, became her compartment. Grandfather and I paid for our seats, and we took Tutu along as hand baggage.

There was enough space for Tutu to look out of the bag occasionally, and to be fed with bananas and biscuits, but she could not get her hands through the opening and the canvas was too strong for her to bite her way through.

Tutu's efforts to get out only had the effect of making the bag roll about on the floor or occasionally jump into the air—an exhibition that attracted a curious crowd of onlookers both at Dehra and Meerut railway stations.

Anyway, Tutu remained in the bag as far as Meerut, but while Grandfather was producing our tickets at the turnstile, she suddenly poked her head out of the bag and gave the ticket collector a wide grin.

The poor man was taken aback. But, with great presence of mind and much to Grandfather's annoyance, he said, 'Sir, you have a dog with you. You'll have to buy a ticket for it.'

'It's not a dog!' said Grandfather indignantly. 'This is a baby monkey of the species macacus-mischievous, closely related to the human species homus-horriblis! And there is no charge for babies!'

'It's as big as a cat,' said the ticket collector.

'Next you'll be asking to see her mother,' snapped Grandfather.'

In vain did he take Tutu out of the bag. In vain did he try to prove that a young monkey did not qualify as a dog or a cat or even as a quadruped. Tutu was classified as a dog by the ticket collector, and five rupees were handed over as her fare.

Then Grandfather, just to get his own back, took from his pocket the small tortoise that he sometimes carried about, and asked, 'And what must I pay for this, since you charge for all creatures great and small?'

The ticket collector looked closely at the tortoise, prodded it with his forefinger, gave Grandfather a triumphant look, and announced, 'No charge, sir. It is not a dog!'

Winters in north India can be very cold. A great treat for Tutu on winter evenings was the large bowl of hot water given to her by Grandmother for a bath. Tutu would cunningly test the temperature with her hand, then gradually step into the bath, first one foot, then the other (as she had seen me doing) until she was in the water up to her neck.

Once comfortable, she would take the soap in her hands or feet and rub herself all over. When the water became cold she would get out and run as quickly as she could to the kitchen fire in order to dry herself. If anyone laughed at her during this performance, Tutu's feelings would be hurt and she would refuse to go on with the bath.

One day Tutu almost succeeded in boiling herself alive. Grandmother had left a large kettle on the fire for tea. And Tutu, all by herself and with nothing better to do, decided to remove the lid. Finding the water just warm enough for a bath, she got in, with her head sticking out from the open kettle.

This was fine for a while, until the water began to get heated. Tutu raised herself a little out of the kettle. But finding it cold outside, she sat down again. She continued hopping up and down for some time until Grandmother returned and hauled her, half-boiled, out of the kettle.

'What's for tea today?' asked Uncle Ken gleefully. 'Boiled eggs and a half-boiled monkey?'

But Tutu was none the worse for the adventure and continued to bathe more regularly than Uncle Ken.

Aunt Ruby was a frequent taker of baths. This met with Tutu's approval—so much so, that one day, when

Aunt Ruby had finished shampooing her hair she looked up through a lather of bubbles and soapsuds to see Tutu sitting opposite her in the bath, following her example.

One day Aunt Ruby took us all by surprise. She announced that she had become engaged. We had always thought Aunt Ruby would never marry — she had often said so herself — but it appeared that the right man had now come along in the person of Rocky Fernandes, a schoolteacher from Goa.

Rocky was a tall, firm-jawed, good-natured man, a couple of years younger than Aunt Ruby. He had a fine baritone voice and sang in the manner of the great Nelson Eddy. As Grandmother liked baritone singers, Rocky was soon in her good books.

'But what on earth does he see in her?' Uncle Ken wanted to know.

'More than any girl has seen in you!' snapped Grandmother. 'Ruby's a fine girl. And they're both teachers. Maybe they can start a school of their own.'

Rocky visited the house quite often and brought me chocolates and cashewnuts, of which he seemed to have an unlimited supply. He also taught me several marching songs. Naturally I approved of Rocky. Aunt Ruby won my grudging admiration for having made such a wise choice.

One day I overheard them talking of going to the bazaar to buy an engagement ring. I decided I would go along too. But as Aunt Ruby had made it clear that she did not want me around I decided that I had better follow at a discreet distance. Tutu, becoming aware that a mission of some importance was under way, decided to follow me. But as I had not invited her along, she too decided to keep out of sight.

Once in the crowded bazaar, I was able to get quite close to Aunt Ruby and Rocky without being spotted. I waited until they had settled down in a large jewellery shop before sauntering past and spotting them as though by accident. Aunt Ruby wasn't too pleased at seeing me, but Rocky waved and called out, 'Come and join us! Help your aunt choose a beautiful ring!'

The whole thing seemed to be a waste of good money, but I did not say so—Aunt Ruby was giving me one of her more unloving looks.

'Look, these are pretty!' I said, pointing to some cheap, bright agates set in white metal. But Aunt Ruby wasn't looking. She was immersed in a case of diamonds.

'Why not a ruby for Aunt Ruby?' I suggested, trying to please her.

'That's her lucky stone,' said Rocky. 'Diamonds are the thing for engagement.' And he started singing a song about a diamond being a girl's best friend.

While the jeweller and Aunt Ruby were sifting through the diamond rings, and Rocky was trying out another tune, Tutu had slipped into the shop without being noticed by anyone but me. A little squeal of delight was the first sign she gave of her presence. Everyone looked up to see her trying on a pretty necklace.

'And what are those stones?' I asked.

'They look like pearls,' said Rocky.

'They are pearls,' shouted the shopkeeper, making a grab for them.

'It's that dreadful monkey!' cried Aunt Ruby. 'I knew that boy would bring him here!'

The necklace was already adorning Tutu's neck. I thought she looked rather nice in them, but she gave us no time to admire the effect. Springing out of our reach Tutu dodged around Rocky, slipped between my legs, and made for the crowded road. I ran after her, shouting to her to stop, but she wasn't listening.

There were no branches to assist Tutu in her progress, but she used the heads and shoulders of people as springboards and so made rapid headway through the bazaar.

The jeweller left his shop and ran after us. So did Rocky. So did several bystanders who had seen the incident. And others, who had no idea what it was all about, joined in the chase. As Grandfather used to say, 'In a crowd, everyone plays follow-the-leader even when they don't know who's leading.'

Tutu tried to make her escape speedier by leaping on to the back of a passing scooterist. The scooter swerved into a fruit stall and came to a standstill under a heap of bananas, while the scooterist found himself in the arms of an indignant fruitseller. Tutu peeled a banana and ate part of it before deciding to move on.

From an awning she made an emergency landing on a washerman's donkey. The donkey promptly panicked and rushed down the road, while bundles of washing fell by the wayside. The washerman joined in the chase. Children on their way to school decided that there was something better to do than attend classes. With shouts of glee, they soon overtook their panting elders.

Tutu finally left the bazaar and took a road leading in the direction of our house. But knowing that she would be caught and locked up once she got home, she decided to end the chase by ridding herself of the necklace. Deftly removing it from her neck, she flung it into the small canal that ran down that road.

The jeweller, with a cry of anguish, plunged into the canal. So did Rocky. So did I. So did several other people, both adults and children. It had become a treasure hunt!

Some twenty minutes later, Rocky shouted, 'I've found it!' Covered in mud, water lilies, ferns and tadpoles, we emerged from the canal, and Rocky presented the necklace to the relieved shopkeeper.

Everyone trudged back to the bazaar to find Aunt Ruby waiting in the shop, still trying to make up her mind about a suitable engagement ring.

Finally the ring was bought, the engagement was announced, and a date was set for the wedding.

'I don't want that monkey anywhere near us on our wedding day,' declared Aunt Ruby.

'We'll lock her up in the outhouse,' promised Grandfather. 'And we'll let her out only after you've left for your honeymoon.'

A few days before the wedding I found Tutu in the kitchen helping Grandmother prepare the wedding cake. Tutu often helped with the cooking and, when Grandmother wasn't looking, added herbs, spices, and other interesting items to the pots—so that occasionally we found a chilli in the custard or an onion in the jelly or a strawberry floating on the chicken soup.

Sometimes these additions improved a dish, sometimes they did not. Uncle Ken lost a tooth when he bit firmly into a sandwich which contained walnut shells.

I'm not sure exactly what went into that wedding cake when Grandmother wasn't looking—she insisted that Tutu was always very well behaved in the kitchen—but I did spot Tutu stirring in some red chilli sauce, bitter gourd seeds and a generous helping of eggshells!

It's true that some of the guests were not seen for several days after the wedding but no one said anything against the cake. Most people thought it had an interesting flavour.

The great day dawned, and the wedding guests made their way to the little church that stood on the outskirts of Dehra—a town with a church, two mosques and several temples.

I had offered to dress Tutu up as a bridesmaid and bring her along, but no one except Grandfather thought it was a good idea. So I was an obedient boy and locked Tutu in the outhouse. I did, however, leave the skylight open a little. Grandmother had always said that fresh air was good for growing children, and I thought Tutu should have her share of it.

The wedding ceremony went without a hitch. Aunt Ruby looked a picture, and Rocky looked like a film star.

Grandfather played the organ, and did so with such gusto that the small choir could hardly be heard. Grandmother cried a little. I sat quietly in a corner, with the little tortoise on my lap.

When the service was over, we trooped out into the sunshine and made our way back to the house for the reception.

The feast had been laid out on tables in the garden. As the gardener had been left in charge, everything was in order. Tutu was on her best behaviour. She had, it appeared, used the skylight to avail of more fresh air outside, and now sat beside the three-tier wedding cake, guarding it against crows, squirrels and the goat. She greeted the guests with squeals of delight.

It was too much for Aunt Ruby. She flew at Tutu in a rage. And Tutu, sensing that she was not welcome, leapt away, taking with her the top tier of the wedding cake.

Led by Major Malik, we followed her into the orchard, only to find that she had climbed to the top of the jackfruit tree. From there she proceeded to pelt us with bits of wedding cake. She had also managed to get hold of a bag of confetti, and when she ran out of cake she showered us with confetti.

'That's more like it!' said the good-humoured Rocky. 'Now let's return to the party, folks!'

Uncle Ken remained with Major Malik, determined to chase Tutu away. He kept throwing stones into the tree, until he received a large piece of cake bang on his nose. Muttering threats, he returned to the party, leaving the Major to do battle.

When the festivities were finally over, Uncle Ken took the unnecessary old car out of the garage and drove up to the veranda steps. He was going to drive Aunt Ruby and Rocky to the nearby hill resort of Mussoorie, where they were going for their honeymoon.

Watched by family and friends, Aunt Ruby and Rocky climbed into the back seat. Aunt Ruby waved regally to everyone. She leant out of the window and offered me her cheek and I had to kiss her farewell. Everyone wished them luck.

As Rocky burst into song Uncle Ken opened the throttle and stepped on the accelerator. The car shot forward in a cloud of dust.

Rocky and Aunt Ruby continued to wave to us. And so did Tutu from her perch on the rear bumper! She was clutching a bag in her hands and showering confetti on all who stood in the driveway.

'They don't know Tutu's with them!' I exclaimed. 'She'll go all the way to Mussoorie! Will Aunt Ruby let her stay with them?'

'Tutu might ruin the honeymoon,' said Grandfather. 'But don't worry—our Ken will bring her back!'

Owls in the Family

One winter morning, my grandfather and I found a baby spotted owlet by the veranda steps of our home in Dehradun. When Grandfather picked it up the owlet hissed and clacked its bill but then, after a meal of raw meat and water, settled down under my bed.

Spotted owlets are small birds. A fully grown one is no larger than a thrush and they have none of the sinister appearance of large owls. I had once found a pair of them in our mango tree and by tapping on the tree trunk had persuaded one to show an enquiring face at the entrance to its hole. The owlet is not normally afraid of man nor is it strictly a night bird. But it prefers to stay at home during the day as it is sometimes attacked by other birds who consider all owls their enemies.

The little owlet was quite happy under my bed. The following day we found a second baby owlet in almost the same spot on the veranda and only then did we realize that where the rainwater pipe emerged through the roof, there was a rough sort of nest from which the birds had fallen. We took the second young owl to join the first and fed them both.

When I went to bed, they were on the window ledge just inside the mosquito netting and later in the night, their mother found them there. From outside, she crooned and gurgled for a long time and in the morning, I found she had left a mouse with its tail tucked through the netting. Obviously, she put no great trust in me as a foster parent.

The young birds thrived and ten days later, Grandfather and I took them into the garden to release them. I had placed one on a branch of the mango tree and was stooping to pick up the other when I received a heavy blow on the back of the head. A second or two later, the mother owl swooped down on Grandfather but he was quite agile and ducked out of the way.

Quickly, I placed the second owl under the mango tree. Then from a safe distance we watched the mother fly down and lead her offspring into the long grass at the edge of the garden. We thought she would take her family away from our rather strange household but next morning I found the two owlets perched on the hatstand in the veranda.

I ran to tell Grandfather and when we came back we found the mother sitting on the birdbath a few metres away. She was evidently feeling sorry for her behaviour the previous day because she greeted us with a soft 'whoo-whoo'.

'Now there's an unselfish mother for you,' said Grandfather. 'It's obvious she wants us to keep an eye on them. They're probably getting too big for her to manage.'

So the owlets became regular members of our household and were among the few pets that Grandmother took a liking to. She objected to all snakes, most monkeys and some crows—we'd had all these pets from time to time—but she took quite a fancy to the owlets and frequently fed them spaghetti!

They loved to sit and splash in a shallow dish provided by Grandmother. They enjoyed it even more if cold water was poured over them from a jug while they were in the bath. They would get thoroughly wet, jump out and perch on a towel rack, shake themselves and return for a second splash and sometimes a third. During the day they dozed on a hatstand. After dark, they had the freedom of the house and their nightly occupation was catching beetles, the kitchen quarters being a happy hunting ground. With their razor-sharp eyes and powerful beaks, they were excellent pest-destroyers.

Looking back on those childhood days, I carry in my mind a picture of Grandmother in her rocking chair with a contented owlet sprawled across her aproned lap. Once, on entering a room while she was taking an afternoon nap, I saw one of the owlets had crawled up her pillow till its head was snuggled under her ear.

Both Grandmother and the owlet were snoring.

Grandfather Fights an Ostrich

Before Grandfather joined the Indian Railways, he worked for some time on the East African Railways, and it was during that period that he had his famous encounter with the ostrich. My childhood was frequently enlivened by this oft-told tale of my grandfather's, and I give it here in his own words—or as well as I can remember them:

While engaged in the laying of a new railway line, I had a miraculous escape from an awful death. I lived in a small township, but my work lay some twelve miles away, and although I had a tent on the works, I often had to go into town on horseback.

On one occasion, an accident happening to my horse, I got a lift into town, hoping that someone might do me a similar favour on my way back. But this was not to be, and I made up my mind next morning to do the journey on foot, shortening the distance by taking a cut through the hills which would save me about six miles.

To take this shortcut it was necessary to cross an ostrich 'camp' or farm. To venture across these 'camps' in the breeding season, especially on foot, can be dangerous, for during this time the male birds are extremely ferocious.

But being familiar with the ways of ostriches, I knew that my dog would scare away any ostrich which tried to attack me. Strange though it may seem, even the biggest ostrich (and some of them grow to a height of nine feet) will bolt faster than a racehorse at the sight of even a small dog. And so, in company with my dog (a mongrel who had adopted me the previous month), I felt reasonably safe.

On arrival at the 'camp' I got through the wire fencing and, keeping a good lookout, dodged across the spaces between the thorn bushes, now and then getting a sight of the birds which were feeding some distance away.

I had gone about half a mile from the fencing when up started a hare, and in an instant my dog gave chase. I tried to call him back although I knew it was useless, since chasing hares was a passion with him.

Whether it was the dog's bark or my own shouting, I don't know, but just what I was most anxious to avoid immediately happened: the ostriches were startled and began darting to and fro. Suddenly I saw a big male bird emerge from a thicket about a hundred yards away. He stood still and stared at me for a few moments; then, expanding his wings and with his tail erect, he came bounding towards me.

Believing discretion to be the better part of valour (at least in that particular situation), I turned and ran towards the fence. But it was an unequal race. What were my steps of two or three feet against the creature's great strides of sixteen to twenty feet? There was only one hope: to wait for the ostrich behind some bush and try to dodge him till he tired. A dodging game was obviously my only chance.

Altering course a little, I rushed for the nearest clump of bushes where, gasping for breath, I waited for my pursuer. The great bird was almost immediately upon me, and a strange encounter commenced. This way and that I dodged, taking great care that I did not get directly in front of his deadly kick. The ostrich kicks forward, and with such terrific force that his great chisel-like nails, if they struck, would rip one open from head to foot.

Breathless, and really quite helpless, I prayed wildly for help as I circled the bush, which was about twelve feet in diameter and some six feet in height. My strength was rapidly failing, and I realized it would be impossible to keep up the struggle much longer; I was ready to drop from sheer exhaustion. As if aware of my condition, the infuriated bird suddenly doubled on his course and charged straight at me. With a desperate effort I managed to step to one side. How it happened I don't know, but I found myself holding on to one of the creature's wings, close to its body.

It was now the bird's turn to be frightened, and he began to turn, or rather waltz, moving round and round so quickly that my feet were soon swinging out almost horizontally. All the time the ostrich kept opening and shutting his beak with loud snaps.

Imagine my situation as I clung desperately to the wing of the enraged bird, which was whirling me round and round as if I had been a cork! My arms soon began to ache with the strain, and the swift and continuous circling was making me dizzy. But I knew that if I relaxed my hold, a terrible fate awaited me: I should be promptly trampled to death by the spiteful bird.

Round and round we went in a great circle. It seemed as if my enemy would never tire. But I knew I could not hold on much longer.

Suddenly the bird went into reverse! This unexpected movement not only had the effect of making me lose my hold but sent me sprawling to the ground. I landed in a heap at the foot of the thorn bush. In an instant, almost before I had time to realize what had happened, the ostrich was upon me. I thought the end had come. Instinctively I put up my hands to protect my face. But, to my amazement, the great bird did not strike.

I moved my hands from my face, and there stood the ostrich with one foot raised, ready to rip me open! I couldn't move. Was the bird going to play with me like a cat with a mouse, and prolong the agony?

As I watched fascinated, I saw him turn his head sharply to the left. A second later he jumped back, turned, and made off as fast as he could go. Dazed, I wondered what had happened.

I soon found out, for, to my great joy, I heard the bark of my truant dog, and the next moment he was jumping around me, licking my face and hands.

Needless to say, I returned his caresses most affectionately! And I took good care to see that he did not leave my side until we were well clear of the ostrich 'camp'.

Return of the White Pigeon

About fifty years ago, on the outskirts of Dehradun, there lived a happily married couple, an English colonel and his beautiful Persian wife. They were both enthusiastic gardeners, and their beautiful bungalow was covered with bougainvillea and *Gul-i-Phanoos*, while in the garden the fragrance of the rose challenged the sweet scent of the jasmine.

They had lived together many years when the wife suddenly became very ill. Nothing could be done for her. As she lay dying, she told her servants that she would return to her beloved garden in the form of a white pigeon so that she could be near her husband and the place she loved so dearly.

The couple had no children, and as the years passed after his wife's death the colonel found life very lonely. When he met an attractive English widow a few years younger than himself, he married her and brought her home to his beautiful house. But as he was carrying his new bride through the porch and up the veranda steps, a white pigeon came fluttering into the garden and perched on a rose bush. There it remained for a long time, cooing and murmuring in a sad, subdued manner.

Every day it entered the garden and alighted on the rose bush where it would call sadly and persistently. The servants became upset and even frightened. They remembered their previous mistress's dying promise, and they were convinced that her spirit dwelt in the white pigeon.

When the colonel's new wife heard the story, she was naturally upset. Her husband did not give any credence to the tale, but when he saw how troubled his new wife looked, he decided to do something about it. And so one day, when the pigeon appeared, he took his rifle and slipped out of the house, quietly making his way down the verandah steps. When he saw the pigeon on the rose bush, he raised his gun, took aim, and fired.

There was a high-pitched woman's scream. And then the pigeon flew away unsteadily, its white breast dark with blood. Where it fell, no one knew.

That same night the colonel died in his sleep. The doctor put it down to heart failure, which was true enough; but the servants said that their master had always kept good health, and they were sure his death had something to do with the killing of the white pigeon.

The colonel's widow left Dehradun, and the beautiful

bungalow fell into ruin. The garden became a jungle, and jackals passed through the abandoned rooms. The colonel had been buried in the grounds of his estate, and the gravestone can still be found, although the inscription has long since disappeared.

Few people pass that way. But those who do, say that they have often seen a white pigeon resting on the grave, a white pigeon with a crimson stain on its breast.

The Parrot Who Wouldn't Talk

'You're no beauty! Can't talk, can't sing, can't dance!'

With these words Aunt Ruby would taunt the unfortunate parakeet, who glared morosely at everyone from his ornamental cage at one end of the long veranda of Grandmother's bungalow in north India.

In those distant days, almost everyone—Indian or European—kept a pet parrot or parakeet, or 'lovebird' as some of the smaller ones were called. Sometimes these birds became great talkers, or rather mimics, and would learn to recite entire mantras or admonitions to the children of the house, such as '*Padho, beta, padho!*' or, for the benefit of boys like me, 'Don't be greedy, don't be greedy!'

These expressions were, of course, picked up by the parrot over a period of time, after many repetitions by some member of the household who had taken on the task of teaching the bird to talk.

But our parrot refused to talk.

He'd been bought by Aunt Ruby from a bird-catcher

who'd visited all the houses on our road, selling caged birds ranging from colourful budgerigars to chirpy little munnias and even common sparrows that had been dabbed with paint and passed off as some exotic species. Neither Granny nor Grandfather were keen on keeping caged birds as pets, but Aunt Ruby threatened to throw a tantrum if she did not get her way—and Aunt Ruby's tantrums were dreadful to behold!

Anyway, she insisted on keeping the parrot and teaching it to talk. But the bird took an instant dislike to my aunt and resisted all her blandishments.

'Kiss, kiss!' Aunt Ruby would coo, putting her face close to the bars of the cage. But the parrot would back away, its beady little eyes getting even smaller with anger at the prospect of being kissed by Aunt Ruby. And on one occasion it lunged forward without warning and knocked my aunt's spectacles off her nose.

After that Aunt Ruby gave up her endearments and became quite hostile towards the poor bird, making faces at it and calling out 'can't talk, can't sing, can't dance' and other nasty comments.

It fell upon me, then ten years old, to feed the parrot, and it seemed quite happy to receive green chillies and ripe tomatoes from my hands, these delicacies being supplemented by slices of mango, for it was then the mango season. This also gave me an opportunity to consume a couple of mangoes while feeding the parrot!

One afternoon, while everyone was indoors enjoying a siesta, I gave the parrot its lunch and then deliberately left the cage door open. Seconds later, the bird was winging its way to the freedom of the mango orchard.

At the same time Grandfather came to the veranda and remarked, 'I see your aunt's parrot has escaped!'

'The door was quite loose,' I said with a shrug. 'Well, I don't suppose we'll see it again.'

Aunt Ruby was upset at first, and threatened to buy another bird. We put her off by promising to buy her a bowl of goldfish.

'But goldfish don't talk!' she protested.

'Well, neither did your bird,' said Grandfather. 'So we'll get you a gramophone. You can listen to Clara Cluck all day. They say she sings like a nightingale.'

I thought we'd never see the parrot again, but it probably missed its green chillies, because a few days later I found the bird sitting on the veranda railing, looking expectantly at me with its head cocked to one side. Unselfishly I gave the parrot half of my mango.

While the bird was enjoying the mango, Aunt Ruby emerged from her room and, with a cry of surprise, called out, 'Look, it's my parrot come back! He must have missed me!'

With a loud squawk, the parrot flew out of her reach and, perching on the nearest rose bush, glared at her and shrieked in my aunt's familiar tones: 'You're no beauty! Can't talk, can't sing, can't dance!'

Aunt Ruby went ruby-red and dashed indoors.

But that wasn't the end of the affair. The parrot became a frequent visitor to the garden and veranda, and whenever it saw Aunt Ruby it would call out, 'You're no beauty, you're no beauty! Can't talk, can't sing, can't dance!'

The parrot had learnt to talk after all!

The Canal

We loved to bathe there, on hot summer afternoons—
Sushil and Raju and Pitamber and I—and there were
others as well, but we were the regulars, the ones who
met at other times too, eating at chaat shops or riding
on bicycles into the tea gardens.

The canal has disappeared—or rather, it has gone
underground, having been covered over with concrete
to widen the road to which it ran parallel for most of
its way. Here and there it went through a couple of
large properties, and it was at the extremity of one
of these—just inside the boundaries of Miss Gamla's
house—that the canal went into a loop, where it was
joined by another small canal, and this was the best
place for bathing or just romping around. The smaller
boys wore nothing, but we had just reached the years of
puberty and kept our *kacchas* on. So Miss Gamla really
had nothing to complain about.

I'm not sure if this was her real name. I think we
called her Miss Gamla because of the large number of

gamlas or flowerpots that surrounded her house. They filled the veranda, decorated the windows, and lined the approach road. She had a mali who was always watering the pots. And there was no shortage of water, the canal being nearby.

But Miss Gamla did not like small boys. Or big boys, for that matter. She placed us high on her list of Pests, along with monkeys (who raided her kitchen), sparrows (who shattered her sweet peas) and goats (who ate her geraniums). We did none of these things, being strictly fun-loving creatures; but we did make a lot of noise, spoiling her afternoon siesta. And I think she was offended by the sight of our near-naked bodies cavorting about on the boundaries of her estate. A spinster in her sixties, the proximity of naked flesh, no matter how immature, perhaps disturbed and upset her.

She had a companion—a noisy peke, who followed her around everywhere and set up an ear-splitting barking at anyone who came near. It was the barking, rather than our play, that woke her in the afternoons. And then she would emerge from her back veranda, waving a stick at us, and shouting at us to be off.

We would collect our clothes, and lurk behind a screen of lantana bushes, returning to the canal as soon as lady and dog were back in the house.

The canal came down from the foothills, from a hill called Nalapani where a famous battle had taken place a hundred and fifty years back, between the British and the Gurkhas. But for some quirky reason, possibly because we were not very good at history, we called it the Panipat canal, after a more famous battle once fought north of Delhi.

We had our own mock battles, wrestling on the grassy banks of the canal before plunging into the water—it was no more than waist-high—flailing around with shouts of joy, with no one to hinder our animal spirits . . .

Except Miss Gamla.

Down the path she hobbled—she had a pronounced limp—waving her walnut-wood walking stick at us, while her bulging-eyed peke came yapping at her heels.

'Be off, you chhokra-boys!' she'd shout. 'Off to your filthy homes, or I'll put the police on to you!'

And on one occasion she did report us to the local thana, and a couple of policemen came along, told us to get dressed and warned us off the property. But the Head Constable was Pitamber's brother-in-law's brother-in-law, so the ban did not last for more than a couple of days. We were soon back at our favourite stretch of canal.

When Miss Gamla saw that we were back, as merry and disrespectful as ever, she was furious. She nearly had a fit when Raju—probably the most wicked of the four of us—did a jig in front of her, completely in the nude.

When Miss Gamla advanced upon him, stick raised, Raju jumped into the canal.

'Why don't you join us?' shouted Sushil, taunting the enraged woman.

'Jump in and cool off,' I called, not to be outdone in villainy.

The little peke ran up and down the banks of the canal, yapping furiously, dying to sink its teeth into our bottoms. Miss Gamla came right down to the edge of the canal, waving her stick, trying to connect with any part of Raju's anatomy that could be reached. The ferrule of the stick caught him on the shoulder and he yelped in pain. Miss Gamla gave a shrill cry of delight. She had scored a hit!

She made another lunge at Raju, and this time I caught the end of the stick and pulled. Instead of letting go of the stick, Miss Gamla hung on to it. I should have let go then, but on an impulse I gave it a short, sharp pull, and to my horror, both walking stick and Miss Gamla tumbled into the canal.

Miss Gamla went under for a few seconds. Then she came to the surface, spluttering, and screamed. There was a frenzy of barking from the peke. Why had he been left out of the game? Wisely, he forbore from joining us.

We went to the aid of Miss Gamla, with every intention of pulling her out of the canal, but she backed away, screaming, 'Get away from me, get away!'

Fortunately, the walking stick had been carried away by the current.

Miss Gamla was now in danger of being carried away too. Floundering about, she had backed away to a point where a secondary canal joined the first, and here the current was swift. All the boys, big and small, avoided that spot. It formed a little whirlpool before rushing on.

'Memsahib, be careful!' called out Pitamber.

'Watch out!' I shouted, 'you won't be able to stand against the current.'

Raju and Sushil lunged forward to help, but with a look of hatred Miss Gamla turned away and tried to walk downstream. A surge in the current swept her off her legs. Her gown billowed up, turning her into a sailboat, and she moved slowly downstream, arms flailing as she tried to regain her balance.

We scrambled out of the canal and ran along the bank, hoping to overtake her, but we were hindered by the peke who kept snapping at our heels, and by the fact that we were without our clothes and approaching the busy Dilaram Bazaar.

Just before the Bazaar, the canal went underground, emerging about two hundred metres further on, at the junction of the Old Survey Road and the East Canal Road. To our horror, we saw Miss Gamla float into the narrow tunnel that carried the canal along its underground journey. If she didn't get stuck somewhere in the channel, she would emerge—hopefully, still alive—at the other end of the passage.

We raced back for our clothes, dressed, then ran through the bazaar, and did not stop running until we reached the exit point on the Canal Road. This must have taken ten to fifteen minutes.

We took up our positions on the culvert where the canal emerged, and waited.

We waited and waited.

No sign of Miss Gamla.

'She must be stuck somewhere,' said Pitamber.

'She'll drown,' said Sushil.

'Not our fault,' argued Raju. 'If we tell anyone, we'll get into trouble. They'll think we pushed her in.'

'We'll wait a little longer,' I suggested.

So we hung about the canal banks, pretending to catch tadpoles, and hoping that Miss Gamla would emerge, preferably alive.

Her walking stick floated past. We did not touch it. It would be evidence against us, warned Pitamber. The dog had gone home after seeing his mistress disappear down the tunnel.

'Like Alice,' I thought. 'Only that was a dream.'

When it grew dark, we went our different ways, resolving not to mention the episode to anyone. We might be accused of murder! By now, we *felt* like murderers.

A week passed, and nothing happened. No bloated body was found floating in the lower reaches of the canal. No memsahib was reported missing.

They say the guilty always return to the scene of the crime. More out of curiosity than guilt, we came together one afternoon, just before the rains broke, and crept through the shrubbery behind Miss Gamla's house.

All was silent, all was still. No one was playing in the canal. The mango trees were unattended. No one touched Miss Gamla's mangoes. Trespassers were more afraid of her than of her lathi-wielding mali.

We crept out of the bushes and advanced towards the cool, welcoming water flowing past us.

And then came a shout from the house.

'Scoundrels! Goondas! Chhokra-boys! I'll catch you this time!'

And there stood Miss Gamla, tall and menacing, alive and well, flourishing a brand-new walking stick and advancing down her steps.

'It's her ghost!' gasped Raju.

'No, she's real,' said Sushil. 'Must have got out of the canal somehow.'

'Well, at least we aren't murderers,' said Pitamber.

'No,' I agreed. 'But she'll murder us if we stand here any longer.'

Miss Gamla had been joined by her mali, the yelping peke, and a couple of other retainers.

'Let's go,' said Raju.

We fled the scene. And we never went there again. Miss Gamla had won the Battle of Panipat.

White Mice

Granny should never have entrusted my Uncle Ken with the job of taking me to the station and putting me on the train for Delhi. He got me to the station all right, but then proceeded to put me on the wrong train!

I was nine or ten at the time, and I'd been spending part of my winter holidays with my grandparents in Dehra. Now it was time to go back to my parents in Delhi, before joining school again.

'Just make sure that Ruskin gets into the right compartment,' said Gran to her only son, Kenneth. 'And make sure he has a berth to himself and a thermos of drinking water.'

Uncle Ken carried out the instructions. He even bought me a bar of chocolate, consuming most of it himself while telling me how to pass my exams without too much study. (I'll tell you the secret some day.) The train pulled out of the station and we waved fond goodbyes to each other.

An hour and two small stations later, I discovered

to my horror that I was not on the train to Delhi but on the night express to Lucknow, over 300 miles in the opposite direction. Someone in the compartment suggested that I get down at the next station; another said it would not be wise for a small boy to get off the train at a strange place in the middle of the night. 'Wait till we get to Lucknow,' advised another passenger, 'then send a telegram to your parents.'

Early next morning the train steamed into Lucknow. One of the passengers kindly took me to the stationmaster's office. 'Mr P.K. Ghosh, Stationmaster,' said the sign over his door. When my predicament had been explained to him, Mr Ghosh looked down at me through his bifocals and said, 'Yes, yes, we must send a telegram to your parents.'

'I don't have their address as yet,' I said. 'They were to meet me in Delhi. You'd better send a telegram to my grandfather in Dehra.'

'Done, done,' said Mr Ghosh, who was in the habit of repeating certain words. 'And meanwhile, I'll take you home and introduce you to my family.'

Mr Ghosh's house was just behind the station. He had his cook bring me a cup of sweet, milky tea and two large rasgullas.

'You like rasgullas, I hope, I hope?'

'Oh yes, sir,' I said. 'Thank you very much.'

'Now let me show you my family.'

And he took me by the hand and led me to a boarded-up veranda at the back of the house. Here I was amazed to find a miniature railway, complete with a station, railway bungalows, signal boxes, and next to it a miniature fairground complete with swings, roundabout and a ferris wheel. Cavorting on the roundabout and ferris wheel were some fifteen to twenty white mice! Another dozen or so ran in and out of tunnels, and climbed up on a toy train. Mr Ghosh pressed a button and the little train, crowded with white mice, left the station and went rattling off to the far corner of the veranda.

'My hobby for many years,' said Mr Ghosh. 'What do you think of it—think of it?'

'I like the train, sir.'

'But not the mice?'

'There are an awful lot of them, sir. They must consume a great many rasgullas!'

'No, no, I don't give them rasgullas,' snapped Mr Ghosh, a little annoyed. 'Just railway biscuits, broken up. These old station biscuits are just the thing for them. Some of our biscuits haven't been touched for years. Too hard for our teeth. Rasgullas are for you and me! Now I'll leave you here while I return to the office and send a telegram to your grandfather. These new-fangled telephones never work properly!'

❁

Grandfather arrived that evening, and in the meantime I helped feed the white mice with railways biscuits, then watched Mr Ghosh operate the toy train. Some of the mice took the train, some played on the swings and roundabouts, while some climbed in and out of Mr Ghosh's pockets and ran up and down his uniform. By the time Grandfather arrived, I had consumed about a dozen rasgullas and fallen asleep in a huge railway armchair in Mr Ghosh's living room. I woke up to find the stationmaster busy showing Grandfather his little railway colony of white mice. Grandfather, being a retired railwayman, was more interested in the toy train, but he said polite things about the mice, commending their pink eyes and pretty little feet. Mr Ghosh beamed with pleasure and sent out for more rasgullas.

When Grandfather and I had settled into the compartment of a normal train late that night, Mr Ghosh came to the window to say goodbye.

As the train began moving, he thrust a cardboard box into my hands and said, 'A present for you and your grandfather!'

'More rasgullas,' I thought. But when the train was underway and I had lifted the lid of the box, I found two white mice asleep on a bed of cotton wool.

❁

Back in Dehra, I kept the white mice in their box; I had plans for them. Uncle Ken had spent most of the day skulking in the guava orchard, too embarrassed to face me. Granny had given him a good lecture on how to be a responsible adult. But I was thirsty for revenge!

After dinner I slipped into my uncle's room and released the mice under his bedsheet.

An hour later we had all to leap out of our beds when Uncle Ken dashed out of his room, screaming that something soft and furry was running about inside his pyjamas.

'Well, off with the pyjamas!' said Grandfather, giving me a wink; he had a good idea of what had happened.

After Uncle Ken had done a tap dance, one white mouse finally emerged from the pyjamas; but the other had run up the sleeve of his pyjama-coat and suddenly popped out beneath my uncle's chin. Uncle Ken grew hysterical. Convinced that his room was full of mice — pink, white and brown — he locked himself into the storeroom and slept on an old sofa.

Next day Grandfather took me to the station and put me on the train to Delhi. It was the right train this time.

'I'll look after the white mice,' he said.

Grandfather grew quite fond of the mice, and even wrote to Mr Ghosh, asking if he could spare another pair. But Mr Ghosh, he learnt later, had been transferred to another part of the country, and had taken his family with him.

Wilson's Bridge

The old, wooden bridge has gone, and today an iron suspension bridge straddles the Bhagirathi as it rushes down the gorge below Gangotri. But villagers will tell you that you can still hear the hoofs of Wilson's horse as he gallops across the bridge he had built a hundred and fifty years ago. At the time people were sceptical of its safety, and so, to prove its sturdiness, he rode across it again and again. Parts of the old bridge can still be seen on the far bank of the river. And the legend of Wilson and his pretty hill bride, Gulabi, is still well known in this region.

I had joined some friends in the old forest rest house near the river. There were the Rays, recently married, and the Dattas, married many years. The younger Rays quarrelled frequently; the older Dattas looked on with more amusement than concern. I was a part of their group and yet something of an outsider. As a single man, I was a person of no importance. And as a marriage counsellor, I wouldn't have been of any use to them.

I spent most of my time wandering along the riverbanks or exploring the thick deodar and oak forests that covered the slopes. It was these trees that had made a fortune for Wilson and his patron, the Raja of Tehri. They had exploited the great forests to the full, floating huge logs downstream to the timber yards in the plains.

Returning to the rest house late one evening, I was halfway across the bridge when I saw a figure at the other end, emerging from the mist. Presently I made out a woman, wearing the plain dhoti of the hills, her hair falling loose over her shoulders. She appeared not to see me, and reclined against the railing of the bridge, looking down at the rushing waters far below. And then, to my amazement and horror, she climbed over the railing and threw herself into the river.

I ran forward, calling out, but I reached the railing only to see her fall into the foaming waters below, where she was carried swiftly downstream.

The watchman's cabin stood a little way off. The door was open. The watchman, Ram Singh, was lying on his bed, smoking a hookah.

'Someone just jumped off the bridge,' I said breathlessly. 'She's been swept down the river!'

The watchman was unperturbed. 'Gulabi again,' he said, almost to himself; and then to me, 'Did you see her clearly?'

'Yes, a woman with long, loose hair—but I didn't see her face very clearly.'

'It must have been Gulabi. Only a ghost, my dear sir. Nothing to be alarmed about. Every now and then someone sees her throw herself into the river. Sit down,' he said, gesturing towards a battered old armchair, 'be comfortable and I'll tell you all about it.'

I was far from comfortable, but I listened to Ram Singh tell me the tale of Gulabi's suicide. After making me a glass of hot, sweet tea, he launched into a long, rambling account of how Wilson, a British adventurer seeking his fortune, had been hunting musk deer when he encountered Gulabi on the path from her village. The girl's grey-green eyes and peach-blossom complexion enchanted him, and he went out of his way to get to know her people. Was Wilson in love with her, or did he simply find her beautiful and desirable? We shall never really know. In the course of his travels and adventures he had known many women, but Gulabi was different, childlike and ingenuous, and he decided he would marry her. The humble family to which she belonged had no objection.

Hunting had its limitations, and Wilson found it more profitable to trap the region's great forest wealth. In a few years he had made a fortune. He built a large, timbered house at Harsil, another in Dehradun, and a third at Mussoorie. Gulabi had all she could have wanted, including two robust little sons. When Wilson was away on work, she looked after their children and their large apple orchard at Harsil.

And then came the evil day when Wilson met the Englishwoman, Ruth, in the Mussoorie mall, and decided that she should have a share of his affections and his wealth. A fine house was provided for her too. The time he spent at Harsil with Gulabi and his children dwindled. 'Business affairs'—he was now one of the owners of a bank—kept him in the fashionable hill resort. He was a popular host and took his friends and associates on shikar parties in the Doon.

Gulabi brought up her children in village style. She came to know stories of Wilson's dalliance with the Mussoorie woman. On one of his rare visits, she confronted him and voiced her resentment, demanding that he leave the other woman. He brushed her aside and told her not to listen to idle gossip. When he turned away from her, she picked up the flintlock pistol that lay on the gun table, and fired one shot at him. The bullet missed him and shattered her looking glass. Gulabi ran out of the house, through the orchard and into the forest, then down the steep path to the bridge built by Wilson only two or three years before. When he had recovered his composure, he mounted his horse and came looking for her. It was too late. She had already thrown herself off the bridge into the swirling waters far below. Her body was found a mile or two downstream, caught between some rocks.

This was the tale that Ram Singh told me, with various flourishes and interpolations of his own. I thought it would make a good story to tell my friends that evening, before the fireside in the rest house. They found the story fascinating, but when I told them I had seen Gulabi's ghost, they thought I was doing a little embroidering of my own. Mrs Dutta thought it was a tragic tale. Young Mrs Ray thought Gulabi had been very silly. 'She was a simple girl,' opined Mr Dutta. 'She responded in the only way she knew . . .' 'Money can't buy happiness,' put in Mr Ray. 'No,' said Mrs Dutta, 'but it can buy you a great many comforts.' Mrs Ray wanted to talk of other things, so I changed the subject. It can get a little confusing for a bachelor who must spend the evening with two married couples. There are undercurrents which he is aware of but not equipped to deal with.

I would walk across the bridge quite often after that. It was busy with traffic during the day, but after dusk there were only a few vehicles on the road and seldom any pedestrians. A mist rose from the gorge below and obscured the far end of the bridge. I preferred walking there in the evening, half-expecting, half-hoping to see Gulabi's ghost again. It was her face that I really wanted to see. Would she still be as beautiful as she was fabled to be?

It was on the evening before our departure that something happened that would haunt me for a long time afterwards.

There was a feeling of restiveness as our days there drew to a close. The Rays had apparently made up their differences, although they weren't talking very much. Mr Dutta was anxious to get back to his office in Delhi and Mrs Dutta's rheumatism was playing up. I was restless too, wanting to return to my writing desk in Mussoorie.

That evening I decided to take one last stroll across the bridge to enjoy the cool breeze of a summer's night in the mountains. The moon hadn't come up, and it was really quite dark, although there were lamps at either end of the bridge providing sufficient light for those who wished to cross over.

I was standing in the middle of the bridge, in the darkest part, listening to the river thundering down the gorge, when I saw a sari-draped figure emerging from the lamplight and making towards the railings.

Instinctively I called out, 'Gulabi!' She half-turned towards me, but I could not see her clearly. The wind had blown her hair across her face and all I saw was wildly staring eyes. She raised herself over the railing and threw herself off the bridge. I heard the splash as her body struck the water far below.

Once again I found myself running towards the part

of the railing where she had jumped. And then someone was running towards the same spot, from the direction of the rest house. It was young Mr Ray.

'My wife!' he cried out. 'Did you see my wife?'

He rushed to the railing and stared down at the swirling waters of the river.

'Look! There she is!' He pointed at a helpless figure bobbing about in the water.

We ran down the steep bank to the river but the current had swept her on. Scrambling over rocks and bushes, we made frantic efforts to catch up with the drowning woman. But the river in that defile is a roaring torrent, and it was over an hour before we were able to retrieve poor Mrs Ray's body, caught in driftwood about a mile downstream.

She was cremated not far from where we found her and we returned to our various homes in gloom and grief, chastened but none the wiser for the experience.

If you happen to be in that area and decide to cross the bridge late in the evening, you might see Gulabi's ghost or hear the hoof beats of Wilson's horse as he canters across the old wooden bridge looking for her. Or you might see the ghost of Mrs Ray and hear her husband's anguished cry. Or there might be others. Who knows?

The Eyes of the Eagle

It was a high, piercing sound, almost like the yelping of a dog.

Jai stopped picking the wild strawberries that grew in the grass around him, and looked up at the sky. He had a dog—a shaggy guard dog called Motu—but Motu did not yelp, he growled and barked. The strange sound came from the sky, and Jai had heard it before. Now, realizing what it was, he jumped to his feet, calling out to his dog, calling his sheep to start for home. Motu came bounding towards him, ready for a game.

'No, not now, Motu!' said Jai. 'We must get the lambs home quickly.' And again Jai looked up at the sky.

He saw it now, a black speck against the sun, growing larger as it circled the mountain, coming lower every moment: a golden eagle, king of the skies over the higher Himalayas, ready to swoop and seize its prey.

Had it seen a pheasant or a pine marten? Or was it after one of the lambs? Jai had never lost a lamb to an eagle, but recently some of the other shepherds had been talking about a golden eagle that had been preying on their flocks.

The sheep had wandered some way down the side of the mountain, and Jai ran after them to make sure that none of the lambs had gone off on its own.

Motu ran about, barking furiously. He wasn't very good at keeping the sheep together—in fact, he was often bumping into them and sending them tumbling down the slope, but his size and bear-like appearance kept the leopards and wolves at a distance.

Jai was counting the lambs; they were bleating loudly and staying close to their mothers. One—two—three—four . . .

There should have been a fifth. Jai couldn't see it on the slope below him. He looked up towards a rocky ledge near the steep path to the Tungnath temple. The golden eagle was circling the rocks.

Suddenly the great bird stopped circling. It dropped a few feet, and then, wings held back and powerful feet thrust out below like the wheels of a plane about to land, it came swooping down, heading straight for a spot behind the rocks.

The eagle disappeared from sight for a moment, then rose again with a small creature grasped firmly in its terrible talons.

'It has taken a lamb!' shouted Jai. He started scrambling up the slope. Motu ran ahead of him, barking furiously at the big bird as it glided away over the tops of the stunted junipers to its eyrie on the cliffs above Tung.

There was nothing that Jai and Motu could do except stare helplessly and angrily at the disappearing eagle. The lamb had died the instant it had been struck. The rest of the flock seemed unaware of what had happened. They still grazed on the thick, sweet grass of the mountain slopes.

'We had better drive them home, Motu,' said Jai, and at a nod from the boy, the big dog bounded down the slope, to take part in his favourite game of driving the sheep homewards. Soon he had them running all over the place, and Jai had to dash about trying to keep them together. Finally they straggled homewards.

'A fine lamb gone,' said Jai to himself. 'I wonder what Grandfather will say.'

❋

Grandfather said, 'Never mind. It had to happen some day. That eagle has been watching the sheep for sometime.'

Grandmother, more practical, put in, 'We could have sold the lamb for three hundred rupees. You'll have to be more careful in future, Jai. Don't fall asleep on the hillside, and don't read storybooks when you are supposed to be watching the sheep!'

'I wasn't reading this morning,' answered Jai

truthfully, forgetting to mention that he had been gathering strawberries.

'It's good for him to read,' put in Grandfather, who had never had the luck to go to school. In his days, there weren't any schools in the mountains. Now there was one in every village.

'Time enough to read at night,' retorted Grandmother, who did not think much of the little one-room school down at Maku, their home village.

'Well, these are the October holidays,' said Grandfather, 'otherwise he would not be here to help us with the sheep. It will snow by the end of the month, and then we will move with the flock. You will have more time for reading then, Jai.'

At Maku, which was down in the warmer valley, Jai's parents tilled a few narrow terraces on which they grew barley, millet and potatoes. The old people brought their sheep up to the Tung meadows to graze during the summer months. They stayed in a small stone hut just off the path which pilgrims took to the ancient temple. At 12,000 feet above sea level, it was the highest Hindu temple on the inner Himalayan ranges.

The following day Jai and Motu were very careful. They did not let the sheep out of their sight even for a minute. Nor did they catch a glimpse of the golden eagle.

'What if it attacks again?' wondered Jai. 'How will I stop it?'

The great eagle, with its powerful beak and talons, was more than a match for boy or dog. The eagle's hind claw, four inches round the curve, was its most dangerous weapon. When it spread its wings, the distance from tip to tip was more than eight feet.

The eagle did not appear that day because it had fed well and was now resting in its eyrie. Old bones, which had belonged to pheasants, snowcocks, pine martens and even foxes, were scattered about the rocks which formed the eagle's home. The eagle had a mate, but it was not the breeding season and she was away on a scouting expedition of her own.

The golden eagle stood on its rocky ledge, staring majestically across the valley. Its hard, unblinking eyes missed nothing. Those strange orange-yellow eyes could spot a field rat or a mouse hare more than a hundred yards below.

There were other eagles on the mountain, but usually they kept to their own territory. Only the bolder ones went for lambs, because the flocks were always protected by men and dogs.

*

The eagle took off from its eyrie and glided gracefully, powerfully over the valley, circling the Tung mountain.

Below lay the old temple, built from slabs of

grey granite. A line of pilgrims snaked up the steep, narrow path. On the meadows below the peak, the sheep grazed peacefully, unaware of the presence of the eagle. The great bird's shadow slid over the sunlit slopes.

The eagle saw the boy and the dog, but it did not fear them. It had his eye on a lamb that was frisking about on the grass, a few feet away from the other sheep.

Jai did not see the eagle until it swept round an outcrop of rocks about a hundred feet away. The bird moved silently, without any movement of its wings, for it had already built up the momentum for its dive. Now it came straight at the lamb.

Motu saw the bird in time. With a low growl he dashed forward and reached the side of the lamb at almost the same instant that the eagle swept in.

There was a terrific collision. Feathers flew. The eagle screamed with rage. The lamb tumbled down the slope, and Motu howled in pain as the huge beak struck him high on the leg.

The big bird, a little stunned by the clash, flew off rather unsteadily, with a mighty beating of its wings.

Motu had saved the lamb. It was frightened, but unhurt. Bleating loudly, it joined the other sheep, who took up the bleating. It sounded as though they had all started complaining at once about the awful state of affairs.

Jai ran up to Motu, who lay whimpering on the ground. There was a deep gash in the dog's thigh, and blood was seeping onto the grass.

Jai looked around. There was no sign of the eagle. Quickly he removed his shirt and vest; then he wrapped his vest round the dog's wound, tying it in position with his belt.

Motu could not get up, and he was much too heavy for Jai to carry. Jai did not want to leave his dog alone, in case the eagle returned to the attack.

He stood up, cupped his hands to his mouth, and began calling for his grandfather.

'Dada, Dada!' Jai shouted, and presently Grandfather heard him and came stumbling down the slope. He was followed by another shepherd, and together they lifted Motu and carried him home.

❊

Motu had a bad wound, but Grandmother cleaned it and applied a paste made of herbs. Then she laid strips of carrot over the wound—an old mountain remedy—and bandaged the leg. But it would be some time before Motu could run about again. By then it would probably be snowing and time to leave these high-altitude pastures and return to the valley.

Meanwhile, the sheep had to be taken out to graze,

and Grandfather decided to accompany Jai for the remaining period.

They did not see the golden eagle for two or three days, and, when they did, it was flying over the next range. Perhaps it had found some other source of food, or even another flock of sheep.

'Are you afraid of the eagle?' asked Grandfather.

'I wasn't before,' replied Jai. 'Not until it hurt Motu. I did not know it could be so dangerous. But Motu wounded it too. He banged straight into it!'

'Perhaps it won't bother us again,' said Grandfather thoughtfully. 'A bird's wing is easily injured—even an eagle's.'

Jai wasn't so sure. He had seen it strike twice, and he knew that it was not afraid of anyone. Only when it learnt to fear his presence would it keep away from the flock.

The next day Grandfather did not feel well. He was feverish and kept to his bed. Motu was hobbling about on three legs; the wounded leg was still very sore.

'Don't go too far with the sheep,' advised Grandmother. 'Let them graze near the house.'

'But there's hardly any grass here,' argued Jai.

'I don't want you wandering off while that eagle is still around,' said Grandmother.

'Give him my stick,' said Grandfather from his bed.

It was an old stick, made of wild cherrywood, which

Grandfather often carried around. The wood was strong and well seasoned; the stick was stout and long. It reached up to Jai's shoulders.

'Don't lose it,' said Grandfather. 'It was given to me many years ago by a wandering scholar who came to the Tungnath temple. I was going to give it to you when you got bigger, but perhaps this is the right time for you to have it. If the eagle comes near you, swing the stick around your head. That should frighten it off!'

*

Clouds had gathered over the mountains, and a heavy mist hid the Tungnath temple. With the approach of winter, the flow of pilgrims had been reduced to a trickle. The shepherds had started leaving the lush meadows and returning to their villages at lower altitudes. Very soon the bears and the leopards and the golden eagles would have the range all to themselves.

Jai used the cherrywood stick to prod the sheep along the path until they reached the steep meadows. The stick would have to be a substitute for Motu. And they seemed to respond to it more readily that they did to Motu's mad charges.

Because of the sudden cold and the prospect of snow, Grandmother had made Jai wear a rough, woollen jacket and a pair of high boots bought from a Tibetan trader. Jai wasn't used to the boots—he wore sandals at other times—and had some difficulty in climbing quickly up and down the hillside. It was tiring work trying to keep the flock together. The cawing of some crows warned Jai that the eagle might be around, but the mist prevented him from seeing very far.

After some time the mist lifted and Jai was able to see the temple and the snow peaks towering behind it. He saw the golden eagle, too. It was circling high overhead. Jai kept close to the flock, one eye on the eagle, one eye on the restless sheep.

Then the great bird stooped and flew lower. It circled the temple and then pretended to go away. Jai felt sure it would be back. And a few minutes later it reappeared from the other side of the mountain. It was much lower now, wings spread out and back, taloned feet to the fore, piercing eyes fixed on its target, a small lamb that had suddenly gone frisking down the grassy slope, away from Jai and the flock.

Now the eagle flew lower still, only a few feet off the ground, paying no attention to the boy. It passed Jai with a great rush of air. As it did so the boy struck out with his stick and gave the bird a glancing blow.

The eagle missed its prey, and the lamb skipped away.

To Jai's amazement, the bird did not fly off. Instead it landed on the hillside and glared at the boy, as a king would glare at a humble subject who had dared to pelt him with a pebble.

The golden eagle stood almost as tall as Jai. Its wings were still outspread. Its fierce eyes seemed to be looking through and through the boy.

Jai's first instinct was to turn and run. But the cherrywood stick was still in his hands, and he felt sure there was power in the stick. He saw that the eagle was about to launch itself again at the lamb. Instead of running away, Jai ran forward, the stick raised above his head.

The eagle rose a few feet off the ground and struck out with its huge claws.

Luckily for Jai, his heavy jacket took the force of the blow. A talon ripped through the sleeve, and the sleeve fell away. At the same time the stick caught the eagle across its open wing. The bird gave a shrill cry of pain and fury. Then it turned and flapped heavily away, flying unsteadily because of its injured wing.

Jai still clutched the stick, because he expected the bird to return; he did not even glance at his torn jacket. But the golden eagle had alighted on a distant rock and seemed in no hurry to return to the attack.

❖

Jai began driving the sheep home. The clouds had become heavy and black, and presently the first snowflakes began to fall.

Jai saw a hare go lolloping down the hill. When it was about fifty yards away, there was a rush of air from the eagle's beating wings, and Jai saw the bird approaching the hare in a sidelong dive.

So it hasn't been badly hurt, thought Jai, feeling a little relieved, for he could not really help admiring the great bird. And now it has found something else to chase.

The hare saw the eagle and dodged about, making for a clump of junipers. Jai did not know if it was caught or not, because the snow and sleet had increased and both bird and hare were lost in the gathering snowstorm.

The sheep were bleating behind him. One of the lambs looked tired, and Jai stopped to pick it up. As he did so, he heard a thin, whining sound. It grew louder by the second. Before he could look up, a huge wing caught him across the shoulders and sent him sprawling. The lamb tumbled down the slope with him, into a thorny bilberry bush.

The bush had saved them. Jai saw an eagle coming in again, flying low. It was another eagle! One had been vanquished, and now here was another, just as big and fearless, probably the mate of the first eagle.

Jai had lost his stick and there was no way in which he could fight the second eagle. So he crept further into the bush, holding the lamb beneath him. At the same time he began shouting at the top of his voice — both to scare the bird away and to summon help. The eagle could not get at them now; but the rest of the flock was exposed on the hillside. Surely the eagle would make for them.

Even as the bird circled and came back in another dive, Jai heard fierce barking. The eagle immediately swung away and rose skywards.

The barking came from Motu. Hearing Jai's shouts and sensing that something was wrong, he had come limping out of the house, ready to do battle. Behind him came another shepherd and—most wonderful of all—Grandmother herself, banging two frying pans together.

The barking, the banging and the shouting frightened the eagles away. The sheep scattered, too, and it was sometime before they could all be rounded up. By then it was snowing heavily.

'Tomorrow we must all go down to Maku,' said the shepherd.

'Yes, it's definitely time we went,' agreed Grandmother. 'You can read your storybooks again, Jai.'

'I'll have my own story to tell,' said Jai.

When they reached the hut and Jai saw Grandfather, he said, 'Oh, I've forgotten your stick!'

But Motu had picked it up. Carrying it between his teeth, he brought it home and sat down with it in the open doorway. He had decided the cherrywood was good for his teeth and would've chewed it all up if Grandmother hadn't taken it from him.

'Never mind,' said Grandfather, sitting up on his cot. 'It isn't the stick that matters. It's the person who holds it.'

Non-fiction

A Knock at the Door

For Sherlock Holmes, it usually meant an impatient client waiting below in the street. For Nero Wolfe, it was the doorbell that rang, disturbing the great man in his orchid rooms. For Poe or Walter de la Mare, that knocking on a moonlit door could signify a ghostly visitor — no one outside — or, even more mysterious, no one in the house . . .

Well, clients I have none, and ghostly visitants don't have to knock; but as I spend most of the day at home, writing, I have learnt to live with the occasional knock at the front door. I find doorbells even more startling than ghosts, and ornate brass knockers have a tendency to disappear when the price of brassware goes up; so my callers have to use their knuckles or fists on the solid mahogany door. It's a small price to pay for disturbing me.

I hear the knocking quite distinctly, as the small front room adjoins my even smaller study-cum-bedroom. But sometimes I keep up a pretence of not hearing anything straight away. Mahogany is good for the knuckles! Eventually, I place a pencil between my teeth and holding a sheet of blank foolscap in one hand, move slowly and thoughtfully toward the front door, so that, when I open it, my caller can see that I have been disturbed in the throes of composition. Not that I have ever succeeded in making anyone feel guilty about it; they stay as long as they like. And after they have gone, I can get back to listening to my tapes of old Hollywood operettas.

Impervious to both literature and music, my first caller is usually a boy from the village, wanting to sell me his cucumbers or 'France-beans'. For some reason he won't call them French beans. He is not impressed by the accoutrements of my trade. He thrusts a cucumber into my arms and empties the beans on a coffee-table book which has been sent to me for review. (There is no coffee table, but the book makes a good one.) He is confident that I cannot resist his 'France-beans', even though this sub-Himalayan variety is extremely hard and stringy. Actually, I am a sucker for cucumbers, but I take the beans so I can get the cucumber cheap. In this fashion, authors survive.

The deal done, and the door closed, I decide it's time to do some work. I start this little essay. If it's nice and gets published, I will be able to take care of the electricity bill. There's a knock at the door. Some knocks

I recognize, but this is a new one. Perhaps it's someone asking for a donation. Cucumber in hand, I stride to the door and open it abruptly only to be confronted by a polite, smart-looking chauffeur who presents me with a large bouquet of flowering gladioli!

'With the compliments of Mr B.P. Singh,' he announces, before departing smartly with a click of the heels. I start looking for a receptacle for the flowers, as Grandmother's flower vase was really designed for violets and forget-me-nots.

B.P. Singh is a kind man who had the original idea of turning his property outside Mussoorie into a gladioli farm. A bare hillside is now a mass of gladioli from May to September. He sells them to flower shops in Delhi, but his heart bleeds at harvesting time.

Gladioli arranged in an ice bucket, I return to my desk and am just wondering what I should be writing next, when there is a loud banging on the door. No friendly knock this time. Urgent, peremptory, summoning! Could it be the police? And what have I gone and done? Every good citizen has at least one guilty secret, just waiting to be discovered! I move warily to the door and open it an inch or two. It is a policeman!

Hastily, I drop the cucumber and politely ask him if I can be of help. Try to look casual, I tell myself. He has a small packet in his hands. No, it's not a warrant. It turns out to be a slim volume of verse, sent over by a visiting DIG of Police, who has authored it. I thank his emissary profusely, and, after he has gone, I place the volume reverently on my bookshelf, beside the works of other poetry-loving policemen. These men of steel, who inspire so much awe and trepidation in the rest of us, they too are humans and some of them are poets!

Now it's afternoon, and the knock I hear is a familiar one, and welcome, for it heralds the postman. What would writers do without postmen? They have more power than literary agents. I don't have an agent (I'll be honest and say an agent won't have me), but I do have a postman, and he turns up every day except when there's a landslide.

Yes, it's Prakash the postman who makes my day, showering me with letters, books, acceptances, rejections, and even the occasional cheque. These postmen are fine fellows, they do their utmost to bring the good news from Ghent to Aix.

And what has Prakash brought me today? A reminder: I haven't paid my subscription to the Author's Guild. I'd better send it off, or I shall be a derecognized author. A letter from a reader: would I like to go through her 800-page dissertation on the Gita? Some day, my love... A cheque, a cheque! From Sunflower Books, for nineteen rupees only, representing the sale of six copies of one of my books during the previous year. Never mind. Six wise persons put their money down for my book. No fresh acceptances, but no rejections either. A postcard from Goa, where one of my publishers is taking a holiday. So the post is something of an anticlimax. But I mustn't complain. Not every knock on the door brings gladioli fresh from the fields. Tomorrow's another day, and the postman comes six days a week.

Bird Life in the City

Having divided the last ten years of my life between Delhi and Mussoorie, I have come to the heretical conclusion that there is more bird life in the cities than there is in the hills and forests around our hill stations.

For birds to survive, they must learn to live with and off humans; and those birds, like crows, sparrows and mynas, who do this to perfection, continue to thrive as our cities grow; whereas the purely wild birds, those who depend upon the forests for life, are rapidly disappearing, simply because the forests are disappearing.

Recently, I saw more birds in one week in a New Delhi colony than I had seen during a month in the hills. Here, one must be patient and alert if one is to spot just a few of the birds so beautifully described in Salim Ali's *Indian Hill Birds*. The babblers and thrushes are still around, but the flycatchers and warblers are seldom seen or heard.

❀

In Delhi, if you have just a bit of garden and perhaps a guava tree, you will be visited by innumerable bulbuls, tailorbirds, mynas, hoopoes, parrots and tree pies. Or, if you own an old house, you will have to share it with pigeons and sparrows, perhaps swallows or swifts. And if you have neither garden nor rooftop, you will still be visited by the crows.

Where the man goes, the crow follows. He has learnt to perfection the art of living off humans. He will, I am sure, be the first bird on the moon, scavenging among the paper bags and cartons left behind by untidy astronauts.

Crows favour the densest areas of human population, and there must be at least one for every human. Many crows seem to have been humans in their previous lives; they possess all the cunning and sense of self-preservation of man. At the same time, there are many humans who have obviously been crows; we haven't lost our thieving instincts.

Watch a crow sidling along the garden wall with a shabby, genteel air, cocking a speculative eye at the kitchen door and any attendant humans. He reminds one of a newspaper reporter, hovering in the background until his chance comes—and then pouncing! I have even known a crow to make off with an egg from the breakfast table. No other bird, except perhaps the sparrow, has been so successful in exploiting human beings.

The myna, although he too is quite at home in the city, is more of a gentleman. He prefers fruit on the tree to scraps from the kitchen, and visits the garden as much out of a sense of sociability as in expectation of hand-outs. He is quite handsome, too, with his bright orange bill and the mask around his eyes. He is equally at home on a railway platform as on the ear of a grazing buffalo, and, being omnivorous, has no trouble in coexisting with man.

The sparrow, on the other hand, is not a gentleman. Uninvited, he enters your home, followed by his friends, relatives and political hangers-on, and proceeds to quarrel, make love and leave his droppings on the sofa-cushions, with a complete disregard for the presence of humans. The party will then proceed into the garden and destroy all the flower-buds. No birds have succeeded so well in making fools of humans.

Although the bluejay, or roller, is quite capable of making his living in the forest, he seems to show a preference for the haunts of men, and would rather perch on a telegraph wire than in a tree. Probably he finds the wire a better launching pad for his sudden rocket-flights and aerial acrobatics.

In repose he is rather shabby; but in flight, when his outspread wings reveal his brilliant blues, he takes one's breath away. As his food consists of beetles and other insect pests, he can be considered man's friend and ally.

Parrots make little or no distinction between town and country life. They are the freelancers of the bird world — sturdy, independent and noisy. With flashes of blue and green, they swoop across the road, settle for a while in a mango tree, and then, with shrill, delighted cries, move on to some other field or orchard.

They will sample all the fruit they can, without finishing any. They are destructive birds but, because of their bright plumage, graceful flight and charming ways, they are popular favourites and can get away with anything. No one who has enjoyed watching a flock of parrots in swift and carefree flight could want to cage one of these virile birds. Yet so many people do cage them.

After the peacock, perhaps the most popular bird in rural India is the sarus crane — a familiar sight around the jheels and riverbanks of northern India and Gujarat. The sarus pairs for life and is seldom seen without his mate. When one bird dies, the other often pines away and seemingly dies of grief. It is this near-human quality of devotion that has earned the birds their popularity with the villagers of the plains.

As a result, they are well protected.

❉

In the long run, it is the 'common man', and not the scientist or conservationist, who can best give protection to the birds and animals living around him. Religious sentiment has helped preserve the peacock and a few other birds. It is a pity that so many other equally beautiful birds do not enjoy the same protection.

But the wily crow, the cheeky sparrow, and the sensible myna will always be with us. Quite possibly they will survive the human species.

And it is the same with other animals. While the cringing jackal has learnt the art of survival, his master, the magnificent tiger, is on his way to extinction.

Bhabiji's House

(My neighbours in Rajouri Garden back in the 1960s were the Kamal family. This entry from my journal, which I wrote on one of my later visits, describes a typical day in that household.)

At first light there is a tremendous burst of birdsong from the guava tree in the little garden. Over a hundred sparrows wake up all at once and give tongue to whatever it is that sparrows have to say to each other at five o'clock on a foggy winter's morning in Delhi.

In the small house, people sleep on, that is, everyone except Bhabiji — Granny — the head of the lively Punjabi middle-class family with whom I nearly always stay when I am in Delhi.

She coughs, stirs, groans, grumbles and gets out of bed. The fire has to be lit, and food prepared for two of her sons to take to work. There is a daughter-in-law, Shobha, to help her; but the girl is not very good at getting up in the morning. Actually, it is this way: Bhabiji wants to show up her daughter-in-law; so, no matter how hard Shobha tries to be up first, Bhabiji forestalls her. The old lady does not sleep well, anyway; her eyes are open long before the first sparrow chirps, and as soon as she sees her daughter-in-law stirring, she scrambles out of bed and hurries to the kitchen. This gives her the opportunity to say: 'What good is a daughter-in-law when I have to get up to prepare her husband's food?'

The truth is that Bhabiji does not like anyone else preparing her sons' food.

She looks no older than when I first saw her ten years ago. She still has complete control over a large family and, with tremendous confidence and enthusiasm, presides over the lives of three sons, a daughter, two daughters-in-law and fourteen grandchildren. This is a joint family (there are not many left in a big city like Delhi), in which the sons and their families all live together as one unit under their mother's benevolent (and sometimes slightly malevolent) autocracy. Even when her husband was alive, Bhabiji dominated the household.

The eldest son, Shiv, has a separate kitchen, but his wife and children participate in all the family celebrations and quarrels. It is a small miracle how everyone (including myself when I visit) manages to fit into the house; and a stranger might be forgiven for wondering where everyone sleeps, for no beds are visible during the day. That is because the beds — light wooden frames with rough string across—are brought in only at night, and are taken out first thing in the morning and kept in the garden shed.

As Bhabiji lights the kitchen fire, the household begins to stir, and Shobha joins her mother-in-law in the kitchen. As a guest I am privileged and may get up last. But my bed soon becomes an island battered by waves of scurrying, shouting children, eager to bathe, dress, eat and find their school books. Before I can get up, someone brings me a tumbler of hot sweet tea. It is a brass tumbler and burns my fingers; I have yet to learn how to hold one properly. Punjabis like their tea with lots of milk and sugar—so much so that I often wonder why they bother to add any tea.

Ten years ago, 'bed tea' was unheard of in Bhabiji's house. Then, the first time I came to stay, Kamal, the youngest son, told Bhabiji: 'My friend is angrez. He must have tea in bed.' Kamal forgot to mention that I usually took my morning cup at seven; they gave it to me at five. I gulped it down and went to sleep again. Then, slowly, others in the household began indulging in morning cups of tea. Now everyone, including the older children, has 'bed tea'. They bless my English forebears for instituting the custom; I bless the Punjabis for perpetuating it.

Breakfast is by rota, in the kitchen. It is a tiny room and accommodates only four adults at a time. The children have eaten first; but the smallest children, Shobha's toddlers, keep coming in and climbing over us. Says Bhabiji of the youngest and most mischievous: 'He lives only because God keeps a special eye on him.'

Kamal, his elder brother Arun and I sit cross-legged and barefooted on the floor while Bhabiji serves us hot parathas stuffed with potatoes and onions, along with omelettes, an excellent dish. Arun then goes to work on his scooter, while Kamal catches a bus for the city, where he attends an art college. After they have gone, Bhabiji and Shobha have their breakfast.

By nine o'clock everyone who is still in the house is busy doing something. Shobha is washing clothes. Bhabiji has settled down on a cot with a huge pile of spinach, which she methodically cleans and chops up. Madhu, her fourteen-year-old granddaughter, who attends school only in the afternoons, is washing down the sitting-room floor. Madhu's mother is a teacher in a primary school in Delhi, and earns a pittance of Rs 150 a month. Her husband went to England ten years ago, and never returned; he does not send any money home.

Madhu is made attractive by the gravity of her countenance. She is always thoughtful, reflective, seldom speaks, smiles rarely (but looks very pretty when she does). I wonder what she thinks about as she scrubs floors, prepares meals with Bhabiji, washes dishes and even finds a few hard-pressed moments for her school work. She is the Cinderella of the house. Not that she has to put up with anything like a cruel stepmother. Madhu is Bhabiji's favourite. She has made herself so useful that she is above all reproach. Apart from that, there is a certain measure of aloofness about her—she does not get involved in domestic squabbles—and this is foreign to a household in which everyone has something to say for himself or herself. Her two young brothers are constantly being reprimanded; but no one says anything to Madhu. Only yesterday morning, when clothes were being washed and Madhu was scrubbing the floor, the following dialogue took place.

Madhu's mother (picking up a schoolbook left in the courtyard): 'Where's that boy Popat? See how careless he is with his books! Popat! He's run off. Just wait till he gets back. I'll give him a good beating.'

Vinod's mother: 'It's not Popat's book. It's Vinod's. Where's Vinod?'

Vinod (grumpily): 'It's Madhu's book.'

Silence for a minute or two. Madhu continues scrubbing the floor; she does not bother to look up. Vinod picks up the book and takes it indoors. The women return to their chores.

Manju, daughter of Shiv and sister of Vinod, is averse to housework and, as a result, is always being scolded— by her parents, grandmother, uncles and aunts.

Now, she is engaged in the unwelcome chore of sweeping the front yard. She does this with a sulky look, ignoring my cheerful remarks. I have been sitting under the guava tree, but Manju soon sweeps me away from this spot. She creates a drifting cloud of dust, and seems satisfied only when the dust settles on the clothes that have just been hung up to dry. Manju is a sensuous creature and, like most sensuous people, is lazy by nature. She does not like sweeping because the boy next door can see her at it, and she wants to appear before him in a more glamorous light. Her first action every morning is to turn to the cinema advertisements in the newspaper. Bombay's movie moguls cater to girls like Manju who long to be tragic heroines. Life is so very dull for middle-class teenagers in Delhi that it is only natural that they should lean so heavily on escapist entertainment. Every residential area has a cinema.

But there is not a single bookshop in this particular suburb, although it has a population of over twenty thousand literate people. Few children read books; but they are adept at swotting up examination 'guides'; and students of, say, Hardy or Dickens read the guides and not the novels.

Bhabiji is now grinding onions and chillies in a mortar. Her eyes are watering but she is in a good mood. Shobha sits quietly in the kitchen. A little while ago she was complaining to me of a backache. I am the only one who lends a sympathetic ear to complaints of aches and pains. But since last night, my sympathies have been under severe strain. When I got into bed at about ten o'clock, I found the sheets wet. Apparently Shobha had put her baby to sleep in my bed during the afternoon.

While the housework is still in progress, cousin Kishore arrives. He is an itinerant musician who makes a living by arranging performances at marriages. He visits Bhabiji's house frequently and at odd hours, often a little tipsy, always brimming over with goodwill and grandiose plans for the future. It was once his ambition to be a film producer, and some years back he lost a lot of Bhabiji's money in producing a film that was never completed. He still talks of finishing it.

'Brother,' he says, taking me into his confidence for the hundredth time, 'do you know anyone who has a movie camera?'

'No,' I say, knowing only too well how these admissions can lead me into a morass of complicated manoeuvres. But Kishore is not easily put off, especially when he has been fortified with country liquor.

'But you knew someone with a movie camera?' He asks.

'That was long ago.'

'How long ago?' (I have got him going now.)

'About five years back.'

'Only five years? Find him, find him!'

'It's no use. He doesn't have the movie camera any more. He sold it.'

'Sold it!' Kishore looks at me as though I have done him an injury. 'But why didn't you buy it? All we need is a movie camera, and our fortune is made. I will produce the film, I will direct it, I will write the music. Two in one, Charlie Chaplin and Raj Kapoor. Why didn't you buy the camera?'

'Because I didn't have the money.'

'But we could have borrowed the money.'

'If you are in a position to borrow money, you can go out and buy another movie camera.'

'We could have borrowed the camera. Do you know anyone else who has one?'

'Not a soul.' I am firm this time; I will not be led into another maze.

'Very sad, very sad,' mutters Kishore. And with a dejected, hang-dog expression designed to make me feel that I am responsible for all his failures, he moves off.

Bhabiji had expressed some annoyance at Kishore's arrival, but he softens her up by leaving behind an invitation to a marriage party this evening. No one in the house knows the bride's or bridegroom's family, but that does not matter; knowing one of the musicians is just as good. Almost everyone will go.

While Bhabiji, Shobha and Madhu are preparing lunch, Bhabiji engages in one of her favourite subjects of conversation, Kamal's marriage, which she hopes she will be able to arrange in the near future. She freely acknowledges that she made grave blunders in selecting wives for her other sons—this is meant to be heard by Shobha—and promises not to repeat her mistakes. According to Bhabiji, Kamal's bride should be both educated and domesticated; and of course she must be fair.

'What if he likes a dark girl?' I ask teasingly.

Bhabiji looks horrified. 'He cannot marry a dark girl,' she declares.

'But dark girls are beautiful,' I tell her.

'Impossible!'

'Do you want him to marry a European girl?'

'No foreigners! I know them, they'll take my son away. He shall have a good Punjabi girl, with a complexion the colour of wheat.'

✿

Noon. The shadows shift and cross the road. I sit beneath the guava tree and watch the women at work. They will not let me do anything, but they like talking to me and they love to hear my broken Punjabi. Sparrows flit about at their feet, snapping up the grain that runs away from their busy fingers. A crow looks speculatively at the empty kitchen, sidles towards the open door; but

Bhabiji has only to glance up and the experienced crow flies away. He knows he will not be able to make off with anything from this house.

One by one the children return home, demanding food. Now it is Madhu's turn to go to school. Her younger brother Popat, an intelligent but undersized boy of thirteen, appears in the doorway and asks for lunch.

'Be off!' says Bhabiji. 'It isn't ready yet.'

Actually the food is ready and only the chapatis remain to be made. Shobha will attend to them. Bhabiji lies down on her cot in the sun, complaining of a pain in her back and ringing noises in her ears.

'I'll press your back,' says Popat. He has been out of Bhabiji's favour lately, and is looking for an opportunity to be rehabilitated.

Barefooted he stands on Bhabiji's back and treads her weary flesh and bones with a gentle walking-in-one-spot movement. Bhabiji grunts with relief. Every day she has new pains in new places. Her age, and the daily business of feeding the family and running everyone's affairs, are beginning to tell on her. But she would sooner die than give up her position of dominance in the house. Her working sons still hand over their pay to her, and she dispenses the money as she sees fit.

The pummelling she gets from Popat puts her in a better mood, and she holds forth on another favourite subject, the respective merits of various dowries. Shiv's

187

wife (according to Bhabiji) brought nothing with her but a string cot; Kishore's wife brought only a sharp and clever tongue; Shobha brought a wonderful steel cupboard, fully expecting that it would do all the housework for her.

This last observation upsets Shobha, and a little later I find her under the guava tree, weeping profusely. I give her the comforting words she obviously expects; but it is her husband Arun who will have to bear the brunt of her outraged feelings when he comes home this evening. He is rather nervous of his wife. Last night he wanted to eat out, at a restaurant, but did not want to be accused of wasting money; so he stuffed fifteen rupees into my pocket and asked me to invite both him and Shobha to dinner, which I did. We had a good dinner. Such unexpected hospitality on my part has further improved my standing with Shobha. Now, in spite of other chores, she sees that I get cups of tea and coffee at odd hours of the day.

Bhabiji knows Arun is soft with his wife, and taunts him about it. She was saying this morning that whenever there is any work to be done Shobha retires to bed with a headache (partly true). Bhabhaji says even Manju does more housework (not true). Bhabiji has certain talents as an actress, and does a good take-off of Shobha sulking and grumbling at having too much to do.

While Bhabiji talks, Popat sneaks off and goes for

a ride on the bicycle. It is a very old bicycle and is constantly undergoing repairs. 'The soul has gone out of it,' says Vinod philosophically and makes his way on to the roof, where he keeps a store of pornographic literature. Up there, he cannot be seen and cannot be remembered, and so avoids being sent out on errands.

One of the boys is bathing at the hand pump. Manju, who should have gone to school with Madhu, is stretched out on a cot, complaining of fever. But she will be up in time to attend the marriage party ...

Towards evening, as the birds return to roost in the guava tree, their chatter is challenged by the tumult of people in the house getting ready for the marriage party.

Manju presses her tight pyjamas but neglects to dam them. She wears a loose-fitting, diaphanous shirt. She keeps flitting in and out of the front room so that I can admire the way she glitters. Shobha has used too much powder and lipstick in an effort to look like the femme fatale which she indubitably is not. Shiv's more conservative wife floats around in loose, old-fashioned pyjamas. Bhabiji is sober and austere in a white sari. Madhu looks neat. The men wear their suits.

Popat is holding up a mirror for his Uncle Kishore, who is combing his long hair. (Kishore kept his hair long, like a court musician at the time of Akbar, before the hippies had been heard of.) He is nodding benevolently, having fortified himself from a bottle labelled 'Som Ras' ('Nectar of the Gods'), obtained cheaply from an illicit seller.

Kishore: 'Don't shake the mirror, boy!'

Popat: 'Uncle, it's your head that's shaking.'

Shobha is happy. She loves going out, especially to marriages, and she always takes her two small boys with her, although they invariably spoil the carpets.

Only Kamal, Popat and I remain behind. I have had more than my share of marriage parties.

The house is strangely quiet. It does not seem so small now, with only three people left in it. The kitchen has been locked (Bhabiji will not leave it open while Popat is still in the house), so we visit the dhaba, the wayside restaurant near the main road, and this time I pay the bill with my own money. We have kababs and chicken curry.

Yesterday Kamal and I took our lunch on the grass of the Buddha Jayanti Gardens. There was no college for Kamal, as the majority of Delhi's students had hijacked a number of corporation buses and headed for the Pakistan High Commission, with every intention of levelling it to the ground if possible, as a protest against the hijacking of an Indian plane from Srinagar to Lahore. The students were met by the Delhi police in full strength, and a pitched battle took place, in which stones from the students and tear gas shells from the police were the favoured missiles. There were two shells fired every minute, according to a newspaper report. And this went on all day. A number of students and policemen were injured, but by some miracle no one was killed. The police held their ground, and the Pakistan High Commission remained inviolate. But the Australian High Commission, situated to the rear of the student brigade, received most of the tear gas shells, and had to close down for the day.

Kamal and I attended the siege for about an hour, before retiring to the Gardens with our ham sandwiches. A couple of friendly squirrels came up to investigate, and were soon taking bread from our hands. We could hear the chanting of the students in the distance. I lay back on the grass and opened my copy of *Barchester Towers*. Whenever life in Delhi, or in Bhabiji's house (or anywhere, for that matter), becomes too tumultuous, I turn to Trollope. Nothing could be further removed from the turmoil of our times than an English cathedral town in the nineteenth century. But I think Jane Austen would have appreciated life in Bhabiji's house.

By ten o'clock, everyone is back from the marriage. (They had gone for the feast, and not for the ceremonies, which continue into the early hours of the morning.) Shobha is full of praise for the bridegroom's good looks and fair complexion. She describes him as being 'gora-chitta'—very white! She does not have a high opinion of the bride.

Shiv, in a happy and reflective mood, extols the qualities of his own wife, referring to her as The Barrel. He tells us how, shortly after their marriage, she had threatened to throw a brick at the next-door girl. This little incident remains fresh in Shiv's mind, after eighteen years of marriage.

He says: 'When the neighbours came and complained, I told them, "It is quite possible that my wife will throw a brick at your daughter. She is in the habit of throwing bricks." The neighbours held their peace.'

I think Shiv is rather proud of his wife's militancy when it comes to taking on neighbours; recently she vanquished the woman next door (a formidable Sikh lady) after a verbal battle that lasted three hours. But in arguments or quarrels with Bhabiji, Shiv's wife always loses, because Shiv takes his mother's side.

Arun, on the other hand, is afraid of both wife and mother, and simply makes himself scarce when a quarrel brews. Or he tells his mother she is right, and then, to placate Shobha, takes her to the pictures.

Kishore turns up just as everyone is about to go to bed. Bhabiji is annoyed at first, because he has been drinking too much; but when he produces a bunch of cinema tickets, she is mollified and asks him to stay the night. Not even Bhabiji likes missing a new picture.

Kishore is urging me to write his life story.

'Your life would make a most interesting story,'

I tell him. 'But it will be interesting only if I put in everything—your successes *and* your failures.'

'No, no, only successes,' exhorts Kishore. 'I want you to describe me as a popular music director.'

'But you have yet to become popular.'

'I will be popular if you write about me.'

Fortunately we are interrupted by the cots being brought in. Then Bhabiji and Shiv go into a huddle, discussing plans for building an extra room. After all, Kamal may be married soon.

One by one, the children get under their quilts. Popat starts massaging Bhabiji's back. She gives him her favourite blessing: 'God protect you and give you lots of children.' If God listens to all of Bhabiji's prayers and blessings, there will never be a fall in the population.

The lights are off and Bhabiji settles down for the night. She is almost asleep when a small voice pipes up: 'Bhabiji, tell us a story.'

At first Bhabiji pretends not to hear; then, when the request is repeated, she says: 'You'll keep Aunty Shobha awake, and then she'll have an excuse for getting up late in the morning.' But the children know Bhabiji's one great weakness, and they renew their demand.

'Your grandmother is tired,' says Arun. 'Let her sleep.'

But Bhabiji's eyes are open. Her mind is going back

over the crowded years, and she remembers something very interesting that happened when her younger brother's wife's sister married the eldest son of her third cousin . . .

Before long, the children are asleep, and I am wondering if I will ever sleep, for Bhabiji's voice drones on, into the darker reaches of the night.

Fragrance to the Air

I would be the last person to belittle a flower for its lack of fragrance, because there are many spectacular blooms such as the dahlia and the gladioli which have hardly any scent and yet make up for it with their colour and appearance. But it does happen that my own favourite flowers are those with a distinctive fragrance and these are the flowers I would have around me.

The rose, of course, is the world's favourite, a joy to all—even to babies, who enjoy taking them apart, petal by petal. But there are other, less spectacular, less celebrated blooms which have a lovely, sometimes elusive fragrance all their own.

I have a special fondness for antirrhinums—or snapdragons, as they are more commonly known. If I sniff hard at them, I don't catch any scent at all. They seem to hold it back from me. But if I walk past a bed of snapdragons, or even a single plant, the gentlest of fragrance is wafted towards me. If I stop and try to take it all in, it has gone again! I find this quite tantalizing, but it has given me a special regard for this modest flower.

Another humble, even old-fashioned flower, is the wallflower which obviously takes its name from the fact that it thrives on walls. I have seen wallflowers adorn a garden wall in an extravagant and delightful manner, making it a mountain of perfume. They are best grown so as to form dense masses which become literally solid with fiery flowers — blood-red, purple, yellow, orange or bronze, all sending a heady fragrance into the surrounding air.

Carnations, with their strong scent of cloves, are great showoffs. In India, the jasmine and the magnolia are both rather heady and overpowering. The honeysuckle too insists on making its presence known. A honeysuckle creeper flourished outside the window of my room in Mussoorie, and all through the summer its sweet, rather cloying fragrance drifted in through the open window. It was delightful at times, but at other times I had to close the window just so that I could give my attention to other, less intrusive smells — like the soft, sweet scent of petunias (another of my favourites) growing near the doorstep, and great bunches of sweet peas stacked in a bowl on my desk.

It is much the same with chrysanthemums and geraniums. The lemon geranium, for instance, is valued more for its fragrant leaves than for its rather indeterminate blue flowers. And I cannot truthfully say what ordinary mint looks like in flower. The refreshing fragrance of the leaves, when crushed, makes up for any absence of floral display. On the other hand, the multicoloured loveliness of dahlias is unaccompanied by any scent. Its greenery, when cut or broken, does have a faintly acrid smell, but that's about all.

Not all plants are good to smell. Some leaves, when crushed, will keep strong men at bay! During the monsoon in the plains, neem pods fall and are crushed underfoot, giving out a distinctive odour. Most people dislike the smell, but I find it quite refreshing.

Of course, one man's fragrance might well turn out to be another creature's bad smell. Geraniums, my grandmother insisted, kept snakes away because they couldn't stand the smell of the leaves. She surrounded her bungalow with pots of geraniums. As we never found a snake in the house, she may well have been right. But the evidence is purely circumstantial.

I suppose snakes like some smells, close to the ground, or by now they'd have taken to living in more elevated places. But, turning to a book on reptiles, I learnt from it that in the snake the sense of smell is rather dull. Perhaps it has an aversion to anything that it can smell—such as those aromatic geranium leaves!

Close to Mother Earth, there are many delightful smells, provided you avoid roadsides and freshly-manured fields. When I lie on summer grass in some

Himalayan meadow, I am conscious of the many good smells around me—the grass itself, redolent of the morning's dew, bruised clover, wild violets, tiny buttercups and golden stars and strawberry flowers and many others I shall never know the names of.

And the earth itself. It smells different in different places. But its loveliest fragrance is known only when it receives a shower of rain. And then the scent of the wet earth rises as though it would give something beautiful back to the clouds. A blend of all the fragrant things that grow upon it.

Garden of a Thousand Trees

No one in his right mind would want to chop down a mango tree. Every mango tree, even if it grows wild, is generous with its juicy fruit, known sometimes as 'the nectar of the gods', and sometimes as the 'king of fruits'. You can eat ripe mangoes fresh from the tree; you can eat them in pickles or chutneys or jams; you can eat them flattened out and dried, as in aam papad; you can drink the juice with milk as in 'mango-fool'; you can even pound the kernel into flour and use it as a substitute for wheat. And there are over a hundred different varieties of the mango, each with its own distinctive flavour.

But in praising the fruit, let us not forget the tree, for it is one of the stateliest trees in India, its tall, spreading branches a familiar sight throughout the country, from the lower slopes of the Himalayas to Cape Comorin.

In Gujarat, on the night of the seventh of the month of Savan (July-August), a young mango tree is planted near the house and worshipped by the womenfolk to protect their children from disease. Sometimes a post of mango wood is set up when Ganesh is worshipped.

If you live anywhere in the plains of northern India, you will often have seen a grove of giant mango trees, sometimes appearing like an oasis in the midst of the vast, flat countryside. Beneath the trees you may find a well and a small temple. It is here that the tired, dusty farmer sits down to rest and eat his midday chapati, following it with a draught of cold water from the well. If you join him and ask him who planted the mango grove, he will not be able to tell you; it was there when he was a boy, and probably when his father was a boy too. Some mango groves are very, very old.

Have you heard of the Garden of a Thousand Trees? Probably not. But you must have heard of the town of Hazaribagh in Bihar. Well, a huge mango grove containing over a thousand trees—some of which are still there—was known as hazari, and around these trees a village grew, spreading in time into the modern town of Hazaribagh, 'Garden of a Thousand Trees'. Anyway, that's the story you will hear from the oldest inhabitants of the town. And even today, the town is almost hidden in a garden of trees: mango and neem, sal and tamarind.

All are welcome in a mango grove. But during the mango season, when the trees are in fruit, you enter the grove at your own peril! At this time of the year it is watched over by a fierce chowkidar, whose business is to drive away any mischievous children who creep into the grove in the hope of catching him asleep and making off with a few juicy mangoes. The chowkidar is a busy man. Even before the mangoes ripen, he has to battle not only with the village urchins, but also with raiding parties of emerald-green parrots, who swarm all over the trees, biting deep into the green fruit. Sometimes he sits under a tree in the middle of the grove, pulling a rope which makes a large kerosene-tin rattle in the branches. He can try shouting too, but his voice can't compete with the screams of the parrots. They wheel in circles round the grove and, spreading their tails, settle on the topmost branches.

Even when there are no mangoes, you will find parrots in the grove, because during their breeding season, their favourite nesting places are the holes in the gnarled trunks of old mango trees.

Other birds, including the blue jay and the little green coppersmith, favour the mango grove for the same reason. And sometimes you may spot a small owl peering at you from its hole halfway up the trunk of an old tree.

Good Day to You, Uncle

On the left bank of the Ganga, where it emerges from the Himalayan foothills, there is a long stretch of heavy forest. There are villages on the fringe of the forest, inhabited by bamboo cutters and farmers, but there are few signs of commerce or pilgrimage. Hunters, however, have found the area an ideal hunting ground during the last seventy years, and as a result, the animals are not as numerous as they used to be. The trees, too, have been disappearing slowly; and, as the forest recedes, the animals lose their food and shelter and move further on into the foothills. Slowly, they are being denied the right to live.

Only the elephants can cross the river. And two years ago, when a large area of the forest was cleared to make way for a refugee resettlement camp, a herd of elephants — finding their favourite food, the green shoots of the bamboo, in short supply — waded across the river. They crashed through the suburbs of Hardwar, knocked down a factory wall, pulled down several tin roofs, held up a train and left a trail of devastation in their wake until they found a new home in a new forest which was still untouched. Here, they settled down to a new life—but an unsettled, wary life. They did not know when men would appear again with tractors, bulldozers and dynamite.

There was a time when the forest on the banks of the Ganga had provided food and shelter for some thirty or forty tigers; but men in search of trophies had shot them all, and now there remained only one old tiger in the jungle. Many hunters had tried to get him, but he was a wise and crafty old tiger, who knew the ways of men, and he had so far survived all attempts on his life.

Although the tiger had passed the prime of his life, he had lost none of his majesty. His muscles rippled beneath the golden yellow of his coat, and he walked through the long grass with the confidence of one who knew that he was still a king, even though his subjects were fewer. His great head pushed through the foliage, and it was only his tail, swinging high, that showed occasionally above the sea of grass.

Often he headed for water, the only water in the forest (if you don't count the river, which was several miles away), the water of a large jheel, which was almost a lake during the rainy season, but just a muddy marsh at this time of the year, in the late spring.

Here, at different times of the day and night, all the animals came to drink—the long-horned sambar, the delicate chital, the swamp deer, the hyenas and jackals, the wild boar, the panthers—and the lone tiger. Since the elephants had gone, the water was usually clear except when buffaloes from the nearby village came to wallow in it. These buffaloes, though not wild, were not afraid of the panther or even of the tiger. They knew the panther was afraid of their massive horns and that the tiger preferred the flesh of the deer.

One day, there were several sambars at the water's edge, but they did not stay long. The scent of the tiger came with the breeze, and there was no mistaking its strong feline odour. The deer held their heads high for a few moments, their nostrils twitching, and then scattered into the forest, disappearing behind a screen of leaf and bamboo.

When the tiger arrived, there was no other animal near the water. But the birds were still there. The egrets continued to wade in the shallows, and a kingfisher darted low over the water, dived suddenly, a flash of blue and gold, and made off with a slim silver fish, which glistened in the sun like a polished gem. A long, brown snake glided in and out among the water lilies and disappeared beneath a fallen tree which lay rotting in the shallows.

The tiger waited in the shelter of a rock, his ears pricked up for the least unfamiliar sound, for he knew that it was at that place that men sometimes sat up for him with guns for they coveted his beauty—his stripes and the gold of his body, his fine teeth, his whiskers, and his noble head. They would have liked to hang his skin on a wall, with his head stuffed and mounted, and pieces of glass replacing his fierce eyes; then they would have boasted of their triumph over the king of the jungle.

The tiger had been hunted before, so he did not usually show himself in the open during the day. But of late he had heard no guns, and if there were hunters around, you would have heard their guns (for a man with a gun cannot resist letting it off, even if it is only at a rabbit—or at another man). And, besides, the tiger was thirsty.

He was also feeling quite hot. It was March and the shimmering dust haze of summer had come early. Tigers—unlike other cats—are fond of water, and on a hot day will wallow in it for hours.

He walked into the water, in amongst the water lilies, and drank slowly. He was seldom in a hurry when he ate or drank. Other animals might bolt down their food, but they were only other animals. A tiger is a tiger; he has his dignity to preserve even though he isn't aware of it!

He raised his head and listened, one paw suspended in the air. A strange sound had come to him with the breeze, and he was wary of strange sounds. So he moved swiftly into the shelter of the tall grass that bordered the jheel, and climbed a hillock until he reached his favourite rock. This rock was big enough both to hide him and to give him shade. Anyone looking up from the jheel might think it strange that the rock had a round bump on the top. The bump was the tiger's head. He kept it very still.

The sound he heard was only the sound of a flute, rendered thin and reedy in the forest. It belonged to Ramu, a slim, brown boy who rode a buffalo. Ramu played vigorously on the flute. Shyam, a slightly smaller boy, riding another buffalo, brought up the rear of the herd.

There were about eight buffaloes in the herd, and they belonged to the families of the two friends Ramu and Shyam. Their people were *Gujjars*, a nomadic community who earned a livelihood by keeping buffaloes and selling milk and butter. The boys were about twelve years old, but they could not have told you exactly because in their village nobody thought birthdays were important. They were almost the same age as the tiger, but he was old and experienced while they were still cubs.

The tiger had often seen them at the tank, and he was not worried by their presence. He knew the village people would do him no harm as long as he left their buffaloes alone. Once when he was younger and full of bravado, he had killed a buffalo—not because he was hungry, but because he was young and wanted to try out his strength — and after that the villagers had hunted him for days, with spears, bows and an old muzzle loader. Now he left the buffaloes alone, even though the deer in the forest were not as numerous as before.

The boys knew that a tiger lived in the jungle, for they had often heard him roar, but they did not suspect that he was so near just then.

The tiger gazed down from his rock, and the sight of eight fat black buffaloes made him give a low, throaty moan. But the boys were there, and, besides, a buffalo was not easy to kill.

He decided to move on and find a cool shady place in the heart of the jungle, where he could rest during the warm afternoon and be free of the flies and mosquitoes that swarmed around the jheel. At night he would hunt.

With a lazy, half-humorous roar — 'a-oonh!' — he got up off his haunches and sauntered off into the jungle.

Even the gentlest of the tiger's roars can be heard half a mile away, and the boys who were barely fifty yards away looked up immediately.

'There he goes!' said Ramu, taking the flute from his lips and pointing it towards the hillocks. He was not afraid, for he knew that this tiger was not interested in humans. 'Did you see him?'

'I saw his tail, just before he disappeared. He's a big tiger!'

'Do not call him tiger. Call him Uncle, or Maharaj.'

'Oh, why?'

'Don't you know that it's unlucky to call a tiger a tiger? My father always told me so. But if you meet a tiger and call him Uncle, he will leave you alone.'

'I'll try and remember that,' said Shyam.

The buffaloes were now well inside the water, and some of them were lying down in the mud. Buffaloes love soft, wet mud and will wallow in it for hours. The slushier the mud, the better. Ramu, to avoid being dragged down into the mud with his buffalo, slipped off its back and plunged into the water. He waded to a small islet covered with reeds and water lilies. Shyam was close behind him.

They lay down on their hard, flat stomachs, on a patch of grass, and allowed the warm sun to beat down on their bare brown bodies.

Ramu was the more knowledgeable boy, because he had been to Hardwar and Dehradun several times with his father. Shyam had never been out of the village.

Shyam said, 'The jheel is not so deep this year.'

'We have had no rain since January,' said Ramu. 'If we do not get rain soon the jheel may dry up altogether.'

'And then what will we do?'

'We? I don't know. There is a well in the village. But even that may dry up. My father told me that it failed once, just about the time I was born, and everyone had to walk ten miles to the river for water.'

'And what about the animals?'

'Some will stay here and die. Others will go to the river. But there are too many people near the river now — and temples, houses and factories — and the animals stay away. And the trees have been cut, so that between the jungle and the river there is no place to hide. Animals are afraid of the open — they are afraid of men with guns.'

'Even at night?'

'At night men come in jeeps, with searchlights. They kill the deer for meat and sell the skins of tigers and panthers.'

'I didn't know a tiger's skin was worth anything.'

'It's worth more than our skins,' said Ramu knowingly. 'It will fetch six hundred rupees. Who would pay that much for one of us?'

'Our fathers would.'

'True, if they had the money.'

'If my father sold his fields, he would get more than six hundred rupees.'

'True, but if he sold his fields, none of you would have anything to eat. A man needs the land as much as a tiger needs the jungle.'

'Yes,' said Shyam. 'And that reminds me — my mother asked me to take some roots home.'

'I will help you.'

They walked deeper into the jheel until the water was up to their waists, and began pulling up water lilies by the roots. The flower is beautiful but the villagers value the root more. When it is cooked, it makes a delicious and strengthening dish. The plant multiplies rapidly and is always in good supply. In the year when famine hit the village, it was only the root of the water lily that saved many from starvation.

When Shyam and Ramu had finished gathering roots, they emerged from the water and passed the time in wrestling with each other, slipping about in the soft mud which soon covered them from head to toe.

To get rid of the mud, they dived into the water again and swam across to their buffaloes. Then, jumping on their backs and digging their heels into thick hides, the boys raced them across the jheel, shouting and hollering so much that all the birds flew away in fright, and the monkeys set up a shrill chattering of their own in the *dhak* trees.

It was evening, and the twilight fading fast, when the buffalo herd finally wended its way homeward, to be greeted outside the village by the barking of dogs, the gurgle of hookah pipes and the homely smell of cow-dung smoke.

The tiger made a kill that night—a chital. He made his approach against the wind so that the unsuspecting spotted deer did not see him until it was too late. A blow on the deer's haunches from the tiger's paw brought it down, and then the great beast fastened his fangs on the deer's throat. It was all over in a few minutes. The tiger was too quick and strong, and the deer did not struggle much.

It was a violent end for so gentle a creature. But you must not imagine that in the jungle the deer live in permanent fear of death. It is only man, with his imagination and his fear of the hereafter, who is afraid of dying. In the jungle it is different. Sudden death appears at intervals. Wild creatures do not have to think about it, and so the sudden killing of one of their number by some predator of the forest is only a fleeting incident, soon forgotten by the survivors.

The tiger feasted well, growling with pleasure as he ate his way up the body, leaving the entrails. When he had his night's fill he left the carcase for the vultures and jackals. The cunning old tiger never returned to the same carcase, even if there was still plenty left to eat. In the past, when he had gone back to a kill he had often found a man sitting in a tree waiting for him with a rifle.

His belly filled, the tiger sauntered over to the edge of the forest and looked out across the sandy wasteland and the deep, singing river, at the twinkling lights of Rishikesh on the opposite bank, and raised his head and roared his defiance at mankind.

The tiger was a lonesome bachelor. It was five or six years since he had a mate. She had been shot by the trophy hunters, and her two cubs had been trapped by men who do trade in wild animals. One went to a circus, where he had to learn tricks to amuse people and respond to the flick of a whip; the other, more fortunate, went first to a zoo in Delhi and was later transferred to a zoo in America.

Sometimes, when the old tiger was very lonely, he gave a great roar, which could be heard throughout the forest. The villagers thought he was roaring in anger, but the jungle knew that he was really roaring out of loneliness.

When the sound of his roar had died away, he paused, standing still, waiting for an answering roar, but it never came. It was taken up instead by the shrill scream of a barbet high up in a sal tree.

It was dawn now, dew-fresh and cool, and jungle dwellers were on the move . . .

The black, beady, little eyes of a jungle rat were fixed on a small brown hen who was pecking around in the undergrowth near her nest. He had a large family to feed, this rat, and he knew that in the hen's nest was a clutch of delicious fawn-coloured eggs. He waited patiently for nearly an hour before he had the satisfaction of seeing the hen leave her nest and go off in search of food.

As soon as she had gone, the rat lost no time in making his raid. Slipping quietly out of his hole, he slithered along among the leaves; but, clever as he was, he did not realize that his own movements were being watched.

A pair of grey mongooses scouted about in the dry grass. They too were hungry, and eggs usually figured in large measure on their menu. Now, lying still on an outcrop of rock, they watched the rat sneaking along, occasionally sniffing at the air and finally vanishing behind a boulder. When he reappeared, he was struggling to roll an egg uphill towards his hole.

The rat was in difficulty, pushing the egg sometimes with his paws, sometimes with his nose. The ground was rough, and the egg wouldn't move straight. Deciding that he must have help, he scuttled off to call his spouse. Even now the mongooses did not descend on that tantalizing egg. They waited until the rat returned with his wife, and then watched as the male rat took the egg firmly between his forepaws and rolled over on to his back. The female rat then grabbed her mate's tail and began to drag him along.

Totally absorbed in their struggle with the egg, the rat did not hear the approach of the mongooses. When these two large furry visitors suddenly bobbed up from behind a stone, the rats squealed with fright, abandoned the egg and fled for their lives.

The mongooses wasted no time in breaking open the egg and making a meal of it. But just as, a few minutes ago, the rat had not noticed their approach, so now they too did not notice the village boy, carrying a small bright axe and a net bag in his hands, creeping along.

Ramu too was searching for eggs, and when he saw the mongooses busy with one, he stood still to watch them, his eyes roving in search of the nest. He was hoping the mongooses would lead him to the nest; but, when they had finished their meal and made off into the undergrowth, Ramu had to do his own searching. He failed to find the nest, and moved further into the forest. The rat's hopes were just reviving when, to his disgust, the mother hen returned.

Ramu now made his way to a mahua tree.

The flowers of the mahua can be eaten by animals as well as by men. Bears are particularly fond of them and will eat large quantities of flowers which gradually start fermenting in their stomachs with the result that the animals get quite drunk. Ramu had often seen a couple of bears stumbling home to their cave, bumping into each other or into the trunks of trees. They are short-sighted to begin with, and when drunk can hardly see at all. But their sense of smell and hearing are so good that in the end they find their way home.

Ramu decided he would gather some mahua flowers, and climbed up the tree, which is leafless when it blossoms. He began breaking the white flowers and throwing them to the ground. He had been on the tree for about five minutes when he heard the whining grumble of a bear, and presently a young sloth bear ambled into the clearing beneath the tree.

He was a small bear, little more than a cub, and Ramu was not frightened; but, because he thought the mother might be in the vicinity, he decided to take no chance, and sat very still, waiting to see what the bear would do. He hoped it wouldn't choose the mahua tree for a meal.

At first the young bear put his nose to the ground and sniffed his way along until he came to a large anthill. Here he began huffing and puffing, blowing rapidly in and out of his nostrils, causing the dust from the anthill to fly in all directions. But he was disappointed because the anthill had been deserted long ago. And so, grumbling, he made his way across to a tall wild plum tree and, shinning rapidly up the smooth trunk, was soon perched on its topmost branches. It was only then that he saw Ramu.

The bear at once scrambled several feet higher up the tree and laid himself out flat on a branch. It wasn't a very thick branch and left a large part of the bear's body showing on either side. The bear tucked his head away behind another branch, and so long as he could not see Ramu, seemed quite satisfied that he was well hidden, though he couldn't help grumbling with anxiety, for a bear, like most animals, is afraid of man.

Bears, however, are also very curious, and curiosity has often led them into trouble. Slowly, inch by inch, the young bear's black snout appeared over the edge of the branch; but immediately as the eyes came into view and met Ramu's, he drew back with a jerk and the head was once more hidden. The bear did this two or three times, and Ramu, highly amused, waited until it wasn't looking, then moved some way down the tree. When the bear looked up again and saw that the boy was missing, he was so pleased with himself that he stretched right across to the next branch, to get a plum. Ramu chose this moment to burst into loud laughter. The startled bear tumbled out of the tree, dropped through the branches for a distance of some fifteen feet, and landed with a thud in a heap of dry leaves.

And then several things happened at almost the same time.

The mother bear came charging into the clearing. Spotting Ramu in the tree, she reared up on her hind legs, grunting fiercely. It was Ramu's turn to be startled. There are few animals more dangerous than a rampaging mother bear, and the boy knew that one blow from her clawed forepaws could rip his skull open.

But before the bear could approach the tree, there was a tremendous roar, and the old tiger bounded into the clearing. He had been asleep in the bushes not far away—he liked a good sleep after a heavy meal—and the noise in the clearing had woken him.

He was in a bad mood, and his loud 'a-oonh!' made his displeasure quite clear. The bear turned and ran from the clearing, the youngster squealing with fright.

The tiger then came into the centre of the clearing, looked up at the trembling boy, and roared again.

Ramu nearly fell out of the tree.

'Good day to you, Uncle,' he stammered, showing his teeth in a nervous grin.

Perhaps this was too much for the tiger. With a low growl, he turned his back on the mahua tree and padded off into the jungle, his tail twitching in disgust.

That night, when Ramu told his parents and his grandfather about the tiger and how it had saved him from a female bear, it started a round of tiger stories—about how some of them could be gentlemen, others rogues. Sooner or later the conversation came round to man-eaters, and Grandfather told two stories which he swore were true, although his listeners only half-believed him.

The first story concerned the belief that a man-eating tiger is guided towards his next victim by the spirit of a human being previously killed and eaten by the tiger. Grandfather said that he actually knew three hunters, who sat up in a machan over a human kill, and that, when the tiger came, the corpse sat up and pointed with his right hand at the men in the tree. The tiger then went away. But the hunters knew he would return, and one man was brave enough to get down from the tree and tie the right arm of the corpse to its side. Later, when the tiger returned, the corpse sat up, and this time pointed out the men with his left hand. The enraged tiger sprang into the tree and killed his enemies in the machan.

'And then there was a bania,' said Grandfather, beginning another story, 'who lived in a village in the jungle. He wanted to visit a neighbouring village to collect some money that was owed to him, but as the road lay through heavy forest in which lived a terrible man-eating tiger, he did not know what to do. Finally, he went to a sadhu who gave him two powders. By eating the first powder, he could turn into a huge tiger, capable of dealing with any other tiger in the jungle, and by eating the second he could become a bania again.

'Armed with his two powders, and accompanied by his pretty, young wife, the bania set out on his journey. They had not gone far into the forest when they came upon the man-eater sitting in the middle of the road. Before swallowing the first powder, the bania told his wife to stay where she was, so that when he returned after killing the tiger, she could at once give him the second powder and enable him to resume his old shape.

'Well, the bania's plan worked, but only up to a point. He swallowed the first powder and immediately became a magnificent tiger. With a great roar, he bounded towards the man-eater, and after a brief, furious fight, killed his opponent. Then, with his jaws still dripping blood, he returned to his wife.

'The poor girl was terrified and spilt the second powder on the ground. The bania was so angry that he pounced on his wife and killed and ate her. And afterwards this terrible tiger was so enraged at not being able to become a human again that he killed and ate hundreds of people all over the country.'

'The only people he spared,' added Grandfather, with a twinkle in his eyes, 'were those who owed him money. A bania never gives up a loan as lost, and the tiger still hoped that one day he might become a human again and be able to collect his dues.'

Next morning, when Ramu came back from the well, which was used to irrigate his father's fields, he found a crowd of curious children surrounding a jeep and three strangers. Each of the strangers had a gun, and they were accompanied by two bearers and a vast amount of provisions.

They had heard that there was a tiger in the area, and they wanted to shoot it.

One of the hunters, who looked even more strange than the others, had come all the way from America to shoot a tiger, and he vowed that he would not leave the country without a tiger's skin in his baggage. One of his companions had said that he could buy a tiger's skin in Delhi, but the hunter said he preferred to get his own trophies.

These men had money to spend, and, as most of the villagers needed money badly, they were only too willing to go into the forest to construct a machan for the hunters. The platform, big enough to take the three men, was put up in the branches of a tall *tun*, or mahogany tree.

It was the only night the hunters used the machan. At the end of March, though the days are warm, the nights are still cold. The hunters had neglected to bring blankets, and by midnight their teeth were chattering. Ramu, having tied up a buffalo calf for them at the foot of the tree, made as if to go home but instead circled the area, hanging up bits and pieces of old clothing on small trees and bushes. He thought he owed that much to the tiger. He knew the wily old king of the jungle would keep well away from the bait if he saw the bits of clothing—for where there were men's clothes, there would be men.

The vigil lasted well into the night but the tiger did not come near the *tun* tree; perhaps he wasn't hungry, perhaps he got Ramu's message. In any case, the men in the tree soon gave themselves away.

The cold was really too much for them. A flask of rum was produced, and passed around, and it was not long before there was more purpose to finishing the rum than to finishing off a tiger. Silent at first, the men soon began talking in whispers; and to jungle creatures a human whisper is as telling as a trumpet call.

Soon the men were quite merry, talking in loud voices. And when the first morning light crept over the forest, and Ramu and his friends came back to fetch the great hunters, they found them fast asleep in the machan.

The hunters looked surly and embarrassed as they trudged back to the village.

'No game left in these parts,' announced the American.

'Wrong time of the year for tiger,' said the second man.

'Don't know what the country's coming to,' said the third.

And complaining about the weather, the poor quality of cartridges, the quantity of rum they had drunk and the perversity of tigers, they drove away in disgust.

It was not until the onset of summer that an event occurred which altered the hunting habits of the old tiger and brought him into conflict with the villagers.

There had been no rain for almost two months, and the tall jungle grass had become a sea of billowy dry yellow. Some refugee settlers, living in an area where the forest had been cleared, had been careless while cooking and had started a jungle fire. Slowly it spread into the interior, from where the acrid smell and the fumes smoked the tiger out towards the edge of the jungle. As night came on, the flames grew more vivid, and the smell stronger. The tiger turned and made for the jheel, where he knew he would be safe, provided he swam across to the little island in the centre.

Next morning he was on the island, which was untouched by the fire. But his surroundings had changed. The slopes of the hills were black with burnt grass, and most of the tall bamboo had disappeared. The deer and the wild pig, finding that their natural cover had gone, fled further east.

When the fire had died down and the smoke had cleared, the tiger prowled through the forest again but found no game. Once he came across the body of a burnt rabbit, but he could not eat it. He drank at the jheel and settled down in a shady spot to sleep the day away. Perhaps, by evening, some of the animals would return; if not, he too would have to look for new hunting grounds — or new game.

The tiger spent five more days looking for a suitable game to kill. By that time he was so hungry that he even resorted to rooting among the dead leaves and burnt out stumps of trees, searching for worms and beetles. This was a sad comedown for the king of the jungle. But even now he hesitated to leave the area, for he had a deep suspicion and fear of the forests further east — forests that were fast being swallowed up by human habitation. He could have gone north, into high mountains, but they did not provide him with the long grass he needed. A panther could manage quite well up there, but not a tiger who loved the natural privacy of the heavy jungle. In the hills, he would have to hide all the time.

At break of day, the tiger came to the jheel. The water was now shallow and muddy, and a green scum had spread over the top. But it was still drinkable and the tiger quenched his thirst.

He lay down across his favourite rock, hoping for a deer but none came. He was about to get up and go away when he heard an animal approach.

The tiger at once leaped off his perch and flattened himself on the ground, his tawny striped skin merging with the dry grass. A heavy animal was moving through the bushes, and the tiger waited patiently.

A buffalo emerged and came to the water.

The buffalo was alone.

He was a big male, and his long, curved horns lay right back across his shoulders. He moved leisurely towards the water, completely unaware of the tiger's presence.

The tiger hesitated before making his charge. It was a long time—many years—since he had killed a buffalo, and he knew the villagers would not like it. But the pangs of hunger overcame his scruples. There was no morning breeze; everything was still, and the smell of the tiger did not reach the buffalo. A monkey chattered on a nearby tree, but his warning went unheeded.

Crawling stealthily on his stomach, the tiger skirted the edge of the jheel and approached the buffalo from the rear. The water birds, who were used to the presence of both animals, did not raise an alarm.

Getting closer, the tiger glanced around to see if there were men, or other buffaloes, in the vicinity. Then, satisfied that he was alone, he crept forward. The buffalo was drinking, standing in shallow water at the edge of the tank, when the tiger charged from the side and bit deep into the animal's thigh.

The buffalo turned to fight, but the tendons of his right hind leg had been snapped, and he could only stagger forward a few paces. But he was a buffalo— the bravest of the domestic cattle. He was not afraid. He snorted, and lowered his horns at the tiger, but the great cat was too fast, and circling the buffalo, bit into the other hind leg.

The buffalo crashed to the ground, both hind legs crippled, and then the tiger dashed in, using both tooth and claw, biting deep into the buffalo's throat until blood gushed out from the jugular vein.

The buffalo gave one long, last bellow before dying.

The tiger, having rested, now began to gorge himself, but, even though he had been starving for days, he could not finish the huge carcase. At least one good meal still remained, when, satisfied and feeling his strength returning, he quenched his thirst at the jheel. Then he dragged the remains of the buffalo into the bushes to hide it from the vultures, and went off to find a place to sleep.

He would return to the kill when he was hungry again.

The villagers were upset when they discovered that a buffalo was missing; and next day, when Ramu and Shyam came running home to say that they found the carcase near the jheel, half eaten by a tiger, the men were disturbed and angry. They felt that the tiger had tricked and deceived them. And they knew that once he got a taste for domestic cattle he would make a habit of slaughtering them.

Kundan Singh, Shyam's father and the owner of the dead buffalo, said he would go after the tiger himself.

'It is all very well to talk about what you will do to the tiger,' said his wife, 'but you should never have let the buffalo go off on its own.'

'He had been out on his own before,' said Kundan. 'This is the first time the tiger has attacked one of our beasts. A devil must have entered the Maharaj.'

'He must have been very hungry,' said Shyam.

'Well, we are hungry too,' said Kundan Singh.

'Our best buffalo—the only male in our herd.'

'The tiger will kill again,' warned Ramu's father.

'If we let him,' said Kundan.

'Should we send for the shikaris?'

'No. They were not clever. The tiger will escape them easily. Besides, there is no time. The tiger will return for another meal tonight. We must finish him off ourselves!'

'But how?'

Kundan Singh smiled secretively, played with the ends of his moustache for a few moments, and then, with great pride, produced from under his cot a double-barrelled gun of ancient vintage.

'My father bought it from an Englishman,' he said.

'How long ago was that?'

'At the time I was born.'

'And have you ever used it?' asked Ramu's father, who was not sure that the gun would work.

'Well, some years back, I let it off at some bandits. You remember the time when those dacoits raided our village? They chose the wrong village, and were severely beaten for their pains. As they left, I fired my gun off at them. They didn't stop running until they crossed the Ganga!'

'Yes, but did you hit anyone?'

'I would have, if someone's goat hadn't got in the way at the last moment. But we had roast mutton that night! Don't worry, brother, I know how the thing fires.'

Accompanied by Ramu's father and some others,

Kundan set out for the jheel, where, without shifting the buffalo's carcase—for they knew that the tiger would not come near them if he suspected a trap—they made another machan in the branches of a tall tree some thirty feet from the kill.

Later that evening, Kundan Singh and Ramu's father settled down for the night on their crude platform on the tree.

Several hours passed, and nothing but a jackal was seen by the watchers. And then, just as the moon came up over the distant hills, Kundan and his companion were startled by a low 'A-ooonh', followed by a suppressed, rumbling growl.

Kundan grasped his old gun, whilst his friend drew closer to him for comfort. There was complete silence for a minute or two—time that was an agony of suspense for the watchers—and then the sound of stealthy footfalls on dead leaves under the trees.

A moment later the tiger walked out into the moonlight and stood over his kill.

At first Kundan could do nothing. He was completely overawed by the size of this magnificent tiger. Ramu's father had to nudge him, and then Kundan quickly put the gun to his shoulder, aimed at the tiger's head, and pressed the trigger.

The gun went off with a flash and two loud bangs as Kundan fired both barrels. Then there was a tremendous roar. One of the bullets had grazed the tiger's head.

The enraged animal rushed at the tree and tried to leap on to the branches. Fortunately, the machan had been built at a safe height, and the tiger was unable to reach it. It roared again and then bounded off into the forest.

'What a tiger!' exclaimed Kundan, half in fear and half in admiration. 'I feel as though my liver has turned to water.'

'You missed him completely,' said Ramu's father. 'Your gun makes big noise; an arrow would have done more damage.'

'I did not miss him,' said Kundan, feeling offended. 'You heard him roar, didn't you? Would he have been so angry had he not been hit? If I have wounded him badly, he will die.'

'And if you have wounded him slightly, he may turn into a man-eater, and then where will we be?'

'I don't think he will come back,' said Kundan. 'He will leave these forests.'

They waited until the sun was up before coming down from the tree. They found a few drops of blood on the dry grass but no trail led into the forest, and Ramu's father was convinced that the wound was only a slight one.

The bullet, missing the fatal spot behind the ear, had only grazed the back of the skull and cut a deep groove at its base. It took a few days to heal, and during this time the tiger lay low and did not go near the jheel except when it was very dark and he was very thirsty.

The villagers thought the tiger had gone away, and Ramu and Shyam—accompanied by some other youths, and always carrying axes and lathis—began bringing buffaloes to the tank again during the day; but they were careful not to let any of them stray far from the herd, and they returned home while it was still daylight.

It was some days since the jungle had been ravaged by the fire, and in the tropics the damage is repaired quickly. In spite of it being the dry season, new life soon began to creep into the forest.

While the buffaloes wallowed in the muddy water, and the boys wrestled on the grassy islet, a big tawny eagle soared high above them, looking for a meal—a sure sign that some of the animals were beginning to return to the forest. It was not long before his keen eyes detected a movement in the glade below.

What the eagle with his powerful eyesight saw was a baby hare, a small fluffy thing, its long pink-tinted ears laid flat along its sides. Had it not been creeping along between two large stones, it would have escaped notice. The eagle waited to see if the mother was about, and as he waited he realized that he was not the only one who coveted this juicy morsel. From the bushes there had appeared a sinuous yellow creature, pressed low to the ground and moving rapidly towards the hare. It was a yellow jungle cat, hardly noticeable in the scorched grass. With great stealth the jungle cat began to stalk the baby hare.

He pounced. The hare's squeal was cut short by the cat's cruel claws; but it had been heard by the mother hare, who now bounded into the glade and without the slightest hesitation went for the surprised cat.

There was nothing haphazard about the mother hare's attack. She flashed around behind the cat and jumped clean over it. As she landed, she kicked back, sending a stinging jet of dust shooting into the cat's face. She did this again and again.

The bewildered cat, crouching and snarling, picked up the kill and tried to run away with it. But the hare would not permit this. She continued her leaping and buffeting, till eventually the cat, out of sheer frustration, dropped the kill and attacked the mother.

The cat sprung at the hare a score of times, lashing out with his claws; but the mother hare was both clever and agile enough to keep just out of reach of those terrible claws, and drew the cat further and further away from her baby — for she did not as yet know that it was dead.

The tawny eagle saw his chance. Swift and true, he swooped. For a brief moment, as his wings overspread the puny, little hare and his talons sank deep into it, he caught a glimpse of the cat racing towards him and the mother hare fleeing into the bushes. And then with a shrill 'kee-e e-ee' of triumph, he rose and whirled away with his dinner.

The boys had heard his shrill cry and looked up just in time to see the eagle flying over the jheel with the little hare held firmly in its talons.

'Poor hare,' said Shyam. 'Its life was short.'

'That's the law of the jungle,' said Ramu. 'The eagle has a family too, and must feed it.'

'I wonder if we are any better than animals,' said Shyam.

'Perhaps we are a little better, in some ways,' said Ramu. 'Grandfather always says, "To be able to laugh and to be merciful are the only things that make man better than the beast."'

The next day, while the boys were taking the herd home, one of the buffaloes lagged behind. Ramu did not realize that the animal was missing until he heard an agonized bellow behind him. He glanced over his shoulder just in time to see the big, striped tiger dragging the buffalo into a clump of young bamboo trees. At the same time the herd became aware of the danger and the buffaloes snorted with fear as they hurried along the forest path. To urge them forward, and to warn his friends, Ramu cupped his hands to his mouth and gave vent to a yodelling call.

The buffaloes bellowed, the boys shouted, and the birds flew shrieking from the trees. It was almost a stampede by the time the herd emerged from the forest. The villagers heard the thunder of hoofs, and saw the herd coming home amidst clouds of dust and confusion, and knew that something was wrong.

'The tiger!' shouted Ramu. 'He is here! He has killed one of the buffaloes.'

'He is afraid of us no longer,' said Shyam.

'Did you see where he went?' asked Kundan Singh, hurrying up to them.

'I remember the place,' said Ramu. 'He dragged the buffalo in amongst the bamboo.'

'Then there is no time to lose,' said his father. 'Kundan, you take your gun and two men, and wait near the suspension bridge, where the Garur stream joins the Ganga. The jungle is narrow there. We will beat the jungle from our side, and drive the tiger towards you. He will not escape us, unless he swims the river!'

'Good!' said Kundan, running into his house for his gun, with Shyam close at his heels. 'Was it one of our buffaloes again?' he asked.

'It was Ramu's buffalo this time,' said Shyam. 'A good milk buffalo.'

'Then Ramu's father will beat the jungle thoroughly. You boys had better come with me. It will not be safe for you to accompany the beaters.'

Kundan Singh, carrying his gun and accompanied by Ramu, Shyam and two men, headed for the river junction, while Ramu's father collected about twenty men from the village and, guided by one of the boys who had been with Ramu, made for the spot where the tiger had killed the buffalo.

The tiger was still eating when he heard the men coming. He had not expected to be disturbed so soon. With an angry 'whoof!' he bounded into a bamboo thicket and watched the men through a screen of leaves and tall grass.

The men did not seem to take much notice of the dead buffalo, but gathered round their leader and held a consultation. Most of them carried hand drums slung from their shoulders. They also carried sticks, spears and axes.

After a hurried conversation, they entered the denser part of the jungle, beating their drums with the palms of their hands. Some of the men banged empty kerosene tins. These made even more noise than the drums.

The tiger did not like the noise and retreated deeper into the jungle. But he was surprised to find that the men, instead of going away, came after him into the jungle, banging away on their drums and tins and shouting at the top of their voices. They had separated now, and advanced single or in pairs, but nowhere were they more than fifteen yards apart. The tiger could easily have broken through this slowly advancing semicircle of men — one swift blow from his paw would have felled the strongest of them — but his main aim was to get away from the noise. He hated and feared noises made by men.

He was not a man-eater and he would not attack a man unless he was very angry or frightened or very desperate; and he was none of these as yet. He had eaten well, and he would have liked to rest in peace — but there would be no rest for any animal until the men ceased their tremendous clatter and din.

For an hour Ramu's father and others beat the jungle, calling, drumming and trampling the undergrowth. The tiger had no rest. Whenever he was able to put some distance between himself and the men, he would sink down in some shady spot to rest, but, within five or ten minutes, the trampling and drumming would sound nearer, and the tiger, with an angry snarl, would get up and pad north, pad silently north along the narrowing strip of the jungle, towards the junction of the Garur stream and the Ganga. Ten years back, he would have had the jungle on his right in which to hide, but the trees had been felled long ago, to make way for humans and houses, and now he could only move to the left, towards the river.

It was after a long time that the tiger finally appeared in the open. He longed for the darkness and security of the night, for the sun was his enemy. Kundan and the boys had a clear view of him as he stalked slowly along, now in the open with the sun glinting on his glossy side, now in the shade or passing through the shorter reeds. He was still out of range of Kundan's gun, but there was no fear of his getting out of the beat, as the 'stops' were all picked men from the village. He disappeared among some bushes but soon reappeared to retrace his steps, the beaters having done their work well. He was now only one hundred and fifty yards from the rocks where Kundan Singh waited, and he looked very big.

The beat had closed in, and the exit along the bank downstream was completely blocked, so the tiger turned into a belt of reeds, and Kundan Singh expected that the head would soon peer out of the cover a few yards away. The beaters were now making a great noise, shouting and beating their drums, but nothing moved, and Ramu, watching from a distance, wondered, 'Has he slipped through the beaters?' And he half hoped so.

Tins clashed, drums beat, and some of the men poked into the reeds with their spears or long bamboos. Perhaps one of these thrusts found a mark, because at last the tiger was roused, and with an angry, desperate snarl he charged out of the reeds, splashing his way through an inlet of mud and water.

Kundan Singh fired, and his bullet struck the tiger on the thigh.

The mighty animal stumbled; but he was up in a minute, and rushing through a gap in the narrowing line of beaters, he made straight for the only way across the river—the suspension bridge that passed over the Ganga here, providing a route into the high hills beyond.

'We'll get him now,' said Kundan, priming his gun again. 'He's right in the open!'

The suspension bridge swayed and trembled as the wounded tiger lurched across it. Kundan fired, and this time the bullet grazed the tiger's shoulder. The animal bounded forward, lost his footing on the unfamiliar, slippery planks of the swaying bridge, and went over the side, falling headlong into the strong, swirling waters of the river.

He rose to the surface once, but the current took him under and away, and only a thin streak of blood remained on the river's surface.

Kundan and others hurried downstream to see if the dead tiger had been washed up on the river's banks; but though they searched the riverside several miles, they could not find the king of the forest.

He had not provided anyone with a trophy. His skin would not be spread on a couch, nor would his head be hung up on a wall. No claw of his would be hung as a charm around the neck of a child. No villager would use his fat as a cure for rheumatism.

At first the villagers were glad because they felt their

buffaloes were safe. Then the men began to feel that something had gone out of their lives, out of the life of the forest; they began to feel that the forest was no longer a forest. It had been shrinking year by year, but, as long as the tiger had been there and the villagers had heard it roar at night, they had known that they were still secure from the intruders and newcomers who came to fell the trees and eat up the land and let the flood waters into the village. But, now that the tiger had gone, it was as though a protector had gone, leaving the forest open and vulnerable, easily destroyable. And, once the forest was destroyed, they too would be in danger.

There was another thing that had gone with the tiger, another thing that had been lost, a thing that was being lost everywhere — something called 'nobility'.

Ramu remembered something that his grandfather had once said, 'The tiger is the very soul of India, and when the last tiger has gone, so will the soul of the country.'

The boys lay flat on their stomachs on the little mud island and watched the monsoon clouds gathering overhead.

'The king of our forest is dead,' said Shyam. 'There are no more tigers.'

'There must be tigers,' said Ramu. 'How can there be an India without tigers?'

The river had carried the tiger many miles away

from its home, from the forest it had always known, and brought it ashore on a strip of warm yellow sand, where it lay in the sun, quite still, but breathing.

Vultures gathered and waited at a distance, some of them perching on the branches of nearby trees.

But the tiger was more drowned than hurt, and as the river water oozed out of his mouth, and the warm sun made new life throb through his body, he stirred and stretched, and his glazed eyes came into focus. Raising his head, he saw trees and tall grass.

Slowly he heaved himself off the ground and moved at a crouch to where the grass waved in the afternoon breeze. Would he be harried again, and shot at? There was no smell of Man. The tiger moved forward with greater confidence.

There was, however, another smell in the air—a smell that reached back to the time when he was young and fresh and full of vigour—a smell that he had almost forgotten but could never quite forget—the smell of a tigress!

He raised his head high, and new life surged through his tired limbs. He gave a full-throated roar and moved purposefully through the tall grass. And the roar came back to him, calling him, calling him forward—a roar that meant there would be more tigers in this land!

The Good Earth

As with many who love gardens, I have never really had enough space in which to create a proper garden of my own. A few square feet of rocky hillside has been the largest patch at my disposal. All that I managed to grow on it were daisies—and they'd probably have grown there anyway. Still, they made for a charmingly dappled hillside throughout the summer, especially on full moon nights when the flowers were at their most radiant.

For the past few years, here in Mussoorie, I have had to live in two small rooms on the second floor of a tumbledown building which has no garden space at all. All the same, it has a number of ever-widening cracks in which wild sorrels, dandelions, thornapples and nettles all take root and thrive. You could, I suppose, call it a wild wall-garden. Not that I am deprived of flowers. I am better off than most city dwellers because I have only to walk a short way out of the hill station to see (or discover) a variety of flowers in their wild state;

and wild flowers are rewarding, because the best ones are often the most difficult to find.

But I have always had this dream of possessing a garden of my own. Not a very formal garden—certainly not the 'stately home' type, with its pools and fountains and neat hedges as described in such detail by Bacon in his essay 'Of Gardens'. Bacon had a methodical mind, and he wanted a methodical garden. I like a garden to be a little untidy, unplanned, full of surprises—rather like my own muddled mind, which gives even me a few surprises at times.

My grandmother's garden in Dehra, in north India, for example: Grandmother liked flowers, and she didn't waste space on lawns and hedges. There was plenty of space at the back of the house for shrubs and fruit trees, but the front garden was a maze of flower beds of all shapes and sizes, and everything that could grow in Dehra (a fertile valley) was grown in them—masses of sweet peas, petunias, antirrhinum, poppies, phlox and larkspur; scarlet poinsettia leaves draped the garden walls, while purple and red bougainvillea climbed the porch; geraniums of many hues mounted the veranda steps; and, indoors, vases full of cut flowers gave the rooms a heady fragrance. I suppose it was this garden of my childhood that implanted in my mind the permanent vision of a perfect garden so that, whenever I am worried or down in the dumps, I close my eyes and conjure up a picture of this lovely place, where I am wandering through forests of cosmos and banks of rambling roses. It soothes the agitated mind.

I remember an aunt who sometimes came to stay with my grandmother, and who had an obsession about watering the flowers. She would be at it morning and evening, an old and rather lopsided watering can in her frail hands. To everyone's amazement, she would water the garden in all weathers, even during the rains.

'But it's just been raining, aunt,' I would argue. Why are you watering the garden?'

'The rain comes from above,' she would reply. 'This is from me. They expect me at this time, you know.'

Grandmother died when I was still a boy, and the garden soon passed into other hands. I've never done well enough to be able to acquire something like it. And there's no point in getting sentimental about the past.

Yes, I'd love to have a garden of my own — spacious and gracious, and full of everything that's fragrant and flowering. But if I don't succeed, never mind — I've still got the dream.

I wouldn't go so far as to say that a garden is the answer to all problems, but it's amazing how a little digging and friendly dialogue with the good earth can help reactivate us when we grow sluggish.

Before I moved into my present home which has no space for a garden, I had, as I've said, a tiny patch on a hillside, where I grew some daisies. Whenever I was stuck in the middle of a story or an essay, I would go into my tiny hillside garden and get down to the serious business of transplanting or weeding or pruning or just plucking off dead blooms, and in no time at all I was struck with a notion of how to proceed with the stalled story, reluctant essay, or unresolved poem.

Not all gardeners are writers, but you don't have to be a writer to benefit from the goodness of your garden. Baldev, who heads a large business corporation in Delhi, tells me that he wouldn't dream of going to his office unless he'd spent at least half an hour in his garden that morning. If you can start the day by looking at the dew on your antirrhinums, he tells me, you can face the stormiest of board meetings.

Or take Cyril, an old friend.

When I met him, he was living in a small apartment on the first floor of a building that looked over a steep, stony precipice. The house itself appeared to be built on stilts, although these turned out to be concrete pillars. Altogether an ugly edifice. 'Poor Cyril,' I thought. 'There's no way *he* can have a garden.'

I couldn't have been more wrong. Cyril's rooms were surrounded by a long veranda that allowed in so much sunlight and air, resulting in such a profusion of leaf and flower, that at first I thought I was back in one of the greenhouses at Kew Gardens, where I used to wander during a lonely sojourn in London.

Cyril found a chair for me among the tendrils of a climbing ivy, while a coffee table materialized from behind a plant. By the time I had recovered enough from taking in my arboreal surroundings, I discovered that there were at least two other guests—one concealed behind a tree-sized philodendron, the other apparently embedded in a pot of begonias.

Cyril, of course, was an exception. We cannot all have sunny verandas; nor would I show the same tolerance as he does towards the occasional caterpillar on my counterpane. But he was a happy man until his landlord, who lived below, complained that water was cascading down through the ceiling.

'Fix the ceiling,' said Cyril, and went back to watering his plants. It was the end of a beautiful tenant-landlord relationship.

So let us move on to the washerwoman who lives down the road, a little distance from my own abode. She and her family live at the subsistence level. They have one square meal at midday, and they keep the leftovers for the evening. But the steps to their humble quarters are brightened by geraniums potted in large tin cans, all ablaze with several shades of flower.

Hard as I try, I cannot grow geraniums to match

hers. Does she scold her plants the way she scolds her children? Maybe I'm not firm enough with my geraniums. Or has it something to do with the washing? Anyway, her abode certainly looks more attractive than some of the official residences here in Mussoorie.

Some gardeners like to specialize in particular flowers, but specialization has its dangers. My friend, Professor Saili, an ardent admirer of the nature poetry of William Wordsworth, decided he would have his own field of nodding daffodils, and planted daffodil bulbs all over his front yard. The following spring, after much waiting, he was rewarded by the appearance of a solitary daffodil that looked like a railway passenger who had gotten off at the wrong station. This year he is specializing in 'easy-to-grow' French marigolds. They grow easily enough in France, I'm sure; but the professor is discovering that they are stubborn growers on our stony Himalayan soil.

Not everyone in this hill station has a lovely garden. Some palatial homes and spacious hotels are approached through forests of weeds, clumps of nettle, and dead or dying rose bushes. The owners are often plagued by personal problems that prevent them from noticing the state of their gardens. Loveless lives, unloved gardens.

On the other hand, there was Annie Powell, who, at the age of ninety, was up early every morning to water her lovely garden. Watering can in hand, she

would move methodically from one flower bed to the next, devotedly giving each plant a sprinkling. She said she loved to see leaves and flowers sparkling with fresh water, it gave her a new lease of life every day.

And there were my maternal grandparents, whose home in Dehra in the valley was surrounded by a beautiful, well-kept garden. How I wish I had been old enough to prevent that lovely home from passing into other hands. But no one can take away our memories.

Grandfather looked after the orchard, Grandmother looked after the flower garden. Like all people who have lived together for many years, they had the occasional disagreement.

Grandfather would proceed to sulk on a bench beneath the jackfruit tree while, at the other end of the garden, Grandmother would start clipping a hedge with more than her usual vigour. Silently, imperceptibly, they would make their way toward the centre of the garden, where the flower beds gave way to a vegetable patch. This was neutral ground. My cousins and I looked on like UN observers. And there among the cauliflowers, conversation would begin again, and the quarrel would be forgotten. There's nothing like home-grown vegetables for bringing two people together.

Red roses for young lovers. French beans for long-standing relationships!

The Garden of Memories

Sitting in the sun on a winter's afternoon, feeling my age just a little (I'm sixty-seven now), I began reminiscing about my boyhood in the Dehra of long ago, and I found myself missing the old times — friends of my youth, my grandmother, our neighbours, interesting characters in our small town, and, of course, my eccentric relative — the dashing young Uncle Ken!

Yes, Dehra was a small town then — uncluttered, uncrowded, with quiet lanes and pretty gardens and shady orchards.

The only time in my life that I was fortunate enough to live in a house with a real garden — as opposed to a backyard or balcony or windswept veranda — was during those three years when I spent my winter holidays (December to March) in Granny's bungalow on the Old Survey Road.

The best months were February and March, when the garden was heavy with the scent of sweet peas, the flower beds a many-coloured quilt of phlox, antirrhinum, larkspur, petunia and Californian poppy. I loved the bright yellows of the Californian poppies, the soft pinks of our own Indian poppies, the subtle perfume of petunias and snapdragons, and above all, the delicious, overpowering scent of the massed sweet peas which grew taller than me. Flowers made a sensualist of me. They taught me the delight of smell and colour and touch — yes, touch too, for to press a rose to one's lips is very like a gentle, hesitant, exploratory kiss . . .

Granny decided on what flowers should be sown, and where. Dhuki, the gardener, did the digging and weeding, sowing and transplanting. He was a skinny, taciturn old man, who had begun to resemble the weeds he flung away. He did not mind answering my questions, but never did he allow our brief conversations to interfere with his work. Most of the time he was to be found on his haunches, hoeing and weeding with a little spade called a 'khurpi'. He would throw out the smaller marigolds because he said Granny did not care for them. I felt sorry for these colourful little discards, collected them, and transplanted them to a little garden patch of my own at the back of the house, near the garden wall.

Another so-called weed that I liked was a little purple flower that grew in clusters all over Dehra, on any bit of wasteland, in ditches, on canal banks. It flowered from late winter into early summer, and it will be growing in the valley and beyond long after gardens have become obsolete, as indeed they must, considering the rapid spread of urban clutter. It brightens up fields and roads where you least expect a little colour. I have since learnt that it is called *Ageratum*, and that it is actually prized as a garden flower in Europe, where it is described as 'Blue Mink' in the seed catalogues. Here it isn't blue but purple and it grows all the way from Rajpur (just above Dehra) to the outskirts of Meerut; then it disappears.

Other garden outcasts include the lantana bush, an attractive wayside shrub, the thorn apple, various thistles, daisies and dandelions. But both Granny and Dhuki had declared a war on weeds, and many of these commoners had to exist outside the confines of the garden. Like slum children, they survived rather well in ditches and on the roadside, while their more pampered fellow citizens were prone to leaf diseases and parasitic infections of various kinds.

The veranda was a place where Granny herself could potter about, attending to various ferns, potted palms and colourful geraniums. She averred that geraniums kept snakes away, although she never said why. As far as I know, snakes don't have a great sense of smell.

One day I saw a snake curled up at the bottom of the veranda steps. When it saw me, or became aware of my footsteps, it uncoiled itself and slithered away. I told Granny about it, and observed that it did not seem to be bothered by the geraniums.

'Ah,' said Granny. 'But for those geraniums, the snake would have entered the house!' There was no arguing with Granny.

Or with Uncle Ken, when he was at his most pontifical.

One day, while walking near the canal bank, we came upon a green grass snake holding a frog in its mouth. The frog was half in, half out, and with the help of my hockey stick, I made the snake disgorge the unfortunate creature. It hopped away, none the worse for its adventure.

I felt quite pleased with myself. 'Is this what it feels like to be God?' I mused aloud.

'No,' said Uncle Ken. 'God would have let the snake finish its lunch.'

Uncle Ken was one of those people who went through life without having to do much, although a great deal seemed to happen around him. He acted as a sort of catalyst for events that involved the family, friends, neighbours, the town itself. He believed in the fruits of hard work: other people's hard work.

Ken was good-looking as a boy, and his sisters doted on him. He took full advantage of their devotion, and, as the girls grew up and married, Ken took it for granted that they and their husbands would continue to look after his welfare. You could say he was the originator of the welfare state; his own.

I'll say this for Uncle Ken, he had a large fund of curiosity in his nature, and he loved to explore the town we lived in, and any other town or city where he might happen to find himself. With one sister settled in Lucknow, another in Ranchi, a third in Bhopal, a fourth in Pondicherry and a fifth in Barrackpore, Uncle Ken managed to see a cross section of India by dividing his time between all his sisters and their long-suffering husbands.

Uncle Ken liked to walk. Occasionally he borrowed my bicycle, but he had a tendency to veer off the main road and into ditches and other obstacles after a collision with a bullock cart, in which he tore his trousers and damaged the handlebar of my bicycle, Uncle Ken concluded that walking was the best way of getting around Dehra.

Uncle Ken dressed quite smartly for a man of no particular occupation. He had a blue-striped blazer and a red-striped blazer; he usually wore white or off-white trousers, immaculately pressed (by Granny). He was the delight of shoeshine boys, for he was always having his shoes polished. Summers he wore a straw hat, telling everyone he had worn it for the Varsity Boat Race, while rowing for Oxford (he hadn't been to England, let alone Oxford); winters, he wore one of Grandfather's old felt hats. He seldom went bareheaded. At thirty he was almost completely bald, prompting Aunt Mabel to remark: 'Well, Ken, you must be grateful for small mercies. At least you'll never have bats getting entangled in your hair.'

Thanks to all his walking Uncle Ken had a good digestion, which kept pace with a hearty appetite. Our walks would be punctuated by short stops at chaat shops, sweet shops, fruit stalls, confectioners, small bakeries and other eateries.

'Have you brought any pocket money along?' he would ask, for he was usually broke.

'Granny gave me five rupees.'

'We'll try some rasgullas, then.'

And the rasgullas would be followed by gulab jamuns until my five rupees was finished. Uncle Ken received a small allowance from Granny, but he ferreted it away to spend on clothes, preferring to spend my pocket money on perishables such as ice creams, kulfis and Indian sweets.

On one occasion, when neither of us had any money, Uncle Ken decided to venture into a sugarcane field on the outskirts of the town. He had broken off a stick of cane, and was busy chewing on it, when the owner of the field spotted us and let out a volley of imprecations. We fled from the field with the irate farmer giving chase. I could run faster than Uncle Ken, and did so. The farmer would have caught up with Uncle Ken if the latter's hat hadn't blown off, causing a diversion. The farmer picked up the hat, examined it, seemed to fancy it, and put it on. Several small boys clapped and cheered. The farmer marched off, wearing the hat, and Uncle Ken wisely decided against making any attempt to retrieve it.

'I'll get another one,' he said philosophically.

He wore a pith helmet, or sola topee, for the next few days, as he thought it would protect him from sticks and stones. For a while he harboured a paranoia that all the sugarcane farmers in the valley were looking for him, to avenge his foray into their fields. But after some time he discarded the topee because, according to him, it interfered with his good looks.

*

Granny grew the best sweet peas in Dehra. But she never entered them at the Annual Flower Show, held every year in the second week of March. She did not grow flowers to win prizes, she said; she grew them to please the spirit of Grandfather, who still hovered about the house and grounds he'd built thirty years earlier.

Miss Kellner, Granny's crippled but valued tenant, said the flowers were grown to attract beautiful butterflies, and she was right. In early summer, swarms of butterflies flitted about the garden.

Uncle Ken had no compunction about winning prizes, even though he did nothing to deserve them. Without telling anyone, he submitted a large display of Granny's sweet peas for the flower show, and when the prizes were announced, lo and behold! Kenneth Clerke had been awarded first prize for his magnificent display of sweet peas.

Granny refused to speak to him for several days.

Uncle Ken had been hoping for a cash prize, but they gave him a flower vase. He told me it was a Ming vase. But it looked more like Meerut to me. He offered it to Granny, hoping to propitiate her; but, still displeased with him, she gave it to Mr Khastgir, the artist next door, who kept his paintbrushes in it.

Although I was sometimes a stubborn and unruly boy (my hero was Richmal Crompton's 'William'), I got on well with old ladies, especially those who, like Miss Kellner, were fond of offering me chocolates, marzipans, soft nankattai biscuits (made at Yusuf's bakery in the Dilaram Bazaar), and pieces of crystallized ginger. Miss Kellner couldn't walk — had never walked — and so she could only admire the garden from a distance, but it was from her that I learnt the names of many flowers, trees, birds and even butterflies.

Uncle Ken wasn't any good at names, but he wanted to catch a rare butterfly. He said he could make a fortune if he caught a leaf butterfly called the Purple Emperor. He equipped himself with a butterfly net, a bottle of ether and a cabinet for mounting his trophies; he then prowled all over the grounds, making frequent forays at anything that flew. He caught several common species — Red Admirals, a Tortoiseshell, a Painted Lady, even the occasional dragonfly — but the high-flying Purple Emperor and other exotics eluded him, as did the fortune he was always aspiring to make.

Eventually he caught an angry wasp, which stung him through the netting. Chased by its fellow wasps, he took refuge in the lily pond and emerged sometime later draped in lilies and water weeds.

After this, Uncle Ken retired from the butterfly business, insisting that tiger hunting was safer.

In Search of the Perfect Window

Those who advertise rooms or flats to let often describe them as 'room with bath' or 'room with tea and coffee-making facilities'. A more attractive proposition would be 'room with window', for without a view a room is hardly a living place — merely a place of transit.

As an itinerant young writer, I lived in many single-room apartments, or 'bedsitters' as they were called, and I have to admit that the quality of my life was certainly enhanced if any window looked out on something a little more inspiring than a factory wall or someone's backyard.

We cherish a romantic image of a starving, young poet living in a garret and writing odes to skylarks, but, believe me, garrets don't help. For six months in London I lived in a small attic room that had no view at all, except for the roofs of other houses — an endless vista of gray tiles and blackened chimneys, without so much as a proverbial cat to relieve the monotony. I did not write a single ode, for no self-respecting nightingale or lark ever found its way up there.

My next room, somewhere near Clapham Junction, had a 'view of the railway', but you couldn't actually see the railway lines because of the rows of washing that were hung out to dry behind the building.

It was a working-class area, and there were no laundries around the corner. But if you couldn't see the railway, you could certainly hear it. Every time a train thundered past, the building shuddered, and ornaments, crockery and dishes rattled and rocked as though an earthquake were in progress. It was impossible to hang a picture on the wall; the nail (and with it the picture) fell out after a couple of days. But it reminded me a bit of my Uncle Fred's railway quarters just near Delhi's main railway station, and I managed to write a couple of train stories while living in this particular room.

Train windows, naturally, have no equal when it comes to views, especially in India, where there's an ever-changing panorama of mountain, forest, desert, village, town, and city—along with the colourful crowds at every railway station.

But good, personal windows—windows to live with—these were to prove elusive for several years. Even after returning to India, I had some difficulty finding the ideal window.

Moving briefly to a small town in northern India, I was directed to the Park View lodging house. There did happen to be a park in the vicinity, but no view of it could be had from my room or, indeed, from any room in the house. But I found, to my surprise, that the bathroom window actually looked out on the park. It provided a fine view! However, there is a limit to the length of time one can spend in the bath, gazing out at palm fronds waving in the distance. So I moved on again.

After a couple of claustrophobic years in New Delhi, I escaped to the hills, fully expecting that I would immediately find rooms or a cottage with windows facing the eternal snows. But it was not to be!

To see the snows I had to walk four miles from my lodgings to the highest point in the hill station. My window looked out on a high stone rampart, built to prevent the steep hillside from collapsing. True, a number of wild things grew in the wall — bunches of red sorrel, dandelions, tough weeds of various kinds, and, at the base, a large clump of nettles. Now I am sure there are people who can grow ecstatic over nettles, but I am not one of them. I find that nettles sting me at the first opportunity. So I gave my nettles a wide berth.

And then, at last, persistence was rewarded. I found my present abode, a windswept, rather shaky, old house on the edge of a spur. My bedroom window opened on to blue skies, mountains striding away into the far distance, winding rivers in the valley below, and, just to bring me down to earth, the local television tower. Like the Red Shadow in *The Desert Song*, I could stand at my window and sing 'Blue heaven, and You and I', even if the only listener was a startled policeman.

The window was so positioned that I could lie on my bed and look at the sky, or sit at my desk and look at the hills, or stand at the window and look at the road below.

Which is the best of these views?

Some would say the hills, but the hills never change. Some would say the road, because the road is full of change and movement—tinkers, tailors, tourists, salesmen, cars, trucks and motorcycles, mules, ponies, and even, on one occasion, an elephant. The elephant had no business being up here, but I suppose if Hannibal could take them over the Alps, an attempt could also be made on the Himalayan passes. (It returned to the plains the next day.)

The road is never dull but, given a choice, I'd opt for the sky. The sky is never the same. Even when it's cloudless, the sky colours are different. The morning sky, the daytime sky, the evening sky, the moonlit sky, the starry sky, these are all different skies. And there are almost always birds in the sky—eagles flying high, mountain swifts doing acrobatics, cheeky myna birds meeting under the eaves of the roof, sparrows flitting in and out of the room at will. Sometimes a butterfly floats

in on the breeze. And on summer nights, great moths enter at the open window, dazzled by my reading light. I have to catch them and put them out again, lest they injure themselves.

When the monsoon rains arrive, the window has to be closed, otherwise cloud and mist fill the room, and that isn't good for my books. But the sky is even more fascinating at this time of the year.

From my desk I can, at this very moment, see the clouds advancing across the valley, rolling over the hills, ascending the next range. Raindrops patter against the window panes, closed until the rain stops.

And when the shower passes and the clouds open up, the heavens are a deeper, darker blue. Truly magic, casements these . . . For every time I see the sky I am aware of belonging to the universe rather than to just one corner of the earth.

The Evil Eye

In northern India, it is called nazar—a glance of malice or envy—and it is held accountable for a wide variety of ailments and disasters.

Recently the milkman's cow went dry. His excuse: his neighbour, who also kept a cow, had been jealous and cast an evil eye which was enough to end the competition! And then there is the man who tells me that his ailing child is growing thinner day by day because a childless person has cast the evil eye upon him.

I do not scoff at these beliefs. Ill will and evil intent cannot be shrugged off lightly. Hate has an aura which quickly permeates the surroundings.

When members of my own household underwent a series of disasters, I was puzzled at the way in which they followed rapidly one after another. Only later did I learn that someone had actually been wishing ill upon us. We were the victims of nazar— a baleful glance from the evil eye of someone who passed us on the road every day.

In India, as in most countries, the popular explanation

for the fairly widespread belief in the evil eye is that it is based on envy or covetousness. It is logical enough to suppose that a man with only one eye is likely to envy a man who has two; the weak and puny envy the good health and good looks of others; the childless woman covets the children of more fortunate women.

One is not surprised to learn that in the ancient Hindu 'Laws of Manu', a one-eyed man is classed with those who are to be treated with caution, possibly because his glance is more concentrated than that of a man with sight in both eyes.

The old prejudice against the one-eyed resulted in Maha Singh, one of the Jaisalmer princes, being disqualified from succeeding to the throne. And when Jaswant Rao Holkar, another powerful Indian prince lost one of his eyes, he remarked: 'I was thought bad enough before—now I shall be looked upon as a guru among rogues!'

The prejudice extends even today to persons with a squint or cast in the eye. Years ago, I knew of an office clerk who suffered from a squint—and the accounts of his fellow clerks always went wrong. They made so many mistakes in their work that they compelled him to cover the offending eye with a cloth during office hours.

The belief that certain persons possess the power of discharging a glance so malefic that it strikes like a dart at the person against whom it is directed, is prevalent in many parts of the world. Many believe that those born on a Saturday, under the unhappy influence of Saturn, have the power to cast an evil eye.

This worldwide belief comes down from remote antiquity. The English word 'fascination' is from the Latin *fascinatio*, which is transliterated from the classical Greek word meaning 'the mysterious bewitching power of the evil eye'. The ancient Egyptians knew and feared the evil eye, carried mascots and muttered protective charms as do the Bedouins and Moors even today.

Montague Summers, the great English student of the occult (whose book *The Vampire* is a classic work), once described how, on a visit to Italy, he was walking with an Italian friend down the Via Roma, the main street of Naples, when he noticed people suddenly begin to scatter in every direction. His friend took him firmly by the arm and guided him into the nearest shop.

'What on earth is up?' asked Summers.

'*Zitto, zitto,*' whispered his friend, putting a finger to his lips.

A tall, well-dressed man, quite a respectable-looking figure, was walking along the empty pavement past the shop window. Summers heard the word *Jettatore* and saw the protective gesture, the pointing horns, made with the hands of those who got out of the way of the mysterious man in the street.

In Italy a *Jettatore* is a man (or woman) with the evil eye, one whose mere presence, whose very shadow, is ill-omened and unlucky enough, but whose baleful glance brings sorrow, sickness and death. Such a person may often be quite unaware of the effect he has on others.

In parts of rural England, sickly or deformed children are still spoken of as wisht—that is, 'ill-wished' or 'overlooked', injured by someone who has cast his or her malevolent gaze upon the sufferer.

An old woman in Somerset once quoted to me from the Bible (proverbs, XXIII. 6): 'Eat not the bread of him that hath an evil eye . . . The morsel which thou hast eaten shalt thou vomit up.'

And she added: 'There's more than one of my neighbours I wouldn't sit down to eat a meal with!'

In Europe you ward off the evil eye by 'making horns'—tucking in the thumb and extending the first and little fingers. In India, one method of avoiding the evil eye is to make on the person likely to be effected a mark which acts as a disguise or distraction. Many people apply kajal to their children's eyes, a device which also serves the practical purpose of protecting them from sunglare! Or a spot is marked in the middle of the forehead, like a third eye—rather like the false 'eyes' on the wings of butterflies, which are meant to distract predatory birds.

Even domestic animals, like cattle and horses are

protected by having brightly-coloured beads round their necks or by marking part of the harness with a single of double triangle. A horse is similarly safeguarded by leaving in the courtyard an earthen pot smeared with streaks of black and white.

Strings and knots, tattooing, precious stones, iron rings made of silver and gold, incense, various grasses or herbs, saliva, blood . . . all have magical or protective properties.

Garlic has been used as a protective in both the East and West. Count Dracula's hypnotic eye was powerless in the presence of a liberal amount of garlic! And in parts of central India, before a young man's marriage, an exorcist crushes pieces of garlic near his eyes or squeezes the juice into his nostrils to expel any evil spirit that might be lurking within.

In some parts of northern India, children who have been the victims of the evil eye are said to be cured by waving garlic and pepper pods round their heads on a Tuesday; these are then thrown into the fire.

Lest all this be dismissed as mere superstition, it would be well to recall that the power of positive and negative thinking has time and again been proved by scientists. In one study, identical barley seeds were planted in pots containing the same soil. All were similarly watered and exposed to sunlight for the same amount of time. But one set received positive thoughts directed at it; the other set received negative thoughts; and the third was left alone.

After fourteen days it was found that the 'blessed' seeds grew slightly better than the ones which received no thoughts at all. The most remarkable thing, however, was that the seeds which were 'cursed' grew only half the size of the others and 62 per cent did not even germinate.

Before scoffing at the power of the evil eye, ponder upon the feats of hypnotism. A powerful mind, using the intensifying apparatus of the eye, is able to influence a mind open to suggestion.

Surely the best way to deal with a baleful glance or negative thought is to reverse the roles, and draw upon one's own latent powers of suggestion, challenge the evil eye, stare it down, set it at naught. Meet it with a steadfast eye!

And should you find a staring match too much of a strain, here's a trick my magic-making grandmother taught me: Don't stare the other person in the eye. Fix your gaze on a point between the eyes, on the bridge of the nose, and keep it there. Your opponent will look away.

April in Landour

Swifts are busy nesting in the roof and performing acrobatics outside my window. They do everything on the wing, it seems, including feeding and making love.

The wind in the pines and deodars hums and moans, but in the chestnut it rustles and chatters and makes cheerful conversation. The horse chestnut in full leaf is a magnificent sight.

*

Amongst the current fraternity of writers, I must be that very rare person, an author who actually writes by hand.

Soon after the invention of the typewriter, most editors and publishers understandably refused to look at any manuscript that was handwritten. A few years earlier, when Dickens and Balzac had submitted their hefty manuscripts in longhand, no one had objected. Had their handwriting been awful, their manuscripts would still have been read. Fortunately for all concerned, these and other famous writers took pains over their handwriting.

Both Dickens and Thackeray had clear, flourishing handwriting. Somerset Maugham had an upright, legible hand, Tagore, a fine flourish. Churchill's neat handwriting never wavered, even when he was under stress. I like the bold, clear, straightforward hand of Abraham Lincoln; it mirrors the man.

Not everyone had a beautiful hand. King Henry VIII had an untidy scrawl, but then, he was not a man of much refinement. Guy Fawkes, who tried to blow up the British Parliament, had a very shaky hand. With such a quiver, no wonder he failed in his attempt. Hitler's signature is ugly, as you might expect. And Napoleon's doesn't seem to know when to stop; how like the man!

When I think of the great eighteenth and nineteenth century writers, scratching away with their quill pens, filling hundreds of pages every month, I am amazed that their handwriting did not deteriorate into the sort of hieroglyphics that makes up the average doctor's prescription today. They knew how to write legibly, if only for the sake of the typesetters.

And it wasn't only authors who wrote with an elegant hand. Most of our parents and grandparents had distinctive styles of their own. I still have my father's last letter, written to me when I was at boarding school over sixty years ago. He used large, beautifully formed letters, and his thoughts seemed to have the same flow and clarity as his handwriting.

In his letter he advises nine-year-old Ruskin about his handwriting:

I wanted to write before about your writing, Ruskin . . . Sometimes I get letters from you in very small writing, as if you wanted to squeeze everything into one sheet of paper. It is not good for you or for your eyes, to get into the habit of writing so small . . . Try and form a larger style of handwriting. Use more paper if necessary!

I did my best to follow his advice, and I'm glad to report that after a lifetime of penmanship, my handwriting is still readable.

Word processors and computers are the in thing now, and I do not object to these electronic aids any more than I objected to the mechanical aid of my old Olympia typewriter, which is still going strong after forty years; the latter is at least impervious to power failures. Although I still do most of my writing in longhand, I follow the conventions by typing a second draft. But I would not enjoy my writing if I had to do it straight on to a machine. It isn't just the pleasure of writing by hand, although that's part of it. Sometimes I like taking my notebooks or writing pads to odd places. This particular entry is being composed on the steep hillside above the cottage in which I live. Part of the reason for sitting here is that there is a new postman on the route, and I don't want him to miss me. For a freelance writer, the postman is almost as important as his publisher. He brings me editorial acceptances or rejections, the occasional cheques and sometimes a nice letter from a reader. I could, of course, sit here doing nothing, but as I have pencil and paper with me, and feel like using them, I shall write until the postman comes and maybe after he has gone, too.

Typewriters and computers were not designed with steep mountain slopes in mind. On one occasion last autumn I did carry my typewriter into the garden, and I am still trying to extricate a couple of acorns from under the keys, while the roller seems permanently stained from some fine yellow pollen dust from the deodar trees. But armed with pencils and paper, I can lie on the grass and write for hours. Provided there are a couple of cheese-and-tomato sandwiches within easy reach.

❊

The smallest insect in the world is a sort of fairy fly and its body is only a fifth of a millimetre long. One can only just see it with the naked eye. Almost like a speck of dust, yet it has perfect little wings and little combs on its legs for preening itself.

That is perfection.

❊

The nice thing about reaching a reasonable age (sixty plus) is that, along the way, one has collected a few pleasant memories. Life isn't always pleasant, but I find it's possible to shut out the darker recollections and dwell instead on life's happier moments. Psychiatrists may not agree with this method. They like their patients to unburden themselves and reveal their childhood traumas. But it's when we cannot escape our childhood traumas that we end up on the psychiatrist's couch.

Anyway, here's an example of being able to relive an old memory without regret:

Last week, after a gap of forty years, I climbed to the little temple of Sirkhanda Devi, a steep climb from the motor road at 8000 feet to the summit at 10,000 feet. Forty years ago I'd walked the thirty-odd miles from Mussoorie to Kaddukhal; there was no motor road then, just a bridle path. Now buses and taxis bring tourists and pilgrims to Kaddukhal, but they still have to climb to the temple. Climbing is good for both body and soul.

The old bridle path has disappeared, but remnants of it can be seen in places. While climbing up from the new road, I came across a little cluster of huts and recognized the one in which I'd spent a night, before tramping on to Chamba. I was just a boy then . . . Of course the old man who'd offered me hospitality was long gone, and his son had moved elsewhere, but there were children in the courtyard, and goats and chickens, and a tall deodar which had been no taller than me on that first visit. So here were memories flooding back in the nicest of ways.

To be perfectly honest, that night in the hut had not been so lovely, for the sheepskin rug on which I'd slept had been infested with vicious fleas and *khatmals*, and I'd stayed awake scratching into the early hours. But see how easy it is to put aside the less pleasant memory. Forget the bugs and think of the moon coming up over the mountains, and life becomes a little more tolerable.

Well, on this second occasion I entered the tiny temple on the hilltop and thanked the Devi for her blessings and told her that life had been good to me since I'd last been there.

I feel drawn to little temples on lonely hilltops. With the mist swirling round them, and the wind humming in the stunted pines, they absorb some of the magic and mystery of their surroundings and transmit it to the questing pilgrim.

Another memory revived when I accompanied the family to the sulphur springs outside Dehra, and discovered that this former wilderness had been turned into a little dhaba township, with the garbage left by tourists and picnickers littering the banks of the stream and being caught up on the rocks.

Here, fifty years ago, I bicycled with my friends,

bathed, and rested in the shade of the ravine. Few people found their way there. Today, it has been 'developed' into a tourist spot, although there is no longer any sign of the hot spring that made it known in the first place. In shock, the spring appears to have gone underground.

All this is progress, of course, and I must confess to being sadly behind the times.

The other day a young Internet surfer asked me why I preferred using a pencil instead of a computer. The principal reason, I told him, was that I liked chewing on the end of my pencil. A nasty habit, but it helps me concentrate. And I find it extremely difficult to chew on a computer.

*

'We should not spoil what we have by desiring what we have not, but remember that what we have too was the gift of fortune'—Epicurus

*

Glorious day. Walked up and around the hill, and got some of the cobwebs out of my head.

Some epigrams (my own, for future use):

A well-balanced person: someone with a chip on both shoulders.

Experience: The knowledge that enables you to recognize a mistake when you make it the second time.

Sympathy: What one woman offers another in exchange for details.

Worry: The interest paid on trouble before it becomes due.

I read these out to my critic and confidant, four-year-old Gautam (Siddharth's younger brother), and he shook his head sadly and responded with *'Kabi Khushi, Kabi Gam!'* Like Mr Dick in *David Copperfield*, he usually comes up with an appropriate response.

❉

Death moves about at random, without discriminating between the innocent and the evil, the poor and the rich. The only difference is that the poor usually handle it better.

I heard today that the peanut vendor had died. The old man would always be in the dark, windy corner in Landour Bazaar, hunched up over the charcoal fire on which he roasted his peanuts. He'd been there for as long as I could remember, and he could be seen at almost any hour of the day or night. Summer or winter, he stayed close to his fire.

He was probably quite tall, but I never saw him standing up. One judged his height from his long, loose limbs. He was very thin, and the high cheekbones added to the tautness of his tightly stretched skin.

His peanuts were always fresh, crisp and hot. They were popular with the small boys who had a few coins to spend on their way to and from school, and with the patrons of the cinemas, many of whom made straight for the windy corner during intervals or when the show was over. On cold winter evenings, or misty monsoon days, there was always a demand for the old man's peanuts.

No one knew his name. No one had ever thought of asking him for it. One just took him for granted. He was as fixed a landmark as the clock tower or the old cherry tree that grows crookedly from the hillside. The tree was always being lopped; the clock often stopped. The peanut vendor seemed less perishable than the tree, more dependable than the clock. He had no family, but in a way all the world was his family, because he was in continuous contact with people. And yet he was a remote sort of being, always polite, even to children, but never familiar. There is a distinction to be made between aloneness and loneliness. The peanut vendor was seldom alone, but he must have been lonely.

Summer nights he rolled himself up in a thin blanket and slept on the ground, beside the dying embers of his fire. During the winter, he waited until the last show was over, before retiring to the coolies' shed where there was some protection from the biting wind.

Did he enjoy being alive? I wonder now. He was not a joyful person; but then, neither was he miserable. I should think he was a genuine stoic, one of those who do not attach overmuch importance to themselves, who are emotionally uninvolved, content with their limitations, their dark corners. I wanted to get to know the old man better, to sound him out on the immense questions involved in roasting peanuts all his life, but it's too late now. Today his dark corner was deserted; the old man had vanished; the coolies had carried him down to the cremation ground.

'He died in his sleep,' said the tea shop owner. 'He was very old.'

Very old. Sufficient reason to die.

But that corner is very empty, very dark, and I know that whenever I pass it I will be haunted by visions of the old peanut vendor, troubled by the questions I failed to ask.

*

Spoke to the Christian writers' group at Deodars, on the subject of writing for a living.

Question: Which, in your opinion, is the best book on Christianity?

'I'd always thought it was the New Testament,' was all I could say.

Reading Was My Religion

In January 1948, Mahatma Gandhi was assassinated.

I had gone to the pictures at one of Dehra's new cinemas—The Hollywood on Chakrata Road—and the film was called *Blossoms in the Dust*; but it had been showing for about ten minutes when the projector stopped running. The lights came on and the manager appeared at one of the doors to announce that news had just been received that Gandhiji, father of the nation, had been shot dead. The cinema would be closed for a week. We were given our money back.

I walked disconsolately home across the maidan, shocked by the event and also a little dismayed that I wouldn't be able to see another picture for at least a week. (And I never did see *Blossoms* in its entirety.) As I was only thirteen at the time, I don't think I could be accused of a lack of sensitivity. As I walked across the vast maidan—it was now late evening—I passed little groups of people talking about what had happened and how it might affect the course of politics in the country.

The assassin belonged to the majority community, and there was undisguised relief that the tragedy would not result in more communal riots. Gandhiji had already become history. Now he was to achieve sainthood.

Oddly enough my sister Ellen took it to heart more than anyone else in the family. She would spend hours drawing pictures of Gandhi. As her eyesight was poor, some of these portraits took weird shapes, but sometimes you could recognize the great man's glasses, chappals and walking stick.

We had moved again. My stepfather was supporting my mother once more, so she had given up the job at Green's, which was about to close down. They had rented a small, rather damp bungalow on the Eastern Canal Road, and I had a dark little room which leaked at several places when it rained. On wet winter nights it had a rather spooky atmosphere: the drip of water, the scurrying of rats in the space between the ceiling and corrugated tin roof, and the nightly visitation of a small bat which got in through a gap in the wall and swooped around the room, snapping up moths. I would stay up into the early hours reading *Oliver Twist* (pinched from Granny's house), *Wuthering Heights* (all in one sitting, during a particularly stormy night) and *Shakespeare's Complete Works*—a lofty volume of the band's plays and poems, which, till then, was the only book in the house that I hadn't read. The print was very small but I set myself the task of reading right through, and achieved this feat during the winter holidays. Of the plays I enjoyed *The Tempest* more than any other. Of the longer poems *The Rape of Lucrece* was the most intriguing but I found it difficult to reconcile its authorship with that of the plays. They were so robust, the poems formalized, watery by comparison.

I realize now that my mother was a brave woman. She stuck it out with Mr Hari who, as a businessman, was a complete disaster. He'd lost on his photographic saloon, which had now been sold by his first wife; he had lost on his motor workshop and he had lost his car sales agencies. He was up against large income tax arrears and he was irregular with all his payments. But he was popular with his workmen and mechanics, as he was quite happy to sit and drink with them, or take them along on his shikar expeditions. In this way everyone had a good time, even though his customers grew more irate by the day. Repair jobs were seldom finished on time. If a customer left a decent looking car with him for servicing, my stepfather would use it for two or three months, on the pretext of 'testing' it, before handing it back to the owner.

But his heart was in the right place. During the communal riots of '47, he, a Hindu, was instrumental in saving a number of Muslim lives, driving friends or employees to safer locations, or even upto the Pakistan border.

He never had a harsh word for me. Sometimes I wish he had!

*

The RAF had undertaken to pay for my schooling, so I was able to continue at BCS.

Back in Simla I found a sympathetic soul in Mr Jones, an ex-Army Welshman who taught us divinity. He did not have the qualifications to teach us anything else, but I think I learnt more from him than from most of our more qualified staff. He had even got me to read the Bible (King James version) for the classical simplicity of its style.

Mr Jones got on well with small boys, one reason being that he never punished them. Alone among the philistines he was the only teacher to stand out against corporal punishment. He waged a lone campaign against the custom of caning boys for their misdemeanours, and in this respect was far ahead of his time. The other masters thought him a little eccentric, and he lost his seniority because of his refusal to administer physical punishment.

But there was nothing eccentric about Mr Jones, unless it was the pet pigeon that followed him everywhere and sometimes perched on his bald head. He managed to keep the pigeon (and his cigar) out of the classroom, but his crowded, untidy bachelor quarters reeked of cigar smoke.

He had a passion for the works of Dickens, and when he discovered that I had read *Nickleby* and *Sketches by Boz*, he allowed me to look at his set of the *Complete Works*, with the illustrations by Phiz. I launched into *David Copperfield*, which I thoroughly enjoyed, identifying myself with young David, his triumphs and tribulations. After reading *Copperfield* I decided it was a fine thing to be a writer. The seed had already been sown, and although in my imagination I still saw myself as an Arsenal goalkeeper or a Gene Kelly-type tap dancer, I think I knew in my heart that I was best suited to the written word. I was topping the class in essay writing, although I had an aversion to studying the texts that were prescribed for English literature classes.

Mr Jones, with his socialist, Dickensian viewpoint, had an aversion for P.G. Wodehouse, whose comic novels I greatly enjoyed. He told me that these novels glamorized the most decadent aspects of upper-class English life (which was probably true), and that only recently, during the War (when he was interned in France), Wodehouse had been making propaganda broadcasts on behalf of Germany. This was true, too; although years later when I read the texts of those broadcasts (in *Performing Flea*), they seemed harmless enough.

But Mr Jones did have a point—Wodehouse was

hopelessly out of date, for when I went to England after leaving school, I couldn't find anyone remotely resembling a Wodehouse character. Except perhaps Ukridge, who was always borrowing money from his friends in order to set up in some business or the other; he was universal.

The school library—the Anderson Library—was fairly well stocked, and it was to be something of a haven for me over the next three years. There were always writers, past or present, to 'discover'—and I still have a tendency to ferret out writers who have been ignored, neglected or forgotten.

After *Copperfield* the novel that most influenced me was Hugh Walpole's *Fortitude*, an epic account of another young writer in the making. Its opening line still acts as a clarion call when I feel depressed or as though I am getting nowhere: 'Tisn't life that matters, but the courage you bring to it.'

Walpole's more ambitious works have been forgotten, but his stories and novels of the macabre are still worth reading—*Mr Perrin and Mr Trail, Portrait of a Man with Red Hair, The White Tower* . . . And, of course, *Fortitude*. I returned to it last year and found it was still stirring stuff.

But life wasn't all books. At the age of fifteen I was at my best as a football goalkeeper, hockey player, athlete. I was also acting in school plays and taking part in debates. I wasn't much of a boxer—a sport I disliked—but I had learnt to use my head to good effect, and managed to get myself disqualified by butting the other fellow in the head or midriff. As all games were compulsory, I had to overcome my fear of water and learn to swim a little. Mr Jones taught me to do the breast stroke, saying it was more suited to my temperament than the splash and dash stuff.

The only thing I couldn't do was sing, and although I loved listening to great singers, from Caruso to Gigli, I couldn't sing a note. Our music teacher, Mrs Knight, put me in the school choir because, she said, I *looked* like a choir boy, all pink and shining in a cassock and surplice, but she forbade me from actually singing. I was to open my mouth with the others, but on no account was I to allow any sound to issue from it.

This took me back to the convent in Mussoorie where I had been given piano lessons, probably at my father's request. The nun who was teaching me would get so exasperated with my stubborn inability to strike the right chord or play the right notes that she would crack me over the knuckles with a ruler—thus effectively putting an end to any interest I might have had in learning to play a musical instrument. Mr Priestley's violin, in the prep school, and now Mrs Knight's organ playing, were none too inspiring.

Insensitive though I may have been to high notes and low notes, diminuendos and crescendos, I was nevertheless sensitive to sound—birdsong, the hum of the breeze playing in tall trees, the rustle of autumn leaves, crickets chirping, water splashing and murmuring in brooks, the sea sighing on the sand—all natural sounds, indicating a certain harmony in the natural world.

Man-made sounds—the roar of planes, the blare of horns, the thunder of trucks and engines, the baying of a crowd—are usually ugly. But some gifted humans have tried to rise above it by creating great music; and we must not scorn the also-rans, those who come down hard on their organ pedals, or emulate cicadas with their violin playing.

Although I was quite popular at Bishop Cotton's, after Omar's departure I did not have many close friends. There was, of course, young A—, my junior by two years, who followed me everywhere until I gave in and took him to the pictures in town, or fed him at the tuck shop.

There were just one or two boys who actually read books for pleasure. We tend to think of that era as one when there were no distractions such as television, computer games and the like. But reading has always been a minority pastime. People say children don't read any more. This may be true of the vast majority, but I know many boys and girls who enjoy reading, far more than I encountered when I was a schoolboy. In those days there were comics and the radio and the cinema. I went to the cinema whenever I could, but that did not keep me from reading almost everything that came my way. And so it is today. Book readers are special people, and they will always turn to books as the ultimate pleasure. Those who do not read are the unfortunate ones. There's nothing wrong with them; but they are missing out on one of life's compensations and rewards. A great book is a friend that never lets you down. You can return to it again and again, and the joy first derived from it will still be there.

I think it is fair to say that when I was a boy, reading was my true religion. It helped me to discover my soul.

Miss Romola and Others

Though their numbers have diminished over the years, there are still a few compulsive daily walkers around: the odd ones, the strange ones, who will walk all day, here, there and everywhere, not in order to get somewhere, but to escape from their homes, their lonely rooms, their mirrors, themselves . . .

Those of us who must work for a living and would love to be able to walk a little more don't often get the chance. There are offices to attend, deadlines to be met, trains or planes to be caught, deals to be struck, people to deal with. It's the rat race for most people, whether they like it or not. So who are these lucky ones, a small minority it has to be said, who find time to walk all over this hill station from morn to night?

Some are fitness freaks, I suppose; but several are just unhappy souls who find some release, some meaning, in covering miles and miles of highway without so much as a nod in the direction of others on the road. They are not looking at anything as they walk, not even at a violet in a mossy stone.

Here comes Miss Romola. She's been at it for years. A retired schoolmistress who never married. No friends. Lonely as hell. Not even a visit from a former pupil. She could not have been very popular.

She has money in the bank. She owns her own flat. But she doesn't spend much time in it. I see her from my window, tramping up the road to Lal Tibba. She strides around the mountain like the character in the old song 'She'll be coming round the mountain', only she doesn't wear pink pyjamas; she dresses in slacks and a shirt. She doesn't stop to talk to anyone. It's quick march to the top of the mountain, and then down again, home again, jiggety-jig. When she has to go down to Dehradun (too long a walk even for her), she stops a car and cadges a lift. No taxis for her, not even the bus.

Miss Romola's chief pleasure in life comes from conserving her money. There are people like that. They view the rest of the world with suspicion. An overture of friendship will be construed as taking an undue interest in her assets. We are all part of an international conspiracy to relieve her of her material possessions! She has no servants, no friends; even her relatives are kept at a safe distance.

A similar sort of character but even more eccentric is Mr Sen, who used to live in the USA and walks from the

Happy Valley to Landour (five miles) and back every day, in all seasons, year in and year out. Once or twice every week he will stop at the Community Hospital to have his blood pressure checked or undergo a blood or urine test. With all that walking he should have no health problems, but he is a hypochondriac and is convinced that he is dying of something or the other.

He came to see me once. Unlike Miss Romola, he seemed to want a friend, but his neurotic nature turned people away. He was convinced that he was surrounded by individual and collective hostility. People were always staring at him, he told me. I couldn't help wondering why, because he looked fairly nondescript. He wore conventional Western clothes, perfectly acceptable in urban India, and looked respectable enough except for a constant nervous turning of the head, looking to the left, right, or behind, as though to check on anyone who might be following him. He was convinced that he was being followed at all times.

'By whom?' I asked.

'Agents of the government,' he said.

'But why should they follow you?'

'I look different,' he said. 'They see me as an outsider. They think I work for the CIA.'

'And do you?'

'No, no!' He shied nervously away from me. 'Why did you say that?'

'Only because you brought the subject up. I haven't noticed anyone following you.'

'They're very clever about it. Perhaps you're following me too.'

'I'm afraid I can't walk as fast or as far as you,' I said with a laugh; but he wasn't amused. He never smiled, never laughed. He did not feel safe in India, he confided. The saffron brigade was after him!

'But why?' I asked. 'They're not after me. And you're a Hindu with a Hindu name.'

'Ah yes, but I don't look like one!'

'Well, I don't look like a Taoist monk, but that's what I am,' I said, adding, in a more jocular manner: 'I know how to become invisible, and you wouldn't know I'm around. That's why no one follows me! I have this wonderful cloak, you see, and when I wear it I become invisible!'

'Can you lend it to me?' he asked eagerly.

'I'd love to,' I said, 'but it's at the cleaners right now. Maybe next week.'

'Crazy,' he muttered. 'Quite mad.' And he hurried on.

A few weeks later he returned to New York and safety. Then I heard he'd been mugged in Central Park. He's recovering, but doesn't do much walking now.

Neurotics do not walk for pleasure; they walk out of compulsion. They are not looking at the trees or the flowers or the mountains; they are not looking at other people (except in apprehension); they are usually walking away from something—unhappiness or disarray in their lives. They tire themselves out, physically and mentally, and that brings them some relief.

Like the journalist who came to see me last year. He'd escaped from Delhi, he told me. Had taken a room in Landour Bazaar and was going to spend a year on his own, away from family, friends, colleagues, the entire rat race. He was full of noble resolutions. He was planning to write an epic poem or a great Indian novel or a philosophical treatise. Every fortnight I meet someone who is planning to write one or the other of these things, and I do not like to discourage them, just in case they turn violent!

In effect he did nothing but walk up and down the mountain, growing shabbier by the day. Sometimes he recognized me. At other times there was a blank look on his face, as though he was on some drug, and he would walk past me without a sign of recognition. He discarded his slippers and began walking about barefoot, even on the stony paths. He did not change or wash his clothes. Then he disappeared; that is, I no longer saw him around.

I did not really notice his absence until I saw an ad in one of the national papers, asking for information about his whereabouts. His family was anxious to locate him. The ad carried a picture of the gentleman, taken in happier, healthier times; but it was definitely my acquaintance of that summer.

I was sitting in the bank manager's office, up in the cantonment, when a woman came in, making inquiries about her husband. It was the missing journalist's wife. Yes, said Mr Ohri, the friendly bank manager, he'd opened an account with them; not a very large sum, but there were a few hundred rupees lying to his credit. And no, they hadn't seen him in the bank for at least three months.

The journalist couldn't be found. Several months passed, and it was presumed that he had moved on to some other town, or that he'd lost his mind or his memory. Then some milkmen from Kolti Gaon discovered bones and remnants of clothing at the bottom of a cliff. In the pocket of the ragged shirt was the journalist's press card.

How he'd fallen to his death remains a mystery. It's easy to miss your footing and take a fatal plunge on the steep slopes of this range. He may have been high on something or he may simply have been trying out an unfamiliar path. Walking can be dangerous in the hills if you don't know the way or if you take one chance too many.

And here's a tale to illustrate that old chestnut that truth is often stranger than fiction:

Colonel Parshottam had just retired and was determined to pass the evening of his life doing the things he enjoyed most: taking early morning and late evening walks, afternoon siestas, a drop of whisky before dinner, and a good book on his bedside table.

A few streets away, on the fourth floor of a block of flats, lived Mrs L, a stout, neglected woman of forty, who'd had enough of life and was determined to do away with herself.

Along came the Colonel on the road below, a song on his lips, strolling along with a jaunty air, in love with life and wanting more of it.

Quite unaware of anyone else around, Mrs L chose that moment to throw herself out of her fourth-floor window. Seconds later she landed with a thud on the Colonel. If this was a Ruskin Bond story, it would have been love at first flight. But the grim reality was that he was crushed beneath her and did not recover from the impact. Mrs L, on the other hand, survived the fall and lived on into a miserable old age.

There is no moral to the story, any more than there is a moral to life. We cannot foresee when a bolt from the blue will put an end to the best-laid plans of mice and men.

La-de-dum-de-dum...

Respect Your Breakfast

'Laugh and be fat, sir!' Thus spoke Ben Jonson, poet and playwright, Shakespeare's contemporary and a lover of good food, wine and laughter.

Merriment usually accompanies food and drink, and laughter is usually enjoyed in the company of friends and people of goodwill. Laugh when you're alone, and you are likely to end up in a lunatic asylum.

'Honour your food,' said Manu, the law-giver, 'receive it thankfully. Do not hold it in contempt.' He did go on to say that we should avoid excess and gluttony, but his message was we should respect what is placed before us.

This was Granny's message, too. 'Better a small fish than an empty dish' was one of the sayings inscribed on her kitchen accounts notebook. She was apt to quote several of these little proverbs, and one of them was directed at me whenever I took too large a second helping of my favourite kofta curry.

'Don't let your tongue cut your throat,' she would

say ominously. 'You don't want to grow up to be like Billy Bunter.' She referred to the Fat Boy of Greyfriars School, a popular fictional character in the late 1930s.

'Just one more kofta, Granny,' I'd beg, 'I promise, I won't take a third helping.'

Sixty-five years later, I'm still trying to keep that promise. I keep those second helpings small, just in case I'm tempted into a third one. I'm not quite a Bunter yet, possibly because I still walk quite a bit. But the trouble with walking is it gives you an appetite, and that means you are inclined to tuck in when you get to the dining table.

Last winter, when I was staying at the India International Centre (IIC), I would go for an early morning walk in the Lodi Gardens, followed by breakfast at the Centre. They give you a good breakfast at IIC, and I did full justice to the scrambled eggs, buttered toasts, marmalade and coffee. I could have done with a little bacon, too, but apparently it wasn't the season for it. Well, when I looked across at the next table I saw a solitary figure breakfasting on watermelon—and nothing else! This made me feel terribly guilty, and I refrained from finishing off the marmalade.

'Aren't you Bond?' asked the man at the next table.

I confessed I was—not the other Bond, but the real one—and it turned out that we'd been at school together, in the dim distant past.

'You were always a good eater,' he said reflectively. 'In fact, you used to help yourself to my jam tarts when I wasn't looking.'

We chatted about our school days and companions of that era, and then he went on to tell me that he was suffering from various ailments—hence the frugal watermelon breakfast. As I wasn't suffering from anything worse than a bruised shin (due to falling over a courting couple in the Gardens) I felt better about my breakfast, and immediately ordered more marmalade and a third toast. When we parted, he urged me to switch to watermelons for breakfast, though I couldn't help noticing that he eyed my scrambled egg with a look that was full of longing. I guess healthy eating and happy eating are two different things.

Diwali, Christmas and the New Year are appropriate times for a little indulgence, and if someone were to send me a Christmas pudding I would respect the giver and the pudding by at least enjoying a slice or two—and sharing the rest!

But strictly speaking I'm a breakfast person, and I stand by another of Granny's proverbs: 'If the breakfast is bad, the rest of the day will go wrong.' So make it a good breakfast; linger over it, enjoy the flavours. And if you happen to be someone who must prepare their own breakfast, do so with loving care and precision. As Granny said, 'There is skill in all things, even in scrambling eggs.'

Simla and Delhi, 1943

We took the railcar to Simla. It was the nicest way of travelling through the mountains. The narrow-gauge train took twice as long and left you covered in soot. Going up in a motor car made you nauseous. The railcar glided smoothly round and up gradients, slipping through the 103 tunnels without subjecting the passengers to blasts of hot, black smoke.

We stopped at Barog, a pretty little wayside station, famous for its breakfasts and in winter, for its mistletoe. We got into Simla at lunchtime and dined at Davico's. Simla was well served by restaurants. Davico's was famous for its meringues, and I experienced one for the first time. Then we trudged off to a lodging house called Craig Dhu, which was to be another of our temporary homes.

The Bishop Cotton Prep School was situated in Chotta Simla, at some distance from the Senior School. The boys were at play when I first saw them from the road above the playing field.

'You can see they're a happy lot,' said my father.

They certainly seemed a good deal noisier (and less inhibited) than their counterparts at the Mussoorie convent. Some spun tops; others wrestled with each other; several boys were dashing about with butterfly nets, chasing a large blue butterfly. Three or four sat quietly on the steps, perusing comics. In those days you had story comics or papers, such as *Hotspur*, *Wizard* or *Champion*, and you actually had to read them.

It was to be a month before I joined the school (admission took time), and in the interim I enjoyed an idyllic holiday with my father. If Davico's had its meringues, Wenger's had its pastries and chocolate cakes, while at Kwality the curry puffs and ice creams were superb. The reader will consider me to have been a spoilt brat, and so I was for a time; but there was always the nagging fear that my father would be posted to some inaccessible corner of the country, and I would be left to rot in boarding school for the rest of my days.

During a rickshaw ride around Elysium Hill, my father told me Kipling's story of the phantom rickshaw — my first encounter with hill station lore. He also showed me the shop where Kim got his training as a spy from the mysterious Lurgan Sahib. I had not read Kipling at the time, but through my father's retellings I was already familiar with many of his characters and settings. The same Lurgan Sahib (I learnt later) had inspired another novel, F. Marion Crawford's *Mr Isaacs*. A Bishop Cotton's boy, Richard Blaker, had written a novel called *Scabby Dixon*, which had depicted life in the school at the turn of the century. And Bishop Cotton, our founder, had himself been a young master at Rugby under the famous Dr Arnold who was to write *Tom Brown's Schooldays*. Cotton became the first headmaster at Marlborough before coming out to India.

All these literary traditions were beginning to crowd upon me. And of course there was the strange fact that my father had named me Ruskin, after the Victorian essayist and guru of art and architecture. Had my father been an admirer of Mr Ruskin? I did not ask him, because at that time I thought I was the *only* Ruskin. At some point during my schooldays I discovered John Ruskin's fairy story, *The King of the Golden River*, and thought it rather good. And years later, my mother was to confirm that my father had indeed named me after the Victorian writer. My other Christian name, Owen, was seldom used, and I have never really bothered with it. An extra Christian name seems quite superfluous. And besides, Owen (in Welsh) means 'brave', and I am not a brave person. I have done some foolhardy things, but more out of ignorance than bravery.

I settled down in the prep school without any fuss. Compared to the Mussoorie convent it was luxury. For lunch there was usually curry and rice (as compared to the spartan meat boiled with pumpkin, the convent speciality); for dinner there would be cutlets or a chop. There was a wartime shortage of eggs, but the school kitchen managed to make some fairly edible omelettes out of egg powder. Occasionally there were sausages, although no one could say with any certainty what was in them. On my questioning our housemaster as to their contents, he smiled mysteriously and sang the first line of a Nelson Eddy favourite — *Ah, sweet mystery of life!*

Our sausages came to be known as 'Sweet Mysteries'. This was 1943, and the end of the War was still two years away.

Flying heroes were the order of the day. There were the *Biggles* books, with a daredevil pilot as hero. And *Champion* comic books featured Rockfist Rogan of the RAF, another flying ace who, whenever he was shot down in enemy territory, took on the Nazis in the boxing ring before escaping in one of their aircraft.

Having a father in the RAF was very prestigious and I asked my father to wear his uniform whenever he came to see me. This he did, and to good effect.

'Bond's father is in the RAF,' word went round, and other boys looked at me with renewed respect. 'Does he fly bombers or fighter planes?' they asked me.

'Both,' I lied. After all, there wasn't much glamour in codes and ciphers, although they were probably just as important.

My own comic book hero was Flying O'Flynn, an acrobatic goalkeeper who made some breathtaking saves in every issue, and kept his otherwise humble team at the top of the football league. I was soon emulating him, on our stony football field, and it wasn't long before I was the prep school goalkeeper.

Quite a few of the boys read books, the general favourites being the *William* stories, R.M. Ballantyne's adventure novels, Capt. W.E. Johns (Biggles), and any sort of spy or murder mystery. There was one boy, about my age, who was actually writing a detective story. As there was a paper shortage, he wrote in a small hand on slips of toilet paper, and stored these away in his locker. I can't remember his name, so have no idea if he grew up to become a professional writer. He left the following year, when most of the British boys began leaving India. Some had grown up in India; others had been sent out as evacuees during the Blitz.

I don't remember any special friend during the first year at the prep school, but I got on quite well with teachers and classmates. As I'd joined in midterm, the rest of the year seemed to pass quickly. And when the Kalka-Delhi Express drew into Delhi, there was my father on the platform, wearing his uniform and looking quite spry and of course happy to see me.

He had now taken a flat in Scindia House, an apartment building facing Connaught Circus. This suited me perfectly, as it was only a few minutes from cinemas, bookshops and restaurants. Just across the road was the newly opened Milk Bar, and while my father was away at his office, I would occasionally slip out to have a milkshake—strawberry, chocolate or vanilla—and dart back home with a comic paper purchased at one of the newsstands.

All those splendid new cinemas were within easy reach too, and my father and I soon became regular cinegoers; we must have seen at least three films a week on an average. I again took to making lists of all the films I saw, including the casts as far as I could remember them. Even today, to reiterate, I can rattle off the cast of almost any Hollywood or British production of the 1940s. The films I enjoyed most that winter were *Yankee Doodle Dandy* (with James Cagney quite electric as George M. Cohan) and *This Above All*, a drama of wartime London.

When I asked my father how the film had got its title, he wrote down the lines from Shakespeare that had inspired it:

> *This above all, to thine own self be true,*
> *And it must follow, as the night the day,*
> *Thou can'st not then be false to any man.*

I kept that piece of paper for many years, losing it only when I went to England.

Helping my father with his stamp collection, accompanying him to the pictures, dropping in at Wenger's for tea and muffins, bringing home a book or record—what more could a small boy of eight have asked for?

And then there were the walks.

In those days, you had only to walk a short distance to be out of New Delhi and into the surrounding fields or scrub forest. Humayun's Tomb was surrounded by a wilderness of babul and keekar trees, and so were other old tombs and monuments on the periphery of the new capital. Today they have all been swallowed up by new housing estates and government colonies, and the snarl of traffic is wonderful to behold.

New Delhi was still a small place in 1943. The big hotels (Maidens, the Swiss) were in Old Delhi. Only a few cars could be seen on the streets. Most people, including service personnel, travelled by pony-drawn tongas. When we went to the station to catch a train, we took a tonga. Otherwise we walked.

In the deserted Purana Kila my father showed me the narrow steps leading down from Humayun's library. Here the Emperor had slipped and fallen to his death. Not far away was Humayun's tomb. These places had few visitors then, and we could relax on the grass without being disturbed by hordes of tourists, guides, vagrants and health freaks. New Delhi still has its parks and tree-lined avenues—but oh, the press of people! Who could have imagined then that within forty years' time, the city would have swallowed huge tracts of land way beyond Ghaziabad, Faridabad, Gurgaon, Najafgarh, Tughlaqabad, small towns, villages, fields, most of the Ridge and all that grew upon it!

Change and prosperity have come to Delhi, but its citizens are paying a high price for the privilege of living in the capital. Too late to do anything about it now. Spread on, great octopus—your tentacles have yet to be fully extended.

❖

If, in writing this memoir, I appear to be taking my father's side, I suppose it is only human nature for a boy to be loyal to the parent who stands by him, no matter how difficult the circumstances. An eight-year-old is bound to resent his mother's liaison with another man. Looking back on my boyhood, I feel sure that my mother must have had her own compulsions, her own views on life and how it should be lived. After all, she had only been eighteen when she had married my father, who was about fifteen years her senior. She and her sisters had been a fun-loving set; they enjoyed going to dances, picnics, parties. She must have found my father too serious, too much of a stay-at-home, happy making the morning butter or sorting through his stamps in the evening. My mother told me later that he was very jealous, keeping her away from other men. And who wouldn't have been jealous? She was young, pretty, vivacious—everyone looked twice at her! They were obviously incompatible. They should never have married, I suppose. In which case, of course, I would not be here, penning these memoirs.

Hill of the Fairies

Fairy hill, or Pari Tibba as the paharis call it, is a lonely, uninhabited mountain lying to the east of Mussoorie, at a height of about 6000 feet. I have visited it occasionally, scrambling up its rocky slopes where the only paths are the narrow tracks made by goats and the small hill cattle. Rhododendrons and a few stunted oaks are the only trees on the hillsides, but at the summit is a small, grassy plateau ringed by pine trees.

It may have been on this plateau that the early settlers tried building their houses. All their attempts met with failure. The area seemed to attract the worst of any thunderstorm, and several dwellings were struck by lightning and burnt to the ground. People then confined themselves to the adjacent Landour hill, where a flourishing hill station soon grew up.

Why Pari Tibba should be struck so often by lightning has always been something of a mystery to me. Its soil and rock seem no different from the soil or rock of any other mountain in the vicinity. Perhaps a geologist can explain the phenomenon, or perhaps it has something to do with the fairies.

'Why do they call it the Hill of the Fairies?' I asked an old resident, a retired schoolteacher. 'Is the place haunted?'

'So they say,' he said.

'Who say?'

'Oh, people who have heard it's haunted. Some years after the site was abandoned by the settlers, two young runaway lovers took shelter for the night in one of the ruins. There was a bad storm and they were struck by lightning. Their charred bodies were found a few days later. They came from different communities and were buried far from each other, but their spirits hold a tryst every night under the pine trees. You might see them if you're on Pari Tibba after sunset.'

There are no ruins on Pari Tibba, and I can only presume that the building materials were taken away for use elsewhere. And I did not stay on the hill till after sunset. Had I tried climbing downhill in the dark, I would probably have ended up as the third ghost on the mountain. The lovers might have resented my intrusion, or, who knows, they might have welcomed a change. After a hundred years together on a windswept mountaintop, even the most ardent of lovers must tire of each other.

Who could have been seeing ghosts on Pari Tibba

after sunset? The nearest resident is a woodcutter who makes charcoal at the bottom of the hill. Terraced fields and a small village straddle the next hill. But the only inhabitants of Pari Tibba are the langurs. They feed on oak leaves and rhododendron buds. The rhododendrons contain an intoxicating nectar, and after dining—or wining—to excess, the young monkeys tumble about on the grass in high spirits.

The black bulbuls also feed on the nectar of the rhododendron flower, and perhaps this accounts for the cheekiness of these birds. They are aggressive, disreputable little creatures, who go about in rowdy gangs. The song of most bulbuls consists of several pleasant tinkling notes; but that of the Himalayan black bulbul is as musical as the bray of an ass. Men of science, in their wisdom, have given this bird the sibilant name of Hypsipetes psaroides. But the hillmen, in their greater wisdom, call the species the ban bakra, which means the 'jungle goat'.

Perhaps the flowers have something to do with the fairy legend. In April and May, Pari Tibba is covered with the dazzling yellow flowers of St John's Wort (wort meaning herb). The paharis call the flower a wild rose, and it does resemble one. In Ireland it is called the Rose of Sharon.

In Europe this flower is reputed to possess certain magical and curative properties. It is believed to drive away all evil and protect you from witches. But do not tread on St John's Wort after sunset, a fairy horseman will come and carry you off, landing you almost anywhere.

By day, St John's Wort is kindly. Are you insane? Then drink the sap from the leaves of the plant, and you will be cured. Are you hurt? Take the juice and apply it to your wound—and if at first this doesn't help, just keep applying juice until you stop bleeding, or breathing. Are you bald? Then rise early and bathe your head with the dew from St John's Wort, and your hair will grow again—if you don't catch pneumonia.

Can St John's Wort be connected with the fairy legend of Pari Tibba? It is said that most flowers, when they die, become fairies. This might be especially true of St John's Wort.

There is yet another legend connected with the mountain. A shepherd boy, playing on his flute, discovered a beautiful silver snake basking on a rock. The snake spoke to the boy, saying, 'I was a princess once, but a jealous witch cast a spell over me and turned me into a snake. This spell can only be broken if someone who is pure in heart kisses me thrice. Many years have passed, and I have not been able to find one who is pure in heart.' Then the shepherd boy took the snake in his arms, and he put his lips to its mouth, and at the third kiss he discovered that he was holding a beautiful princess in his arms. What happened afterwards is anybody's guess.

There are snakes on Pari Tibba, and though they are probably harmless, I have never tried taking one of them in my arms. Once, near a spring, I came upon a checkered water snake. Its body was a series of bulges. I used a stick to exert pressure along the snake's length, and it disgorged five frogs. They came out one after the other, and, to my astonishment, hopped off, little the worse for their harrowing experience. Perhaps they, too, were enchanted. Perhaps shepherd boys, when they kiss the snake-princess, are turned into frogs and remain inside the snake's belly until a writer comes along with a magic stick and releases them from bondage.

Biologists probably have their own explanation for the frogs, but I'm all for perpetuating the fairy legends of Pari Tibba.

The Elephant and the Cassowary Bird

The baby elephant, another of Grandfather's unusual pets, wasn't out of place in our home in north India because India is where elephants belong, and in any case our house was full of pets brought home by Grandfather, who was in the Forest Service. But the cassowary bird was different. No one had ever seen such a bird before — not in India, that is. Grandfather had picked it up on a voyage to Singapore, where he'd been given the bird by a rubber planter who'd got it from a Dutch trader who'd got it from a man in Indonesia.

Anyway, it ended up at our home in Dehra, and seemed to do quite well in the sub-tropical climate. It looked like a cross between a turkey and an ostrich, but bigger than the former and smaller than the latter — about five feet in height. It was not a beautiful bird, nor even a friendly one, but it had come to stay, and everyone was curious about it, especially the baby elephant.

Right from the start the baby elephant took a great interest in the cassowary. He would circle round the odd creature, and diffidently examine with his trunk the texture of its stumpy wings; of course, he suspected no evil, and his childlike curiosity encouraged him to take liberties which resulted in an unpleasant experience.

Noticing the baby elephant's attempts to make friends with the rather morose cassowary, we felt a bit apprehensive. Self-contained and sullen, the big bird responded only by slowly and slyly raising one of its powerful legs, all the while gazing into space with an innocent air. We knew what the gesture meant: we had seen that treacherous leg raised on many an occasion, and suddenly shooting out with a force that would have done credit to a vicious camel. In fact, camel and cassowary kicks are delivered on the same plan, except that the camel kicks backward like a horse and the bird forward.

We wished to spare our baby elephant a painful experience, and led him away from the bird. But he persisted in his friendly overtures, and one morning he received an ugly reward. Rapid as lightning, the cassowary hit straight from the hip and knee joints, and the elephant ran squealing to Grandfather.

For several days he avoided the cassowary, and we thought he had learnt his lesson. He crossed and recrossed the compound and the garden, swinging his trunk, thinking furiously. Then, a week later, he appeared on the veranda at breakfast time in his usual cheery, childlike fashion, sidling up to the cassowary as if nothing had happened.

We were struck with amazement at this and so, it seemed, was the bird. Had the painful lesson already been forgotten, that too by a member of the elephant tribe noted for its ability never to forget? Another dose of the same medicine would serve the booby right.

The cassowary once more began to draw up its fighting leg with sinister determination. It was nearing the true position for the master-kick, kung-fu style, when all of a sudden the baby elephant seized with his trunk the other leg of the cassowary and pulled it down. There was a clumsy flapping of wings, a tremendous swelling of the bird's wattle, and an undignified getting up, as if it were a floored boxer doing his best to beat the count of ten. The bird then marched off with an attempt to look stately and unconcerned, while we at the breakfast table were convulsed with laughter.

After this the cassowary bird gave the baby elephant as wide a berth as possible. But they were forced not to coexist for very long. The baby elephant, getting bulky and cumbersome, was sold to a zoo where he became a favourite with young visitors who loved to take rides on his back.

As for the cassowary, he continued to grace our veranda for many years, gaped at but not made much of, while entering on a rather friendless old age.

A New Flower

It was the first day of spring (according to the Hindu calendar), but here in the Himalayas it still seemed mid-winter. A cold wind hummed and whistled through the pines, while dark rain-clouds were swept along by the west wind only to be thrust back by the east wind.

I was climbing the steep road to my cottage at the top of the hill when I was overtaken by nine-year-old Usha hurrying back from school. She had tied a scarf round her head to keep her hair from blowing about. Dark hair and eyes, and pink cheeks, were all accentuated by the patches of snow still lying on the hillside.

'Look,' she said, pointing. 'A new flower!' It was a single, butter-yellow blossom, and it stood out like a bright star against the drab winter grass. I hadn't seen anything like it before, and had no idea what its name might be. No doubt its existence was recorded in some botanical tome. But for me it was a discovery.

'Shall I pick it for you?' asked Usha. 'No, don't,'

I said. 'It may be the only one. If we break it, there may not be any more. Let's leave it there and see if it seeds.' We scrambled up the slope and examined the flower more closely. It was very delicate and soft-petalled looking as though it might fall at any moment.

'It will be finished if it rains,' said Usha. And it did rain that night—rain mingled with sleet and hail. It rattled and swished on the corrugated tin roof; but in the morning the sun came out. I walked up the road without really expecting to see the flower again. And Usha had been right. The flower had disappeared in the storm. But two other buds, unnoticed by us the day before, had opened. It was as though two tiny stars had fallen to earth in the night.

I did not see Usha that day, but the following day, when we met on the road, I showed her the fresh blossoms. And they were still there, two days later, when I passed by, but so were two goats, grazing on the short grass and thorny thickets of the slope. I had no idea if they were partial to these particular flowers, but I did know that goats would eat almost anything and I was taking no chances.

Scrambling up the steep slope, I began to shoo them away. One goat retreated, but the other lowered his horns, gave me a baleful look, and refused to move. It reminded me a little of my grandfather's pet goat who had once pushed a visiting official into a bed of nasturtiums; so I allowed discretion to be the better part of valour, and backed away.

Just then, Usha came along and, sizing up the situation, came to the rescue. She unfurled her pretty, blue umbrella and advanced on the goat shouting at it in goat language. (She had her own goats at home.) The beast withdrew, and the flowers (and my own dignity) were saved.

As the days grew warmer, the flowers faded and finally disappeared. I forgot all about them, and so did Usha. There were lessons and exams for her to worry about, and rent and electricity bills to occupy a freelance writer's thoughts.

The months passed, summer and autumn came and went, with their own more showy blooms; and in no time at all, winter returned with cold winds blowing from all directions.

One day I heard Usha calling to me from the hillside. I looked up and saw her standing behind a little cluster of golden star-shaped flowers—not, perhaps, as spectacular as Wordsworth's field of golden daffodils but, all the same, an enchanting sight for one who had played a small part in perpetuating their existence.

Where there had been one flowering plant, there were now several. Usha and I speculated on the prospect of the entire hillside being covered with the flowers in a few years' time.

I still do not know the botanical name for the little flower. I can't remember long Latin names anyway. But Usha tells me that she has seen it growing near her father's village, on the next mountain, and that the hill people call it 'Basant', which means spring.

Although I am just a little disappointed that we are not, after all, the discoverers of a new species, this is outweighed by our pleasure in knowing that the flower flourishes in other places. May it multiply!

Poetry

Boy in a Blue Pullover

Boy in a faded blue pullover,
Poor boy, thin, smiling boy,
Ran down the road shouting,
Singing, flinging his arms wide.
I stood in the way and stopped him.
'What's up?' I said. 'Why are you happy?'
He showed me the nickel rupee-coin.
'I found it on the road,' he said.
And he held it to the light
That he might see it shining bright.
'And how will you spend it,
Small boy in blue pullover?'
'I'll buy—
I'll buy a buckle for my belt!'
Slim boy, smart boy,
Would buy a buckle for his belt
Coin clutched in his hot hand,
He ran off laughing, bright.
The coin I'd lost an hour ago;
But better his that night.

We Three

We three,
We're not a crowd;
We're not even company—
My echo,
My shadow,
And me.

Granny's Tree-Climbing

My grandmother was a genius. You'd like to know why?
Because she could climb trees. Spreading or high,
She'd be up their branches in a trice. And mind you,
When last she climbed a tree, she was sixty-two.
Ever since childhood, she'd had this gift
for being happier in a tree than in a lift;
And though, as years went by, she would be told
That climbing trees should stop when one grew old
And that growing old should be gone about gracefully
She'd laugh and say, 'Well, I'll grow old disgracefully.
I can do it better.' And we had to agree;
For in all the garden there wasn't a tree
She hadn't been up, at one time or another
(Having learned to climb from a loving brother
When she was six) but it was feared by all
That one day she'd have a terrible fall.
The outcome was different; while we were in town
She climbed a tree and couldn't come down!

We went to the rescue, and helped her descend . . .
A doctor took Granny's temperature and said,
'I strongly recommend a quiet week in bed.'
We sighed with relief and tucked her up well.
Poor Granny! For her, it was more like a season in hell.

Confined to her bedroom, while every breeze
Whispered of summer and dancing leaves.
But she held her peace till she felt stronger
Then sat up and said, 'I'll lie here no longer!'
And she called for my father and told him undaunted
That a house in a treetop was what she now wanted.
My dad knew his duties. He said, 'That's all right
You'll have what you want, dear, I'll start work tonight.'
With my expert assistance, he soon finished the chore:
Made her a tree house with windows and a door.
So Granny moved up, and now every day
I climb to her room with glasses and a tray.
She sits there in state and drinks mocktails with me,
Upholding her right to reside in a tree.

Love's Sad Song

There's a sweet little girl who lives down the lane,
And she's so pretty and I'm so plain,
She's clever and smart and all things good,
And I'm the bad boy of the neighbourhood.
But I'd be her best friend forever and a day
If only she'd smile and look my way.

In a Strange Cafe

Waiter, where's my soup?
On its way, sir, loop the loop!
Straight from our famous cooking pot,
Here it comes, sir, piping hot!
But waiter, there's a fly in my soup.
That's no fly, sir,
That's your chicken.
The smaller the chicken the better the soup!
Please take it away.
I'll just have the curry and a plate of rice . . .
The curry's very good, sir, full of spice!
Waiter, what's this object that's floating around?
Just a small beetle, sir,
Homeward bound!
Never mind the curry, just bring me some bread,
I have to eat something before I'm in bed.
What's on the menu? Hungarian Goulash?
I suppose it's served up with beetles and mash.

In a Strange Cafe

Isn't there anything else I can eat?
Yes sir, you could try the crow's feet.
Highly recommended and good for the teeth.
All our best guests
Are most happily fed here.
And where are they now?
All happily dead, sir.

If Mice Could Roar

If mice could roar
And elephants soar,
And trees grow up in the sky;
If tigers could dine
On biscuits and wine,
And the fattest of men could fly!
If pebbles could sing
and bells never ring
And teachers were lost in the post;
If a tortoise could run
And losses be won,
And bullies be buttered on toast;
If a song brought a shower
And a gun grew a flower,
This world would be nicer than most!

My Best Friend

My best friend
Is the baker's son,
I gave him a book
And he gave me a bun!
I told him a tale
Of a magical lake,
And he liked it so much
That he baked me a cake.
Yes, he's my best friend —
We go cycling together,
On bright, sunny days,
Or in rain and bad weather.
And if we feel hungry
There's always a pie
Or a pastry to feast on,
As we go riding by!

The Cat Has Something to Say

Sir, you're a human and I'm a cat,
And I'm really quite happy to leave it at that.
It doesn't concern me if you like a dish
Of chicken masala or lobster and fish.
So why all these protests around the house
If for dinner I fancy
A succulent mouse?
Or a careless young sparrow who came my way?
Our natures, dear sir, are really the same:
Flesh, fish or fowl, we both like our game.
Only you take yours curried,
And I take mine plain.

As a Boy

As a boy I stood on the edge of the railway-cutting,
Outside the dark tunnel, my hands touching
The hot rails, waiting for them to tremble
At the coming of the noonday train.
The whistle of the engine hung on the forest's silence.
Then out of the tunnel, a green-gold dragon
Came plunging, thundering past—
Out of the tunnel, out of the dark.
And the train rolled on, every day
Hundreds of people coming or going or running away—
Goodbye, goodbye !
I haven't seen you again, bright boy at the carriage
    window,
Waving to me, calling,
But I've loved you all these years and looked for you
    everywhere,

As a Boy

In cities and villages, beside the sea,
In the mountains, in crowds at distant places;
Returning always to the forest's silence,
To watch the windows of some passing train . . . .
Mountains in my blood.

The Demon Driver

At driving a car I've never been good—
I batter the bumper and damage the hood—
'Get off the road!' the traffic cops shout,
'You're supposed to go *round* that roundabout!'
'I thought it was quicker to drive straight through.'
'Give us your licence—it's time to renew.'
I took their advice and handed a fee
To a Babu who looked on this windfall with glee.
'No problem,' he said, 'your licence now pukka,
You may drive all the way from here to Kolkata.'

So away I drove, at a feverish pitch,
Advancing some way down an unseen ditch.
Once back on the highway, I soon joined the fray
Of hundreds of drivers who wouldn't give way:
I skimmed past a truck and revolved round a van
(Good drivers can do anything that they can)
Then offered a lift to a man with a load—
'Just a little way down to the end of this road.'

As I pressed on the pedal, the car gave a shudder:
He'd got in at one door, got out at the other.
'God help you!' he said, as he hurried away,
'I'll come for a drive another fine day!'
I came to that roundabout, round it I sped
Eager to get to my dinner and bed.
Round it I went, and round it once more
'Get off the road!' That cop was a bore.
I swung to the left and went clean through a wall,
My neighbour stood there—he looked menacing, tall—
'This will cost you three thousand,' he quietly said,
'And send me your cheque before you're in bed!'
Alas! my new car was sent for repair,
But my friends gathered round and said, never despair!
'We are all going to help you to make a fresh start.'
And next day they gave me a nice bullock-cart.

Read More in Puffin

The Room of Many Colours: A Treasury of Stories for Children

Ruskin Bond

'The subtle nuances in Ruskin Bond's writing can be experienced while reading the collection of tales brought together in this treasury of stories for children. Bond's ability to get across the richness of childhood experience gives these tales unusual insight and universality' — *The Hindu*

For over five decades, Ruskin Bond has written charming tales that have mesmerized readers of all ages. This collection brings together his finest stories for children in one volume. Filled with a rich cast of characters and superb illustrations, *The Room of Many Colours: A Treasury of Stories for Children* is a must-read for all Ruskin Bond fans.

WATER
MUSIC

A Cape Cod Story

Marcia Peck

SEA CROW PRESS
amplifying voices

To my parents: Marion Hadley Peck and Samuel Watson Peck
For Dave and Hadley

IN A NET OF BLUE AND GOLD

When the moored boat lifts, for its moment,
out of the water like a small cloud—
this is when I understand.
It floats there, defying the stillness to break,
its white hull doubled on the surface smooth as glass.
A minor miracle, utterly purposeless.
Even the bird on the bow-line takes it in stride,
barely shifting his weight before resuming
whatever musing it is birds do,
and the fish continue their placid, midday
truce with the world, suspended a few feet below.
I catch their gleam, the jeweled, reflecting scales,
small dragons guarding common enough treasure,
And wonder how, bound to each other as we are
in a net of blue and gold,
we fail so often, in such ordinary ways.

Jane Hirshfield

BEAUFORT SCALE

A SCALE FOR MEASURING THE FORCE OF WIND

PROLOGUE

The bridge at Sagamore was closed when we got there that summer of 1956. We had to cross the canal at Buzzards Bay over the only other roadway that tethered Cape Cod to the mainland. That was the summer the cello proved to be my steadiest companion, although I would have had it otherwise. My mother had to make do without a piano of her own, which did not auger well: music had always been her refuge. And my father was dead set on building a cottage—built the *right* way, which was to say, better than Uncle George's—when we couldn't afford it. We thought we spotted the *Andrea Doria* moments before it sank. And I discovered the small ways in which people try to rescue each other.

Our property fronted a salt pond whose fertile waters hatched clams the size of a toenail, infant eels no bigger than a bobby pin, and young crabs so fragile you could crush them between two fingers. When they matured, they found their way to the creek, an outlet booby-trapped with rocks from an old abandoned mill, and followed it out to Pleasant Bay, that vast shallow body of water which, like a long adolescence, spanned

1

the distance between our pond and the full-fledged, fathomless ocean.

Tides filled and emptied our small world and I tried to figure out who belonged to whom. I longed to belong to my mother. But I learned that summer that she was like a teacup, spilled out and upside down on the saucer, and she couldn't right herself. She thought she was mad at my father; she didn't recognize that fiercer winds than his tore at her. All summer the storm gathered and gathered, took its breath from every direction we thought we knew, and lashed us into spindrift.

And all the while, surrounding us, holding us up like the sea we floated on, was the music.

1
LIGHT AIR

Beaufort Number 1
Wind speed 1-2 MPH
direction of wind shown by smoke but not by wind vanes

*I*n the pre-dawn darkness I heard the clink of cup on saucer, porcelain to porcelain. Unmistakably my mother's. Not the sound of Daddy's solid mug or the dependable syncopation of his footsteps, one leg polio-short.

She touched my shoulder. "Wake up, Lily. Daddy wants you to help him pack the car." She clicked on the light.

"I'm awake." I opened my eyes to the hot New Jersey morning.

But she was on her way out the door, bent forward so not to spill.

I hurried to dress in the clothes I had laid out the night before. The last few weeks of sixth grade had inched by. But now, at last, we were returning to the Cape, as we had each of

3

the five summers since Daddy bought the property—our property—across the pond from Uncle George's cabin. Fifteen acres at one hundred dollars an acre, every dime he had. At the end of each summer, when we left to return to New Jersey, I had cried to myself in the backseat because I knew I'd never love another place like I loved our woods and pond.

I heard my sister Dodie in the hallway. Two turned-out legs of equal length, ballet straight. The door to her room closed. I brushed my teeth, closed my suitcase, and carried it downstairs. The morning was already sweltering.

My mother stood at the counter, buttering bread for sandwiches by the kitchen light, but everything else on our block was dark and quiet. No dogs barked, no lawnmower whined, no fragments of bickering or smell of donuts frying in hot fat wafted through the open windows. Just the whir of the DeMeo's window fan next door, covering up their snores.

Outside, Daddy was sitting on the bumper of the '53 Pontiac, tying a rope around the big canvas tent. His thick shock of black hair fell forward as he worked. I had always been told I had his forehead, the unruly low hairline that came to a widow's peak and made an actual hair-do an impossibility. Clean-shaven even at that hour, he worked by the square of light from the kitchen window. Toolbox, hip boots and typewriter lay on the grass. He cinched his knot and looked up.

"Lily. Just in time. Sun will be up soon." He whispered in case the neighbors were light sleepers. "I need the big things first." He stowed the bulky tent.

I picked up the heavy box containing all his best tools, freshly oiled, sharpened and arranged in compartments.

Dodie let the screen door swing shut and bumped her suitcase down the steps. Daddy put an alarmed finger to his lips. I handed him her suitcase.

"Next, your cello."

Of all the things over which my parents fought, on this subject there was no disagreement: they would find a way to bring my cello. No matter how long and complicated the list, no matter how full the car, they made room for music. As a boy my father had helped his father with his piano-moving business. Grampy Grainger thought moving pianos was honest work, but *playing* a piano was heaven's own miracle. Daddy, the compliant one of Grampy's two sons, faithfully trudged off to his weekly piano lesson taught by a neighbor only marginally capable of furnishing the basics. Despite her efforts he never progressed beyond simple hymns, which was progress enough to strike joy into Grammy Grainger's Baptist heart. But he knew there was more to music, and he knew that practice was the way to get there. Practice, and a good teacher. And he had lined up just such a summer teacher for me. Mr. Metcalf, he was told, was "the best." I got my cello from the house, conspicuously minding the door, which Daddy rewarded with an approving nod.

"Now something this size." He formed his hands around an imaginary box. I handed him my mother's sewing basket. "Good eye," he whispered.

I went back inside for two pieces of toast. One for each of us, which we ate while we worked.

He loaded the trunk and when it was full, brought the lid down tentatively. Satisfied my cello was safe, he leaned on the hatch until it clicked shut. Then he packed the backseat, higher and higher. Folding cots for Dodie and me, the kerosene lamp, my mother's piano music, the books and papers he would need to work on his dissertation.

When every crevice was filled, he spread a foam pad on top just behind the front seat. Dodie brought out the bag of sandwiches and we climbed in. She was small for thirteen, and skinny, which was fortunate because there was scarcely room for us and we had to scrunch down between the mattress and the roof. But it seemed a snug enough roost for the long trip. We were like a pair of earrings stretched out on the little square of cotton that comes in the box with expensive department-store jewelry.

My mother was the last to leave the house just as dawn broke. Through the kitchen window we could see her draw a glass of water and drink it down. More a methodical gesture than a thirsty one. She turned slowly in a circle and looked around the room, paying out her glance like a fisherman letting out line. Ever since Easter when my grandmother, BerthaMelrose, picked a fight with my father—a fight even my grandfather, Tucker, couldn't remedy—there had been a reluctance about my mother. Music was the only thing she really put her heart into. But even her piano playing now sounded hesitant and unnerved. She was stuck on the same passages, over and over.

"Blow the horn," I said.

"We've got plenty of time," Daddy answered. As if he weren't itching to get going too. As if he had known all along that in a minute she would swiftly—all at once—switch off the light, lock the door behind her, and join us. "All set?" Daddy started the car. "Lydia?"

She settled her purse at her feet.

He pulled out of the driveway.

I slid onto my stomach, my nose at the back of her powder-scented neck, and watched as we turned from our mapled neighborhood onto the Avenue. All the stores were dark.

I was eleven, two years younger than Dodie, and didn't understand why the Cape meant something different to my mother than it did to Daddy. My mother, in spite of a soft spot for the Transcendentalists, was hardly enthusiastic about "the rustic life." That would mean pumping water, heating water, carrying water, no phone, no electricity, chilly visits to the outhouse in the dead of night while regretting that last cup of tea or cocoa. No piano of her own, available whenever she wanted to practice. But she had also read *The Outermost House*, had devoured *The House on Nauset Marsh*, two books you couldn't read without falling in love with Cape Cod, and hoped things would improve. One day she, too, would sip the genteel pleasures afforded one with time to observe the small miracles of nature.

Daddy insisted there was nothing like the rigors of the great outdoors to test one's mettle. But even for him the prospect of living in a tent all summer long had lost its glamour. We had been tested enough. Change jars had been filled and taken to the bank, an architect had been consulted: the time had come to build a house. Our house would not be lavish, but it would be solid, at least as good as Uncle George's, and when it was done, my mother—like Aunt Fanny—wouldn't have to rough it anymore. No more washing dishes on the picnic table while the gnats chewed on her face and neck. No more sponge baths. No more worrying about a tent that was never meant to last this long. And it would be no mere cottage but a proper home, with room for a piano.

The architect estimated the cost at $2500, and we were still a good five hundred short. My father was a thorough man. Teaching high school mathematics had taught him economy; his maritime forefathers had taught him prudence. And so it was unlike him to become so excited about this house, drawn up on large, impressive blueprints, that he would begin construction without really knowing how he could pay for it all.

My mother suspected the initial expense was only the beginning, and the scrimping and saving had barely begun. A house had to be kept up: painted, furnished, cleaned, wired, plumbed, roofed, curtained, lit and heated. Then there was the matter of how close it was to Uncle George. The house became the crucible for every disagreement my parents had. I thought their arguments were all about money, but I was wrong. Once decanted, they left two layers of sediment. One was the trouble with BerthaMelrose, my mother's mother. (My mother, never given to baby-talk, called my grandmother BerthaMelrose— given name and surname all run together, just like that. It was as if she sensed from an early age that little about the formidable BerthaMelrose inspired terms of endearment.) The other was the trouble with Uncle George, my father's brother. For my mother the house proved my father would never outgrow Uncle George's little contests. She didn't know how a decent man like my father could wind up with a brother like Uncle George.

But perched atop all our belongings in the backseat, it seemed to me we were just plain lucky. We were about to escape the New Jersey heat, traffic jams on the Garden State, the rotting smells that drifted over from the Meadows. A two-months' vacation was supposed to make up for a schoolteacher's modest paycheck. To *me*, it more than compensated. I recognized a blessing when I saw one. Like having been born an American instead of, say, a Communist.

Daddy turned onto the cobbled road along the Passaic River, a streak of sludge between factories on either bank. We headed north, then east.

Beyond the shoulder of Route 17 a dark oily soup marked the Meadows, thirty thousand acres of marshland and garbage. My mother had to go to the bathroom and so we gassed up at a station on a pad of concrete fringed with bits of broken glass. Cars whizzed by, rushing to appointments in New York City. The sky was light. It was going to be a scorcher.

Finally my mother came out, zipped and buttoned, but squinting self-consciously nonetheless. Dodie drew an imaginary dividing line between us. She staked her pencils, paper, and book of crosswords on her side, giving herself more than half the space, but when I started to say so, my mother said we were going to be in the car ten hours and we had better find a way to get along.

"The girls will be fine. Won't you, girls?" said Daddy. "They can look for license plates. This will be the best trip ever. I'm sure of it." He turned and winked at me. A wink to make me his partner in the job of proving him right.

"Let's just get there," my mother said, as though she were going to the dentist. Resolved to see it through, poised for any nasty surprises.

I let Dodie's Mason-Dixon line stand, but not without giving her a look, which was wasted because she had already started to read. I stacked my two books carefully to one side. My mother took out her gardening catalogue.

"We could try to get the alphabet," I said to Dodie.

"Not now." She turned the page. It was hard to get Dodie away from a book. For her, reading was a time-saver. It took her out of the fray, avoided messy conversations, taught her the least strenuous method of understanding the world. I watched her eyes flit from line to line. She resembled my mother's side of the family: delicate-boned, nearsighted and fair, prone to sunburn and an annual case of poison ivy that blistered and itched and spread from her toes to her eyelids even though she wore gloves to keep from scratching. I was a Grainger—everybody said so—with my ruddy cheeks and wide feet. As common and solid as a slab of Nova Scotia granite, with speckled gray eyes to match. But I had my mother's hands and her long fingers. Good hands for the cello, my father insisted.

Daddy found a station playing classical music on the radio. "Maybe you can get some time on Fanny's piano." Aunt Fanny's out-of-tune upright. Uncle George said she neglected to tune it so she could blame the blankety-blank piano for all the sour notes that came out of her violin. But Uncle George missed the point. When Aunt Fanny played the violin a beatific smile over-took her features as if she were listening to something heavenly, magical. She wasn't the least bit aware that everything she played came out sounding equally atonal, like modern music. "She'll be happy for the company."

"Maybe. Or I could use the one at the church," said my mother, who would rather go without than Wear Out Her Welcome. She would not want it said she had imposed. Not even on family. Especially not on family. Even though Uncle George only came down on weekends and there was little danger of running into him mid-week.

I hung over her shoulder. She had the catalogue open to photographs of flowers in "warm tones." I pointed to some big splashy tulips.

"They bloom too early," my mother answered, not looking up. "They'd be gone before we got there." She turned the page.

"Momma!" I said. The caption under a camellia read "well-bred," a description I was sure would appeal to her.

"Wrong climate. Besides, you have to plant something that fits the spot." She opened to the page her thumb was marking. An old-fashioned trumpet vine climbing on a barn. "Something like this, maybe. For the new house. On a trellis against the shingles." She gave my father an inquiring look. "Weston?"

"Whatever you want," my father answered.

"Aren't you even going to look?"

"Lydia, I'm driving."

I looked at my mother. Her lips went tight, a hyphen across her face. She turned away, closed the catalogue and looked out the window. We were crossing the George Wash-ington Bridge. I craned my neck to glimpse the spans, high as steeples, to see what opportunities for humoring her might be found up there.

My father pointed suddenly to a ferry on the river. Sunlight glinted off a handful of cars pulling out into the current from the Weehawken wharf. "Bet they wish they were headed where *we* are going." A little too enthusiastic.

My mother studied a speck of lint in her lap.

He cocked his head at her. "Really. Plant whatever you want. Anything is OK with me."

"Never mind." A sizzle in her voice, like saliva on a hot iron. Because she had made this overture: to be a part of things. The house could be his, but she could bring to it a garden. A trumpet vine on a trellis. But he hadn't shown any interest.

"And what? You're interested in which nuts and bolts I'm going to use on the house? Two-penny nail. Finishing nails. Carpenter screws...."

"No, Weston. You could *pretend*."

"Lydia...." My father lifted his hands and let them drop back to the steering wheel. He shook his head. "I'm interested. What do you want to show me?"

"Nothing," said my mother. "Nothing at all." Stiff like starched crinolines. "I don't know why we are talking about it anyway. I don't know how we're going to pay for any of this." Iron nice and hot.

Everybody was quiet. Daddy too, because he didn't know either, even though she didn't have to remind him. Dodie, oblivious, worked a crossword puzzle. My mother watched the car in front of us. A foghorn on the Hudson lowed to its drove of boats. We turned north, away from that isolated note. My father guided the car through Westchester, then onto the Merritt Parkway.

It would all get worked out, I told myself. Once the house was built my parents would wonder why they ever worried. They would laugh and say to each other, *Why didn't we do that a long time ago?* Once and for all the house would prove we belonged. We were no mere tourists; we were summer *residents*. I'd be able to make believe New Jersey was temporary, merely a present condition of my father's employment. The teaching job taken just before I was born. We should have stayed in Boston, for by now it was clear that the move hadn't panned out the way they expected. None of Daddy's original hopes had materialized. The pay didn't go as far as he thought, the students didn't study as hard, my parents had made few friends, the really good music was in New York, a distance of eleven miles that might as well have been a hundred. They missed the familiar. Daddy even missed Grammy Grainger's high expectations and they both missed Grampy Grainger's elaborate, homespun compliments that put a smile even on my mother's lips. A disbelieving smile, but a smile nonetheless. The one person my mother did *not* miss was Uncle George, who could get my father's goat over the smallest thing. And the worst part, according to her, was that my father always fell for it.

By the time my father began to wish he had stayed in Boston, he had tenure, and quitting didn't make sense anymore. My mother tried to make the best of it, but her shyness could not make itself at home in the hubbub of New Jersey's Italian and Jewish neighborhoods. She thought she should embrace all cultures, the less familiar the better, and she disapproved of her inability to gab with the neighbors or to like garlic or gefilte fish. New Jersey only served to highlight her shortcomings. I thought that in some way she regarded it as a failing on my part that I had been born there.

"Look, Mommy...." She liked to be called Mommy. "Look, your favorite road."

She didn't respond.

"How come?" I asked.

"How come what?"

"How come it's your favorite?" I could recite the answer.

She half turned to me, her mouth puckered with impatience. Then she let out a sudden sigh, as if deciding to allow herself to be managed. "No telephone wires. No power lines. They buried them."

"Spared no expense," said my father. "That's why we pay all these *tolls*."

My mother's lips thinned again. He'd picked the wrong time to tease her. "He was kidding," I piped up. "You were kidding, weren't you, Daddy?"

My mother shushed me with a scowl.

"Reach down and get me a sandwich, would you, Lily?" he asked. This relieved me, because my parents never ate during a *serious* fight.

"Any one?"

"Any one at all."

I passed him a chicken sandwich. He held it with his left hand resting on the steering wheel and peeled back the waxed paper.

"I thought we'd get a bunch of shells and crush them up for the walkway. We'll have to have a walkway to the front door," he said between bites. "I imagined some bayberry bushes next to the house, and maybe a wild rose. A wild rose for sure. Honey?" He looked over at my mother. "You pick it. Color. Bloom. Tell me the exact genus and phylum and I'll find it if I have to drive all the way to Hyannis."

"Well, maybe." She softened. Her fingers rifled a corner of the catalogue. "You'd have to build a fence for a wild rose. But you can't have bayberries next to the house. They wouldn't do well." The garden was her department.

"That's OK. Then we'll put them down near the water."

"Yes." We were passing a big unpainted Connecticut barn with wide gaps between the slats for drying tobacco leaves. "They could go near the water."

She took out her lipstick and pulled down the visor mirror. I settled back behind her shoulder and watched her inspect her hairdo now that the bayberries had been settled. Medium length, medium color. And fine, so that it left little strands of down in her hairbrush. She wasn't pretty in a glamorous way, but she had what her father, my grandfather Tucker Melrose, called "the good looks of intelligence." A perfectly respectable, perhaps even superior, kind of beauty. Tucker said apologetically she couldn't escape her Puritan stock, for which he accepted full responsibility. Generations of pious, educated people molding her brow and chiseling her cheekbones too sharply, draining the color from our identical, quartz-gray eyes; ancestors who were buried at Lexington and Concord and Salem so long ago that their headstones were no longer legible. They had come not long after the Mayflower and over the years had married other established, reliable families. Boring church-goers with complexions like mash, as Tucker told it. What we needed was a scalawag. Or a floozy. Someone to add spice and fire, some *zest* to the family genes. My mother always said that was why her hair had no body, even though she pinned it up every night with bobby pins. Too many pilgrims.

She blotted her lips together, adjusted her glasses and crimped a wave at her temple with tentative fingers. She had pretty hair. Dodie officiously called it strawberry blonde, but I thought it was more like maple syrup from Tucker's woods. The first draw down in spring when the sap ran pale and the flavor was mild.

She let the stiffness go out of her face. She didn't even say anything when my father bought fireworks at a roadside stand in Connecticut. Fifteen dollars worth and they hardly filled a brown paper bag.

Every year my mother predicted that Providence, which couldn't be avoided, would make a long, hard trip longer and harder. And she was right again. Traffic outside the State House seized up behind an overheated car. We crawled. Uncle George had called long distance from Boston to say the bridge at Sagamore was being repaired, necessitating a detour along the crowded business strip at Buzzards Bay, past cranberry stores and saltwater taffy stands, to the only other bridge that linked Cape Cod to the North American continent.

The car grew stuffy and hot. By the time we crossed the canal, bits of bread and broken-pointed pencils littered the mattress upon which Dodie and I crouched. Our space, which had seemed cozy at the start of the trip, now felt cramped and confining. I couldn't stretch in any direction. Every time I moved, my mother said I bumped her. Dodie had grown irritable and selfish.

"You're over the line," she said.

"No I'm not."

"Move it," she demanded.

I pressed a crease in the center of the mattress and placed my foot defiantly at its edge. "There. Satisfied?"

Dodie eyed my foot sullenly and placed hers next to mine, close but not touching. "I'm watching you," she said.

I looked out the window. The hardwood forests of New York and Connecticut had given way to stands of stunted pine. Where earlier the edge of the blacktop had been a clean, straight hem, it now was ruffled with sand. The roof of the Pontiac sopped up the afternoon sun and squeezed it out on Dodie and me, every drop. I opened the window and let the wind finger my hair. I wondered if my cousin Nicole, who was between Dodie and me in age, would only want to be friends with Dodie this year for the sole, unfair reason that Dodie was older.

"Almost there," my father said.

The hot breeze had relaxed to something more forgiving. The clean light cast a watercolor wash over all the greens and browns and blues of the landscape. I pictured fishing with my father, raking clams, swimming until my skin flaked white with salt.

I wondered what this Mr. Metcalf would be like, if he would be strict, if he would like me, if he would think I was good enough at last to play in the talent show at St. John's. Finally I felt the air soften to that saline sweetness which cushioned the cries of the terns, which carried the tantalizing scent of something distant and wonderful, which caused the cormorants to lift off and wing slowly out to sea.

We had all summer.

2
LIGHT BREEZE

Beaufort Number 2
Wind Speed 4-7 MPH
wind felt on face, leaves rustle, wind vane moves

The driveway wasn't in yet when we arrived, and so we parked between two pine trees at the bottom of the hill and lugged everything up the path through the woods.

Piece by piece Daddy began to pry things out of the backseat so that we could finish before dark. I picked up my duffel bag along with the precious jug of fresh water for priming the pump and started up the hill.

A new layer of pine needles carpeted the ground. The fox's hole was still there. A tree was down. Weather had cured and colored the woods since I last saw them, iced them over, blown and dampened them. Spring runoff had made little gunnels in the path.

The trees were mostly pitch pines—scrub pine, Daddy called them—and oaks. Our land encompassed the highest point in the

17

township, scant as the elevation was. The deed read "fifteen and three quarters acres more or less," sizable enough to swell my father's voice with pride. When you had something so priceless, what was an acre here or there?

The property faced the pond, then ran a quarter mile along a tidal creek. This creek—navigable only at high tide—would be the source of many good times, Uncle George had assured Daddy. We would get in our boats—if he could ever talk Daddy into replacing our old "piss-bucket" rowboat—and take picnics to Pochet or to an island in Pleasant Bay, or sail the bay all the way out to the ocean. But the frontage on the pond was the real reason Uncle George had called Daddy when it came up for sale. So we could have our own place, facing his. Us on one side. Uncle George, Aunt Fanny, Digory and Nicole on the other. All summer. Close. But not touching.

The pond was about the size of a city block. Bigger. It fed us a harvest of fish, crabs, and mollusks, rocked us with the rhythm of its tides. It held us up when we learned to swim. We rowed across it, swam in it, walked around it, and watched the sunset burn down to a lavender ash on its surface.

My father emptied the car. Draped with satchels, I trailed Dodie up and over the hill to the clearing. There, a safe distance from the shore, tucked at an angle against a hummock tufted with sedge, sat the Playhouse, peaceful and undisturbed.

The Playhouse, where my parents slept, towed from Boston last summer by Grampy Grainger to augment our aging tent, had all the ingredients of a real house: shingles weathered silver by the salt air; windows with forest green trim, the many coats of paint checkered with age; a tarnished brass knocker in the shape of a tall ship sailing across the green wooden door. But all only ten by fourteen. Aunt Fanny had seen Beacon Hill bathrooms that were bigger. A shock of honeysuckle, artfully transplanted from Aunt Fanny's garden, encircled the door like frizzy hair and you had to duck to enter. The screen door had swollen in the jamb and when Daddy yanked it open there was a flutter of leaves. Embarrassed to be caught napping, the Playhouse roused itself to greet us.

"We're here," I announced unnecessarily.

Daddy worked the key into the rusted lock, jiggled it to the left and jiggled it to the right. Finally the door swung open. My mother didn't want everyone tracking in sand and so Daddy passed me his bundles and he and Dodie went back for another load. I ducked through the damp and fragrant honeysuckle. My mother edged past me, her arms stacked with blankets. She opened the pullout bed on the far wall and looked for signs of mice. Satisfied, she began to line the top drawer of the tiny bureau with newspaper.

I waited for her to tell me what to do. To the left of the door stood two chairs and a card table. Over that hung the dish cupboard. The kerosene stove snuggled against the opposite wall with two folding chairs for when Aunt Fanny and Uncle George came for a foursome of bridge. An icebox was built into the wall and it had a front door so that you could open it from inside the Playhouse, and a back door so that when you wanted to slide in a block of ice, you could do so from outside, without dripping on the floor.

A trinket pretending to be a whole cabin.

"I can manage here, Lily," my mother said. "You go help Daddy."

"I could unpack the dishes and arrange them on the shelves."

"That's all right. I'll do it."

I started back down the path. The oak leaves were the soft green of ripe pears. I heard the car door open. Daddy said something I couldn't make out. I stopped and looked back toward the Playhouse. The path was empty in each direction. Quickly I detoured along a faint trail that fell away down the slope toward the pond. Not far from the main path, underbrush concealed the massive base of an oak from which three trunks grew like three notes of a chord. I had discovered it one day last summer when standing-up-to-Uncle-George was the subject of a heated disagreement between my parents. From this outpost I could listen at a nosy but discreet distance. It was a black oak. Daddy believed that eventually our forest would go entirely to oak. In the old days Cape Cod timber had been cleared first for farming, later to supply soda ash for the Sandwich Glass Works. When the settlers found out how little would grow in the poor soil and the glassworks finally closed, the pitch pines were the first to come back, earning themselves the nickname "pioneers." But oaks gradually infiltrated. They had one big advantage: their seedlings could flourish even in the shade of the parent tree. It would take generations, but eventually this one trait would give them the upper hand over other species. I named mine Triple Tree.

I couldn't say why I hadn't told Dodie. I probably worried that once she knew about it, it wouldn't be mine anymore. "It'll be *ours*," she would say. But I had a feeling "ours" would mean more hers than mine. Now my feet found the footholds they had learned by heart and carried me up into the branches.

I slid my hand over the bark. "I'm back," I whispered.

And the tree, crusty as bread from Grammy Grainger's oven, returned the pressure of my hand. It reassured me that everything would work out. Our cottage would get built and after that my parents could stop worrying. The whole summer stretched before me. Here I was, safely out of reach of the communists, the Pope and the Garden State Parkway. Most of all, I wanted to deserve these blessings. I was willing to work hard to get into the talent show. (That would get my cousin Nicole's attention.) But I also had an inkling that humility was supposed to be a virtue. And so I amended my prayer, if that's what it was, to make me deserving, but not to know it.

Then, before I was missed, I picked my way back to the path and on down to the car.

Daddy and Dodie were still sorting gear. He placed in my arms a box of pots and pans, utensils and extra dishes. Again and again Dodie and I trudged up the hill with all our belongings gripped in a fist, wedged under an arm, balanced against a hip, cradled on a shoulder, dangled from an elbow. The pine needles made a fat cushion under my feet. I wanted to take off my shoes and feel the sand between my toes. It would take a few days for calluses to form. But before long the soles of my feet would grow so tough, I could step on pinecones sharp as broken glass without noticing. Like the Wampanoags, a local Indian tribe, I'd be able to find the path by feel alone. I would learn which plants were edible, to Dodie and Nicole's astonishment. I would feel like a creature sprung from the woods themselves.

I carried cots to the knoll where the tent would go. I put my father's typewriter and my mother's sewing basket in the Playhouse. We had stopped on Route 6 for a block of ice, which Dodie and I carried up between us in the dishpan. Finally all that was left was my cello, and Daddy said I should leave it in the car until morning, when I could put it in the tent, our large army surplus tent big enough for me to practice in, sitting on my cot with a block of wood on the floor to keep my sharp endpin from poking a hole in the canvas.

It was dusk before Dodie and I could take the path down to the pond. Seaweed, washed ashore by winter tides, bearded the beach. Eelgrass grew like stubble along the perimeter. Apart from Uncle George's, the only other houses on the pond belonged to year 'round people who kept to themselves. There was plenty to keep us busy without ever leaving our own kingdom of fifteen and three quarters acres more or less— although I suspected my mother, with just a little encouragement, might have liked to make a friend or two.

The pond was just large enough to water ski in a tight circle behind Uncle George's new speedboat. And it was just small enough to shout across. Essential, because we didn't have anything so extravagant as a telephone. Dodie climbed a lichen-covered boulder on the beach, cupped her hands to her mouth and bellowed, "Nicole!"

I could see a lamp burning at Uncle George's, indicating they had arrived from Boston ahead of us.

"Nicole!" She drew out the "o" until it trailed off and she sounded like she was falling down a well. The sun was setting behind the pines on the far shore; a wisp of breeze crinkled the flat surface of the water and carried the sound of her voice into the purple sky.

We waited.

"Let me," I said, and I started to step up onto the rock.

Dodie put out an arm barring my way. "You can call tomorrow." Just as she drew a deep breath to call again, we spotted movement in the trees. A figure tumbled down the hill and raced to the end of my uncle's wharf.

"See....you....tomorrow," slid across the still surface of the pond.

Candlelight already flickered in the Playhouse window when we ascended the hill. We heard my parents' voices.

"...can wait 'til morning to prime the pump. No sense fighting with it in the dark," said my father.

We went inside. They were sitting at the table. "We saw Nicole," said Dodie.

"We'll have to do something about breakfast," said my mother.

My father was trimming the wick on the lamp. "Fanny will feed us. She'd be glad to."

"Nicole said she'd see us tomorrow," I said, eager to put a plan into place.

My mother barely glanced at me. "Ellis' Market opens early. We could drive into town for groceries first thing."

Daddy frowned. My mother could be counted on to resist

the attraction, strong as a magnet, Uncle George exerted on the rest of us.

"Can't George wait one day?" she said.

One breakfast—a simple bowl of cereal would have done nicely—had gotten complicated. Daddy lit the lamp and blew out the candle.

"Have it your way, Lydia," he sighed. I watched the kerosene flame light his face. He seemed to be evaluating two tastes, both bitter. Then he said, "But you know, it's my brother you're talking about."

One day last summer Uncle George had announced he was tired of acting the host, providing the food and drinks all the time and he'd be over for a lobster dinner. He showed up and sat there until my father poured him a glass of Canadian Club and made a pot of corn chowder. And then Uncle George left without eating it, saying if he'd wanted corn chowder, he could have made it himself.

The flame smoked. Daddy trimmed the wick. "Lydia, it's late."

But my mother didn't want to fight after all. "Fine. We'll go to George's."

Daddy put away the matches. "Look. George may be a louse. Nobody says otherwise. But I'm not automatically guilty by association, Lydia." He stood up. "Shall we get the tent set up?" he said to me.

"What does that mean?" asked my mother.

"Lydia," he despaired. "I've been driving all day. Can we worry about it tomorrow? I'll go to Ellis' in the morning. Just make a list."

"No. We'll go to George's."

"No. It's settled."

He walked us up the short path to the knoll. It was cooling off. I watched the familiar hiccup in his gait as his lame left leg swung out, thrust forward, took his weight, and passed it quickly over to his muscular right leg. He was strong and could walk as long and as far as anyone. But his childhood polio had prevented him from running or dancing or playing a sport. Uncle George had been the athlete. That made him the winner, by default. But he didn't seem to know it. He made everything a competition. Daddy said that's why he married Aunt Fanny. He wanted a wife as smart, as educated, as blue-blooded as my mother. A shy beauty to inspire the respect of more cultured men than he. I think what made my mother the maddest was not that Uncle George was a louse (I filed that word carefully away for future use) but that he got away with it.

Dodie and I cleared the ground of twigs and pinecones. Then we unrolled the large square canvas. Daddy got the poles ready. It was a big tent. In the beginning all four of us slept there, four cots all in a row, no extra inches anywhere to walk around. Then Grampy Grainger took the Playhouse in payment for moving a piano to Brockton. He and Uncle George and Daddy dragged it out to the Cape behind Grampy Grainger's truck (slow as a horseshoe crab, six gears operated by two big iron levers that disappeared into a hole in the floor), carried it in pieces through the woods, and put it all together again. At first I thought the Playhouse was meant for Dodie and me. It would have been just our size. But Daddy told me that Dodie and I got to have the tent all to ourselves. He put it that way, to make it sound like a special treat. And so I tried to think about how roomy it would be, instead of how cozy it had been before, when my parents put us on notice every night that we had better not wake them up too early, and I would lie awake mornings listening to their dream-busy breathing. Dodie and I did our best not to complain. Uncle George always said there were two kinds of people in the world: those who get ulcers and those who give them to other people. I didn't have to be told which it was better to be. Complainers—clearly—were ulcer-givers. Dodie and I would strive to be ulcer-getters. Anyway,

Daddy said the tent had kept our country's fighting men dry under the worst conditions possible, and so it would surely do the job for two lucky girls under the starry Atlantic sky.

He set up the center pole and fitted the spokes into the corners. He unfurled the large awning, tied one corner to a pine tree to which, two years ago, he had nailed a mirror and a tiny shelf for his shaving things. The lichen-covered shelf was still in place. He got the cots opened up, and Dodie and I piled them with sheets, blankets and quilts.

"There. You'll be plenty warm."

"Couldn't you sleep here with us, Daddy?" I asked, even though I knew the answer.

"No, Lily. We'll be in the Playhouse."

"But what if something happened," I pressed. "You wouldn't hear us."

"Of course we would. Besides, it's only for this summer. By next year we'll have the new house. Now go to sleep."

"Maybe Dodie and I could sleep in the Playhouse. We wouldn't take up any room, would we Dodie?"

"Lily." Meaning, that's-the-end-of-it. He gave the center pole a tug and, satisfied that it was secure, he kissed us goodnight and tied the flap closed behind him.

I listened until I thought I could hear the Playhouse door swing to. "Dodie?" I waited. No answer. "Dodie?"

"What?"

"Are you asleep?"

"What do you think?"

"You want to move our cots together?"

"If you'll scratch my arms."

"I'll scratch yours if you'll scratch mine," I negotiated.

"You do me first."

"All right," I acquiesced. "But I'm going to keep count tonight." I swung my feet to the chilly floor, already gritty with sand, and shoved my cot to the other side of the tent, next to hers. I brushed the sand from my feet and huddled back under the covers. Dodie stuck one arm, sleeve pulled up, across my stomach. I began to scratch lightly, almost a tickle, the way she liked it. Up, down, three, four. Up, down, seven, eight, to fifty. Then the other arm. I could feel the hairs prickle with cool air as I pushed my sleeve up and stretched my arm to Dodie. One, two…. We were really here. I began to warm up against the taut canvas of my cot, safe under the slack canopy of the tent. "Lighter," I asked. Up, down, five, six….

Next I knew it was morning.

3

GENTLE BREEZE

Beaufort Number 3
Wind Speed 8-12 MPH
leaves and small twigs in constant motion; wind extends light flag

The morning air was luffing the tent walls, drawing the canvas gently in and releasing it again, like the idle propulsions of a jellyfish moving through calm water. A faint, sticky odor of sap and the rotting musky scent of low-tide decay drifted in on the breeze. I could hear the soft wooden clunking of halyards against a mast and the water drowsily slapping the bulkhead of a moored sailboat. A bobwhite whistled. Two notes ending with a question mark.

From the direction of the Playhouse came the screech of metal on metal, someone—it would only be Daddy—rapidly working the pump handle. It stopped and I heard a gurgle. He would be pouring fresh water down the wellhead. Then the pumping began again in quick jerks. There was a knack to it and so he always did it himself. Twice he paused, added more water and resumed pumping. The hollow screech drew down to a sucking sound. The pumping slowed; the strokes lengthened. There was a sputter, and finally the noise of a stream spewing from the spout and splattering onto the ground.

Dodie stirred. "What time is it?"

"I'm not sure. Eight?" I stretched. "We should get up."

She burrowed into her blankets. My mother, who as a new parent had diligently sought the advice of experts, once reported the unlikely theory that children—contrary to popular misconception—did not grow gradually, a little bit at a time, but in spurts, overnight. Dodie took that to mean it was important never to get up too early. You could stunt your growth.

I moved my feet to a cool section of the sheet and measured myself against the length of the cot. In a month I would turn twelve, but I had no clear idea of what this would mean beyond having to pay full price at the movies. My hope was that I would wake up on my birthday and discover that I was now strong, smart and funny, but I was in the dark as to how to lay the groundwork for such a transformation. In the meantime the Cape's every nuance was a hone on which to sharpen my senses. I could tell time by the light: the pink luster of morning, diamond hard noon, amethyst evenings. I knew the temperature by sound and by feel: the hot dry ratchet of grasshoppers, low pressures that lifted the hairs on my arm, those moody overcast days with air as smooth and chill as pencil lead. In every sound and smell I dared find happiness, as if happiness were as prevalent as the taste of salt.

At the risk of stunting her growth, I shook Dodie's cot. "Daddy's up already. We should help him put the boat in."

She sat up with a jerk. "What time is it?"

"I don't know. Eight maybe."

She threw the covers back and reached for her clothes. "You coming or not?"

It was early afternoon before we had finished oatmeal from

Ellis' Market, I had done my practicing and my mother was seated in the stern of the Clamshell (a bit tippy, but no Piss-Bucket, no matter what Uncle George said) with her score to the Beethoven violin sonatas tucked under her arm. Dodie pushed off and we each took an oar. I dipped mine cleanly into the khaki water to match her steady strokes. The day was clear and calm. A marsh hawk checked our progress from the top branch of a pine on the southern shore. Uncle George's mooring was empty. He'd be out for a spin already. Uncle George may have been a thorn in my mother's side, yet he and Aunt Fanny and Nicole were the hub around which our summer turned. If a day went by without seeing one of them, it was a day that lacked for something. We may have arrived. We may even have unpacked. But until we had set foot across the pond, we weren't really *there*.

Nicole was standing in the water up to her ankles waiting for us when we scraped bottom on the beach.

"Hi, Aunt Lydia!" She reached into the bow for the anchor and drove it into the sand. Her every move was swift and decisive, but the tiniest bit uncoordinated, so that she reminded me of a marionette. Not quite in charge of all her extremities. She excelled at math, never read a book for pleasure and followed every utterance with a startled silver-blue stare, like a landed codfish weighing its options. Wisps of sun-soaked blond curls escaped from the rubber band that holstered her ponytail. She glowed, iridescent-eyed and haloed.

My mother, dungarees rolled to her shins, stepped out of the Clamshell, careful not to get her music wet. "You've grown!" she said to Nicole. Brightly, even though I knew that of all the George Graingers, Aunt Fanny was the only one she really felt related to. "Is your mother home?"

"She's been waiting for you all morning."

Nicole stood first on one bare foot, then on the other until my mother was partway up the hill, safely out of earshot. Then she turned her attention to Dodie. "So what took you so long? Fartface here slow you down?" Nicole may have been good at math, but cuss words were her specialty. "Come on, we've got stuff to do."

She led us to the rear of the boathouse, where a freshwater spring bubbled from a pipe in the hill. An old Wampanoag trail ended here according to Aunt Fanny, who found amazement in unexpected places. She maintained that the trail crossed the entire width of the Cape all the way from Brewster, and Indians had used it as a route from Massachusetts Bay to the Outer Shore. She had an aerial photograph and had traced a zigzag line for me with her prematurely arthritic forefinger. "Admittedly it's faint," she said. I couldn't make out anything at all but pretended I could because the trail and the spring both seemed to please her so. "Lourdes has nothing on us," she said conspiratorially, as if letting me in on a very fine secret.

The water wandered around and under the boathouse to the beach, where it made foot-numbing rivulets through the sand. It was sweet, and cold enough to make your temples hurt on the hottest days.

Nicole squatted like a frog, twisted her mouth up under the spout, and gulped. Wet-faced and self-assured, she stood up and pushed Dodie toward the pipe.

"Drink," she commanded.

Dodie swung her neckerchief to the back, knelt and drank. Dainty little quaffs, like a fawn. Tidy and obedient. Starting off on the right foot. When she was through, she lay back against the bank. "What'll we do now?"

"My turn," I said.

Nicole was redoing her ponytail.

"My turn for a drink of water," I repeated.

"Sure. Go ahead." She snapped the elastic band into place.

I straddled the pipe and cupped my hands underneath. Nicole dipped her face close to mine. "It's not *waughter*," she corrected me, concentrating the word in the front of her mouth like a wad of chewing tobacco. She sounded like one of those union organizers for the dockworkers. She poked me with an outstretched finger to indicate this information merited my close attention. "It's *wahtah*." She straightened up with satisfaction. Her ponytail quivered. The approved pronunciation. Evidence that her Boston citizenship was a rare and exclusive accomplishment.

By Nicole's geography the United States of America consisted of Cape Cod, Boston and the rest of New England (except of course Connecticut, obviously a New York appendage) plus a few unimportant but necessary outposts like the Empire State Building and Washington, DC. She had a cat named Thoreau and had never left the state. I was separated from her once and for all by my accent. When I opened my mouth to speak she smelled New Jersey: salami from Newark's Italian neighborhoods, kreplach and garlic pickles from the Oranges. I could change how I dressed, how I combed my hair, I could cultivate a pout or a slouch, but try as I might I could not rinse New Jersey from my speech.

I wiped my mouth.

"Good," she said as if I had expressed a willingness to comply even though I hadn't said a word, "Because we have to choose a meeting place."

"Where?" Dodie pushed her glasses up her nose and did a handstand—pale, white legs scissored smoothly into the air—against the steep bank. She floated for a moment and then let her arms collapse. She finished on her back, feet uphill, head down, glasses crooked.

"Someplace where Digory can't get us," said Nicole. For as hateful as Nicole's older brother was, he still provided us this essential service: we spent the summer avoiding him.

"How about the pump-house?" I offered up my best suggestion, out to demonstrate how much I had matured in one year, how worthy of Nicole's friendship I had become. Despite diction.

She rejected the pump-house. Too easy for Digory to stumble onto us.

"Where is he anyway?" asked Dodie. Keeping track of him was a reflex, like looking both ways before crossing the street.

"Applying for a job at Livingstone's."

"Digory is going to *work*?" I said. I was in Advanced English and had only just learned the meaning of oxymoron. But Nicole only nodded, apparently having had more time than I to get used to the idea.

Dodie suggested the old tennis court.

"Too near the road." Nicole flopped to the ground, rested her head against Dodie's shoulder, and put her feet up too. They were quiet for a while, thinking. Twins. Dodie was born in Boston and lived there two whole years before my parents moved to New Jersey. When Dodie pronounced *water*, she sounded like a Minuteman. Pride of the nation. I was the only one completely from New Jersey. Every inch. Nicole wasn't a Cape Codder either, to be precise. The canal, built between 1909 and 1914, severed the Cape from the mainland shortening the trip for ships going north or south. People who lived in Plymouth or Scituate or Boston might think of themselves as Cape Codders, but a purist would know they were giving themselves airs. A stickler could even cast doubt on the pedigrees of Falmouth and Hyannis. They weren't the *true* Cape: the fishing villages of Truro and Wellfleet, or Chatham with its whaling history.

But Nicole was untroubled by petty distinctions. She began to hum, a contented little monotone. A satisfying solution was bound to turn up for a fully vested daughter such as herself, flanked by two eager and devoted handmaidens.

I leaned against the boathouse, two New Jersey feet flatly on the ground. Four symmetrical Yankee feet nestled side by side among the Queen Anne's Lace on the bank. "I know a place," I said finally.

Nicole looked at me. "Well?"

Dodie looked at me.

"It's a tree."

"A tree?" They exchanged skeptical glances.

"It's sort of a triple tree," I went on, wishing I would stop. "It's got three trunks." For some reason I couldn't clamp my mouth shut. "We could each have one," I finished.

"So where is this tree?"

"Across the pond."

"Where?" Nicole pressed.

"Back from the shore." Vague, in case it wasn't too late to recant. "You can't see it from here."

Nicole pondered this. "Mm. That could work," she mused. Two feet came to the ground. Then the other two. Two faces turned right side up, pointed expectantly at me. "That could work very well." She was gaining momentum. "Let's see. Triple Tree. I like that. I know. We'll call it Secret Hideout In Triple Tree. SHITT, for short."

"How come I've never seen this tree?" said Dodie.

"It's there," I said.

"You take us to it tomorrow," said Nicole.

Transaction complete. Everything settled.

"Right now we'll do the initiation," she went on. "You'll have to be a member."

"Member of what?"

She pushed me to my knees and pointed to a spot on the ground. "Dodie, you stand there." Then she faced the spring and began to gesture authoritatively.

"What about Dodie? Doesn't she have to kneel?"

"She's *already* a member," she said, clearly tired of explaining the obvious.

33

I looked into Dodie's face, pleased at this confirmation we would be *members* of something. An official threesome.

"Here," Dodie said. She untied her neckerchief. Until now this had been Nicole's show. "You need this." She tied it around my waist. I could tell she was making things up as she went along.

"Do you promise to uphold all the rules of the club in absolute secrecy, forever, so long as you live?" continued Nicole.

"I do," I said ardently. "What are the rules?"

"To uphold the rules," said Nicole brusquely.

"But...."

"*Do* you?" She was beginning to sound exasperated. "Usually you have to take off all your clothes. 'You take off all your clothes and swear naked under a knife....'" she intoned like an incantation. "But we can skip that part today," she continued, businesslike. "So swear."

"Swear what?" I asked, imagining it necessary to be precise.

"I do!"

"I do." Just then I heard an outboard motor coming up the creek. "I do," I repeated, but Nicole had turned toward the sound. When it entered the pond, Uncle George's boat tore into high gear and sped toward the dock. His new boat. His big boat with 40-horse power. So everyone could hear him coming.

"OK, that's it." She stomped one foot in the wet sand, flipped her curls at us and darted up the hill, leaving a deep footprint that was already filling with water from the spring. Dodie and I leapt to follow. We traversed the slope to the steps. When we neared the house, the engine cut out abruptly. In the silence that followed I could hear music. Piano arpeggios. The clip-clop of violin notes earnestly trotting to keep up.

Nicole gestured for us to be quiet and waved us over to the stone chimney at one end of the cabin, which she climbed quickly and effortlessly. She managed to be, not graceful, but practiced. Habitual, even. Again her hand flapped for us to follow. Dodie and I climbed more slowly, choosing our hand-holds and using the friction of our bare feet. We hoisted ourselves up onto the roof.

Nicole crouched low and eyed us to do the same. She put an urgent finger to her lips and took up a position where she could observe the steps to the pond.

I sat down against the chimney, hands behind my head. The shingles were warm, a radiant, satisfied temperature. I basked. The three of us, members at last of the same genus and phylum. Even if it meant sharing my tree.

Aunt Fanny and my mother were playing Beethoven. The piano part progressed from bar to bar, steady and sure. Loud notes loud. Soft notes soft. Fast notes evenly spaced. All the right sharps and flats.

The violin stuttered along behind, timid but persistent. There wasn't any piece of music Aunt Fanny wouldn't under-take to learn. She would potter away at it hour after hour, trans-ported, bow zigging and zagging like the rickrack that trimmed her apron. Uncle George bought her an expensive instrument. To soften the assault to his ears, he said. To give her a fighting chance at making it sound like a violin at all. But he said later that he should have known all along Stradivarius was no match for Aunt Fanny.

It wasn't really a Stradivarius.

The violin faltered. My mother paused while Aunt Fanny's fingers scurried to catch up.

Dodie crawled over to me and sat down. We heard Uncle George coming up the hill talking animatedly. Right behind him Gloria mounted the steps holding up the hem of her skirt. Gloria, his right hand at the printing company. They were laughing.

I started to wave, but Nicole gave me a menacing glare. "Don't let them see us," she hissed.

She had a point. Uncle George wouldn't like us fooling

around on his roof. For him, children—even if unseen and unheard—were a nuisance. All except for Nicole, who had naturally curly golden hair like a halo and could ask him for anything.

They were almost up to the house.

Gloria's silvery laugh rang all the notes of the scale, like progressively sized bells. "I've got to hand it to you, George. He had it coming." She had tried to downplay her Boston accent ever since her husband, the Irishman, lost his job and left her with newborn twins. That was eleven years ago. (The twins, who spent summers with their father, were my age.) She said good riddance, even though she didn't know where their next meal was coming from. She took diction lessons as part of a program to better herself. To go far in life, she said, you had to enunciate. But she had only gone as far as landing a job at Uncle George's printing company, where profits immediately climbed. Everyone knew he couldn't run the business without her.

I peeked in time to see them clear the top step and "Hoohoo" through the window.

"OK ladies," Uncle George hollered. "Time for some *real* music."

The door slammed. The music stopped.

"Lydia!"

"Hello George. We were just finishing," said my mother, even though they were in the middle of the piece. Some piano keys banged as if the music had fallen. Then her voice brightened. "Gloria. I didn't know you were down this week." She liked Gloria. Both my parents did. "She's doing a marvelous job of raising those twins," my father said once in contradiction to BerthaMelrose's charge, among other things, that Gloria was over-sexed. Gloria was unlike anyone else we knew. For one thing, she *dressed*. Her clothes were practically costumes: all black, or a paint box of primary colors. Dry Clean Only. With jewelry for each outfit. My mother laughed at Gloria's jokes, tried to stick up for Gloria when people called her a buttinsky or a flirt. "She's only trying to get by, just like the rest of us," my mother would say. "Gloria's not so bad," or "Maybe we don't know the whole story."

Gloria was practically part of the family.

And she was the only one who could get away with chewing out Uncle George, which she did regularly over the way he treated Aunt Fanny.

"Just for the day," said Gloria. "But don't stop on our account. I love to hear you play."

"I should be getting back."

"So Weston can put you to work?" Uncle George said. "Have a cup of coffee. Fanny, put on some coffee. I want Lydia to hear my new record."

"Let me do it, Fanny," said Gloria. "It won't take a minute."

"You must have got in pretty late," said Uncle George. "Fanny was hoping you'd come by for breakfast. Weren't you, Fanny?"

Aunt Fanny murmured something indistinct, and I heard the soft screech of a rag wiping rosin from violin strings.

"Even if she's too polite to say so." Uncle George had a way of phrasing things so that you couldn't tell if it was a compliment or a complaint.

The clatter of cups came from the kitchen.

Nicole frowned, listening. She had forgotten about Dodie and me.

"George told me about your plans for the new cottage," said Gloria over the sound of running water.

"We have to see what we can afford," said my mother.

"It's good of George to keep Gloria up to date," said Aunt Fanny, who sometimes failed to follow the conversation.

Uncle George said, "I'll ignore that, Fanny."

"Did I say something wrong?" said Aunt Fanny with an innocence which, except that it came from Aunt Fanny herself, I would have said verged on sarcasm.

"I thought Weston said he's starting construction," said Uncle George, true to his word about ignoring Aunt Fanny.

"Yes," said my mother once it became clear that Uncle George was addressing her.

"He'll have to put the driveway in first," Uncle George speculated, suddenly engrossed in my father's plans, giving the matter his full attention. "Tell him to watch out for that patch of soft sand halfway up the hill. He'll have to go around that. If he wants me to...."

"I'm sure he has it in hand."

"Oh yes, I'm sure he does," he said way too agreeably. What he really meant was, *No one can tell Weston his business.*

My foot had fallen asleep. I tried to change position, but Nicole shushed me again.

"Coffee!" said Gloria.

"I really must...."

"Put your music down, Lydia. You can't turn down a cup of Gloria's coffee. It's made now. Gloria, talk to Lydia."

"In a minute, George. There must be cookies here somewhere."

"In Fanny's cupboard? Asparagus and lima beans. Tell me if I'm wrong."

"I don't want coffee. I'd prefer tea," said Aunt Fanny.

"That's it, Fanny. Be particular," said Uncle George. "Well, speak up. Everyone's listening now." No one spoke. "Now can I play my record? What about it, Fanny, is the 1812 Overture beneath you?" Uncle George could leave a person dangling between two subjects, one as disconcerting as the other.

"You are pushing it, George," said Gloria as close as anyone ever dared come to criticizing him.

I readied myself for the tirade to follow, but Uncle George only replied, "Ah, here it is. Listen to this. Muskets from West Point. Authentic! Stereophonic sound. I guarantee you haven't heard anything like this." Once again all enthusiasm, pitching his idea of a good classical barnstormer.

"I don't have anything against Gloria's coffee," said Aunt Fanny.

"That's OK, Fanny. I'll put the kettle on," said Gloria.

"Damn it, Fanny," said Uncle George, holding fast to the spotlight.

I felt Nicole move next to me. She wiped her face on her sleeve. I leaned toward her. For a minute I thought she was crying, but just then the 1812 Overture blasted from the hi-fi directly under me, sudden as shrapnel. I jumped a foot. So did Dodie and Nicole. Three girls hit the roof with three loud thumps. Nicole was on her feet in a flash. Then Dodie. I knew immediately we had given ourselves away.

"What was that?" shouted Uncle George over the music. Then he must have grabbed the needle, because there was horrible noise as it ripped across the record. Followed by silence. A big loud silence.

"Damn," bellowed Uncle George.

By the time I struggled to my feet, Nicole and Dodie were down the chimney. They gained the woods before Uncle George banged out of the door.

"So! It's you!" The moment I hit the ground he had me by the wrist. Tight.

My mother appeared at the door with her music under her arm. "I'm sorry, George. We were just going." She looked at me as if I had slammed the piano lid on her fingers.

I knew Uncle George had a temper; that came as no surprise. I knew he had claws sharp as fishhooks. But I usually escaped his notice. Dodie said later that he was just showing off for Gloria. But something about my mother's being there made it worse. I knew it immediately. She looked from me to Uncle George and back to me again.

"Well, no harm done." Uncle George released me.

"All the same," said my mother.

"No, really." They went back and forth, with an odd formality, observing some protocol unknown to me. Uncle George seemed to be waiting for her to say something.

But she didn't.

At last he said, "Don't pay any attention to me. Your company means a lot to Fanny."

A small wind sighed through the pine trees and played over my mother's carefully composed features, lifting her loose hair. She looked down.

"I love your shells, Fanny," said Gloria from inside. "George, forget about the girls. See what Fanny's collected."

"I have to go now." My mother stepped past Uncle George and me. "Good-bye Fanny," she called. Then she started down the steps toward the beach.

"Tell Wes I'll be over to see the plans," Uncle George called after her. "First thing."

I followed her.

"What was she doing up there anyway?" I heard him say to Aunt Fanny. "She breaks her neck, then where will I be? And my damn record's ruined."

My mother traversed the hill to the beach. Dodie and Nicole were nowhere to be seen. "Forget about the girls," Gloria had said. Girls, *plural*. Gloria knew it hadn't been my fault alone. I trailed my mother past Aunt Fanny's dubious Indian trail, past the spring running clear and cold. At water's edge four black snails left furrows in the wet sand, a laborious effort to keep pace with the outgoing tide. My mother lifted the anchor by its rope and let it fall into the bottom of the boat. I climbed into the stern. She pushed off, took both oars and began to row toward home.

A year earlier we went to an auction in Chatham and my mother placed the winning bid (two dollars) on a cardboard box labeled "miscellaneous items." It was a frivolous thing to do and made her almost giddy. The miscellaneous items turned out to be a pencil sharpener, some gummed labels, a ball of twine, a large brass key and a platter, long and slender like the Cape itself, real porcelain with an unidentifiable fish painted on it. It wasn't even chipped and my mother heralded it as a Significant Find. She said she'd put it on the mantle over the fireplace when our house was done. She said we may not be able to afford a lobster dinner, but we had the platter to put it on.

I didn't know why I remembered that now, except that it seemed so long ago. I knew she thought I had proved her point about Uncle George. We weren't welcome, or at least he never wanted it forgotten that it was his to say if we were or weren't. And I had given him just the opening he needed to spell it out. W-E-R-E-N-apostrophe-T.

When we got back to our side of the pond, she went to the Playhouse. Daddy was typing in the woods. Dodie's scarf was still around my waist. I followed the path to the knoll, then the fainter path to my tree. It was waiting. A trickle of fresh sap bled from a knothole. I took a sharp branch, scratched the inside of my hand and pressed it to the bubble that had formed. Making us blood brothers. I climbed into Triple Tree, now its official name, and found a place on my favorite branch. I put my sticky hands around its trunk, lay my cheek against the crusted bark, and tried to explain that I had to share it now.

4

MODERATE BREEZE

Beaufort Number 4
Wind Speed 13-18-MPH
wind raises dust and loose paper, small branches move

y grandfather Tucker's earliest known ancestor, Winthrop Melrose, crossed the Atlantic in 1640, twenty years too late for the family to lay claim to a Mayflower pedigree, although BerthaMelrose was at times known to hedge. By 1765 Winthrop's descendants, scattered all the way from Lynn, Massachusetts to Boothbay, Maine, had had plenty of time to cultivate an independent streak.

In 1765 Archibald Grainger, on the other hand, was a newly arrived colonist. A simple workingman, he had little knowledge of high-minded notions such as Liberty and Equality and even less interest in the trouble brewing over the Stamp Act. He considered the renegades who called themselves Patriots a threat to the peace and stability he was working hard to find. For him the King stood for precious order.

And so Melrose and Grainger, Patriot and Loyalist-by-default, found themselves on opposing sides of the Revolution. Persona non grata by the time the smoke cleared, Archibald fled to Nova Scotia, where subsequent Graingers had little material wealth, but contented themselves with the good opinion of their God-fearing neighbors and enough root vegetables to share with those less fortunate than themselves. They paid little attention to the world beyond their rocky maritime province. Grampy was working as a blacksmith when he met Grammy, who impressed him with her gracefully stockinged ankle if not her Christian zeal. But despite Grammy's religious fervor, God broke their hearts twice. After burying two small children in the Acaciaville cemetery, they put their savings into a new start on ten acres south of Boston—from whence their Loyalist ancestors had once fled—and brought two boys successfully to adulthood. Weston, the intelligent one. And George, the crafty one.

Like spoils of that long ago war, my sister Dodie and I had been divvied up early on between the two families. Possessed of good taste and breeding without ever being showy, a bit highstrung and delicate, firmly educated: these were the avowed Melrose characteristics for which Dodie—it was agreed—showed natural affinity. Graingers occupied a different domain. They were robust, adaptive, and practical, tempered by the rigors of shoeing oxen and eking out a living from the stingy Nova Scotia soil. They were handsome like my father and had a streak of devilry like Uncle George, the result of too many generations of piety, too seriously served up. My rugged constitution placed me in the Grainger camp. That, and the fact that it was the only one left.

Daddy inherited Grampy Grainger's conviction that music embodied a transforming magic. But he had never been able to tap into that magic with his own attempts at learning an instrument. Grammy Grainger considered any music other than church music suspect, and certainly not a profession. Hymns were well and good, but music was not the arena in which she intended my father to excel. He was to be the family's first College Graduate, not a journeyman musician. Whatever the reason, Daddy's talent on the piano, to his extreme disappointment, never rose above plodding.

The cello was his favorite instrument. He said I had the hands of a cellist, which pleased me. It made me feel suitable. Like a photograph suitable for framing or wine suitable for drinking. I imagined my father saying to a new acquaintance, "Lily is my daughter. She has the hands of a cellist," implying that this alone would be enough to invoke their good opinion.

But no matter how much he liked the cello, he believed all instruction began with the piano. In an orderly universe arithmetic came before algebra, you couldn't be a scholar without Latin, and the keyboard formed the basis of every musical education.

And so when I was old enough to reach the pedals, he asked my mother to teach me the piano. My mother didn't view music as a transforming experience so much as a reliable friend. One that welcomed—and rewarded—her efforts. She had majored in music in college and was heartened to discover there was something she was good at. She thought the music of the masters might explain something about the world she struggled otherwise unsuccessfully to understand. She didn't mind long hours of solitary practice. In fact she found it soothing. Now and then she caught glimpses of what she thought might be greatness in the famous composers and she hungered after more such glimpses, but had been unable dependably to reproduce them. She was skilled, but still striving for an elusive brilliance.

When my father put her to work as my piano instructor, she balked. It was hard enough for her to find thirty minutes in a day for her *own* respite at the piano. And she said it never worked when parents tried to teach their own children. She'd rather hire Miss Zarzeszna, who was known to be good with five-year-olds. But Daddy said why give the job to just anybody down the street when the best pianist in the whole state lived here, right under our own roof.

At first I liked having my mother all to myself for that half hour. Despite her misgivings she sat gamely on the bench next to me and showed me the fingerings, urged me on, willed me to find the correct notes. One at a time at first. But as I progressed, the notes came in threes and fours and worse. Handfuls of notes. She moved to a chair next to the piano bench as I struggled to translate the black specks and blobs on the page into commands, delivered to my fingers before they hesitated, stumbled, or fell on the wrong keys altogether.

She would listen, intent with purpose at first, then taut with anticipation of the wrong notes she came to expect, finally rigid with frustration. Within a year my lessons had become sporadic, then deteriorated into a few words of instruction shouted from the kitchen while she boiled potatoes or scraped carrots. We continued like that until at last, one Friday night after I turned eight, my father brought home a half-size cello and told me I'd meet my new teacher in the morning.

And so Joseph Furia rescued my mother.

From the start I liked the cello better. For one thing there was only one staff to read, not two. And only one note at a time on that staff. (Appallingly, chords were to come later.)

Mr. Furia was a squat man with a small mustache and heavy eyebrows. Where any normal person would have hair, he was as bald and shiny as an eel. Instead his hairs grew, dark and curly and thick as kelp, on the backs of his hands. In his small basement studio he planted himself behind his cello—a black one all nicked and scarred—and attacked it with the same urgency with which some people gorged on chocolate before having to give it up for Lent. His tone was coarse, his phrases blunt. But he took my lessons seriously. I no sooner walked into the room but what he plunged into the business of building my technique as if we were in constant danger of falling behind schedule. He gave me his full attention, and soon I was able to match the slant of my fingers or the angle of my wrist to the pictures and diagrams in the yellowed method book that he periodically pointed to with the tip of his bow.

Daddy had stayed out of my piano lessons. He said that was my mother's department, even though the whole thing had been his idea. But the cello was different. Now it was his turn to pull up a chair and supervise, to my mother's relief. He was full of pointers, but they all boiled down to one principle: Repetition. Do it over and over, and eventually I'd get it. Again. And again. And again. He wasn't so interested in the subtle little habits that made practice time productive. He had more faith in total time served. An uncomplicated method and in his estimation— although it had done nothing for his own budding musicianship —universally effective.

Nobody else I knew had to spend the summer practicing an instrument, but when I asked why I had to and Dodie didn't, he answered, "Dodie is Dodie. You are you." Which, whatever it meant, sounded final to me.

"Besides," he added conspiratorially, "you have a gift."

It didn't seem right that a "gift" brought with it so much drudgery, until I realized one day that I had never heard Daddy tell Dodie *she* had a gift. Its value shot up and I rededicated myself to the task.

He said that where I had done an hour a day in winter, I could do two in summer. With a good teacher I could accomplish twice as much in half the time. He said that summer was precisely when I *had* the time to work hard, and that by doing so, maybe someday I'd get good enough to learn the crown jewel of all the cello repertoire, the Dvořák Cello Concerto.

When Daddy listened to Dvořák—Dvořák was his favorite

composer—he leaned way back in his chair and closed his eyes. Music seemed a powerful thing, to be able to take him away from his work like that.

Joseph Furia was well and good for winter, but for the strides I would be making this summer, no mere artisan would do. An outstanding teacher was needed. And so he was pleased when he found that he could place my training in the hands of Alphius Metcalf, an elderly man who came from Boston each summer and took a room at Rose Acres Cottage in Wellfleet.

My mother would drive me. Daddy had his hands full with his dissertation, the supervision of my practicing, and the house (he had hired a carpenter, but every nail he himself hammered would cut costs.)

On the day of my first lesson, we left early to allow plenty of time to get there. My mother seemed to welcome a reason to fix her hair, apply a touch of lipstick and close the Playhouse door behind her. Daddy was off to a good start on his paper; Uncle George was away. She had said nothing more about the roof incident. (Dodie saw no injustice in the fact she got off scot-free, and attributed her successful getaway to a naturally superior swiftness and cunning. I allowed her smug assessment to stand, grateful only that nothing more had come of it.)

We drove out the dirt road, turned right, skirted town and went north at the rotary. My mother wasn't a nervous driver, but a careful one, guiding the impressively wide Pontiac down narrow stretches of Route 6. She refused to hurry. She looked left and right, murmuring over what was planted in window boxes, disapproving of a new trim color, admiring a sloop anchored in Town Cove.

She exclaimed over the sweetbriars growing on (practically crushing!) a wooden fence by what was left of the Captain Ryder place. You could just make out the old foundation. She pulled to the side of the road to let an accumulation of cars pass us. One turret still stood in a curious state of good repair amidst the stone rubble.

"It was a whaling captain's mansion," my mother said, in answer to my obvious curiosity and eased the car back onto the road. She liked Cape Cod's architecture and she liked history. And she *especially* liked a house with a history.

"Whose ship was lost at sea," I said. To see if she felt like a game. To see if she had forgiven me for Uncle George's. To try to get over being nervous about meeting Mr. Metcalf.

She let her eyes swing from the fender over to me. "Off the coast of Siberia," she said, deciding to play.

"Where they had rescued a Spanish princess."

"And were...."

"Sunk by pirates!" I blurted, out of turn.

She slowed for a car in front of us to turn down Nauset Road. "I don't think they have pirates off the coast of Siberia," she said.

"Really?" I squinted at her in the glare of the windshield, unsure if I had spoiled things.

My mother accelerated again. "Oh, why not? OK. Pirates." She warmed again to the game. "And the captain's widow burned down the house, looking for the treasure she knew was hidden there."

"And she still lives in the tower," I added, trying not to skip a beat.

"Which would make her three hundred and fifty years old!" my mother scoffed. She was pretty when she laughed. There was a small chip in the center of her front tooth, which she confessed she got from habitually opening bobby pins with her teeth in spite of BerthaMelrose's warnings. It gave her smile a naughty look, like a confirmation dress with a missing button.

She slowed down, turned off Route 6 and steered up the tree-lined blacktop into Wellfleet. Low-slung clapboard buildings hugged the hill as if to avoid attracting the attention of easterlies that constantly shifted and sculpted the Truro dunes.

My mother liked Wellfleet, with its widows' walks and antique stores. She parked in front of the First Congregational, which had the only steeple clock in the world that struck ships' bells. This was according to my grandfather, Tucker, who collected clocks. My lesson was at three o'clock, which would be —I did the calculation—six bells. We were early, and so I slipped my hand into hers and we walked up Main Street. Clapboard, unlike the standard Cape Cod weathered shingle, had to be painted, which gave Wellfleet an impractical, but cared for, air. My mother stopped in front of Windward Antiques, the only building whose paint was blistered and beginning to peel.

We went inside.

Windward Antiques was chockerblock full. There were framed botanical prints, tarnished brass instruments of navigation, furniture smelling of beeswax, breakable lamps with frayed silk shades, pewter items of all kinds, a tattered lace shawl, and a mottled clock face without its case. A bell tinkled and dust motes skirmished in a beam of sunlight when I closed the door behind me. My mother stepped tentatively across the plank floor toward a porcelain figurine standing on a drop leaf table.

Something stirred behind a desk in one corner of the room, a wrinkled woman wearing sensible shoes and a fresh dusting of face powder. She made a small noise, half rattle, half purr, by way of greeting.

My mother's hand, which she had reached out to touch the figurine, hovered uncertainly, and strayed instead toward her hair. She didn't pause over the luster of old wood or run her hand across a cool porcelain surface when people were watching. It was too personal. She nodded and idly picked up an iron trivet.

"Oh look," I said. I stopped in front of a glass vase. It was blue—rich people would call it a "vahze"—and I thought I recognized the design.

She turned.

"It's just like BerthaMelrose's," I said.

Like the one my mother had found in an antique store in Montclair and intended to give my grandmother for Easter before BerthaMelrose up and left, ruined everything, and my mother blamed my father. Genuine Sandwich glass.

But at the mention of BerthaMelrose my mother said, "We should get going, Lily." A hint of impatience in her voice. The antique store had somehow ceased to be a good idea.

"Looking for anything special?" asked the old woman behind the desk.

I thought the vase might link me in a favorable way to my mother's law: Simple is good; old is better; simple and old is best. And I was about to say something along those lines when I discovered, on a shelf beneath a large gilt mirror, a fan. A fan made of ostrich feathers, stuck in a dusty pitcher. Six plumes that spilled extravagantly over the rim. I forgot about the blue vase and BerthaMelrose both. I thought it was the most lavish thing I had ever beheld. It was a musty pink, and in it I saw not merely a dress-up accessory, but—as they would say in the courts of Europe—a true accoutrement. A sort of royal scepter and magic wand, all in one. I reached for it gingerly.

"Dust catcher," said my mother from the doorway.

"Six dollars," said the woman. "It's very old."

I turned pleading eyes toward my mother.

"That's a dollar a feather," my mother said to me with an indignation intended for my ears if not the shopkeeper's.

"Please?" I begged.

But she was out the door with her purse tucked under her arm. The bell tinkled loudly behind her. I stole a look at the woman in the corner, convinced that she would be annoyed if I rang the bell again. But it couldn't be helped. "Good-bye," I mumbled, opened the door and left before she could say anything, leaving my magic wand behind, and unable to explain what had happened to the good feeling in the car.

Six immodest feathers at one troublesome dollar apiece. Even more than I wanted the fan, I wanted my mother to want me to have it.

We took my cello from the car in silence and walked the half block off Main Street. Rose Acres was an ancient-looking house so shaded by an enormous maple tree that passing through the vine-covered picket fence was like entering a cave. My mother made me shake the sand out of my shoes and tap them against the stone stoop before I entered. Inside, murmurs of conversation, like lullabies, reached us as we passed the parlor and creaked up the thinly carpeted stairs to Mr. Metcalf's room on the second floor. We didn't speak until we had gained his doorway. Mr. Metcalf was a guest, and we were guests of *his*. We came and went as if our right to be there was a tenuous one.

She knocked. The door opened and Mr. Metcalf stood smiling at me. I would find out that a smile was practically his only expression. He looked as if something had just then struck him funny. "Come in. Come *in*," he said through little gurgles. Understated little chortles on the verge of becoming full-fledged laughs.

From the cool, dark interior of the central hallway we emerged into his gabled corner room. I could think of few people as old as Alphius Metcalf. He had not missed a summer at Rose Acres since the Depression. He was tall and willow slender. His eyes were round—he had the perpetually startled look of a seagull—and each pale iris was fogged by a creamy film. Nearly everything about him was white: his skin the color of typing paper; his linen vest and trousers; the porcelain wash basin and water jug; the painted spool bed and chenille bedspread, unwrinkled and geometrically straight. His hair no doubt would have been white too, had he had any other than a few wisps in his ears. He had a long, tapered nose, the bones of which were covered so transparently that it looked as if he had barely enough skin to reach to its tip. On the far side of the room an eyelet curtain had been looped to one side of the open window, which faced the big maple outside. That tree must have been a music lover, because its branches pressed right up to the casement, clamoring to get in. The room smelled of lavender water.

"Ah, Mrs. Grainger. So nice to meet you." Mr. Metcalf bobbed and bowed to my mother. They exchanged *how-do-you-do's* and *um's* and *yes indeed's*, and I could see that, whatever she had expected, he was an improvement on it. She asked him to call her Lydia, and then she took up her position on a small wooden chair beside the bedstead. She didn't *occupy* the chair, not like someone invited to make herself comfortable. She perched on it. It wasn't just the straightness of the chair. Even in Mr. Metcalf's moon white presence, my mother remained watchful.

"And you must be Lily. My dear." Mr. Metcalf clasped his hands together as he surveyed me. "We have lots to do. *Lots* to do." He said this as if it pleased him no end, and was sure I would feel exactly the same.

I was doubtful. But there was something infectious about his optimism. And he seemed truly unaware that he was unmistakably odd.

My mother began to knit. I unpacked my cello.

"We have wonderful things to work on this summer," he continued and patted a stack of étude books on his dresser with evident glee. "There is Dotzauer and Popper. Oh, and Ševčík! We mustn't overlook our technique. Without technique, we can make no music…."

Mr. Metcalf's voice rustled on.

I liked him. He had a gentle, weightless way. It seemed a simple thing, to try to play the right notes in the right order and have him say, "Why Lily, that's fine. So fine. I can see you are going to do excellent work. Oh, this is going to be such a summer!"

He kept in constant motion, demonstrating, admonishing, encouraging, cajoling. His dry fingers curled over my right hand, correcting Mr. Furia's stiff old-fashioned position, steering and molding my fingers into a living, breathing bow grip. He observed my posture from every corner of the room. He took my head in his hands and wobbled it from side to side. "Tension banished. *Now* the music can sing. Once again." He conducted my phrases, stabbing the air with his bony knuckles, eyes lifted heavenward, and his long nose sailed past my shoulder like the prow of a ship.

"Yes, yes. Music first, my Lily. Our fingers will follow," he chuckled.

He played a Capriccio for me. The notes leapt and danced and even the curtain of his cataracts could not conceal the delight in his eyes. No tired old hack, Mr. Metcalf. He gave a *performance*. His bow flew, his fingers pumped up and down the strings, he ended with a flourish. I thought I would like making my cello sound like that, so....*Spanish*.

I broached the subject of the talent show at St. John's. The audience would cheer after a piece like that. He said maybe. Possibly. It would depend on me. We mustn't get ahead of ourselves, but he would see. He would see.

At the end of my lesson he said that each week, if I played well, he would do a trick for me. That week he asked if I had ever heard the magnificent call of the Ruby Throated Warbler.

I hadn't.

Then that *must* be today's trick. It was *such* a good one. He trilled and whistled and jiggled his Adam's apple with his fore-finger until it sounded like a whole lexicon of birds.

On the way home my mother said that music should be its own reward and, anyway, she had never heard of a Ruby Coated whatever-it-was.

But I could tell she really liked Mr. Metcalf. It was to let me know she was no pushover. And only a spoiled girl would beg for an ostrich plume fan.

5

FRESH BREEZE

Beaufort Number 5
Wind Speed 19-24 MPH
small-leaved trees begin to sway; crested wavelets form on inland
waters

All the wood for the house was on order at Nickerson Lumber, but couldn't be delivered until the driveway went in, so Daddy lost no time. Cobb's Excavation bulldozed the most direct route from the road. But the Pontiac immediately sank up to its hubcaps in the soft sand, just as Uncle George had predicted. Merrill Cobb had to come back and cut a wider curve around and over the hill. The architect's estimate had not allowed for the second driveway. It cost us double.

Once the driveway was redone, Daddy hired Brewster Concrete to pour the slab for the house. Uncle George and Digory came over to watch the truck drive in with its big revolving belly. At 15, Digory was nearly as tall as Uncle

George. He had watery eyes that darted from side to side like minnows and a ragged, high-pitched voice that sounded like he had a wad of phlegm in his windpipe. Uncle George hoped one day Digory would learn the printing business, but so far the only thing he showed any aptitude for was pinching baseball cards from Livingstone's. Trucks held his interest, though. The bigger the better. Eddie, the driver of the cement mixer, backed carefully up to the foundation which had already been leveled and framed, while Daddy and Digory stood on either side guiding him into position.

Uncle George had seen cement mixers before, and so he sat down at the picnic table where my mother was washing dishes. He unrolled the blueprint, anchoring three corners with three rocks. Recognizing an opportunity to get back in his good graces, I smoothed the last corner and placed a pair of pliers there. Dodie and Nicole were in the Playhouse wrapping each other's hair in rags to make Scarlet O'Hara ringlets. (I vowed not to submit to another haircut until mine too reached the necessary, eligible length.)

Uncle George smacked his hands together and buffed them enthusiastically against each other. "Well! Big day! Let me get a look. Mother always said I could have been an architect, but I was more of a concept man. Thank you, Lily."

I had not seen Uncle George since the day he ruined his record because we were on his roof. He was being extra jovial to show my mother he could let bygones be bygones.

"Wish Weston had used my man, though. Your guy, this Pearce fellow, he's probably perfectly good." He tapped the sand from his shiny business shoes. "It's not that...." His voice trailed off.

As mad as my mother sometimes got at my father for succumbing to Uncle George's tug of war, she knew whose side she was on. As jealous as she was that Daddy would drop everything the minute Uncle George beckoned, Uncle George couldn't get her to say a single bad thing about my father. She set the soapy dishes one by one on the table. When Uncle George paused, she replied, "I'm sure he looked into it."

"Oh, my brother dots his I's all right," he said, winking as if they were confederates, pretending they found my father mutually amusing. "So what have we here?" He bent over the blueprint, disregarding my mother's failure to wink back.

She tossed the soapy water on a spruce sapling, then pumped a pan of rinse water.

All of a sudden the cement mixer started up. Dodie and Nicole came out to watch. Little knobs of hair and rags stuck from their heads like grenades. Eddie told everyone to stand back while he got ready to pour. Then he and my father stood on either side of the chute and coaxed the elephant-colored mud out onto the ground in yielding, fat folds. Everything Eddie needed to go about his business seemed to reside in his lumpy thigh pockets, including the cigarettes which he drew from the package, hung from his lower lip, and lit, one after the other, by striking a kitchen match with his thumbnail. My father handed him tools and helped him level the cement, but Eddie did all the finish work. It had to be "just so," he said, which apparently included the ash which kept falling from his cigarette onto the soft, damp surface. Later Dodie and Nicole, finished ringlets drooping like long apple peelings, looked on as Eddie squinted at me through the smoke that curled up to his eyes and asked, "Ready, Princess?" Then he swung me off my feet and held me over his knee so that I could reach over and sink my hand into the firm, wet mud without disturbing our flawless, even foundation.

Before everyone left, Eddie lit one last match with a disinterested flick of his thumb, held it to his cigarette, and I saw Uncle George take Digory aside and overheard him say, "You can't cut corners, Dig. Uncle Wes tries to save a dime and this time there'll be hell to pay." He laced his fingers together and snapped them apart. "The first good storm, and that main beam will pull apart like toothpicks. See if I'm right."

My mother must have heard him too, because after supper she got out the blueprint while Daddy cleaned crabs on a piece of newspaper. "Aren't all main beams alike?" she asked as she poured over the drawings.

Daddy said, "Yes and no." Ours was going to be *stronger* than most. A new (and better!) design. Three two-by-sixes, side by side, bolted together clear through every eight feet. Professionally engineered.

My mother rubbed her forehead as she took this in and tried to reconcile it with the plans in front of her. "I don't think George should bring Gloria around." She was in one of those moods, finding trouble under every stone. "Fanny's not strong. It's not right."

"There's a kettle of fish we don't want to mess with," said my father.

Even though most people didn't approve of Gloria, my parents really liked her. My father thought she filled a gap that Aunt Fanny had failed in some way to close. Gloria had been the Rock of Gibraltar during Aunt Fanny's six weeks of "rest" on the locked floor of Massachusetts General a few years ago. To spare Aunt Fanny any embarrassment, no one mentioned it now; even though everyone said at the time a breakdown was nothing to be ashamed of. I was a little alarmed that my mother brought Gloria up, because there was a certain equilibrium on the other side of the pond that even I could tell was better left undisturbed.

And I liked Gloria.

"Your brother talks behind your back," she said finally, rolling up the blueprint.

"Are we back on George? I thought it was the center beam."
My father gathered up the newspaper with the discarded crab
shells. "What exactly is it? Lydia?"

"You are the *one* person who could say something."

"What have you got against George?" He wiped his hands on
a towel.

"You didn't hear him crowing about the driveway? Right, as
usual?"

At that my father grew suddenly angry. He threw the towel
down. "Lydia, what do you want? You keep at me and at me.
What is it you want? Shall we forget the house? Is that it? We'll
pay for the cement and there it can sit for all I care. Is that what
you want?"

He went in the Playhouse and came back out with the car
keys in his hand. He got in and shut the door hard. Sand spurt
from the wheels as he drove down the driveway.

———

Before everyone had left, Nicole announced that she would set
aside the following day to inspect Triple Tree. She arrived the
next morning right after breakfast. I had imagined a somewhat
dramatic unveiling, something with a certain amount of pomp.
But in the end Nicole and Dodie were preoccupied with finding
their way through the underbrush without catching poison ivy,
and they came upon my magnificent oak without much fanfare.
Nicole pronounced it satisfactory and proceeded to divvy it up.
Dodie hadn't quite got over the fact that she didn't discover it
first, but magnanimously—even risking the appearance of
correcting Nicole—proclaimed it *very good,* an opinion I knew
she would retract in a flash if she caught me gloating, which I—
with some effort—did not do. One of the three trunks shot up
quickly away from the others and then looped out forming a

good place to sit with access to higher branches. Dodie took that one because she didn't mind heights. Nicole claimed the branch that grew almost horizontally and stretched at an alarming angle toward the pond. I chose the lowest, a thick arm that hugged the hill before tilting judiciously to the sun.

Nicole positioned herself on her own branch and took a box of stove matches out of her pocket. She motioned Dodie and me over. Once we were balanced on either side of her, she slid the cover off the matches and emptied them into a corner of her shirt. "All right. Now." She stuck one hand into the pile and clutched a fistful of matches, instructing Dodie and me to do the same. We did. A few strays remained in her lap. With her free hand, she held up my wrist and squinted at my portion. She took her time, turning my fist this way and that. She did the same with Dodie's. Then she picked up one match and added it to mine, two went into Dodie's handful, and the rest she scooped into her own pile. "There. Now they're even," she said decisively. "Let's get started."

I eyed my somewhat shy portion, waiting for Nicole to explain.

"Go on. You saw him." Nicole took a match from her pile and flicked it with her thumbnail. Nothing happened. "You try it."

So that was it. We were to perform Eddie's trick. I gripped a match in my fist and snapped its sulphur head smartly with my thumbnail. It didn't light.

"Don't rub it. *Fire* it."

"I am." I tried again, harder. The wooden shaft broke in two.

"Here. Like this," said Nicole. She tried again. The white tip snapped off.

Dodie's tongue poked the corner of her mouth—an aid to concentration—but she was having no better luck. "He must do something to his nail. Boys know certain tricks."

Nicole disagreed, insisting we only had to get the hang of it.

I tried again. This time it crackled and I dropped it. Failure only fueled our zeal.

"If I were a boy," Nicole mused, "I'd have my own charter boat, and I'd take people deep sea fishing." She pronounced it *chahtah* boat.

"You don't *have* to be a boy to do that." Dodie was no tomboy, but she liked to think up ways girls were just as good as boys. "Besides, if you were a boy you'd have to join the army first. Army first. Then fishing." Always tidy.

"So?" Nicole broke another match.

I had a sudden vision of uniforms and foxholes and loud explosions and soldiers with smudged faces bleeding on stretchers. A combination of fear and pity welled up in me for all boys, Digory notwithstanding.

"So I'm glad I'm not a boy," said Dodie.

"It's only for two years," said Nicole. "And anyway, girls have to have the babies."

A chill went through me. Having a baby was so unbearable you had to be put to sleep. And we all had heard about "cruelty on the maternity wards." Doctors tied their patients' legs together so they could finish dinners at the country club. It was in the Saturday Evening Post. Our actual understanding of childbirth, admittedly deficient, consisted of one irrefutable fact: it was horrifying down to every detail. I debated which was worse, babies or war, but in the end I thought girls had the slim advantage. You didn't sign up to *die*.

"They're both bad," I said. And that seemed to settle it.

Unlit, broken matches were piling up in our laps. Nicole came closer to succeeding than any of us when she got a sulphur splinter caught under her nail just as it cracked into flame. She howled and sucked on her thumb.

Dodie laughed, but Nicole glowered at her so she stopped.

That day, the day Triple Tree became only one-third mine, we stayed in the branches the whole afternoon, and our feet never touched earth. Nicole let Dodie braid her hair and then practiced smoking a cigarette she had lifted from Uncle George's glove compartment. (Striking a match effortlessly against the bark.) She had a package of M&Ms in her pocket, which she divided evenly, counting them out into two waiting palms. Through the afternoon I held them one at a time in my patient mouth until the candy coating crumbled away and the warmed chocolate spilled over my tongue. Sweet chocolate in *equal* shares. Two thirds of us thought it was better to be a girl. By a hair. The future had its uncertainties, but at least signing up to fight Communists wasn't one of them.

Nicole decreed that we would meet every afternoon, swimming from her beach and mustering at Triple Tree on alternate days. That was to be our routine. Everything organized.

———

Every day after breakfast I went to the tent, unpacked my cello, rosined my bow and practiced two hours. It took about thirty minutes to do scales and arpeggios, then an hour for études, and finally the last half hour I could work on the Capriccio Mr. Metcalf had played for me. I had a long way to go before it would be good enough even to ask my mother to try the accompaniment with me, let alone to play it in public.

Weekdays, when the breakfast dishes were done, my mother rowed across the pond to play Aunt Fanny's piano. I practiced two hours but she played all morning. First she played sonatas with Aunt Fanny. By the time I put my cello away and walked around the pond to find Dodie and Nicole, she was barely warmed up. When Aunt Fanny tired, packed her violin in its case, and secured the latches, my mother brought out her own pieces for piano alone. Brahms, Ravel, Bach. Even a little Gershwin. Racy music. And Beethoven. Always Beethoven. "I've almost got the exposition," she would say, working out a difficult passage. On the prowl for wrong notes or imprecise rhythms. But once she had the nuts and bolts in place, then she went after the music. She sought out a more expressive tempo, a longer phrase, a different articulation which might better reveal what it was Beethoven meant to say. To see if he would say it to *her*. When BerthaMelrose insisted that my mother learn the piano, she did so because a certain rudimentary knowledge of music was an obvious requirement of any well-versed girl's education. No one expected my mother to get so good.

———

The beginning of July we went into town to get canning jars and cheesecloth at Snow's Hardware so that my mother would be all set to put up jelly as soon as the beach plums ripened. Afterwards we went into Murray's Fabrics, where she took a long time examining all the bolts of material squeezed into the tiny cottage. She touched, stroked, measured, kneaded, priced and wished, but didn't buy anything. Before we went home, she let Dodie and me look in Watson's.

"May I help you?" said the lady wearing a sweater set.

Dodie tried on dungarees, rigid dark cloth that folded like lengths of planking. I drifted over to the rack of dresses. Girls' sizes six through fourteen. As if girls came in even numbered ages. The row of hems got progressively longer as the numbers got higher.

They had three varieties of school outfits made from sturdy gabardine in colors that wouldn't show the dirt. And one other dress, hanging on the peeling bar. A two-piece dress. A blue cotton pinafore with a foamy white dotted-swiss topping like whipped cream.

"You may try it on, but that's all," said my mother.

"Excellent for the price," said the lady. "Only twenty-five dollars."

63

My mother closed her gray eyes, already sorry she let me try it on but-that's-all.

"It's a twelve. Room to grow," I told her to show what a sensible girl I was, standing in front of the three-way mirror in the corner of the store. Arms like airplane wings so not to deflate the dotted-swiss. Picturing myself on stage at the talent show.

Dodie edged herself into view in the mirror, jeans rolled up at the ankles. The legs were too wide and the waist too small. To zip them, she sucked in a shop-dusty breath, sucked so hard she wheezed. She cocked her head to one side. "They're perfect. Don't you think so?" The beginnings of a poison ivy rash showed under the cuffs.

"OK, girls," said my mother, waiting.

"You look better in red," said Dodie as the lady helped me unbutton the dotted-swiss apron and unzip the crisp blue cotton. "I look good in green," she said and stepped out of the legs like two stiff blue funnels.

OK girls.

Dodie folded the jeans into fourths and returned them to the shelf.

I hung the dress, two pieces carefully arranged on one hanger, back up on the gray metal bar.

My family didn't have many rituals, but the few we did observe, we took to heart. We celebrated graduations and anniversaries at Moy Bing's, where we ordered Sweet and Sour Pork, Moo Goo Gai Pan, two portions of Egg Foo Young, and the boiled rice that came at no extra charge. We never opened Christmas presents on Christmas Eve like some of the Catholics we knew, but only on Christmas morning. In order. One at a time. Fireworks were for the Fourth of July and-not-one-day-sooner.

And so come the Fourth, we still had the entire bag, transported across two state lines, kept dry on a shelf in the Playhouse and untouched since Connecticut. Sparklers, firecrackers and rockets. The full fifteen dollars worth. Let Uncle George see if he could top that.

If there was an offshore breeze, we had to light them from our beach, so that stray sparks would drift harmlessly out over the pond. A westerly wind would mean we celebrated at Uncle George's, where parties were more fun. We laughed more, sang songs around the piano, and ate salted nuts (but did *not* pick out the cashews) from little bowls. We stayed later.

And so as soon as I woke up, I went outside to check. Blue sky. A light breeze moved the pine needles. Barely a riffle, but *from the west*. I woke up Dodie and together we ran to the beach.

"Three....o'clock...." Nicole called back. "Come at three."

We sprinted back up the hill. Dodie had to peel potatoes for potato salad. I banged on the Playhouse door to see if Daddy was ready to go for clams.

"Wind's from the west. Nicole says we should come at three. Can I come in?"

"May I," my father corrected.

My mother frowned into the light that fell across the bed when I opened the door. "How's the tide?" asked my father.

"Pretty low," I answered.

"We need it dead low."

"It's past the rock."

"OK. We should go." He sat up, reached for the clock on the dresser and began to wind it. "How many clams can you eat?" he said, smiling, to my mother.

"We weren't invited."

We both looked at her.

"I had no invitation to George's." She said it quietly. Just a rustle of leaves. A quiet ambush.

Daddy's smile guttered for a moment like a candle in a draft but didn't go out. "What do you mean, we weren't invited? He's my brother."

"You know what I mean." She threw the blanket back and swung her feet to the floor. She poured some water from the pitcher into the wash pan, splashed her face, and squeezed some toothpaste onto her toothbrush.

Daddy sat immobile on the bed. "Of course we're invited," he said. "Besides, *we've* got the fireworks."

She lifted the toothbrush to her mouth. "All the more reason for him to *invite* us."

This time Daddy's smile flickered out. He let out his breath in a rush. "Oh Lydia. What do you need? An engraved invitation?" He gripped his thin leg with both hands and lifted it to the floor. "'May we have the pleasure of your company....?' Is that it? Are you above a simple family get-together?"

"Common courtesy would do," my mother snapped and started to brush her teeth in short, staccato motions.

I supposed that she was still mad at Uncle George because he tried to get her to make fun of my father for dotting his "I's", or else because he turned out to be right about the driveway, or because now he had scared her about the strength of the main beam. Or all of those things.

My father stood up, keeping one hand on the dresser until he found his balance. There was always an uncertain moment when he launched his weight onto his feet, as when a newborn foal lurched up onto all fours. Daddy's leg was no more than a spindle, hinged in the middle by a bulbous knee. The sight of it below his bathing suit or undershorts shot currents of pain through my chest. It was as slender and brittle as a stalk. If it hurt, he never said so. Nor did he complain that it embarrassed him. But it embarrassed me. I wasn't embarrassed for him in public. He didn't care what people thought. He never let it stop him from wearing a bathing suit at the beach. No, I hurt for him in the quiet, private moments, like this one, when my strong father's leg seemed less a deformity than a frailty. Next to his sturdy, muscled right leg, his left was as thin as my arm.

I looked away.

"You're right," he said finally, conciliatory. "An invitation would not be out of order. But it's summer. Maybe if you had a brother you'd understand. Can't we just go without all this... this...." He paused. Then he lowered his voice further, to an even softer, beseeching level. "You wouldn't want to disappoint Fanny. Fanny would be so disappointed." He almost crooned. He was a good singer. He hitched his good leg into a better position so that he could assemble a hopeful face in comfort.

My mother lowered her toothbrush. "No. I don't want to disappoint Fanny." She sagged. "Poor Fanny," she added, almost as a reflex.

Daddy reached for his shirt. He caught my eye and gave an imperceptible nod toward the pond. I backed out the door and went to fetch the clam rake and pitchfork from the tool shed.

He was already at the boat when I got to the beach. I set the things in the bow of the Clamshell and together we half lifted, half dragged it into the water. We didn't really need the boat because at low tide we could walk the shoreline to the creek, but it was easier not to have to lug the bucket along. And it meant we could go on digging without keeping an eye on the time; we could always row back if the tide came in.

We had the pond to ourselves. The July water was already warm as we waded over to the sandbar where the creek emptied in.

Daddy picked a spot and turned up a forkful of mud and sand. I bent over the pitchfork and ran my fingers through, letting clumps of sand dissolve away. We wanted a full bucket. He dug a few holes before he struck a "producer" as he called it. I fingered the clams, sifting out the live ones, discarding empty shells. We worked in silence except now and then he said *You missed one* or *Too small.* I kept the bucket in the rowboat on short anchor, and pulled it along next to us. We worked our way over to the drop-off, where the sand bar fell away precipitously to murky depths.

"What do you think is on the bottom?" I asked. Nicole might be able to ask Uncle George *for* anything, but I could ask my father *about* anything. My father didn't boast; he gave real answers.

"Bottom of what?"

"The pond."

"I don't know. Same as here, I guess. Keep the broken ones. We'll use them for bait."

"But it gets so mucky. And seaweedy. Do you think things grow on the bottom?"

"Like what?"

"I don't know."

"I don't think so, Lily. There may be a couple of old shoes and some anchor rope. That's about all."

"A shipwreck?" I asked hopefully.

Daddy laughed out loud. "It'd have to be a pretty small ship. We'd have to call it a 'boatwreck.' You can leave that big one for seed. The smaller ones make better eating anyway."

I put back a large, fat clam.

"I'll tell you the most interesting fact about the bottom," he said. "Did you know that if there's a really cold winter and the pond freezes, the water under the ice stays at thirty nine degrees? Exactly thirty nine degrees?"

I had no idea whether 39 degrees was supposed to be hot or cold.

"Think of that. These clams can count on thirty-nine degrees all winter long. The Waldorf Astoria doesn't have a thermostat that steady."

The Waldorf Astoria, that bastion of prosperity and permanence. "Daddy...." I was working around to what was really on my mind. "Daddy, do you think our house will last?"

He stopped digging. "Of course it will, Lily. Why?"

"I don't know. I just wondered."

"You bet it will. When my dissertation has sold a million copies, the house will still be like brand new. See if it isn't. You just take care of your practicing. I'll look after the house. Don't you have a lesson tomorrow?"

I nodded. We continued in silence while I brooded on one overwhelming question: How to warn him the main beam was going to split apart like toothpicks?

Our bucket was nearly full when we heard an outboard engine fire up. Uncle George closed the distance between his wharf and us in the time it took me to straighten up and shade my eyes.

"Hallooo," he called out and cut the engine just the other side of the drop off. The wake from his speedboat stirred the water around our feet. I steadied the dinghy.

"Perfect day, huh?" he shouted.

"George, you've muddied the water," said Daddy.

"As usual. You forgot to say 'as usual.' Why break your back digging clams when you can buy a boatful up to Ellis' for a dollar?"

"You eat yesterday's clams. Lily and I," here Daddy winked at me, "we like them fresh, don't we, Lily?"

As a matter of fact I didn't really like clams one bit, however fresh. For an instant I recognized another unexpected opportunity to get on Uncle George's good side. "I don't really like clams," I could have said and tipped the tide in Uncle George's favor. But of course I did no such thing.

I had decided on an inconclusive nod when luckily, before I could answer, Uncle George said, "Oop. There's Gloria." He throttled his motor into high and lurched away, circled the pond twice at top speed, streaked to his dock, and then cut the engine as abruptly as he had left us.

"Might as well quit for today," Daddy said. "Water's too stirred up. We've got enough."

———

We had too much to carry to row across the pond to Uncle George's, and so we put everything into the Pontiac and drove. When we got there, Daddy and I carried the bucket of steamers between us to the house. My mother brought the potato salad, and Dodie trumpeted the arrival of the fireworks. Uncle George and Digory were playing cards in the breezeway.

Uncle George's house had started as a one-room cabin that had been added onto like a scrabble game, from the center out. First he built a sleeping porch on the pond side. Screened against bugs. Next came a porch. He wanted to put it across the front of the cabin so he'd have more of a buffer between him and "all the damned company," referring to the occasional visit by Aunt Fanny's mother. But Aunt Fanny got him to put it by the garden, and it smelled of wild rose and Sweet William all summer. Then he built an ell on the opposite side so that Gloria would have a place whenever she came. But Aunt Fanny's cousins, the French McKenzies, used it once, and Uncle George said he could hardly sleep for the sound of people sponging off him. So he added another whole addition with three bedrooms, one each for him and Aunt Fanny and Nicole (Digory now had the entire sleeping porch to himself) because Aunt Fanny preferred a room of her own. The addition had a bathroom with running water, and he called it Bunker Hill. Bunker Hill abutted the porch, which now had to be called a breezeway, and Aunt Fanny had to move her trellis. Over time the name came to mean the whole conglomeration. Bunker Hill.

Aunt Fanny called to us through the open kitchen window,

where she stood shucking corn. Gloria's car was gone. We set the bucket in the breezeway, in the shade. Daddy put water on for the clams, my mother sliced watermelon, and I washed my hands to help Aunt Fanny. At five-foot two Aunt Fanny stood not much taller than I, which was too bad because she rejected the prevailing fashion that to be "petite" was a virtue. She wanted to be tall. Instead of an apron she was wearing a bathrobe dizzily flowered with periwinkle blossoms over her housedress. Her shoulder-length hair was the same pale brown as a Bartlett pear. She had green eyes that seemed to curl in on themselves like tightly closed fronds of a fern. She had one French grandparent, a fact that had lent to her initial mystique, but which Uncle George had since come to view as a deliberate affectation. She had a crumpled voice, a head full of little-known facts and an old-fashioned face—part angel, part sprite —much like the ones in the art book she brought with her from Boston every year. She must have wondered sometimes how her degree in French from Radcliffe prepared her for life with Digory, Nicole and Uncle George. The closest thing she came to a harsh word was an occasional droll, "Why, that's naughty, Nicole. Naughty." This she uttered with a bewildered little laugh as if to say she knew she was play-acting at a highly amusing role for which she had been decidedly miscast.

At last she took off her housecoat and rang the ship's bell for dinner.

By then everyone was starving. The picnic table had been extended with some long planks and a sawhorse. She draped a sheet over the whole apparatus for a tablecloth. I took a plate and found a place on the bench. There were two bowls of clam broth on the table and little Pyrex dishes of drawn butter. My father came out of the cabin bearing Aunt Fanny's lobster pot, full to the brim with steaming clams, and everybody dug in.

Whatever my parents' disagreement about being issued a proper invitation, they were not going to let it spoil their steamers. Even Digory wanted some. Daddy scooped a pile onto each plate, but I pulled mine away and stuck instead to corn and watermelon. My mother pulled open a clam, pinched the skin from the neck, speared it with her fork, and swished it in a bowl of the broth they had been steamed in, to rinse the sand off. My parents were particular about this. It couldn't be plain water even though the broth was at least as sandy as the clams themselves.

Digory sat down next to me. "What's the matter," he said. "Don't you like clams?"

I pretended not to hear him.

"Which part don't you like?" His voice was something between a rasp and a whine and he was careful to reveal nothing about himself save for whatever could be inferred from his expression, which ranged from a smirk to a sneer. "The neck?" He pursed his lips and squeezed out the rubbery neck of a clam so that it looked like the flicking tongue of a lizard. "Or the stomach?" Then he opened his mouth wide, displaying the sewage inside.

"Chew with your mouth closed," said Nicole, never nonplussed.

Uncle George said, "Last time I was in New York, I ordered clams and you know what they brought me?"

"What?" said Daddy.

"Cherrystones. The menu said 'clams' and they brought cherrystones."

"You ought to know better, George."

"I do. I sent them back."

Daddy laughed. "You were just baiting them. You only ordered clams to make a point."

"'Baiting them.' That was good, Weston," said Aunt Fanny, who never missed a pun.

Nicole was chewing on her tongue in concentration as she peeled the membrane back from the neck of a clam.

Digory followed my gaze, leaned over and whispered conspiratorially in my ear, "You know what that is? That's the foreskin."

I inched away from him, certain that whatever he had said, it couldn't be good.

"I told the guy, 'This isn't a clam, this is a quahog,'" said Uncle George. "He looked at me like he'd never heard of a quahog."

My father wiped his fingers on his napkin. "He probably hadn't."

"I've heard," said Aunt Fanny, "that the Italians eat mussels. Is that true, Weston?"

"The Italians will eat anything," said Uncle George.

"Careful. You start to sound like a bigot," said my father.

"Well, I know enough not to eat mussels."

"You know what you get if you add S-H to bigot?" said Digory.

No one responded.

"Big shot. You get big-shot," said Digory.

"Who cares," said Nicole.

"I had mussels once," said my mother with a sideways glance at my father. She had been quiet 'til now.

"You've eaten mussels?" said my father.

"And so have you. That time at the DeMeo's."

"Those were mussels?"

"You had seconds."

Uncle George hooted. "I'll bet they slipped you some carp, too."

"They were delicious," said my mother.

"Well, forget clams," said Uncle George. "Give me lobster. That's what I say. A steal at two fifty a pound."

"Money isn't the only measure of what's good," said my father, defending our clams, every last one dug by hand and kept cool and fresh in a shaded bucket of seawater.

"Pay attention, mother." (Uncle George meant Aunt Fanny.) "Here comes our philosophy lesson."

"I'm interested in philosophy," said Aunt Fanny, who graduated summa cum laude.

"By all means, enlighten us," said Uncle George, who never finished college.

Daddy reached into the pot and put a handful of cost-free steamers on my mother's plate. He *had* taken a philosophy class. He knew how hard it was to study while working as night operator at the telephone exchange, where between calls he catnapped on a cot. When the switchboard lit up, he had to stay awake while the callers talked so that he could unplug them when they finished. "Then I'll say this, George," Daddy said. He paused to loosen his belt one notch. "Money can't buy a better meal. Just because it costs more doesn't make lobster any the finer. A measure of Beethoven sounds no better in the ear of a wealthy man. And there is no clam anywhere tastier, fresher, or more perfectly cooked than the one you are swallowing right now."

It was a whole speech.

Uncle George watched my father with stingy eyes and chewed for a minute. When Daddy graduated, Uncle George took over the job at the telephone office and earned enough money to start a small (and quick to thrive) printing business. My mother's father, Tucker, who also had an office in Stanhope Street, helped him set up his bookkeeping. That was the first intersection of the two families. Melrose and Grainger. In spite of their age difference, Uncle George and Tucker got along, played a hand of poker now and then on weekends. Tucker introduced him to my mother, but she was intrigued instead by Uncle George's older brother, the studious one who loved music and bore his limp without complaint. Uncle George built up his business. Became successful. A self-made man.

One who didn't need a lecture.

He got up and tossed his plate into the bag at the end of the table. "What would you know about what money can buy?" he said to my father. "You never spend any."

There was a moment of silence while the meanness of what he said sank in. Digory fished in the butter dish for a clam that had fallen off his fork.

My mother spoke first. "You gave me the best ones," she said, and spooned the clams from her plate onto Daddy's. "Here. You have these."

"I'm sure that can't be true, George," said Aunt Fanny. "Weston is very generous," she faltered.

Tucker would never have admitted he was disappointed that my mother chose Uncle George's brother, but even after my parents were married, Tucker and George remained the better pals. Uncle George was more Tucker's type. He followed ball scores, flirted with the waitress whatever her age, pretended not to keep track of who owed whom what. He based his likeability on professing to lack all intellectual prowess. But when it suited him, he had brains enough to exploit any advantage to clinch a deal.

"It's OK, Fanny," said my father.

And he let it go at that, but it was clear that there had been some kind of contest, and that my father was right, but Uncle George had won.

Then my mother said, as if in answer to something somebody had asked even though no one had spoken, "No, I couldn't eat another bite. Girls, would you clear, please?"

Uncle George knew how to win points with a well-timed concession. "At least we know a clam from a quahog. Best steamers I ever ate." Which came out sounding almost like an apology.

By now the platter was piled high with shells dripping juice and congealed butter onto the bedsheet tablecloth. Digory knocked over his Coke, which mingled with the watermelon stains, and everyone forgot about lobster at two-fifty a pound.

"Don't worry," said Aunt Fanny, mopping up. "We'll hang it in the Metropolitan. Pablo Picasso has nothing on us." She stood back, smiling at the mess, and after a moment it struck her even funnier because her shoulders rippled while she laughed to herself.

After supper my father passed out firecrackers. Digory got a tin can out of the garbage and lit a two-incher under it. When it exploded, it blasted the can twenty feet into the air and I burnt my fingers trying to catch it. I hopped around on one foot, sucking on my poor fingers (which made them sting worse), and Dodie and Nicole thought I was funny, so I did it again.

Then my father brought out the real rockets. We hiked down to the pond and stood in the dusk on Uncle George's wharf. Nicole and Dodie got in the rowboat and paddled a few feet from shore.

Daddy wanted it good and dark. Uncle George, noting my impatience, said, "Let the man take his time, Lily. Your father is in charge. Then we'll know the job is done right."

Anyway, we couldn't hurry the night. My mother lit a cigarette. Nicole and Dodie circled the wharf in the boat. The oars creaked quietly in the oarlocks. We fixed our attention on the fading light.

"I don't know what happened to me," Uncle George said, almost to himself. "Weston was always the smart one. Anything that ever happened, I did the poorest job of anybody." It was the seductive beginning to one of his stories. A story to pass the time. A story to get us back on his side.

"Perhaps, George, you'd like to entertain us while we wait," said Aunt Fanny.

"What's the matter, Fanny? You sick of my stories?" Uncle George could spin a yarn, each ultimately about how he got the better of somebody. He turned to my mother. "Did I ever tell you how I met the Earls?"

"I don't know the Earls," said my mother, which Uncle George took to be an invitation to begin.

He looked briefly at each of us, to raise the curtain. "It was during the war, with rationing."

"The rationing part is important," said Aunt Fanny.

"You want to tell it, Fanny?"

"We want you to tell it," I obliged him. My parents, on their own, did not give themselves to reminiscing. After a meal they didn't sit around the table over a second cup of coffee, rest their feet on a chair, and linger aloud over the past. Not that they hadn't had good times. I knew for instance that my father had once owned a red convertible. A car without a single practical feature. But they never said, "Remember that red convertible?" It was almost as if they were afraid it would make things worse now to remember how they had romped through happier days. Days when they had more money. Or if they didn't, it hadn't mattered so much. When Uncle George's ribbings tasted merely salty, not bitter.

"All right then. I was boarding the train to Boston...."

He told the story of how a Mrs. Earl, traveling alone, had accepted his newspaper. It was wartime and newspapers were scarce.

My father set the rockets down, took my mother's hand in his, and leaned back against a wharf post.

When the advantageously married Mrs. Earl learned that the kind traveler who so willingly shared his newspaper didn't have a way home from the station, she insisted on offering him a ride. What could he do but accept and help her in turn with her luggage? Her husband was waiting there with a chauffeur. Of course Uncle George didn't want to take them out of their way, but they insisted they'd be honored to drop him off. So honored that they invited him in for a Scotch before sending him home.

"I told Eleanor Earl, anytime you want help with your baggage, give me a call." Uncle George laughed as though he had said something really funny. "She knew I was joking. We got along. But something was wrong with him. I don't know what." Uncle George tilted his head evasively, implying he was too polite to suggest Mr. Earl wasn't all there. "He had money, but I think she would have liked to have had someone more...more...."

"More like you?" said Aunt Fanny.

"Fanny was so impressed, she said...." Now he warbled in falsetto, "'Oh, how could you? Those were the Earls.' And I said...." His voice rose with excitement as he approached the punch line. "I said, 'They may be the Earls, but they were *honored* to meet *me*.'"

Everyone laughed this time.

There followed an encouraging silence, in case there was more to the story. But he only sat looking out over the water. His smile faded. Finally he sighed and said, "I don't have to worry about people like the Earls."

I loved Uncle George's stories, even when they didn't appear to have a point. The point of this one seemed to be that in spite of all their money—any passerby might have taken him for Mrs. Earl's porter—he had something the Earls prized. Something more than a newspaper. But we knew (wink) that a newspaper and a little charm was good as gold in wartime. Uncle George (wink) was too worldly to care that he was out of the Earls' league. Uncle George knew how to garner extra credit for telling a joke on himself.

What Uncle George did *not* want anyone to take from his story was this: that he was afraid people were right when they said he married "up." He was afraid Aunt Fanny was better than him. And Aunt Fanny, like Mr. Earl, wasn't even all there.

By then nobody could find the box of matches in the dark, but my mother produced hers. I stood up to get a better view. Uncle George lit the first rocket, then Daddy, with a space in between to make them last. Daddy's was pink and gold, and shot deep into the sky; it looked like it was falling into a wishing well, with stars at the bottom for the glint of coins.

It was cooling off by then and the bugs had gone. Partway out a fish broke the surface of the pond with a small slap. Nicole said it was a flounder, but I didn't bother to correct her. Flounder were bottom feeders.

When there was one cherry bomb left, Daddy insisted that Uncle George do the honors and Uncle George insisted back. In the end Daddy lit the fuse ceremoniously—Dodie and Nicole tied up at the wharf—and threw it as far as he could out into the pond. It was supposed to create a real explosion, but not much happened. I thought I saw a few bubbles. Uncle George said it was a dud, and Daddy looked so disappointed I worried he'd been cheated. I told him maybe he could stop on our way back to New Jersey and get his money back, but he said it didn't really matter. He gave everyone a sparkler and we formed a glittering procession up the hill to the house.

I was lingering outside to see my sparkler down to its last fraction of an inch when Digory said, "Hiya, Squirt," through the open kitchen window.

I looked up and got a sudden drenching full in the face. My one rationed sparkler fizzled out.

He held up an empty glass. "Oh, sorry," he said with a malevolent snicker. "I didn't know the window was open."

I looked around. It was just the two of us. Digory, with a high-pitched voice like an underpowered motor, and me.

Groping for an equally wise-aleck retort and coming up short, I stumbled to the front of the cabin. Outside the door I stopped to wipe my face before Nicole or Dodie could see. Digory would never have thrown water on Dodie or Nicole.

Aunt Fanny came to the door. "Coming inside?"

"I'm coming." The front of my shirt was all wet.

"Something wrong?" she asked.

"No, I...." I tried to slip past her, but she tucked me under her arm and drew me to the picnic table.

"Really?" Aunt Fanny held me firmly. She was stronger than she looked. "Princess Anne wouldn't hold it in. She'd tell what was on her mind."

Princess Anne wasn't the kind of person people played tricks on. Or if they did, she probably got even.

"So?" Two fern-green eyes whispered, *Tell. Tell.*

"Digory threw water on me," I said finally. There it was. On top of everything, I was a crybaby too. And all of a sudden everything seemed an effort. Trying to keep up with Nicole, learning the cello, trying to make my mother smile. From my mother I knew that the heart beat in three-quarter time. From my father I knew that the number of petals on most flowers conformed to the Fibonacci number series. I was pretty sure I could swim across the pond without stopping; I could name the stars in the Summer Triangle. But I didn't know how to be the kind of person Digory didn't pick on. What could Aunt Fanny do?

"Why, Lily," she said finally, "I don't understand. You're upset because Digory threw water on you?"

My shoulders twitched in a guilty little shrug. Overhead, branches shifted. Pine needles licked the night air. No one liked a tattletale.

"And you didn't do something to prompt him to do that?"

"No." Laughter erupted from inside the cabin. I wanted to take back my accusation.

"You didn't do anything."

"No, I didn't. I really didn't. I was just coming...."

"You didn't say something to him?" she probed.

I sensed a trap. It must be that I provoked Digory, and she would defend him. "No, I didn't say anything," I sighed. "May I go now?"

She pulled me back under her arm. "Then *he's* the one who should be crying."

I looked up, confused. I couldn't imagine Digory crying. Aunt Fanny was studying my face. I studied hers to see if she was kidding.

"You said you did nothing to him. That means he bullied you for no reason." She looked at me squarely to see if I was following.

I wasn't. Then little by little, a startling new idea began slowly to take shape in my mind.

"*He's* the one who should feel bad," she said at last, confident she had reached the correct conclusion. The summa cum laude conclusion. "For having done such a mean thing. Not you." She brushed drops of water from my hair. "You are a fine girl, Lily. Digory is a rascal."

She made a bashful sound, not quite laughter. She smelled of perfume from the small cobalt blue bottle on her dresser. Evening in Paris, to remind herself that to be one of the French McKenzies was to be part of something ongoing and fine. She could see Picasso in a soiled tablecloth. She could hear Beethoven in the wheezings of her violin.

And she meant that I hadn't deserved it.

That was when the tears came. Not because Digory was a jerk, but because Aunt Fanny had been so nice to me. I didn't know why she would take my side against Digory, but what she had said threw off sparks, so brilliant was the rightness of it. The less people listened to her, the more she understood. She understood *me*. I dried my eyes and kissed her on her fragrant, one-fourth French cheek.

Inside, Digory was sitting at the piano working a crossword puzzle. Nicole was setting up a game of Monopoly on the floor next to him. A grass rug covered the floorboards. When Dodie folded it back to make a flat surface for the game, there were patterns of sand where the rug had been, and she had to sweep it up with the dustpan and brush before we could play.

Aunt Fanny joined my mother, who was washing out the lobster pot at the kitchen sink.

Uncle George smacked his hands together with forced enthusiasm as if the evening would sputter and die without a good revving up from him. "How about a highball."

My mother said, "I think it's time to head home. I'll just finish the dishes."

"Come on, deah," said Uncle George, exaggerating his accent and doing a little two-step. "The night is young."

Dodie rummaged through the Monopoly pieces and pulled out the shoe. I nudged the cat, Thoreau, to make room for myself. He looked up briefly, stretched against my leg, and went back to sleep. I settled for the flatiron, and placed it on the board. "Come on, Mama. Just a little longer?"

She looked doubtfully at my father. "Well, maybe just one." He was stretched practically prone on a chair that was too small for him, his hands clasping the back of his head against the wall. He balanced on the two back legs, and his feet reached nearly to the center of the room. His eyes were partly closed and he was smiling. "A small one," she specified.

Uncle George put a Glenn Miller record on the hi-fi. The needle missed the first couple of bars and "In the Mood" abruptly filled the room. He took a bottle from the cabinet, and with his forearm bulldozed the clutter from the counter: rocks and colored glass, sand dollars, a piece of driftwood that looked like a dolphin. Some shells fell to the floor and broke.

"Fanny's dustcatchers," said Uncle George and swept the pieces into the corner with his foot.

I saw my mother bristle.

"Your turn," said Nicole.

I rolled the dice and moved my gamepiece.

Aunt Fanny said, "I think the music's too loud."

But Uncle George wasn't listening. Into four tall glasses he poured Canadian Club, added ice cubes and topped them with gingerale. "Come and get it," he called.

"Do you want to buy it?" said Nicole.

"What?"

"Do you want to buy Oriental?" she repeated, drumming her fingers.

I gave her a hundred dollars and bought Oriental.

My mother had her arms up to the elbows in a pan of soapy water. Aunt Fanny was drying the silverware, but they couldn't talk above the hi-fi.

"No dishes tonight, girls," Uncle George shouted above the music. He waltzed around the counter and untied Aunt Fanny's apron. He was only just beginning to have fun.

Aunt Fanny shook him off and retied a bow. "George Grainger, go get squiffy yourself if you want. We're busy."

"Squiffy!" Uncle George guffawed. "Did you say 'squiffy'?"

Aunt Fanny smiled tentatively. "Was that funny?"

"I might get stinko, Fanny. I might even get swacked. But I definitely won't get *squiffy*. Now will you take off that apron?"

"Did I say something funny?" she persisted.

"Can't hear you," Uncle George sang louder.

The corners of his mouth tipped merrily upward on either side of his nose. He was always quick to say he had an aquiline nose, making it sound like he got it from a statue in a museum; but in point of fact it was hooked, so hooked that it gave all his expressions an extreme look, an exclamation point dead center of his face, there to punctuate his every mood. And right now he was really having fun.

"Lydia, show Fanny how to have a good time, would you?" He tango-ed up to my mother and took her by one soapy hand. "Fanny, look here. It's a *holiday*."

My mother stiffened. She sent a distressed, helpless look in the direction of my father. She was trying to keep a grip on the

83

evening before Uncle George went too far and it all came to no good. But she would want to appear game. So that no one could say later, *It was all Lydia's fault. She kept everyone from enjoying themselves.*

Uncle George took a step toward her. She backed into Aunt Fanny and stepped on her toe. Aunt Fanny squealed in pain. Digory stood up from the piano and kicked the Monopoly board, sending the pieces scattering.

"Quit it!" I yelled.

"Now look what you've done," said Nicole.

My father's chair came to the floor with a bang. "How about a hot game of Scrabble, Fanny?"

But he was too late. "I think we should go," my mother said coldly, no longer paralyzed.

"That's it," said Uncle George, seizing the offensive. "Drink my booze, then leave. When was the last time I had a drink at your house? How about it Weston?" Uncle George, the life of the party. Everybody's Sugar Daddy. But then when he finally got his way, he accused people of taking advantage of him.

The room went cold. My mother, seeking a way to make it his fault, aimed a pointed look at my father, who was helping me pick up Monopoly pieces. Because in her search for someone to blame, Uncle George wasn't hers to fight with. My father would have to do. Glenn Miller blared from the record player.

"Amo, amas, amat, amamus…." Aunt Fanny, at a loss, stepped from the kitchen conjugating verbs.

"Hey, just kidding," Uncle George said to my mother. "Just kidding." He held up his arms for her to dance. "Is the moon out tonight…." he crooned.

"Hujus, hujus, hujus."

"You see? Fanny, here, is so fired up she's taken to babbling. Come on, Fanny. Nobody here speaks Greek. Tell Lydia to dance with me."

My mother hesitated. Then, unexpectedly, the fight went out of her. A succession of expressions passed across her face. Repulsion, fascination in the face of such vitality. Jealousy that in spite of their barbs, the two brothers were close, and in the life of an only child there was no equivalent. Grudging admiration and the wish that she could be more like him: more egotistical, more careless, more cussed, more unladylike, more irrepressible, more *sure* of herself. Given the choice between refusing Uncle George and dancing with Uncle George, she must have judged the Uncle George she danced with to be the less dangerous. Hold your enemies close, Uncle George himself used to say. She looked embarrassed. She looked self-conscious. She looked sad. And then she danced with him.

Pretty soon my father got to his feet and asked Aunt Fanny to dance. She uttered a coy, "Oh, my." Uncle George and my mother stopped dancing and turned to watch. Aunt Fanny did an awkward little curtsey, girlish and pleased.

Everyone knew that my father didn't dance. His polio had come too early in his life. He had never even played softball, or bowled. Aunt Fanny flattened the corner of the rug by the ruined Monopoly game and positioned herself to dance. Daddy stood facing her, game and uncertain.

"That's it, Fanny! Give it all you've got," called Uncle George.

"No, Fanny," said my mother so deliberately that Uncle George stopped short. My mother stepped forth. She spoke with a calm as if from the eye of a hurricane, a forceful, irresistible calm. "I'd like to dance with Weston."

Nobody moved.

Then Aunt Fanny relinquished her spot next to my father with a confused half-bow.

My mother moved close to him. "Weston?" she said sternly.

"Lydia."

They put their arms up and took the first few tentative steps. They shuffled; it hardly amounted to dancing. They staggered.

85

They shambled. They bumped against each other. And then they smiled at each other. "Well, get to it, George," my father berated his brother. "This is your party."

Uncle George sallied up to Aunt Fanny. "I believe the honor is mine, Madam?" He flashed a dazzling smile. It was hard to tell when Uncle George was pulling your leg. As he swung Aunt Fanny into his arms, he said over his shoulder, "But I warn you, brother dear, next is a polka."

Nicole was up then, and Dodie with her. They gripped each other's shoulders, nuzzled their foreheads together, and skipped from foot to foot. Nicole lifted her knees high in a caricature of old-time dancing. Dodie had had ballet, and pointed her toes.

That left only Digory and me, and I would sooner have gone to church than dance with him. And so I added myself to Dodie and Nicole's twosome. We hopped and bobbed, three little buoys on high seas.

"I didn't know you had it in you," Uncle George shouted to my father halfway through the number. He had taken ballroom dancing and knew the correct steps.

"I don't," my father shouted back. My mother had propped her shoulder under his, and fairly hobbled him around the room. The clarinet blared louder, and then an accordion played the chorus very fast. We swirled and bounced and collided, and finally my father tripped and collapsed on the couch. And my mother fell on top of him, laughing.

Then the band played "Good Night Irene" and Aunt Fanny sang along in her quaky voice, and the others joined in.

Tired, I curled up on the rug, lay my head against Thoreau, and felt the music vibrate through the floor.

"It was Latin, George," my father said as we were leaving. "Not Greek."

Later, after Dodie and I had gone to bed, I got up to go to the outhouse. There was no moon, but the stars were bright. Candlelight shone through the Playhouse window, and so I peeked in. My mother sat on the daybed, and my father was listening to her, bending slightly over her. He seemed to be taking a big breath of her. In one hand he held her breast, cupped, like the bowl of a pipe.

I hurried on.

6
STRONG BREEZE

Beaufort Number 6
Wind Speed 25-31 MPH
large branches move; telegraph wires whistle; umbrellas difficult to
control

*J*ellyfish had come in on June tides, as well as bluefish, flounder, small stripers, hornpout and the rumble of guns from the naval air station at Quonset Point, where trainees ran missions to fire on Target Ship, a decommissioned Liberty Ship scuttled on a shoal near Eastham for the purpose of shelling practice. By July the jellyfish pirouetted from the pond, heading for cooler water, and we could spot eels snaking in along the floor of the creek. Daddy was partial to eel. No one else would eat them no matter how enthusiastically he smacked his lips and declared their dense, oily flavor a delicacy. He fished for them regularly in spite of the ribbing he took from Uncle George, who said *he* wouldn't feed them to the *cat*.

My mother spent afternoons picking huckleberries for jelly. A warm-up for the real thing: beach plums when they ripened at the end of summer. I became Daddy's fishing partner. I would peer over the side of the Clamshell and watch my drop-line disappear into the hypnotic goldgreen water, striated and flecked like the iris of an eye. The best fishing, he told me, was at the mouth of the creek just when the tide was turning, between the sandbars, those two fangs through which the ocean pushed the tide into our little pond and sucked it out again.

Otherwise we could navigate the creek to the bay, but we had to do it with the tide. Depart on the ebb tide, return on the flood. No point in waging a battle that couldn't be won. Creek tides had powered a mill there once. A careful navigator like my father could pick his way through the old timbers and rocks that were left submerged when it was torn down. But the tide had to be high enough and it had to be going the right way. When rowing in the pond, I gave the creek a wide berth, for I had been warned that the current could catch me and suck me past the millstone, past the Indian mound, past the Boys' Camp, down the bay, maybe even all the way to Monomoy and out to sea.

One day Daddy and I caught the outgoing tide to fish off Viking Spit. The air was warm and still, and the water carried us like a slur over moving notes, smoothly past a ripple here or an eddy there. Sea Lavender was in bloom, milkweed pods were beginning to open, and the grasses and firs along the shoreline came in gradations of green as varied and comprehensive as a chromatic scale, with one clear tone of blue above.

We anchored off the Spit and baited our lines with clams. I let mine out until I felt the soft thud of the sinker striking bottom, and then drew up six inches or so, just as Daddy did, and waited for the tug. We sat like that, not needing to talk. I slapped at a horsefly. Daddy pointed at a sandpiper picking for fleas in the mud. The boat lurched whenever he yanked on his line. "Bite?" I asked when he pulled it up. He held up a barren hook and shook his head, chagrined over losing what surely had been a monumental catch. When he needed a fresh clam, he slid the paring knife through the slit until it severed the muscle that held the two halves of the bi-valve together. I used the rubbery neck because it was easier to thread onto the hook and harder for a fish to steal. When I felt a nibble, I was to jerk my line to set the hook, pull it in hand over hand, pinch the eel with my thumb and forefinger in the soft spot just behind its jawbone, pinch hard, so that I could work the hook out of its mouth while it writhed and curled up my arm. Any other method was like trying to hold onto a greased snake. It couldn't be done.

But we weren't having any luck and the sun was getting low.

"Tide's changed," said Daddy. "Shall we head back?"

I had to go in the bushes first, so I wound up my fishing line and he put me ashore. Eelgrass needled my feet. A yellow-jacket tagged along. They were harmless as long as you ignored them. And so ignore him, I did. I found a thicket of beach plums, untied my bathing suit and crouched behind the bushes.

While he waited, Daddy set the fishing tackle and oars on the beach and then dipped one gunwale in shallow water to fill the bottom of the boat. He rocked the dinghy, sloshing the water from side to side, rinsing it clean, then tipped it completely over. He braced himself on his good leg and flipped the boat right side up again, lifting it clear so it landed with a splash, all emptied out. It was one of the reasons he didn't want a bigger boat. He didn't need hoses, trailers, winches and a whole afternoon to bring ours in for the winter or to keep it primed with a coat of dark green paint.

My persistent yellow-jacket darted to and fro. A companion joined him. They began to whiz this way and that, winged marauders, drawing orbits around me like schoolbook diagrams of frantic atoms. Trying to get me to provoke them.

Still ignoring them (almost) I pulled up my bathing suit,

hurrying, elbows tight inside the wasp orbits. Reaching behind my neck to tie my bathing suit with wasp-nervous fingers, trying to keep my balance in the beach plums on uneven ground. Loose sand gave way beneath one sinking foot and suddenly the air around me went dark with hornets. The first sting caught me on the arm. I shrieked and bolted blindly in the direction of the boat, even as I heard my father's steady voice shout, "Don't panic." Spears of beach grass stabbed my feet. Batting the air with one hand, clutching my still untied suit with the other, I careened into the water.

"Get your head under!" Daddy shouted.

Arms like pinwheels thrashed the water. I submerged and kicked and churned and finally, when I had no breath left, I slowed. I trod water and wiped my eyes to see if I was clear.

Daddy waded out to his chest and brought the dinghy up next to me. "You all right?"

"I think so." In a whimpering, stung voice. I tied my bathing suit. Cold, salt-heavy creek water holding me up. One small inadvertent swallow a sweet salve on my throat, which was tight with cowardice. I had never been stung before. The welts hurt, but not as much as I feared they would. Not as much as the sight of the wasps themselves with their convict stripes and pinched waists and swivel eyes and stinger, armed and cocked to harpoon unsuspecting persons just going to the bathroom.

I hauled myself into the stern.

"How many times did they get you?"

"I don't know. Three, I think."

He brushed a straggler from his neck. When it came back he crushed it between his fingers and flicked it into the water. "They must have a nest in the grass."

That was when we saw the two boys in a canoe, pulling against the tide. One was a skinny boy about eight or nine, with freckles. The other I guessed to be my age, but taller than other boys. He j-stroked to keep the canoe flush with the current.

"Undertow's pretty strong here," Daddy called to them.

"Yes, sir," said the tall boy. The j-stroker. He let the canoe lose a little ground to stay even with us.

"Looks like you're managing."

"Yes sir. I think we'll make it all right."

"Camp let you boys come up here against the tide?"

"To be honest, sir," he answered, "We don't have permission." He said it straight out, just like that.

"Well," said my father, impressed in spite of himself with the boy's directness. "Well then. You'd better take it on in before you are missed."

"Yes sir." An obedient smile for my father. "We'll do that." Then he grinned at me. "Any bites?"

"Bites?" My fishing line lay coiled beside me, the empty bucket at my feet. I came to the slow-witted conclusion that I was being teased. Fish weren't biting; the bees were. A hungry swarm, chasing people who provoked them *by mistake* from behind a couple of skimpy beach plum bushes. "Oh, bites," I said, meaning to convey a certain savvy nonchalance, but achieving at best something wary and noncommittal. My eye was swelling; my foot stung.

Green eyes teased me. One stroke, another stroke, to keep the canoe alongside.

"Yes," I said, still guarded, in a faded blue bathing suit. Not red, the color Dodie had decreed I looked good in. "Lots."

"Come on, Nick," said the skinny, freckled boy. "Let's go."

Nick nodded at me (maybe it was a wink) and dug his paddle deeply into the current. They moved slowly but smoothly through the water toward the Namequoit landing.

———

My father hated to go home skunked. He said right now he was getting skunked on his dissertation, and he'd be jiggered if he was going to get skunked fishing, too. And so on our way home he put his line out at the mouth of the creek while I went for a swim to relieve the stinging, and he caught three nice eels, each about the size of my arm. We beached the boat and carried the eels in a pail between us up the hill.

"What'll you do if you don't finish?" I asked as he hammered a nail through the snout of the smallest eel into the outhouse wall.

"Don't finish what?"

"Your dissertation."

"I won't get my degree, that's what." He took the pliers and began to rip back the skin.

"Do you think it hurts?"

"What? The eel?"

I nodded.

"No. No central nervous system." He sounded very sure.

"Can I try it?"

"May I." He handed me the pliers.

"What happens if you don't get your degree?" I tugged tentatively on the pliers.

"Here, you have to put your weight behind it," he said. "Like this." He braced his bad foot against the outhouse shingles.

I took the pliers in both hands and let my weight hang from them.

"Ow!" Daddy yelped.

I jumped and lost my grip. The pliers popped off the eel and I fell backwards to the ground.

"You can't skin an eel down there, buckaroo." He laughed and gave me a hand up.

This time I gripped tighter and peeled back about three inches, exposing the raw red pulp underneath. The body hung limp now. I handed him the pliers. "But what *does* happen if you don't get your degree?" I persisted.

"Nothing, Lily. I won't get my raise, that's all. And we need it to pay the bills. I'm going to finish. I'm counting on it."

I thought this over while he finished skinning the second eel. "How do you learn that?" I asked at last.

"Learn what?"

"How to pay bills."

"There's nothing to learn."

"But you have to know how to write checks. And you keep everything in columns in your ledger. How do you know what to put in the columns? How do you know how much money you need?"

"Whoa." He dislodged the nail with the prong end of the hammer and tossed the stripped eel into the bucket. Then he put away his tools in the outhouse and faced me. "All in good time," he said. "You learn it all in good time." He picked up the bucket and started up the path to the Playhouse.

I fell in behind him. "Aren't you going to do the last one?"

"No, we'll boil that one for chowder." We skirted the new house. Rows of two by fours stood like bleached bones awaiting a plywood skin. "Remember before your first cello lesson, you told me you didn't want to go because you didn't know how to do it?"

I nodded.

"But I made you. And you found out that your teacher didn't expect you to know. Otherwise he wouldn't have a job to do." He stopped for a minute, sighted down the unfinished wall, and then continued. "First you learned how to hold the cello. Then the bow. Then you practiced open strings, then scales. A step at a time. That's how it goes, Lily. Same with bills and cleaning fish and writing a dissertation and building a house." He took a breath. "A step at a time."

"Who teaches you?" I asked after a minute, not quite satisfied. "Do they teach you how to pay bills in school?"

My father smiled and nudged me with his fist. "No, Worry-pants, they don't. Your parents are supposed to teach you that. Come on. Let's cook up these eels."

He set the bucket on the picnic table and washed his hands at the pump. Then he pumped an inch or so of water into a kettle. He went into the Playhouse and came out carrying the kerosene stove, a precaution against my mother's complaints against strong odors.

He lit the stove. When the water boiled, he took the lid off the pot, pinched the eel behind its jawbone and tried to wrestle it in. It twisted and wrapped itself around his wrist.

I pried the coils from his arm, but that eel did not want to get boiled. Together we slid it under the lid, clamped the cover on and held it down hard. Inside, the eel thrashed and thumped like it was going to buck the kettle off the burner. At last it was still.

———

At supper my mother ladled steaming hot corn chowder into three bowls while she, Dodie and I sat at the picnic table and waited for Daddy to finish frying up his two remaining eels. Even outdoors it went up your nose like a strong ointment. He was humming to himself, spatula in his right hand, adjusting the flame with his left. A thickness of cheesecloth (four corners tied together) stained and bulging with cooked huckleberries hung from the pine tree and dripped blackpurple into a bowl. I sank a spoon into my corn chowder and left it there until Daddy sat down.

In our family we were required to observe only very few points of etiquette. The Melrose pedigree was unassailable which, Tucker maintained, gave them a certain elbowroom when it came to table manners. (BerthaMelrose, for her part, was less concerned about our manners than she was that we might damage her *things*.) My mother thus felt free to make her own decisions about which customs were based in logic and which were not, and she enforced or ignored them accordingly. The few which made the cut: we were expected to clean our plates (after all, there were people starving in Armenia who would be *grateful* to have our food.) We were to wait for everyone to sit down before starting to eat. (She was inexplicably fond of this one. It was like waiting for the conductor of an orchestra to give the downbeat.) And it was advised we not talk with our mouths full. In fact my mother's one golden rule of table manners—avoid any behavior that might make the person sitting next to you throw up—pretty much covered it. Along with finishing our food so the Armenians wouldn't get it.

Daddy shut off the kerosene burner, slid his eels from the frying pan onto a plate, sat down, made a show of tucking his napkin under his chin and took his first enthusiastic bite. "Anybody want some?"

My mother made a face.

My chowder had reached a nice edible lukewarm. I ate a spoonful. "Not me," I said.

"No," said Dodie.

"Not *I*. No *thank you*," said my father. Because unlike certain superficial manners, *grammar* was not optional. "All the more for me, then. They don't get fish like this in New Jersey." He severed the head and tossed it into the garden.

My mother made no attempt to disguise her distaste. "I don't think an eel can be considered a fish at all, by the look of it."

But my father insisted it was. Fins, gills, the whole works. He had a cookbook—admittedly slim—devoted entirely to this one catch.

A seagull landed in the garden, snatched the eel's head and flew to the woodpile, trailing some vertebrae from its beak.

"Daddy says eels are an ancient life-form," I said, attempting to score points for Daddy.

"If you were a fish, Lily," said my father, "what fish would you be?"

"A bluefish," said Dodie promptly. "I'd be a bluefish."

"Plus a reason. You need at least one reason," Daddy advised her even though he had asked *me*.

"Because it's blue."

"How about you, Lily?"

"That's not a reason."

"Hey. You know the rules."

A person's reason stood, no matter how stupid.

I thought about it. A bluefish was nice. My father always called it his lucky day if he caught a bluefish. "A bluefish, I guess."

"You can't pick bluefish," said Dodie. "I already said it."

"She doesn't *have* to pick something different. Besides, I asked her first," he said, restoring fairness.

Dodie opened her mouth to protest but my father said this was a game, not a contest, a distinction that was apparently supposed to put a stop to bickering.

"That's OK. I'll be a porpoise," I said, confident I had made a better choice anyway.

"A porpoise isn't a fish," said Dodie sanctimoniously, and Daddy backed her up.

I looked at my mother.

"Don't look at me," she said. "I'm not in this."

"Why not? What fish would you be?" Daddy asked her.

"I don't want to play."

"But Mama," I urged.

She looked at my father. "You first, then."

"OK. I'd be a striped bass," he said without hesitation. "Because they're fun to catch."

"Not an eel?" said my mother. She blew on her chowder, forgetting it was already cold.

"I'll be an eel," I jumped in, in case Daddy had noticed the sarcasm.

"Maybe *you* would like to be an eel?" my father teased my mother, ignoring people whose turn it wasn't.

She drew up her knees, hugged her bare legs and watched the gull on the woodpile. "No. Finnan Haddie. That's my favorite." Refusing to be teased.

Somehow—I didn't know how—the game had shifted. It was just between the two of them.

"That's not a fish. It's a recipe."

"Nevertheless." She waved some gnats away. Along with his objection.

"Disqualified."

"Oh, all right." She grew thoughtful. Then she picked trout. Definitely a trout. Daddy pressed for specifics. After a moment more she brightened and said, "Rainbow. Because they're hard to catch."

Simultaneous nods. They both found this answer highly satisfying.

"That leaves you, Lily." The clear bubble that had enclosed them dissolved.

By then I knew my answer. "Starfish," I said.

"I thought you were an eel," said Dodie.

"Because…." prompted my father.

Why did I pick starfish? I liked the way it sounded. Then I thought of an answer I knew he would approve of. "Because it has five arms and five is a Fibonacci number."

"Bravo!" said Daddy. "You see? The reason says at least as much as the choice." He sieved the last slender fish bones through his teeth and made of them a latticework on the edge of his plate while I avoided the dark look I knew Dodie would be casting in my direction. "Lily's growing up. How old are you going to be? Have you thought about what you'd like for your birthday?"

I hesitated. I knew what I wanted, but if I couldn't have it, it would feel worse to have actually asked for it.

"No?"

"I guess I'd like a dress for the talent show." A blue dress with a whipped cream apron. Excellent for the price.

"Don't you have a dress?"

I *had* packed a dress. There was nothing wrong with my dress. When it was Dodie's, I had actually coveted it. A less greedy girl would have been content with one perfectly good dress. But I forged ahead. "The one at Watson's...."

"That dress was twenty five dollars," said my mother.

My father's eyes widened.

"Maybe Tucker and...." I had been putting some thought into this.

"No, Ma'm. Your grandfather is not made of money." My mother guessed my little scheme.

"I don't think that." But I had exhausted all other ideas for making that dress mine.

"That dress wasn't so great," said Dodie.

The evening had turned cooler. Daddy tossed his scraps into the garden. Another gull snatched them up. Or maybe the same one, hogging everything. No one made a move to do the dishes. No one took up the cause of my birthday dress. Shock at mention of the price tag still flickered in Daddy's eyes.

My mother rubbed her bottom lip. Back and forth. Just when I thought the subject was closed, she said, "You may write to them that you are saving toward a dress. That way they might decide to contribute, and the amount is up to them."

Not an entirely promising plan, but it boasted one distinct advantage: she backed it. I would write the letter before she could change her mind.

Supper was over, but no one was quite ready to leave the table. Daddy got a jar of nails and spread them out on a piece of newspaper to sort. My mother offered to show us the material she bought for Playhouse curtains.

"You're making curtains for the Playhouse?" asked Daddy.

The evening breeze was cool but gentle and she missed the note of disapproval. "I got a very good price. Here, I'll show you." She went inside and came out with a package wrapped in brown paper.

My mother had been a perfunctory seamstress when she was growing up. But faced with the need for curtains and drapes when they moved to New Jersey, she rolled up her sleeves and tackled the project. She labored over tuck-points and valances. She developed patience she didn't know she had, and looked forward to a visit to the fabric store. Materials didn't have to be expensive to be of good quality, she would insist, casting her eye over the bolts of fabric, testing textures and weights between her fingers. At Murray's I would steer her toward flamboyant prints in bold colors, but she would reject them without a second look. My mother's choices spilled over with understated grace. Thirty years later a pair of curtains she had lined carefully with muslin and sewn with her straight, tiny stitches, would not have puckered or faded. Save for their softness after many launderings, they would not be dated in any way.

She unwrapped the package and unfolded a simple blue and white design in cotton. Price-worthy cotton.

"I'm just wondering why you're making curtains for the Playhouse when we won't even use it next year. And we need every penny now."

Now she heard it. The criticism. "Actually I do want to use it...." She began and faltered.

His eyebrows shot up. "Oh?"

She hesitated. She fingered a corner of the material. She had thought of getting a piano, she said at last. The Playhouse could be a studio. It was just an idea. So she could take students. Or.... She studied a spot on her thumbnail.

"Or what?"

"I could become an accompanist."

An accompanist. I wasn't even sure what she meant. Was that a profession?

Everyone's eyebrows went up. Waiting for her to elaborate. She hadn't ever said she wanted to become an accompanist.

"An accompanist," said my father. "*Here?*"

For which my mother had no answer.

"Well, go ahead and do what you want. Make the curtains."

His permission, as my mother well knew, was beside the point. Fabric that was cut to measure was non-returnable.

Daddy made piles of nails. I watched my mother in the fading light. I wondered what she must have been like when she was my age. I knew she had had braces; she had a cat named Timothy. Last summer, when BerthaMelrose cleaned out the attic, she sent a packet of letters my mother had written home from music camp in Maine, where reveille was early, showers were cold, and character-building was mentioned in a prominent position on the camp stationary. (My mother had not told me I could read the letters, but she hadn't told me I *couldn't* either.) In her small, economical hand-writing she had written BerthaMelrose weekly reports with a detailed accounting of what she had spent on thread to mend a button, writing paper, a gift for a friend, a new piece of music which could only be ordered from Boston. She told what measures she was taking to insure her good health. She wrote how hopeless she was with a canoe! How varied the crafts! The funny things the other girls did! She was so forthcoming, so full of high spirits. A lone daughter away from home, constructing a persona for sour BerthaMelrose, whom she hoped to win.

As if reading my thoughts, my mother said, "I think I might write to BerthaMelrose and Tucker and invite them down for Lily's birthday."

The sun was setting behind Uncle George's. Daddy counted out a pile of screws. "BerthaMelrose won't come."

"I'll offer to make reservations."

"You watch. Her arthritis will take a sudden turn for the worse. Or more likely she'll have urgent business in her garden."

"They'll come," she said.

My father said good. If they came, then Tucker could bring the loan.

"What loan?" said my mother.

"Well, I totaled everything up. We're about a thousand short."

"What loan?"

"I asked him if he could tide us over." As if it were self-evident.

My mother, who had been running a fork along the wood grain of the table, stopped. "You what?"

Fights, I decided, were like rain. It was hard to tell exactly when they began.

"Oh, Lydia. You agreed." My father gave an exasperated sigh.

"You said *maybe* you'd ask."

"Meanwhile we have *costs*."

That didn't make them Tucker's responsibility, she said, a darkness gathering on her face.

"He'll pay Tucker back when he gets his raise," I interjected. To clear things up. "It's all worked out."

My mother turned in my direction. Turned not just her head, but at the waist as though her neck had gone suddenly stiff. For a long moment that was the only indication she had heard me. Her narrowed eyes pierced an object just beyond my left shoulder.

"Lydia." My father tried to capture her attention.

But she was fixed on whatever it was just behind me. Her lips moved. Testing out replies she hadn't yet decided on. Then she picked this one, the one with a big stinger in its backside.

Because she had heard me after all. Because I, too, wanted to go over her head and tap Tucker for money.

"I have two daughters. And one of them likes to interfere."

Everything. Stopped.

I wondered how it was possible to forget for stretches at a time that I had a sister and her name was Dodie. I wondered how long it took to earn a thousand dollars. I wondered why, when you hold your breath, your heart doesn't stop beating.

She drew furrows on the table with the tines of her fork. "Nobody has told me what we are going to do if my parents don't help us pay for this house," she said to her plate after one of her daughters straightened the green ribbon on her ponytail. Because she looked good in green. And the other daughter, after a very long time, took a breath. "A loan we had no business asking for in the first place."

I dug a trench in the sand with my toe. I hoped Daddy would know what to say. Finally he crumpled his napkin into a ball and dropped it to the table. "You mean *I* had no business asking for."

"Is that why we eat eels? We can't afford a proper dinner?"

"No, Lydia. *I* eat eels. Not you. I eat what they won't even serve in restaurants. Not good enough for BerthaMelrose, who needs *reservations*. Just about right for the likes of me."

"What is that supposed to mean?"

"It means, Lydia, I wish you didn't put yourself above other people." He got up from the table. "It's unattractive."

Just then a bold gull flapped to the ground near us, looking for more scraps.

Daddy stretched his plate out and banged it with his knife. "Scat! Beat it!"

It eyed him and then lifted itself into the air and flew heavily away. The second gull followed.

"I've got about a half hour of light. I have work to do." He put down his plate and started in the direction of his typing tree.

But before he got far he stopped and turned back. "I didn't really mean that, Lydia. It's just that...."

"Go do your work," my mother interrupted him. Her voice was bitter. She wasn't about to let him off with a preëmptive apology.

He turned and limped up the hill.

She lit a cigarette, leaned back against the pine tree and looked out over the pond, studying some clouds that were vying to extinguish the setting sun. The fight seemed to replay itself across her face. The water was glassy. It was getting dark.

For once I wished Daddy would prove to be wrong. I wished BerthaMelrose and Tucker *would* come for my birthday. I sensed that my mother needed very badly to be right. It was more than curtains, more than the money. She needed something with BerthaMelrose to get fixed. But Daddy had good reason to doubt BerthaMelrose would ever visit us again. BerthaMelrose was a fussy woman. Travel slowed her circulation. She had to arrange for someone to water her plants and feed the cat. The thought of a neighbor entering her house, sitting on her chairs, using her bathroom, was an odious one. That was her word. Odious.

Easter clinched it.

The week before Easter my mother had cleaned house. She polished the kitchen floor, aired the rooms, moved Dodie into my room and fixed up Dodie's room for my grandparents. She picked daffodils from the garden and snapped off branches of cherry blossoms. She even took our winter clothes to the attic. And she toasted almonds.

First she blanched them in boiling water. I helped her slip them out of their skins. They were slippery inside their wet suits, and sometimes they shot across the kitchen as if they'd been fired from a sling. We giggled, my mother and I. Then she sprinkled them with Wesson oil and salt, and roasted them in the oven.

Oh, those almonds tasted good.

My father, who knew my grandmother's talent for disappointing my mother, stood in the kitchen doorway looking thoughtful. "I hate to see you get your hopes up, Lydia," he cautioned her.

"It's only for a few days," said my mother, assuming this show of concern had more to do with his own dread of a visit from BerthaMelrose.

BerthaMelrose and Tucker arrived on Good Friday in time for dinner. My mother served leg of lamb, conscientiously roasted to the recommended 145 degrees.

We ate on the dining room table with the lace tablecloth and the good water glasses. I liked lamb pink, the way my mother liked it, but BerthaMelrose said it was bloody. I saw a look pass between my parents and then my father carved all the outside slices for her. Less pink, but crusty with salt and pepper. His favorite part.

The next morning I got up early to help Daddy make egg custard for breakfast. But BerthaMelrose was up ahead of us. She hadn't slept a wink, she said. The mattress in Dodie's room was lumpy as a gravel pit.

My father listened without comment as he broke eggs into the mixing bowl. BerthaMelrose paused and a second layer of dissatisfaction settled over her face.

"Well?" she said to my father.

My father slid the custard into the oven and turned to face her. "It's only two nights," he said at last.

When my mother came down, she offered to swap rooms. "It's no trouble," she insisted.

But my father, who hated to see BerthaMelrose turn him out of his own bed, made one disastrous mistake: he frowned.

"I see I am not welcome," said BerthaMelrose.

My mother went rigid. Tucker disappeared into the living room with yesterday's *Newark Evening News*.

Too late, Daddy saw the stricken look on my mother's face. But once a fight was ferreted out, BerthaMelrose chased it down. Daddy's hesitation was just the excuse she needed to declare she could have predicted this would be the extent of his hospitality.

My father wrenched his eyes from my mother. "I think you've gone too far," he glowered at my grandmother.

BerthaMelrose turned her back and, stiff-ankled, went upstairs to pack their things.

My mother rushed to follow her. I waited in the kitchen with Daddy while my mother's stricken voice, pleading, imploring, as chilling as a draft, poured down the stairway.

My grandparents drove back to Boston that day, before my mother had the chance to play the Debussy piece she had been preparing for the occasion. Tucker was apologetic, but there was no changing BerthaMelrose's mind. My mother waved to them as they backed out of the driveway. She stood at the curb and waved as they drove down the street. She stood there until they were out of sight. Then she walked back to the kitchen and turned eyes full of hatred on my father. "You did this," she said to him in slow, measured tones.

"Good riddance," said my father, "if that's how BerthaMelrose thinks she can behave." Still not hearing the full glint of steel in my mother's voice.

"You had no right." She was livid.

Then the pressure that had built since BerthaMelrose arrived finally exploded. It was as if white-hot steam burst from a ruptured valve and scalded the whole house. Dishes rattled. Piano strings vibrated as the explosion echoed from room to room. And every sound seemed to make my mother madder.

I went to my room. Dodie went to hers. I pulled a pillow over my ears until, after a long while, the shouting stopped, the house grew quiet, and all the loose objects—the dishes in the cupboard, the doorknocker, the piano lid—dared not to make a sound.

Now my mother stubbed out her cigarette and lit another. She said in measured tones, "I don't think I'll do the dishes tonight. I think I'll just break them against that tree." She indicated a large rough pine.

Dodie lifted a plate to her shoulder. "OK." Mistakenly thinking she was joking.

My mother grabbed for the plate. She gave Dodie a black look and Dodie set it back on the picnic table.

"You won't have to wash mine," I said, licking my bowl. "See. It's clean."

"Don't count on BerthaMelrose and Tucker coming for your birthday. Just because I ask them doesn't mean any of it will work out."

"I know."

Suddenly she looked tired. Shadows deepened under her eyes. She made brooding circles in the ashtray with the tip of her cigarette.

And so to bring her back from wherever she had gone to, to prove I didn't think Tucker was made of money, I leaned back just like her, picked up my knife and pretended to smoke it. I held it casually to one side, as I had seen Greta Garbo do it. My mother really liked Greta Garbo.

Her eyes shifted ever so slightly to include me in her gaze. I stretched out my arm and took another elegant puff from my "cigarette."

"I guess you think you are pretty smart." She turned towards me. "A real sophisticate."

I couldn't tell what she was getting at, but I thought this was a promising beginning, and so I exhaled again.

"And smoking. It's so *attractive.*"

An unfamiliar stratagem in her tone confused me. I could tell she was leading up to something.

"Here. Have a puff on mine." She held out to me a freshly lit Pall Mall.

I froze. Something in her manner told me this was not a friendly game among equals. On the other hand, what could be so hard about it? I watched her lift the cigarette to her lips and draw deeply. She inhaled with a long, satisfied swelling of her chest. With her thumb and ring finger she slowly plucked a stray shred of tobacco from the tip of her tongue, looking straight at me the whole time. At last she exhaled and extended the cigarette to me again.

"Go ahead. Have the whole thing," she said grandly.

A glance at Dodie did nothing to help me decipher what change had taken place. I accepted the cigarette, took it gingerly between my fingers. Smoke coiled upward from the hot orange tip.

"Go ahead, glamour-puss," said Dodie, quick to perceive which side offered the more promising alliance.

And so I brought the cigarette to my mouth, sucked briefly and discharged the bitter smoke triumphantly into the air.

"Oh no," said my mother. "Take a good drag. *Inhale* it. Like this." She lit another cigarette. "Hmmm?" she coaxed.

Now there were two cigarettes going.

"Oh," I said. Smoke was stinging my eyes. "Sure."

This time I adopted a practiced pose. I held the cigarette as my mother did, hand opened flat along my face. Again I drew on the cigarette. I felt the bitterness enter my mouth. I felt my throat open; I felt my shoulders rise to give it space.

Then my insides convulsed.

Smoke exploded from my mouth in gut-wrenching spasms. I erupted from the table. The pot of corn chowder overturned and knocked my mother's coffee cup to the ground. My eyes watered, my nose stung. Air scraped down my throat, then scraped out again in fractured coughs. My mother whacked me on the back.

"All right. All right. Now, now."

"It went down the wrong pipe," I gasped. The look of smug superiority had left Dodie's face. Something else startled her mouth open and rounded her eyes. Panic. Maybe a little pity.

"So," my mother said, "smoking isn't all it's cracked up to be."

My coughing subsided, but I had not been able to cough up this lesson: that my mother had ventured to ask for what she wanted. A studio of her own in the Playhouse, so that she could become an accompanist. And that her disappointment was an acrid and dangerous thing.

———

Before bed Daddy got out the bottle of Calamine lotion and painted our stings by lamplight in the Playhouse. To my surprise he had at least a dozen and he hadn't even mentioned it. "You got away with something at supper, you know." He dabbed the cotton on my eyelid.

"I did?" I braced for what might follow.

"Starfish is a crustacean."

"Oh." Considering everything, this little piece of information arrived as a relief.

Just before I fell asleep, I realized why I chose a starfish. Because when people found them washed up on the beach, they picked them up and kept them.

7

MODERATE GALE OR NEAR GALE

Beaufort Number 7
Wind Speed 32-38 MPH
whole trees sway; walking against wind difficult

*T*ucker Melrose was a redhead. No one knew exactly with whom the carrot color had originated—there were occasional hints of a possible barbarous Viking explanation—but it had been a consistent mark of Melrose men since Winthrop Melrose straggled over from England twenty lamentable years *after* the Mayflower.

A bit embarrassed by the family's relative success in business, my grandfather instead derived satisfaction from the Melrose name's long history in New England. His grandfathers and great grandfathers and cousins twice and thrice removed had gained a foothold not merely in the New World or in the Colonies, but where it counted, in Boston and its environs. Salem, Quincy, Plymouth. Longevity was the Melrose wealth: by the time they dressed up as Indians and dumped British tea into Boston Harbor in an act of civil disobedience, they had been here a century and a half. It meant Tucker didn't need to feel inferior to anyone, no matter how distinguished. Or how flush.

Shy with women, Tucker was a man's man. His college record confirmed a lackluster intelligence, a special talent and enthusiasm for cards, and a passing interest in the workings of government. He met my grandmother when both were on the verge of having missed out on marriage. Her father, Bartholomew Simpson, was not English at all, but a hard-hearted Scot, a Presbyterian who had come to this country to teach Divinity at Harvard. Her father's Oxford education and Harvard credentials somewhat—but not entirely—mitigated the fact of Miss Bertha Simpson's relatively recent emigration and *Scots*, not English, ancestry. Melroses, after all, valued intelligence and prided themselves on being broad-minded. And at least she wasn't Irish.

Tucker did well during the Depression, running the credit department of a candy company. By the time I was born, he had been elected to the state legislature, which seemed to require very little of his time. He smoked cigars, could tell a joke, and never missed a Red Sox game on the radio, all of which served to foster his popularity both in the State House and in the eyes of his two adoring granddaughters.

Tucker would not let us down. Perhaps BerthaMelrose had failed to inherit any measure of generosity from her parsimonious father. But Tucker was different. It was true I had never known him to discuss the particulars of personal financial matters, his or ours. In fact silence on that topic might as well have been the eleventh commandment. But I held fast to the vision of Tucker, the impish and highly likeable carrot-topped legislator, and my father—Grammy Grainger's favorite—solving all our problems with a bank draft and a handshake.

———

The day after I learned that smoking was not all it was cracked up to be, my mother wrote BerthaMelrose inviting them to come for my birthday later in August, with an offer to make reservations. I wrote my own letter to them and took a long time getting the wording just right, replete with certain clues. I told them I was practicing my cello every day and that I hoped someday to get as good on cello as my mother was on piano. I wanted to play in the talent show at St. John's Episcopal and was trying to win my teacher's permission. Finally worming my way to the point, I told them about the dress I had seen at Watson's. It was rather expensive, but *perfect* for the performance. *I have a birthday coming, so you never know,* I wrote. Cryptic enough to meet my mother's requirements, but not *too* cryptic. I was saving all my pennies, I hinted, in case I was in for a big disappointment. I underlined the word *disappointment* and drew some tears in the margin. On the flap of the envelope I wrote the initials SWAK, and very small underneath, in case they didn't know what that meant, I translated *Sealed with a Kiss.*

The letter crinkled with promise in my pocket.

My mother held hers in her hand as side by side we walked the quarter mile to our mailbox out on Route 28, she in one tire track and I in the other, separated by the strip of weeds in the middle. The day was warm and walking raised a damp shine on her face. She still had a scar like a white skid-mark on the inside of her arm where she had burned herself on the oven rack at Easter. As she walked she tapped the letter against her leg. She wore a sleeveless blouse that showed her freckled arm from her long fingers to her soft upper-arm, that skim of flesh that shimmied ever so slightly when she struck loud notes on the piano. Threads of sea-green veins showed at her wrist.

The letter tap-tapped against her leg and she filled her lungs with oxygen, as if a deep breath could clear an unpleasant aftertaste. "Smell the bayberry?" she said as we passed a man scraping barnacles from the bottom of a boat on Dr. Poole's shore.

She had been quiet all morning. Daddy had carried his blanket and typewriter up into the woods to his favorite tree. There was no mention of the loan or of making the Playhouse into a studio. The air smelled good, but I couldn't pick out bayberry. "I think so," I lied. There had also been no mention of smoking. We were all pretending last night's dinner had been like any other.

"Here." She reached down and picked a small branch of stiff green leaves with a cluster of small gray berries. "Here's what you do." She took her thumbnail and scraped the waxy coating from one of the berries and held the branch to my nose.

I inhaled. The leaves smelled of the sachet she kept in her drawers. Even here on the road to the mailbox with her shirt sticking to her in the heat, she was wrapped in that delicate scent. My dress would smell of sachet, too. I would keep it folded in her bureau in the Playhouse. At home in New Jersey she sometimes let me iron her hankies and put them away in her drawer. There, I took my time furtively trying on her jewelry, running my hands over her satin slip with the lace trim, fluttering the nylon stockings through the air like streamers. I practiced clasping the stays on her garter belt, careful to put everything back just as it had been, mystified how she knew to ask if I had been going-through-her-things. I loved to watch her gather a nylon into an accordion between her fingers, slip it over her toes, ease it past her heel and unfurl it along her leg and over her knee, so careful not to snag it with a fingernail. I was still a little girl when, one night, she was taking off her bra while undressing for bed and I reached up, patted and joggled her breasts and called them her powder puffs. She steered me firmly out of the room, closed the door and finished putting on her nightgown alone, letting me know her powder puffs were hers, not mine.

We put our letters in the mailbox. One atoning for Easter. One sealed with a manipulative kiss.

Every afternoon we walked to the mailbox together. And every day the mailbox was empty. Not completely empty. Dodie got a postcard from a girl who lived on our block in New Jersey. The light bill came, along with telephone and gas. All from New Jersey because of course at the Cape the only light we had were daylight and the kerosene lamp, and there was no charge for shouting from our beach across the pond to call Nicole. But no letter with a Boston postmark.

After a week my mother shuffled through the small packet of envelopes in her hand and said it was too soon to expect a reply.

After a few more days she said, "They have things to do, you know," even though I hadn't said a word. "They can't be expected to drop everything just because you are having a birthday."

July grew hot and by the end of the third week the asphalt burnt our feet when we reached the pavement, but the box was still empty of answers from BerthaMelrose and Tucker.

———

By late July my fingers were more callused than my bare feet. Mr. Metcalf said I was making progress. My mother and I had our first run through of Capriccio at Aunt Fanny's so that I could begin to see how the parts fit together. My counting was lax, and she told me that I should take a good look at her part on my own so that I would know what to listen for. Periodically Daddy took time out from typing on *The Mathematics of Music*— this was the new title of his dissertation—to check on me. I had done all the fast passages slowly, working on coordination because, as Mr. Metcalf had stated, my left hand seemed not to have made my right hand's acquaintance. Now I was trying to speed it up little by little, with limited success.

Daddy came in one morning just as I had gotten all twisted up on the fiery coda.

"What's this, Lily? Getting a little ahead of yourself?" He sat down on the cot and told me to slow down. "Try it ten times. But slowly." He had a real feeling for the concrete aspects of music: key signature, metronome markings and practice habits that could be precisely measured.

"I *have* done it slowly," I objected, surprised by the appalling whine in my tone.

"So?" Graingers didn't whine.

It began to dawn on me that there would always be another ten times and another ten. "Couldn't I skip a day?" I said. Dodie was at Triple Tree with Nicole, who had managed to come by another filter-tipped cigarette. (Nicole, who was getting quite accomplished with Uncle George's Lucky Strikes, had renamed our club *Smokers' Hideout at Triple Tree,* preserving the desired acronym.) Later they were going to forage for a Ladies' Slipper to transplant to Aunt Fanny's garden. She needed cheering up lately.

"Skip a day!" He sounded genuinely alarmed.

I poked some grains of sand on the floor with the tip of my bow.

"It would take two days just to get back to where you left off."

"After just one day?" This was an even bigger job than I thought.

"There's only one way to get where you are going, Lily. You know what that is."

"Yes," I said doubtfully. He meant the ten times. I made little tic-tac toes in the sand.

"Ask Rubenstein," he continued, as if that explained everything. "Ask Heifetz how much *he* practices. Or any of the Greats. Go ahead. Just ask them."

It didn't occur to me that I had no way of asking the Greats. This whole conversation had gotten much too serious.

I blew sand from the tip of my bow, placed it on the strings and began. I was on the third repetition when we heard my mother dragging the metal laundry tub up the path to the clothesline Daddy had strung between two trees. He left.

I finished and added a pencil mark to the row of slashes in the margin of my music.

"Need help?" I heard him ask.

I started my fourth repeat. By the fifth their voices had risen. I could hear them clearly even over my sixteenth notes.

"Well, it's too late. I *did* ask him," I overheard him say.

"We could cut back."

"You should have said that last spring."

"This was your idea," said my mother. "Not mine."

"Come again?"

No reply from my mother. I took the pencil and marked a slash for number five and started again. Softly.

"Besides, they can afford it." Daddy's voice again. "Tucker would want to know if we were in trouble."

"*Are* we in trouble?"

There was a pause. I stopped playing altogether.

"No."

Another pause.

"I notice you didn't see fit to ask your own parents."

"Lydia. Use your head." His parents didn't *have* any money. He said it didn't take a genius to figure *that* out.

He had done it now. He shouldn't have said *Use your head.* Sure enough, she began to strafe him with words like *threadbare* and *pinchpenny.* Now I played louder to drown her out. But over the music I still heard *can't manage our affairs...humiliate me...just so you can call them tight-fisted.*

Then my father burst in. "That's right," he said. "Tight-fisted. You bet she is. I can't make it up to you that BerthaMelrose cares for no one but herself." He was yelling now. He said it was a mystery to him how such a selfish person as BerthaMelrose gave birth to so fine a woman as my mother. It was her one act of generosity, he said.

"What gives you the right..." shouted my mother.

I put my cello down and went to the door of the tent. "Stop shouting!" I shouted at her. "Why won't you just let Daddy take care of it?" I could feel the indentations from the steel string on my fingertips.

She stopped and a look of surprise came over her. She turned her head ever so slightly to include me in her vision. Eyebrows arched. Eyebrows arched in search of sedition.

"It's all right, Lily," said my father. "Finish your practicing."

I looked from one to the other.

"It's all right, cowgirl," he said again. "I'll be there in a minute."

She was still regarding me with interest. Tucking something away, I thought, for future reference. That I blamed their fights on her.

I went back inside and picked up my cello. I thought it was generous of my father to attribute their fights to BerthaMelrose when my mother's attacks were so mean. I wondered what would happen to us if we couldn't pay. Once a friend in my class "lost their house," and my mother gave me money to take her for lemon ice the day their furniture was auctioned. A house was a big thing to lose. Daddy was right. Tucker would want to help us. I could understand why my mother might not want to ask Bertha-Melrose. BerthaMelrose made us walk sideways down her stairs so our heels wouldn't scuff the risers. But Tucker was different.

I picked up my bow and a chilling new note entered my

mother's voice. "I don't suppose," she said coldly, "you've spoken to George about Gloria."

"Lydia...." My father's pleading voice moved slowly down the path. I stopped playing. The Playhouse door slammed. It slammed again. Then there was silence. I had lost track of which number I was on. I started over. Nothing worked right. My bow scraped the wrong string and my fingers stumbled over each other. When I looked up, Daddy was in the doorway, his face drawn. A pinched and threadbare face pretending everything was all right.

"I'll get it, Daddy." He sat down on Dodie's cot. I muddled the measures again.

"No." He lifted his lame leg with his hands to move his foot. "No, Lily. Try again."

I tried again.

"Better." But it wasn't better. "You should do that section until I say stop."

I played the passage two or three times through; then he got up and left.

I remembered days when he would come to the tent and listen at the door, smiling. "Got the wind at your back today, eh Lily?" he would say, and his smile made me not mind that the cello was hard and the hours went slowly.

I repeated the bars over and over. He didn't come back. I tried playing each note ten times in a row, then the next note, making the passage ridiculously simple. Hoping he would catch me at that game. I listened for him. Nothing. I tried it backwards. I traced the shadow of a pine bough on the tent wall with the tip of my bow. He had vanished. Finally I packed up. I looked in the Playhouse, the new house (nearly ready for the roof) and the outhouse. At last I checked the knoll. No typewriter noise.

When I crested the hill I spotted him under the black oak, legs splayed on a blanket, papers tossed aside, playing solitaire.

To get to Wellfleet we had to pass Blackfish Creek, named for the pilot whales that periodically stranded in the shallows along the shore north of Eastham. No one drove that stretch of road without a long look no matter how long it had been since the last stranding. It was said that the whales beached themselves deliberately and died, not from lack of food or water, but from their own body weight, pressing on their lungs and heart. The mates of stranded whales would linger in the waters offshore long after it was certain their partners were lost. People who lived in the area knew this because they heard the singing, lonely songs of animals who lived in the ocean but were mammals, like us.

Near the end of July the *Cape Codder* reported that a pod of mothers and juveniles had been discovered milling in the shallows, the first such incident in a number of years. Townspeople —with a certain amount of self-importance that theirs was the chosen beach—had convened a small flotilla of skiffs and trawlers and herded or towed as many as they could back out to sea. There was a photo on the front page. The rest were trapped on the beach when the tide went out and were abandoned there to die.

These were the hopeless cases my mother and I encountered on the way to my lesson that afternoon. The day I found out that we were in trouble because Daddy said *No, we weren't.*

It was hot and Route 6 was empty. During the drive my mother had kept her preoccupied eyes steadfastly on the road as though evidence could be found there for bolstering her case against my father. So that she could re-argue all the ways my father was wrong about BerthaMelrose, making my father the unreasonable one and BerthaMelrose the misunderstood one. But as we approached Wharf Road, she slowed down. Eight black mounds loomed out of the shallows like hulls of grounded ships. She stopped the car on the shoulder and let it idle for a minute. No one was around. It was hard to see anything clearly. She squinted in the direction of the whales, then looked up and down the road. She pondered a minute. Finally she turned off the ignition.

"I suppose I should take a look," she said. This was a distraction worthy enough to interrupt her brooding.

I popped open my door.

"You stay here."

"Please?"

"I'll be right back."

She crossed the road and stood at the edge of the water, hand indecisively on her hip.

"Can you see anything?" I called.

She glanced at me momentarily and then reached down to remove her shoes.

I got out of the car and crossed the road. She was out on the flats by the time I got my shoes off and waded out to her.

"I thought I told you to stay in the car." Then her whole face shrank at the smell. "Stay close, you understand?"

We hiked up our shorts and waded out to the first whale, smaller than I expected a whale would be, and tipped partly on its side. Fiddler crabs scuttled from under my feet. A couple of horseshoe crabs moved at a prehistoric pace through the shallow water, each dragging one brutal spike which served for a tail. We were near the naval base and a plane droned in the distance, flying low.

The tide was going out. There were white splotches all over the whale. A pus wound on its back expelled a swarm of flies, which fanned out like fireworks and settled back down again. Two expressionless eyes, partially submerged, were filmed over. My mother moved around it, keeping a distance and averting her face. She went on to the next one.

I followed her to each dead whale, unsure if there might be a recommended code of conduct to cover a situation such as this. The Catholics would have known what to do. They would have known what words to say. The smell was dense and putrid. I left a few cautious feet between each whale and me. We had now joined the ranks of what my mother normally dismissed contemptuously as the Morbidly Curious.

"This one's alive." She was standing by the one furthest from shore. She moved in closer to it and poked its dry black skin tentatively with her finger. She bent down and looked into its face and then scooped some water up in her shirttail and flung it upward. Its head became a glistening dark watermelon. The whale moved a slender, pointed fluke. It was alive. She nudged it with her foot. "Swim, baby. Go on, swim."

I thought a sound came from his throat. "Mom, I don't think...."

She nudged it harder. "Lily, help me."

She leaned a shoulder into him. "Swim," she urged. I splashed him—I supposed it was a him although I didn't really know—with water and pushed with her. He was stuck fast. We could sooner have pushed Cape Cod to Block Island, the two of us. "Go on. Swim!" My mother sounded sterner. In the distance I could hear the guns at the naval base, low and dissonant, a sound like someone laying his forearms on the bottom notes of a piano. She looked up briefly in that direction and shaded her eyes. "Damn it, swim!" She slid her hand into the whale's mouth and tugged on its jawbone.

"Let's go, Mom. We can't do anything." I was beginning to feel all-alone out there.

A car on the road slowed.

"You can swim," she demanded. She strained against the thick skin. Then she stepped back. To take stock. Or to start over.

"It's no use, Mom," I cried. "Let's go."

"Need some help?" a man called from the road.

She dug her shoulder into the whale's side.

"It's OK," I called uncertainly. Daddy would know what to do. Dodie would know what to do. Even Aunt Fanny would know what to do. I did not.

"Let's go now. We should go. Mama?"

The car drove away.

Her hands clenched. Her jaw worked. "Swim!" she ordered again.

Sand gave way under my foot. I teetered, and all at once I could see us, as if I were looking down from a great distance, standing up to our knees in water on the edge of nothing more than a shifting sand dune, tiny bits of glass piled in the shape of an arm, an elbow and a fist. The easterly most point of the United States. Fragile as a piecrust. Adrift far out to sea.

"You're being…." I floundered. I cast about for the right thing to say, *something* to say, and I grasped the worst words I could have chosen. "Daddy wouldn't like this."

"Daddy wouldn't like it?" she yelled. She shoved the whale with the heel of her hand. "*Daddy* wouldn't like it?" And then she kicked it. Her foot went out. Water sprayed us.

I tried to step between her and the whale. "Get out of here!" she shouted, either at me or at the whale, I wasn't sure which. She dug both feet into the sand and strained against it. "*Daddy* can't even stand up for *Aunt Fanny*."

"Momma." My voice trembled.

But she seemed not to know I was there. Another car passed. Still she strained against the whale.

"Momma!" I said again. Louder.

Her eyes narrowed. "It's none of your business," she said, jaw clenched, to the daughter who liked to interfere. The daughter who gave up piano because there were too many notes, who thought we had formed a tremulous alliance when we *colluded* on a scheme to solicit money from Tucker. She drew her leg back, preparing to punish whales, *this* whale, for giving up, because giving up meant something worse than simple rage. She wavered momentarily on the other foot, seeking her balance in the water. Her shorts were wet up to the waist.

"Stop it!" I cried. I wanted a mother who kissed me goodnight. I wanted a mother who would teach me the names of flowers. I wanted a mother who took my face in her long-fingered hands and saw her own. I wanted *my* mother, as I thought she used to be.

I caught hold of her foot. We fell into the water. She twisted and thrashed. Salt stung my eyes. I threw myself on top of her and tried to pin her arms.

"Leave me alone," she shrieked. Fury had grabbed her like an undertow, pulling her deeper and deeper. Her foot jerked to her chest, a wedge against me.

"Daddy's girl," she spit at me. And shoved me from her. Her knee caught me in the stomach, but it was her words, her saved-up hope-splitting words, that made me gasp for breath.

"Stop," I tried to say, but it came out choked.

She went slack. I tried to get up but stumbled back on top of her. She pushed me away. I rolled off her, coughed and leaned back against the whale, whose heart still beat, however faintly. But I didn't care now. I elbowed, hard, the thick carcass with satisfying disdain.

"Stupid fish," my mother hissed.

"It's not a fish," I said spitefully.

She picked up a handful of wet sand. I flinched, but she heaved it past me and it hit the whale with a tired slap. Without any force or will in the arm that threw it.

The whale made a soft downward noise, almost a sigh. And from the bay, some ways out, I heard a cry of utter loneliness, a solo voice, like a cantor wailing, but less earthly, rising and falling in plainsong, too pure a grief to come from anything merely mortal. It seemed connected only to sadness itself.

"I know it's not a fish," she said.

. . .

Back in the car I held still while my mother scoured my head dry with a towel. Her lips moved, forming words, but she said nothing out loud. She made me take off my wet clothes and put on my bathing suit. She took the towel to my body, hard like sandpaper. The towel hurt. Her hands hurt me. It made me glad. It put our hurts together, skin to skin.

I took my lesson in my bathing suit. My mother's knitting chair stood empty; she waited in the car while her shorts dried. I played my Capriccio, a dull-hearted reading with fingers stiff as stumps.

Mr. Metcalf never said a word.

Afterwards my mother took me into Windward Antiques and bought me the ostrich plume fan. "Don't tell your father," she warned. I supposed she meant about the six dollars.

8

FRESH GALE OR GALE

Beaufort Number 8
Wind Speed 39-46 MPH
twigs break off trees, progress is generally impeded

*I*f you thought of summer as the trajectory of one of Digory's boomerangs, then the beginning of August was the turn-around point, when the momentum was no longer carrying us farther out into vacation, but back towards New Jersey and school. Midsummer.

We were still waiting to hear from BerthaMelrose and Tucker, but that wasn't necessarily a bad sign, I reasoned. It could mean they were trying to work it out. When they came, Tucker would be full of stories and would give my mother a puff on his cigar. And in his vest pocket would be the money for the dress I'd wear at the talent show. "She plays so well," people in the audience would say of me in that dress. I'd play like Pablo Casals.

Of course I knew that the dress couldn't really improve my

performance. I knew I didn't fool my mother when I implied as much in Ellis' Market one day. She took two cans of soup from the shelf, dropped them into the cart and did not say what I knew she was thinking: she could tell when people were kidding themselves.

Neither of us told my father about what happened at Blackfish Creek. Not even that we had seen the whales. I wasn't sure exactly what had gone wrong, but I was certain I was not a daughter he could be proud of. Since that day my mother and I had been tiptoeing around each other, as if a critical patient in the next room shouldn't be disturbed.

Mr. Metcalf wanted Capriccio memorized and so I spent a little extra time each morning trying to play it by heart. The trickiest spots were those when the music was the same, but in a different key. My fingers just didn't see the logic in that. So far I hadn't made it all the way through once without breaking down, but I persevered. Mr. Metcalf said I had enough senses to worry about with Hearing and Touch. I'd thank him when I could cross off *Sight*.

Daddy hired a mason to construct the chimney. It was to separate the kitchen from the living room with a raised hearth to sit on (my mother's wish.) The whole chimney took only two days. Mr. Cavanaugh, wearing white overalls, slathered on mortar like icing on a cake. Slap went a dollop of cement. On went the brick. He tapped it into place with the heel of his trowel. Then with a flick of the blade he sliced off any excess, plopped it back into his bucket, laid his level across the brick and studied the bubble.

I watched, transfixed. Slap went the cement, on went the brick. Tap-tap with the trowel. Slice, trim, plop. Higher and higher. As metronomic as a Kreutzer étude.

"All with one tool," Daddy marveled.

Not counting the level.

After that Mr. Gill declared it was time for the roof, and August unleashed a heat wave. Mr. Gill brought an apprentice to help with this momentous step. A young apprentice with a dull expression and good balance. Daddy held the ladder as they climbed up and straddled ceiling joists ten feet off the ground. The apprentice steadied the collar beams while Mr. Gill hoisted the ridge pole into place, perspiring, trembling with the effort, never taking his eyes off the spot where it finally was all to come together in an upside down V.

"You make it look easy as shucking corn," Daddy told him when they finished. He fairly glistened with high spirits. I didn't know why it should astonish me so, that now it looked like a house, that it had graduated from a schematic to an abode. Drawing distinctions, Daddy said we technically couldn't call it a roof until it had been sheathed, tar-papered and shingled. But it was up. He got a bottle of ale he had been saving for the occasion out of the icebox and split it with Mr. Gill. He gave a swallow in the bottom of a glass to the sweaty, underage apprentice, who chucked it down before Daddy could change his mind.

Mr. Gill pulled his chin thoughtfully and critiqued his own work: Not bad. "Not half bad," he said, chattier than he'd been all summer.

According to him the house was half done. The ridgepole ran the whole length, straight and true as the keel of a scull. Beams dipped out to either side like two rows of evenly spaced oars. I stood next to Daddy and let my eyes travel from the foundation all the way up to the peak, back down and along the eaves, over the struts, and I saw how everything connected finally to the massive center beam. The roof elicited oohs and ahhs, but the core of the whole structure was that central girder, the spine that held everything up and to which everything attached, *three* two-by-sixes, side-by-side, bored through and clamped together by big galvanized bolts. Professionally engineered. A beam that ran the length of the house. Uncle George's splitting-apart-like-toothpicks beam.

Daddy finished the last of the ale.

"Wouldn't it be stronger," I asked, "if it had just one big thick beam?" Anxious whether I had achieved the right degree of offhandedness to conceal my big fear.

Daddy took Mr. Gill's empty glass and turned to me. "What's this? What about the beam?" Eyes on me like searchlights. "Listening to Uncle George, I see."

Anyone who had left well enough alone could have stood firmly on two steady feet. *I* shifted weight from one leg to the other, worrying a scrap of hair by my ear.

"Lily, what you want to do is, you want to know something about everything and everything about something. Uncle George, now he thinks he should know everything about everything."

He flung the last drops from the glasses onto the ground. There was only one thing Daddy couldn't stand. It wasn't laziness, it wasn't forgetfulness, it wasn't even whining. What upset him most was if I didn't put my trust in him.

"Anybody can nail two boards together," he continued. "But that doesn't make him an authority. The difference between Uncle George and me is that I'm not ashamed to say so. Place your faith in education, Lily. I paid good money for an out-and-out architect. Go with the expert. Not Uncle George's hot air."

Caught doubting, I managed a nod, squirmed, and wished I could forget Uncle George's words. *You can't cut corners to save a dime, Dig. There'll be hell to pay.*

"I'll tell you what," Daddy said, suddenly brighter. "Put these glasses on the picnic table and go get me an egg out of the icebox."

I hesitated, wondering what an egg had to do with anything.

"Shimmy, shimmy," he said.

Mystified, I ran to do what he asked. Mr. Gill started to load up his truck.

"OK," he said when I came back. "Now how hard do you think it is to crush this egg between your palms?" He gave it a little toss and caught it.

"Not hard." Anybody knew that.

"All right then. Show me. But you have to hold it end to end. It has to be end to end. Got it?"

I positioned the egg between my hands.

"That's it. Now try to break it. Push as hard as you can. Go on."

I didn't know what could be the point, but he said to do it, and so I did. I squeezed.

"Push hard. What's the matter? Harder." He was smiling.

I strained as hard as I could. I gritted my teeth, bulged my eyes and grunted for maximum effect. The egg held.

"What, no luck? Lace your fingers. Go for some leverage."

Daddy was obviously enjoying himself, so I did as I was told. I grimaced and cocked my arms at the elbows and dug my feet into the ground. He was getting the better of me, but I didn't mind.

"So," he said brightly. He plucked the egg from my fingers and held it to the light. "Learn anything?"

I thought it was a pretty good trick, but I doubted that's what he meant. "I think so," I said.

"And?"

"An eggshell is stronger than it looks?"

He laughed heartily. "That's my little Einstein." His face settled into a thoughtful smile. "A lot of things are stronger than they look. It's no trick, Lily. It's physics. Now, no more fretting about the house. OK?"

The Cape was full in the hot breath of August, a long exhale, forged on the Midwestern plains, which scudded across the Adirondacks and deposited a haze over the coastline on its way out to sea.

Dodie, Nicole and I convened daily. Mornings we wore a path to Triple Tree. Afternoons we swam off Uncle George's wharf. Periodic explorations of the woods up and over the hill yielded an occasional glimpse of a spirited game taking place on the sandlot baseball diamond belonging to the boys' camp. But I didn't spot Nick, the boy in the canoe.

My father bet us we couldn't swim across the pond without stopping. All the way from our beach to Uncle George's. And so we launched ourselves ceremoniously one afternoon with the intent to prove him wrong. We waded gingerly through the soft dark mud, one wary foot at a time like three circumspect herons, out to the drop-off and—since our undertaking seemed to call for an appropriately grand by-word—"put out to sea." Aunt Fanny put in from the far shore in her small sailboat to provide encouragement and cheer us on. She tacked expertly beside us even though the Lusitania was said to be notoriously hard to handle. My father followed us in the Clamshell, should rescue be required. Halfway there Dodie began to lag. Nicole circled her twice. But we were all accomplished doggie-paddlers and made the far shore without mishap.

Flush with success, we decided our next expedition should be a walk into town for a Saturday matinee. On the appointed morning I put off breakfast and raced through my practicing. I cheated on arpeggios, dashed through Capriccio and told myself I'd iron out the mistakes tomorrow.

My mother was in the Playhouse when Dodie and I went to tell her we were setting out for Nicole's. The fabric for the curtains was laid out on the bed. White peonies on a navy blue field, three little curtains for three tiny windows. Meant to last. A chasm had opened between us since the day she kicked the whale. In place of solid ground there now was a tentative formality. And an occasional peace offering: the ostrich plume fan, or an unaccustomed interest in my opinion. Today it took the form of three one-dollar bills, which she pinned to the inside of my shorts pocket for ice cream and the movie. More than enough. Her treat.

"How will you get home?" She took a sip of coffee and placed her cup on the table.

We had not anticipated this detail. "Walk?" said Dodie.

"I've got to go to Ellis'. I can pick you up." She unspooled a length of thread, and with that we were gone.

"Bring the change!" she called after us.

Nicole, Dodie and I left Bunker Hill by noon. We skirted the crumbling clay tennis court that used to belong to the old girls' sailing camp and circled behind Norgeot's cranberry bog. The Norgeot boy, whose overtures of friendship Digory consistently ignored, waved to us from where he worked on his knees in the bog. We came out on the main road the other side of Virginia Carman's house, where Aunt Fanny took her weekly violin lessons.

Town was three miles. Nicole took the lead, setting a crisp pace. Then Dodie. I matched the rhythm of my steps to the sunburnt backs of Dodie's legs. Heat vapors rose from the pavement. I brushed a green-headed horsefly from my shoulder. It landed on my arm. I slapped it. It circled and landed on my arm again. This time I squeezed it and felt its sides crack and buckle between my fingers much like I thought Daddy's egg should have done. A yellowish soup spilled out. I wiped my hands on my shorts and felt the crinkle of the three dollars in my well-heeled pocket.

We cut through St. John's Episcopal, where Aunt Fanny attended church every summer because, she said, it was the prettiest church on Cape Cod and so God was sure to be in attendance. Uncle George didn't go. He said St. John's was Episcopal and that made it practically Catholic. I wondered if you had to cross yourself in an Episcopal church. And if you did, did she?

We rested behind the little chapel so that Dodie could catch her breath. She picked a honeysuckle blossom. We hovered over her while she pinched off the very tip and carefully drew out the pistil. She put the tiny drop of nectar that formed to her lips. A drop of honey pilfered from the Episcopal Church.

"Have you ever thought of becoming a nun?" I asked. I knew a girl who went to parochial school and swore not all nuns were mean and strict and old. One of her teachers wore lipstick and mascara and made dedicating your life to Christ sound like a wonderful thing. Mysterious, simple and clear-cut, everything all mapped out for you. A nun would not find herself scrapping over a half-dead whale.

"And get my head shaved?" said Nicole. She leaned on her hand against the wall. "N-O. No." For Nicole, certainty was a virtue. She climbed on a rock and boosted herself up to peer in a window.

"I like those blue habits the French nuns wear," Dodie ventured. She rested, back to the wall.

Nicole's arms were taut with holding herself up. "They're OK."

I said, "But a nun has no worries, ever." She was so intent on peeping, I wasn't sure she was even listening. "If you were a nun, you'd always know you were doing the right thing."

"Oh no, you wouldn't," said Nicole, paying attention after all. "You have to believe you are always sinning. Otherwise you are committing the sin of pride. Get it? No matter what, it's a sin." She rapped on the window. "Hey, in there."

Dodie started to her feet. "What are you doing?"

"Nothing. Nobody home." She hopped down from the window. She thought of herself as a swash-buckler, with a flashy nickname like *Renegade* or *Bounder*.

"Anyway, you've got to be Catholic to be a nun," said Dodie, always practical.

"Of course if you're Catholic, you're already on God's good side," said Nicole. She headed back out to the road. "Catholics have it made. 'Hail Mary full of grace blessed art thou....'"

"Don't," said Dodie, suddenly concerned.

"Why not?"

"Just don't."

We were coming around the end of Crystal Lake, all scrubbed and freshwater-transparent. I thanked Dodie silently: the Hail Mary wasn't ours to recite. I didn't think God necessarily watched over every little thing we did or said, but saying the Hail Mary without meaning it was bound to attract undue attention. I *was* curious, though, if Nicole really knew all the words.

She let it drop. "Who's in the talent show this year?" Like Uncle George, she knew how to change the subject before a conversation had time to go against her.

"I'm playing in it," I said. Last year the best act was Uncle George and Gloria's soft shoe. Gloria wore a sequined halter-top and circle skirt. I pictured myself performing on the makeshift stage in front of all those people, and my hands went suddenly sweaty. I wondered if I would be ready, and how I would know I was ready. Or if I would ever feel ready. Did grown-ups? Maybe that was the mark of a professional: forging ahead, ready or not.

"That last ten percent takes as much work as the first ninety," Mr. Metcalf told me at my last lesson. "That's how hard it is— once you get it up to a certain level—to eke out those last tiny improvements. But they make all the difference. It's that last ten percent that separates the men from the boys." He gave me the OK to play in the show after I surprised both of us by making it through Capriccio memorized *and* up to tempo. But it still needed Character. Character was what made one piece sound different from all others. Character was to be the aim of my last ten percent.

"It's *Spanish*, Lily. Where is that hot blood?" he half shouted over the music. "Anyone you were ever mad at, let's hear it. Who has insulted you? Get even! Faster. Louder. Stop! Big dramatic pause…. Now dig in. Race to the end." He flung his arms through the air like a brutal Genghis Khan. "You have only a poor little wooden cello, and it is your mighty sword. Avenge yourself!"

"I hope Camp Namequoit does a skit again," said Dodie. "That was really funny last year."

"Are you going out for it?" I asked Nicole.

"Me? No. I don't have a talent," she said readily, without any apparent regret.

A convertible carrying two couples, sitting close, passed us. Summer people. Otherwise the road was empty.

A trickle of sweat rolled down my back. "I'll probably get a new dress, one I saw in Watson's," I said.

"Really?" said Nicole. Interested.

Dodie turned to look at me, eyes widened in surprise.

"Yes," I went on, having captured Nicole's attention. "Bertha-Melrose and Tucker are getting it for me. For my birthday." This was more than I meant to say, strictly speaking.

"That's funny. My father says BerthaMelrose is the stingiest person in the whole world," said Nicole.

"That's an exaggeration." Curiously, I found myself defending BerthaMelrose.

"See?" said Nicole. "You agree. You didn't say 'you're lying.' You just said I exaggerated. Maybe she's not the stingiest person in the whole world. Just the western *hemisphere*." She had an exasperating knack for being right, even when she didn't know it.

"You'll see when they get here," I said for lack of a better answer.

"When?"

"For my party."

"Where are they staying?"

I wondered if she was worried BerthaMelrose would have to stay with them. "My mother is making reservations." I stepped over a patch of briars and bumped into Dodie. "They're coming."

Nicole raised her pinkie finger, arched her eyebrows, and uttered in a shrill falsetto, "Oh but I couldn't. My delphiniums are in bloom!"

It took me a second to realize who she was being. She wasn't imitating my grandmother. She was imitating Uncle George imitating my grandmother.

"BerthaMelrose isn't like that." I said, although she had her to a tee. Not the voice and the pinkie. But the delphiniums.

"My father says BerthaMelrose never lets Tucker come over for cards anymore. And they used to play all the time."

Even though my father was by rights Tucker's son-in-law, Uncle George was the one Tucker got along with best. My father wasn't much for poker. "Tucker can do anything he wants," I said.

Dodie was kicking pinecones without saying anything.

We walked on. Dodie, every inch BerthaMelrose's favorite— red-haired, near-sighted, with her soft teeth and allergies— Dodie hadn't said a word at all. The day was turning into a scorcher. BerthaMelrose would have done her gardening early. Her mulch would be raked, her delphiniums deadheaded, and now she'd be drinking an iced tea on her screened-in porch.

"Well," I said at last, "maybe Gloria will come." I wasn't sure why I said it, but it felt like I had just given in, made a concession. Admitted Nicole might be right about BerthaMelrose.

But Nicole's next words weren't those of somebody who knew she had gotten the better of me. Instead she was abrupt and grumpy. "Gloria's not coming."

Not smug. Not charitable. Just grumpy.

"She can't come?"

"She's just not."

"You mean she's busy?"

"She's just not."

Nicole was setting a good pace. We were more than halfway to town. It was starting to feel important to have Gloria at my party.

Then it hit me, and I didn't know why I hadn't seen it before. Aunt Fanny didn't like Gloria. Aunt Fanny didn't like Gloria, and Nicole was on Aunt Fanny's side. And it hadn't occurred to me before that Aunt Fanny *had* a side. Not one separate from my parents' or Uncle George's.

I looked at Dodie, who still had nothing to say. Her eyes were on the ground in front of her.

"Oh, I get it," I said, meaning to appease the fervor in Nicole's voice. For lack of something better to say.

And for some reason that was all it took. That seemed to satisfy her. Her expression changed from defiant to bored. She snapped a branch from a forsythia bush and swung it like a scythe at all the underbrush. She turned suddenly up a dirt road to the left and said, "Follow me."

I hesitated. Dodie itched her ankle with the toe of her sneaker.

"*This* way," Nicole commanded, while still managing to look disinterested. She obviously expected us to obey, even while she didn't appear to care one way or the other. That's what made her irresistible: our conviction that, whatever it was, she'd do it with us or without us. Her mesmerizing indifference.

Dodie shrugged.

I started up the narrow ruts behind her. It was the way to the town dump. I had been there often with Daddy. At the other end of the road a little spur ran into town behind the lumberyard. We walked for some minutes. Now Nicole's mood changed again. She led, swinging her arms and putting a little hitch in her step in time to a tune whistled in snatches through her teeth. As we walked I gradually became aware that some other sound was swelling over the hum and whir of insects. A rougher, insistent sound, which grew louder the closer we got to the dump. We rounded the last bend and Nicole held up a hand to indicate we had arrived.

"This is it," she said. She had to raise her voice.

A whole kingdom of garbage stretched before us. Thousands of seagulls clamored and thieved over acres of foul-smelling leftovers, shrieking over their greedy good luck. Bits of refuse littered the road.

Nicole stretched out an arm grandly, taking in the entire sight, and breathed deeply. Dodie shielded her eyes. The hot sun poured over us like melted butter. I bent over to pick up something that glittered near Nicole's foot.

"What's that?" said Dodie.

I blew the dirt from it.

"Garbage picker," said Nicole.

It was a little gold earring, squashed, like somebody had driven over it. Fake gold. I could see where the finish was chipped.

Nicole reached for it. "Let me see that." I handed it to her. She held it up close to her eyes for a minute, and then stuffed it in her pocket even though I was the one who had found it.

A pick-up truck pulled in and braked at the edge of the pit. A man in fishing waders got out and began tossing trash bags from the rear of his truck. Gulls flapped heavily into the air, barked at him, scattered, regrouped and settled again a little farther away.

I looked over the edge. Where we stood, fresh garbage came right up to the lip. Tin cans half full of slimy water, brown bottles, green bottles, clear bottles, broken bottles, newspapers soaked with engine oil, rusted bedsprings, old tires, a turntable that looked brand new, sofa cushions with the stuffing popping out, grocery bags ripped open and stained with grease. Everything nobody wanted left to molder in the sun.

"Here's good," said Nicole, motioning toward a scrawny grove of locust trees back a few feet from the rim. She flopped down, felt her pocket, and brought out a fistful of matches. She reached in again and withdrew three cigarettes.

The man in waders got back in his truck and drove away, raising a dust that hung suspended, then coated our tongues and hair.

I looked at Dodie. She looked away and sat down beside Nicole, letting me know I was on my own. I sat.

Smoking had to get easier. Everyone said so. "You got three," I said stupidly, doing my best to deepen my voice to a more experienced, veteran-sinner timbre. Instead, it squeaked out, the little mewling of someone who still slept with a teddy bear and on occasion secretly rode an imaginary horse named Thunder.

She paid no attention to me. She divvied up the matches and doled them out along with the cigarettes. I held out the fleeting hope that Eddie's thumbnail method would fail to light a single match. Nicole struck hers on a rock. It fired. She lit her cigarette.

"Ahhh...." She leaned back against the tree trunk, one hand behind her head. She exhaled lazily.

"Here goes." Dodie lit her cigarette. She pulled on it, sucked in her breath briefly, and exhaled. Efficient. Unromantic. I gaped at her, deserted. She had done this before. My goody-goody sister with the Melrose myopia and her poison ivy complexion. My sister, a smoker. She pushed her glasses up her nose. They slid down again on a bead of sweat. She crossed her legs Indian fashion and began to pick at the skin that was peeling on her thighs.

Nicole was watching me.

I placed the third cigarette between my lips and struck a match with my thumbnail. Nothing happened.

"Magic Fingers here needs a light," said Nicole.

She reached over and took the cigarette from my lips and placed it between hers. She held the glowing nose of her cigarette to mine and dragged. Then she took mine out of her mouth, inspected the tip, puffed on it twice and handed it back to me.

"Uh, thanks." I watched the cigarette burn and felt Dodie's eyes on me.

A cigarette burns very slowly. I sat with Tucker once while he smoked a cigar on the bench next to the barn—a leisurely smoke by the finest barn in Hillsborough. Tucker had all the patience in the world when in possession of a lit cigar. He said a good cigar was the secret weapon of every successful politician (and he was a state legislator, so he would know.) Essential to getting elected. Which led me to ask him who he wanted for president. Tucker told me that the way a person votes was a profoundly private matter, one any responsible citizen kept strictly to himself. But if I was willing to give my solemn oath that it would remain just between the two of us, he thought he could see his way clear to confide in me and in me alone that General Eisenhower was his man. I, of course, was proud to have the inside line on the election and I took it as a real compliment that Tucker trusted me and me alone with his secret. I would have liked to have been as much Tucker's as Dodie was.

Nicole flicked the ash from her cigarette. "Well?"

I tapped off the ash from mine.

Finally I put the cigarette to my lips and pulled on it gingerly. Rolling my tongue back, I made space for the smoke, held it in my mouth and expelled it in a long thin stream. Flies buzzed in my ears. Smoke went up my nose. The garbage made little cooking noises. Bubbles breaking in a simmering kettle. The smell went up my nose and down my throat in a hot gust. I realized I had skipped both breakfast *and* lunch. Dodie had stopped peeling her leg and was watching me carefully.

Nicole beat time impatiently with her foot. "You didn't inhale. You have to inhale. No point in smoking if you don't inhale. Like this." She dragged deeply on her cigarette and inhaled. Then she leaned toward me, rolled her lips back and pumped out three big ropey smoke rings. Her mouth formed an "O" which dilated and contracted in regular spasms. She looked like a flounder.

"Oh," I said noncommittally. My head started to pound. My stomach clenched with hunger. My neck was damp and I was having trouble focusing on Nicole through the haze. "Oh sure," I said. I lifted the cigarette to my mouth. My hand felt heavy and slow.

"She inhaled." It was Dodie's voice, sudden, decisive.

"No she didn't."

"She inhaled. I saw her."

Nicole opened her mouth, then shut it. She looked at Dodie without moving. Dodie looked back. A standoff between Uncle George's favorite and Tucker's favorite.

And me. Daddy's girl.

Finally a pure white gull landed in the dirt beside Nicole's foot. "Beat it," she said. She picked up a handful of sand and pitched it at the bird. It moved a sluggish distance away. "Geez, the birds are retarded. It's from all this garbage."

"Yeah," said Dodie. "Come on. Let's go."

She stubbed out her cigarette. I did the same.

Nicole lodged hers against her thumb, aimed at the bird and fired it off with a flick of her middle finger. "Goddamn gulls." It missed.

We started up the road toward town. I breathed the woodsy air. In through the nose. Out through the mouth. We had about a half a mile to go, and it took that long before my legs felt solid enough to support my full weight.

We cut through the woods and came out at Livingstone's Pharmacy, where Digory had gotten a job as a soda jerk. He had a book open on the counter and didn't look up until the three of us were seated at the fountain. He had the hat and everything.

"What'll it be, Princess?" he said to Nicole with a facetious little explosion on the letter P in Princess. Digory was a bookworm with a mean streak.

"Three coffee frappes," I ordered.

He swiveled in my direction. "Oh. A high roller." His words came out as if spurts from a spigot.

"We'll take extra flavor," said Nicole.

"And plenty of ice cream," I added. I was working up the idea that the dump had been some kind of test that I had passed with flying colors. It had all turned out fine. Money in my pocket was making it easy to assert myself. In fact the three dollars were producing in me a somewhat euphoric haze of fraternity.

Digory flipped open the bin and began to scoop ice cream into the metal blender container. A little smirk lifted one side of his face. When he had added the milk and coffee syrup, he clicked the "on" button, then came over and planted himself in front of me. "So. Who's stronger? Boys or girls?"

"Girls," said Nicole.

Digory kept his eyes on me. "Girls. Right, Ace?"

I hesitated. I didn't know how I had suddenly become the focus of Digory's attention.

"Right, Ace?" he repeated. His teeth needed brushing.

"Right," I said to make him go away.

A miscalculation, because he placed his elbow on the counter, his face close to mine, and said, "Good. Then let's arm wrestle." He was positively gleeful.

"She didn't mean *brute* strength," said Nicole.

As far as I knew I hadn't meant *anything*.

"Of course, if you're chicken...." he wheedled.

I was chicken if I didn't wrestle and a sure loser if I did. Exultant, he removed his elbow and stood up slowly. His eyes flicked restlessly in random directions. He stopped the blender and poured the frappes. Now he was suddenly full of information about the movie, how scary it was. Nicole browsed through the shelf of perms, sipped her frappe, unconcerned. The Camp Namequoit bus pulled up in front of the theater. Boys in their camp tee shirts started to file off.

"Come on, the movie's going to start," said Dodie.

I finished my shake, unpinned my pocket and got out the money. Digory leaned over the counter so close I could smell his breath.

"It's so scary," he said, "last Saturday night a *grown man* wet his pants."

I started to get up, but he put his hand over the glass I was still holding. We froze like that a moment before I realized I could take my hand away. I pulled it quickly behind me. It felt like it had been in one of those mystery boxes where you're supposed to reach in and blindly touch whatever's inside.

"Oh, get lost," Nicole said and tossed her curls at him.

"Yeah," I said, summoning all my nerve. "Get lost." And I handed him the money.

He put his hands up. "It's on the house," he laughed evilly. "Candyface."

The Namequoit boys were already inside when we hurried into the darkened theater. The newsreel announcer was describing authoritatively in his familiar, fatherly baritone all the steps that our government was taking to manage radioactivity, infectious disease, the Red Threat, the fail-safe protections promulgated on my very own behalf. We moved cautiously down the aisle. Nicole prodded us to the front. Dodie went first, stopping every few rows to whisper, "Here?" Heads turned in our direction.

Nicole shoved me into the third row. I sat down next to a little boy smeared with chocolate and smelling of pee. Dodie took the seat next to me. A pool of Coke had dried on the floor and every time I moved, my foot made a loud smacking noise. The person behind me began to kick my chair rhythmically. My head hurt from drinking the milkshake too fast, and my stomach, now full, felt scrambled and sodden. All around me people were eating popcorn with a relentless, hypnotic chewing.

The newsreel ended and some boys in the back cheered. A kernel of popcorn hit me on the cheek. The titles started and a glassy-eyed young girl appeared, wandering in the desert all alone. More popcorn showered us; this time it landed in Dodie's lap. She turned around.

"It's the Namequoit boys," she said, giving them a cold, scornful shoulder.

I turned. There was the boy, Nick, three rows back. Canoeing-without-permission Nick. The j-stroker. He was slouched in his seat with one foot on the back of the chair in front of him. "It was him," he mouthed to me in the flickering light and pointed to the boy next to him. The boy next to him was laughing. Nick hit him in the arm and made a face that said, *He's hopeless.* I faced quickly front.

"Don't pay any attention to them," said Dodie.

I snuck another look. Nick was watching the movie. But before I could look away, he turned his bag of popcorn upside down to prove it was empty. To confirm future innocence. He smiled the smile of a mischief-maker, nothing like Digory's leer.

I tried to concentrate on the story. After the girl with the teddy bear, there was an elderly scientist and his levelheaded daughter—of whom he was very proud—and these gigantic, radiation-soaked ants that were living in sewers. Realistic monsters that made a ghastly chirping a lot like crickets, a sound all the more menacing for its familiarity. The police wore gas masks that made them look just like the ants.

The milkshake felt like a fist in my stomach. The air in the theater had become close and suffocating. My skin was cold, but at the same time I had begun to sweat, and my head throbbed.

James Arness tapped a cigarette out of a full pack, lit it and blew out a thoughtful stream of lung-blackening smoke. The harsh, burnt taste of tobacco scraped at the back of my throat. I shifted my feet and produced the smacking noise. I felt my stomach tighten. I pressed my hands together. I knew I could keep it down if I concentrated. I clutched my knees. I trained my eyes on the exit sign. That was what you were supposed to do if you were seasick, fix on a distant point.

My ashen mouth ran suddenly with saliva. The fist in my stomach liquefied and began to slosh this way and that. And then it began to lurch up into my chest. It twisted upward in spasms.

I leaned over to ask Dodie to let me out.

"What?" she said.

I started to climb over her.

Up, up a big wave. A towering, cresting wave.

A breaking wave.

And I threw up. Right into her lap.

"Holyshit!" exclaimed Nicole.

"Oh Lily. Oh no." Dodie sounded like she was moaning.

They got to their feet, scrambled to the aisle and started for the rear exit, followed by every eye in the place. I lunged after them and stumbled out, the whole humiliating length of the theater, past the Namequoit boys, past the usher, past the ticket booth and out into the blinding Saturday afternoon sunshine.

Dodie stood looking at the vomit glistening down her shorts and legs.

"I'll get a towel," I offered.

She made a sound of revulsion, unable to speak.

"That's disgusting," said Nicole, to whom words came easily. She talked the ticket lady into letting them back in to rinse off in the bathroom.

"Don't ever do that again," said Dodie over her shoulder as they disappeared inside. As if I had done it on purpose.

It was suddenly very quiet. The ticket lady stacked quarters in her booth. Alone, I leaned against the little iron fence that enclosed the pocket cemetery next to the theater and waited for everything to settle down and stop spinning. I would have given anything for a sip of Coke to take away the taste in my mouth. I noticed for the first time that I had a scrape on my leg. My mother wouldn't be by to pick us up until the movie was over. I'd be standing there waiting when the theater let out. When the Namequoit boys came out to board their bus.

Two nondescript gray eyes struggled to stay dry. I trained them on the headstone nearest me and stood there, I didn't know how long, before the mottled inscription registered in my consciousness. The writing was wearing away, but I could still read "Mrs. Thankful, wife of John Jarvis." She was seventy-two and eight months when she died. It didn't give the year. There was no explanation for why Mrs. Thankful had a different name from her husband's. I began to worry I looked like a loiterer, and so I studied another grave, pretending to have business there.

Little by little the trilling in my ears subsided.

My mother drove up just as Dodie and Nicole came back out arm in arm. She was early.

"You're wheezing," she said to Dodie with a quizzical look for why we weren't still inside with the rest of the moviegoers.

"No I'm not," said Dodie.

Nicole soon dashed any hope I might have had of down-playing my plight. She rushed to give a full account of every detail. "All over everybody." She pinched her nose. "You should have seen…." She seemed as if she could go on at some length with real enthusiasm, but my mother interrupted her.

"That will do," she said to Nicole. Nicole, with the squashed, fake-gold earring in her pocket.

My mother turned off the ignition. Her face was dimpled with anger. I wasn't sure whether it was on Nicole's account, or because I had wasted the movie admission by leaving early or because I had gotten Dodie's shorts vomity, and she had to make Dodie take them off before we got in the car.

She thrust an envelope at me. I recognized the handwriting.

"What did she say?" I said, hope wicking in me.

"You read it."

"Are they coming?"

"Read it."

I opened it slowly and unfolded the page. I read:

Dear Lydia,

We got your invitation. I'm afraid it is too hot this summer to make the trip from Boston. I'm sure you'll understand. The garden has been glorious, but now it's beginning to fade. The enclosed is for Lily, for her birthday. Would you see that she gets it? Tucker sends his best, as do I.

Love, Mother

Inside was a check for five dollars.

They weren't coming.

"We have a stop to make," my mother said in a clipped staccato. "Are you too sick?"

Maybe she was mad because my hint had been so underhanded and BerthaMelrose was forced to prove she didn't fall for tricks.

"No," I said in as bright a tone as I could falsify. I folded the letter and returned it to its envelope. Five and no/100ths dollars. I had two dollars and twenty-five cents leftover from the movie. I fought not to cry in front of Nicole. I looked out the window. Across the street a woman was wheeling a baby carriage.

My mother started the car. *I told you,* she would say. But I had to go and pin everything on false hopes. She let out the clutch and the car lurched forward. She wound out the gear and shifted with a jerk. Without slowing down she passed right by the side street with Ellis' Market, where I assumed her errand must be. She braked suddenly and turned sharply at the Howard Johnson's, neglecting to signal her turn.

She drove straight to Murray's. "You wait here," she said to Dodie and Nicole. "Lily, you come with me."

Inside, she stabbed at bolts of fabric with furious fingers. She snagged a callus on some satin. She ran her hand over the bumps on some dotted-swiss; rubbed an unknown cloth, puckered like an orange peel; crushed the polished cotton to see how badly it would wrinkle.

"Five dollars won't even pay for the *buttons,*" she said finally, biting off the last word.

Five dollars would have bought a barrel of buttons. That was when I realized she wasn't angry with me. Not over anything I had done at all. Dodie's shorts were ruined; I spent seventy-five cents on a movie we didn't watch. But she was mad at Bertha-Melrose.

Little by little the textures of the materials worked to soften her. The rise and fall of her shoulders slowed to a normal ebb and flow. I followed her from table to table, a little burr on her heels. And she gradually remembered that she liked the colors and smells and dust-devils of little low-ceilinged Murray's. She stopped at the pattern drawer. "What about this?"

"It's nice." On the cover was pictured a dress that looked a little like the one in Watson's.

"Or this?" She held out another.

Slowly it came to me that we were shopping for me. She was going to sew a dress. For me. A dress that was to take the place of the one I wanted so badly I schemed for it. And I knew this dress, for all her trying, would not be as good as the one in Watson's. I felt suddenly shabby. I would pretend it was better, of course. I reached a downhearted hand into the drawer and pulled out pattern after pattern, none the dress I had imagined. Finally I handed her one with a full skirt, scoop neck, a wide notched collar, and a sash that tied in a bow at the back.

She read the instructions. "I think I can do this." She scanned them again. "Yes. I think I can."

I watched her study the steps. I could see that she was trying to make something up to me. A dress, my dress, was taking shape in her mind's eye, and I shouldn't spoil it. Even though I already hated this dress. Hated myself for hating it. Pitied her that she would try so hard with so little and it would fall so short.

She helped me pick out the best organdy in the store—white, with small blue rosebuds—while Dodie and Nicole waited in the car. "A very nice print," said Mr. Murray. We bought matching thread, a zipper, a mother-of-pearl button and a length of narrow velvet ribbon to trim the neck.

As she was paying, she looked over her glasses at me and said, "Don't let Nicole get away with too much."

The five dollars plus the two twenty-five in my pocket almost covered it. We were a dollar and a half short, but my mother took it from the grocery money. She said we'd never miss it.

9

STRONG GALE

Beaufort Number 9
Wind Speed 47-54 MPH
slight structural damage occurs; shingles may blow away

*M*y mother had laid out the fabric for my dress on her bed, read the pattern, pinned the tissue-thin paper to the material, measured, then repinned and remeasured, and was steeling herself to make that first mortal cut, when Aunt Fanny stopped over with some bad news. Virginia Carman told her at her violin lesson that Mr. Metcalf had been in a car accident. Hit from behind by a refrigerated truck loaded with cod on its way from the Provincetown fish pier to Boston.

"Always signal your turn," said Mr. Metcalf when we entered his hospital room, as if in mid-conversation. "If I had signaled my turn, I'd be on the porch of Rose Acres playing pinochle this very minute." His skin was so transparent that I expected to see through to his organs, like the drawings in biology books.

Business was slow on the accident ward at Cape Cod Hospital. Except for a man whose bruised face looked like crushed grapes, Mr. Metcalf was their only customer. He was propped against pillows, his legs thin as Popsicle sticks under the sheet. He was encased in a plaster cast from his armpits to his hips. But when he saw us, his face scrolled through its variety of expressions—most of them radiant—as enthusiastically as ever. A hospital stay was a serious business, I knew. But he looked quite well. My mother made the drive all the way to Hyannis because she knew in all probability we would be his only visitors. He had a broken back.

"From now on I'm a confirmed signaler. Dear Lily, here I am, proof positive that everything that happens is an opportunity to improve oneself." He closed the books and music that littered his bed and handed my mother pencils, erasers, and his reading glasses.

She set the things on his table. "I'm so sorry about your injury." We had come prepared to commiserate with Mr. Metcalf over his misfortune. Now she tried to adjust to the unexpected buoyancy of his mood.

"Oh, but it's not so bad as it sounds. There's no *pain*. It will just take time to mend. A cracked thoracic vertebra." He spoke as if this was cause for some excitement. "Well, fractured," he corrected himself. "Not broken. In any case, not *severed*."

"Are you well looked after?" my mother asked, steering Mr. Metcalf from the uncomfortably intimate mention of specific body parts.

"Never better. This is the best thing that could have happened." He fingered the cast on his chest with his left hand and bowed the air with his right. "I've wanted to write a composition of my own for so long. Now's my chance! Now I have the time to do it. Six months. Right here. Flat on my back."

I could see my mother struggle with herself. Some part of her wanted him to succeed. But another part was thinking, How could he be so....*cheerful*? Still, she would not think it her place to discourage him. "Why, that's wonderful," she said out loud, leaving him to discover the hopelessness of his plan all by himself.

"I know what you're thinking. How could I possibly become a composer when I can't even get out of bed to sharpen my pencil? But music will *speed* my recovery, you see." He paused to let the truth of this sink in. And then he remembered that he was not a composer yet but still a teacher. My teacher. "But how's my star pupil? How's that Capriccio coming?"

"Fine." I remembered the jelly jar filled with marigolds I was holding, and placed them on the windowsill. "These are for you, Mr. Metcalf."

"Lily, dear girl. You'll have to finish the summer without me. I wanted to hear you play at the talent show. Good thing we worked so hard. You'll be ready. I know you will. But what about the high D? Are you reaching it? Are you remembering to take time to get there?"

And he asked me about the slow introduction. Was I pacing my ritard? Was I establishing enough contrast in the fast section? Extra bite with the bow might help. How about the sixteenths? Were they more even with our new fingering? I must be sure I was listening to the piano. Every note. That was my lifeline, he insisted. "You'll have to put on the finishing touches without me. This is the test. And I know you're up to it."

He patted my hand and, through his teeth, inhaled a wet spot from the corner of his mouth. "Come close. I have something important to tell you."

I bent over him. I had expected the hospital to be sickening in some way. Bathroom smells. Iodine. People not fully dressed looking weak and faint, making me feel weak and faint. The possibility of blood. But this was Mr. Metcalf. Lavender water and skin like fresh tracing paper Mr. Metcalf. Weak, but not faint. For the first time since we entered the room, I brought my whole self in.

Without waiting to find out what he wanted to tell me, I told him what had been troubling me from the moment I learned of his accident. "I don't know if I'll be ready for the show if you aren't getting me ready." Everything I had worked for seemed suddenly in doubt.

Mr. Metcalf looked at me a long time before he answered. The lines on his face deepened; his eyes grew sad. I thought perhaps he was in pain after all. Finally he said, as if it were self-evident, as if he could take no credit for it, "You are going to have to do it on your own, my Lily. You will be alone on that stage. But that was always to have been the case. And even if the accident hadn't happened, one day you will have to be your own guide. You must do it now, is all."

I stood transfixed, trying to take in that Mr. Metcalf was letting me go.

"Remember this. Music comes from here and here." He tapped his forehead with his finger and then clutched the span of plaster over his heart. "Head and heart. Head and heart. Prepare like a scientist. But *play* like a *gypsy*. When you rosin your bow and step out onto the stage, there are no limits to what you can say with your cello. No plaster cast holding *you* back."

He looked at me a moment with milky eyes and then with difficulty tried to change his position.

My mother bent to help him. "Lily is very lucky to have worked with you." She straightened his pillow.

My mother had noticed the get-well cards on his night table. She noticed that his pencils needed sharpening. She even noticed that his calluses were dry and took the tube of hand cream from her purse and placed it by his bed. But she didn't notice how Mr. Metcalf had drawn a little arc over the two of us, connecting me to him like notes in a phrase.

10

WHOLE GALE OR STORM

Beaufort Number 10
Wind Speed 55-63 MPH
trees uprooted; considerable structural damage occurs

The Atlantic was our ocean, and so we watched the heavens rise, not set. My mother said a full moon breaking the surface of the Atlantic was every bit as spectacular as any Pacific sunset (although, so far as I knew, she had never set foot west of the Catskills.) The August moon was her favorite. July was a bustling month, its heavens brisk and to the point. Constellations, compact and precise, etched themselves into the sky like acid on metal. August, however, yielded a watercolor moon, plump and languid, which emerged from the ocean with a lack of haste, as though it had gorged on too many clams dipped in drawn butter, too many blue-claw crabs and too many sweet ears of corn. We decided on a clambake at Nauset Beach to watch this drowsy, round-cheeked cherub peep over the horizon. The days were already growing shorter.

To please Aunt Fanny, who was suffering frequent headaches lately, Uncle George made a special trip from Boston midweek. Only Digory, who was washing dishes at the Southward Inn now, couldn't come. Uncle George arrived without Gloria this time, which would have pleased my mother more if it had been on account of a talking to by my father, proof my father could stand up to Uncle George. But there was no sign my father had spoken to him about it. Gloria had stayed behind simply because she was busy.

We drove to Wellfleet, turned east across the heath on a back road that wound through scraggy clumps of sandwort and poverty grass and parked at the dead end. From there we carried two picnic hampers, a thermos, three jars of home-squeezed lemonade, binoculars, cutlery and a container of Aunt Fanny's favorite pickles down the steeps of sand to the unregulated beach below, empty except for one surf caster way up near the lighthouse.

Uncle George and Daddy got to work digging a pit and lining it with rocks. They lay down a fire, a good hot one, to heat the stones.

At the water's edge Nicole and Dodie rolled up their dungarees and taunted the waves to catch them. They draped their arms over each other's shoulders, anchored to the ocean by their shadows long as ropes in the evening sun.

I helped my mother spread out blankets near the fire. I was sticking close, building on my belief that her mood had evened out somewhat. I thought the improvement was due at least in part to my determination to make a success of our Capriccio rehearsals. "It's coming along," she had said to me when we finished rehearsing at Aunt Fanny's only that morning after finally making it through the piece without a major mishap. Aunt Fanny by contrast seemed more upset over little things than usual. They settled themselves on the blankets and I stretched out on my stomach next to them and counted waves.

Every seventh was supposed to be a big one. The escarpment already cast us in shadow.

Daddy and Uncle George let the blaze die back and now they swept the embers aside. They spread a layer of seaweed over the hot rocks and strew clams over that. A final layer of seaweed, loudly hissing and snapping, topped off the "oven," a fumarole spewing clouds of steam. A two-man job.

They sat back down on either side of the fire, each with a cold beer, debating the necessity of frequent oil changes, reminiscing about the old Model T Grampy kept for farm work. Each rested an arm on one bent knee. Brothers. One with hair plentiful and dark, parted like a coffee bean down the middle. The other's beginning to thin, a weaker brew. Both normally combed and hair-tonicked, both now tousled. Daddy was handsomer than Uncle George. But they looked more alike than I realized. Except for the declarative length of Uncle George's nose and his high forehead, except for Daddy's scholarly glasses and his one wasted leg, they could be twins.

"I hear a little rattle when I play my violin," said Aunt Fanny. "I think it's only the G string. It comes and goes."

My mother murmured something indistinct. She poured lemonade into a paper cup.

"I wonder if it could be the string. I think it might be the string. I haven't changed them recently." Aunt Fanny was wearing a sweater even though the evening sun was still really hot.

"Gee, Fanny, I don't know. Maybe Weston...."

Daddy was trying to fix Uncle George's pocketknife.

"I thought it might be coming unglued, but I can't find any openings. I looked. I looked carefully. I don't think it's the glue. I hope it's not the glue."

I sat up. "Is it OK if I have a pickle?"

"Maybe it's not exactly a rattle. It might be more of a buzz," said Aunt Fanny. She fidgeted with the lid of her basket. "Pickles would be in here somewhere," she said absently and pawed the clasp. "If I can just get it open."

"Let me," said my mother and flicked open the latch.

Aunt Fanny's hand strayed uncertainly to her forehead. Nicole and Dodie ran past, kicking up sand. Aunt Fanny began to rummage through her hamper in search of pickles.

"Here, have one of these," my mother said. She opened a jar of gherkins from our basket and handed them to me.

"Because if it's the glue, I'd have to get it fixed in Boston," Aunt Fanny said, both hands fitfully rifling the contents of her basket.

My mother frowned. "That could take some time." She looked in my father's direction. Daddy sometimes had a way with Aunt Fanny.

I spotted Aunt Fanny's dill spears under a towel. "That's OK, Aunt Fanny. These are fine." I bit into a gherkin.

"Oh dear, I should never have left it out of the case. But I can't…. How *much* time?" Aunt Fanny banged the cover shut. Then she seized the hamper suddenly and shook it.

The three of us sat there, surprised. Little things, I'd been told, were the culprits that landed Aunt Fanny on the locked ward at Mass General. Things as innocuous as misplaced keys, confusion over dialing a phone number, a few days spent in bed when she wasn't sick, the use of all her violin music to start a fire in the fireplace. I couldn't think of what to say. My mother still had the screw cap from the pickle jar in her hand. She glanced over at my father and Uncle George—she would accept even Uncle George's help if it meant Aunt Fanny would stop scaring her, if she would just get hold of herself—but they were tending the fire. So she put her hand on Aunt Fanny's shoulder. "That's OK, Fanny," she said. "I've got pickles."

My mother's reassurance must have done the trick, because Aunt Fanny took off her shoes, arranged her feet under her and seemed determined to say no more about it. "Your piece is sounding very nice," she said to me in an effort to cover up her little outburst. "Debussy is one of my favorite composers." I caught my mother's eye. Capriccio wasn't by Debussy. It wasn't even French. "I was wondering if you'd play duets with me again? I could send for music."

I said *Yes, I'd like that,* and meant it. It got lonely, always practicing on your own. Aunt Fanny and I could help each other out. She sipped her lemonade. "You're a good girl, Lily. We must work hard to deserve whatever talent the good Lord gave us." It didn't seem fair that the good Lord gave Aunt Fanny so little when she loved it so much. She slipped into a reverie, humming softly to herself. My mother took out her knitting.

We had the beach to ourselves. Dodie and Nicole, searching for skipping stones, ponytails bobbing in sync, dungarees wet to the knees. Aunt Fanny, buttoning and rebuttoning the skirt of her shirtwaist dress. My mother, in her sun-bleached slacks, wanting to be the one to cheer Fanny up. Counting on inspiration to strike. Daddy and Uncle George, engaged in the precision art of seafood preparation, squinted identical squints at the sun-sequined water. The scent of sea-things rose from the cooking pit. The surf rolled in at pensive intervals, each breaker emerging, growing, cresting, reaching for us before draining back and disappearing into the formless expanse of ocean.

The sun was sinking.

All at once Uncle George pointed to a speck on the horizon, something glittering brightly and moving slowly to the south-west, trailing a column of smoke. An ocean liner, he speculated, judging by the way it was lit up when it wasn't even dark yet. Headed for the Sound. But my father said we wouldn't be able to see the shipping lanes from here; no vessel of any size would travel in so close.

"Where are those binoculars?" said Uncle George. "Lily, find those binoculars for me, would you?"

Whatever it was, it was winking out of sight. Uncle George

stood to get a better view. Daddy started to get to his feet but couldn't get the necessary leverage in the sand, so Uncle George stretched out a hand and pulled him up, his whole weight. "Fanny, you saw the paper. What's docking tomorrow?"

Aunt Fanny roused herself. "Docking? You mean ships?"

But Uncle George was busy focusing the eyepiece. "Two to one it's the Queen Mary."

Daddy shaded his eyes with one hand. "Save your money. Anyway it's gone now."

"You're right. I should know better." Uncle George lowered the binoculars. "Lily, don't ever bet your father. You'll get snookered every time."

Daddy, laughing good-naturedly, raised an innocent face. "Not true," he protested.

"Like the time your father was supposed to call me to dinner," said Uncle George, still pretending to address me. "Did I ever tell you that one?"

It was one of my favorites. I relished Uncle George's depiction of my father as a wrongdoer. It was so unlikely.

"You cooked your own goose, not me." My father fended Uncle George off, but he was laughing.

Uncle George (this was his side of it) went skating one Sunday when the hollow behind the potato field had filled with rain and frozen over. A misdemeanor because Uncle George understood full well that reading the bible and playing hymns on the piano were the only activities sanctioned on Grammy Grainger's Sabbath. Come time for dinner, Grammy sent Daddy to find Uncle George. But instead of summoning him promptly, Daddy gave Uncle George to believe dinner was still an hour off.

"Then do you know what my dear brother, *your* father, did?" said Uncle George, peering at me. Gathering his public into his fold. Daddy and I appeared to be the only ones listening.

I did know. "No, what?"

158

"He told Mother, 'I *tried* to get him to come. He just wouldn't listen to me!'"

Daddy laughed out loud.

Grammy made Uncle George pick a good stout switch from the lilac bush and his legs burned for days.

"You've got some imagination." That was my father's entire defense. The best thing about the story was how much they both seemed to enjoy it. I wondered if my father didn't sometimes wish *he* could have been the one to go skating on the Sabbath. I almost thought I detected some delight in this account of his wicked self just a little. And that Uncle George was actually indulging him. Wes, the impish one. Wes, the devil. Wes, who gave Uncle George a shellacking.

Uncle George put the binoculars away. They each took a swig of beer and positioned themselves again on either side of the fire. The Grainger boys. One always up to no good. Grampy Grainger's boy. Grampy kept a bottle of hooch in the barn supposedly unbeknownst to Grammy—*nothing* was unbeknownst to Grammy—for the occasional medicinal nip.

The other, Grammy's life's work. It was one thing for George to follow in Grampy's exasperating footsteps. But it wouldn't do for her Weston. Grammy had not lived a good life for naught, and she had other plans for my father. Plans that didn't include Uncle George. One of her sons, in spite of her best efforts, exhibited all the signs of a backslider. And one of her sons was natural born College Material. Then along came that awful sickness that nearly ruined everything. All those months my father lay with his fever on the sofa in the parlor of the house on South Main Street while Grammy gave him alcohol baths and fixed his favorite foods. A thick slice of ham baked with mustard, brown sugar and curdled milk. Potatoes from the root cellar, roasted in their skins and basted with butter. The tender shreds of meat from the freshly wrung neck of one of their laying hens.

Uncle George was left to his own devices.

Grammy, girded with the memory of two small graves in the Acaciaville Cemetery, and unwilling to accept God's will for her Weston, her oldest, who had promised to be so robust, Grammy loved Daddy more. She made no bones about it. And once he recovered, she saw to it that she had saved no ordinary soul, but one worth all the fuss. She didn't know exactly how his life would go, only that he should go far.

Uncle George pushed the blanket of seaweed aside with a stick and a pillow of steam rose from the clams underneath. He may have been jealous that Daddy knew Trigonometry, he may have been jealous that Daddy had more waterfront, but I had never guessed that Uncle George might be jealous of Daddy's polio leg.

"Now there's a mess of clams," said my father.

"No argument there," said Uncle George.

It was a miracle they liked each other at all.

We ate until the pit was empty and our stomachs were full. I tried a clam and discovered it wasn't as disgusting as I expected. Then we watched night fall around us. The storm-sheared dune rose vertically behind us, cutting us off from the rest of the world. Nicole lay on her back. One toe touched Uncle George's foot. She used Dodie's lap for a pillow. My mother had one hand on Dodie's foot and the other worried arm around Aunt Fanny's shoulder. Daddy sat shoulder to shoulder with Uncle George. I insinuated myself under his other arm. On that strip of beach— flanked to the east by the ocean that stretched for three thousand miles and broke in foam at our feet, and on the west by our slender arm of disintegrated rock that shifted with every storm and tide, overhead by the three stars of the elongate Summer Triangle—on that narrow strip of unregulated beach, everyone was touching.

Uncle George said he'd give a dollar to whoever saw the moon first.

"Whomever," said Aunt Fanny.

"For God's sake, Fanny."

Aunt Fanny brought a hand to her mouth. She seemed startled that she had spoken.

"There it is," said my mother. "There's the moon."

I wondered how that slice of brilliance could have appeared in so small an instant when I let my eyes wander.

"I'll have to owe you," said Uncle George.

"I don't want your dollar," said my mother.

"That's all right. Weston's going to owe me when we find out that really was the Queen Mary. I'll clean up on that one."

"I never took that bet."

"We may never know what boat it was," observed Aunt Fanny.

"It was a ship, Fanny," said Uncle George, "and my brother is a piker."

Aunt Fanny began to pack her picnic hamper. "Why...why...."

"Out with it, Fanny. What?"

Aunt Fanny knitted her brow, prepared a sentence, and then drew herself up. "Weston is very kind. I think you are being untoward."

Uncle George guffawed. "Untoward? Is that the best you can do?" He was positively delighted. "No wonder we can't get along. Lydia is my witness. I'm not *untoward*. I'm an out and out SOB, Fanny. I'm the real thing."

A boast everyone endorsed except Aunt Fanny, who said, "I think...what I meant was...it's just that if I had to send my violin to Boston, I don't know when I'd get it back."

"Good God, are you still fretting?" said Uncle George. "Come on. Let's go home. I'll buy you a damn Strad." He threw back his head, faced the streak of silver that now slit the ocean in half, and howled long and loud into the roar of the surf.

———

When my mother and I arrived the next day at St. John's Episcopal for the one and only dress rehearsal, a small group of performers were already gathered by the makeshift stage. A platform had been set up in the churchyard. Next to it stood an old upright piano that had been half carried, half rolled out from the Sunday school room. The group included about a dozen Camp Namequoit boys. The rector was sitting on the edge of the stage, and from a radio held on his lap came the excited, staticky voice of a newscaster. My mother set my cello under a tree and we joined the circle.

"The *Andrea Doria* went down last night," the rector explained. "Just south of Nantucket." It had collided with the *Stockholm*, a smaller ship owned by the Swedish-America Line.

The *Andrea Doria* was a jewel of a ship, we learned from the broadcast. Brand new, a floating palace, built to the latest specifications—no expense spared—and powered by steam turbines. Engineered for utter safety. Now at the bottom of the ocean. This was as grand a disaster as the Titanic, except there was reason to hope for more survivors, the accident having occurred so close to land. Practically in our backyard.

He bent his ear to the radio and then switched it off. "It will come in clearer later, when the signal switches to Boston. They don't know anything yet. People are waiting at the piers in New York harbor for rescue ships. But nobody knows anything. Nobody knows more than that."

The rector decided to say a prayer, and so we bowed our heads and while he prayed I said my own benediction for the *Andrea Doria*, the "darling" of the Italian Line, whose gilt and marble ballrooms, crystal chandeliers, lockers full of caviar and champagne, and perhaps whose jeweled and tuxedoed passengers were at that moment being washed by tides fathoms deep off Nantucket Island.

When he finished, even the Namequoit boys were quiet. The sky had started to cloud over. No one knew quite how to begin the rehearsal after so solemn a moment, but pretty soon the camp music director looked at the weather and said we ought to start. He played a couple of tentative chords on the piano. The rector went inside and the counselor mounted the stage to call out the order of the program. A tap dancer was first. Then a barbershop quartet. Someone had some magic tricks. Then me. And last, the Namequoit boys were to sing *There is Nothing Like a Dame*.

My mother found a bench and I sat down next to her. The boys were horsing around. One of them was doing an Al Jolson imitation. Then I noticed Nick sitting on a fence rail watching the magician assemble his props.

I leaned against my mother and waited my turn.

The magician had some trouble getting his table set up so that the tricks would work, and so I was called. My mother stepped to the piano and I sat on a stool in the center of the stage. I looked out at the people there. The tap dancer had left already. The magician was tapping on something with a screwdriver underneath his table. The camp boys were tossing a ball out in the street. My mother began the introduction and I counted my eight bars rest, as we had practiced at Aunt Fanny's. Then I dug into the Capriccio just as Mr. Metcalf had instructed me, trying to imagine the sound starting deep in my bones. It sounded scrawny, played outdoors, like the thin buzzing of insects. I forgot my fingering in the spot where the melody returned in a different key. But my mother kept playing, and even played my missing notes, too, to get me back on. And so I forged ahead without stopping. Which was what I thought Mr. Metcalf would have wanted me to do, since it was the dress rehearsal. When I was almost at the end, a few drops of rain fell. A gust of wind blew my mother's music from the piano, and the camp counselor shouted to one of the boys, "Get the tarp!"

I stood up uncertainly. People started rushing around. The rector shouted that he would open the sanctuary. I felt a raindrop and climbed down from the stage to put my cello away. Just then two boys carrying chairs bumped into me and knocked the bow out of my hand. I reached for it and the wind toppled my case. One boy stopped short and picked it up. It was Nick.

"Here. In here." He took my cello case and dashed for the nearest door.

I ran behind him and followed him hesitantly inside. The door slammed behind me just as thunder cracked across the sky and the rain started in earnest.

I fumbled with my cello and my bow and tried to catch my breath. We were in some kind of storeroom. The walls were lined with racks of hanging robes and shelves stacked with folded garments, some red velvet, others white satin with gold threads. They had a Catholic look about them, and the disembodied word *vestments* came to mind. For some reason I was focused on terminology, as if terminology could explain my present situation. I had never been in an Episcopal church before. I had never been in an Episcopal church with a boy I didn't know before. Not with any boy.

Nick leaned the case against the wall and pointed to my cello. "You should dry it off."

Rain sheeted from the outside eaves. I stood there, unable to move or speak.

"Then use this." He took off his t-shirt and held it out to me. "My dad's a bass player. You should dry it off."

I made myself take it from him. It was white, a little damp, and felt warm in the drafty room. Camp Namequoit abutted our land where the creek widened to the bay; it was a world not more than a ten-minute walk away. Yet we had never spoken to a single person there until the mortifying day Nick asked me if I got any 'bites.'

"I remember you from the canoe," I said finally.

I rubbed my cello dry and slipped it in its case. He didn't answer. He was surveying the contents of the room.

"Did you get in trouble that day?"

"No. I've been trying all summer to get sent home. But I never do anything bad enough."

"Why?"

"I don't know. They keep giving me one last chance."

"I mean, why do you want to get sent home?"

"Oh. They'd have to send me to my dad."

"Oh," I said, although this explained nothing. I loosened my bow and placed it in its pocket.

"My mom's on her honeymoon." Something flickered across his face. A momentary defiance that steeled his jaw. "And anyway," he added quickly, "camp is boring."

It took me a minute to understand and when I did, I felt immediately sorry for him. Gloria was the only divorced person I knew, but—apart from her—everyone knew that respectable people didn't get divorced. I was having trouble squaring this with Nick, who seemed perfectly nice. His t-shirt was balled up in my hand. I handed it back to him.

"I liked your dad," he said. The defiance, or whatever it was, was gone. "He seemed nice."

"Yours plays bass?"

"In a band," he said proudly.

"Maybe he'll come get you."

He started to pull his shirt on.

"Wait," I said. "You have a tick."

"Where?"

"Here." I touched it lightly, just below his shoulder blade, off to the side.

He tried to reach it.

"Wait a second," I said. "You're supposed to do it with a match." I drew a matchstick from the ample supply in my

165

pocket. (I had been practicing.) "You'll have to lift up your arm."

He did.

I drew back. He had hair under his arm. Not a lot. Some. Growing in a swirl, close to the skin.

"Don't burn me." Half teasing. My attention was riveted to the fine moss that curved like a nautilus under his arm.

I averted my eyes and flicked the match ineffectively with my thumbnail. Nick took it and snapped it once against his front tooth. It fired instantly. It burnt to his fingers while I gaped at him. He shook it out, lit another and handed it to me.

I blew out the flame and touched the embered head to the brown tick. "Didn't work."

"Just go ahead and pull it off."

"I'll try again." If you didn't do the job right, the head could remain embedded, sucking a person's blood. I got my left index finger under the hind end of the tick and lifted it away from Nick's back. He struck another match, blew it out fast and I pressed it to the tick.

"Ow!" yelled Nick.

"I'm sorry!" I dropped the match.

He bent around to me. "Just kidding," he laughed. The tick relaxed its hold and came away between my fingers. "Let me see the bugger," said Nick. His left arm dropped to my shoulder as he bent close. I could smell his hair. It smelled sandy and damp and near. He held still and studied the tick.

"It's a male," he said at last.

"How can you tell?"

"Males have suspenders. See?" He pointed to two parallel white lines down the tick's back. He held my fingertips lightly. Sun had bleached the tips of his eyelashes. "Females have a necklace."

I bent to look. His head came close to mine. There was the

soft hush of his breath. He smelled faintly salty. The freckles on his nose met my cheek. His hair brushed my forehead.

The door opened.

"Lily! I couldn't find you anywhere," said my mother. The rain had stopped.

I shook the tick from my finger. I had forgotten she'd be looking for me. My cello was still leaning against the wall. Nick was holding his balled-up t-shirt. Through the window I could see some boys wheeling the piano back to the main door.

"Mom. This is Nick." Nick, from a broken home. Nick pulled on his shirt. "He goes to the boys' camp."

My mother looked from him to me, to my cello.

Nick nodded at my mother and then me. "See you." And he left.

That night after supper we went to Aunt Fanny's to listen to the news on the radio. Most passengers had been picked up by rescue ships. A miracle. A navy transport and a tanker had taken some, as well as the *Stockholm*. The Swedish twin-diesel was damaged but seaworthy. But by far the greatest number of survivors had been taken onto the *Ile de France*, which upon hearing the distress call had reversed course forty-five miles out to sea and returned to the *Andrea Doria's* side. All night the great matron had beamed her searchlights onto the crippled princess, as if the strength of that tether could lengthen her life. All night she had sent her boats back and forth because the *Doria* listed so severely that her own boats were useless, had gathered the bewildered, the injured, the grieving, and, when the tether failed, had stayed to see the young ship go down. After the *Andrea Doria* rolled to her side, after her bow slipped beneath the surface, after her stern upended and heaved underwater leaving a whirlpool of debris, the *Ile de France* circled the spot, sounded her siren, half-masted her colors, and dipped her flag. The *Andrea Doria's* last rites.

Such were the reports. My mother listened more intently than anyone, and I didn't know what held her more in thrall: the young Italian princess or the Grande Dame who tended her.

For days the Globe sold out before noon. We hovered over the radio, sucking in reports of heroism (and cowardice) aboard the *Andrea Doria*. Convinced, as we were, that we had seen her from Nauset Beach, all lit up and steaming full throttle toward her destiny only hours before the collision, we followed the news as closely as if the accident had happened in our own pond. As if we had a personal stake in the fate of all the passengers, from the beaded and gloved martini-drinkers in first-class to the smudged, tubercular immigrants in steerage. The captain, whom I pictured with a small, inconsequential limp, had refused to board the last lifeboat. He intended to go down with his ship, as captains were supposed to do. But he was so well thought of, so loved by the crew, that his officers threatened to remain on board with him, also to drown, if he didn't permit himself to be taken from the bridge. And so he sacrificed his honor to save their lives, for the sake of their wives, mothers and children.

The most miraculous story was that of a fourteen-year-old girl who had been sleeping when the crash occurred. When it ripped into the *Andrea Doria*, the prow of the *Stockholm* slid right under the girl's berth. She should have been mangled by tons of steel. Her body should have dropped into the sea through the gaping hole left when the *Stockholm's* powerful reverse engines wrenched the ship away, grinding and scraping along the hull of the *Andrea Doria* with a terrible noise. But when the two ships broke apart, she had been deposited on the *Stockholm* forecastle, injured and unconscious, but alive. She was found by daylight in the wreckage there, the girl whose name mysteriously couldn't be located on any *Stockholm* passenger list.

———

Uncle George went back to Boston convinced he had won his bet with Daddy—*Andrea Doria, Queen Mary, what's the difference?* —and that Daddy, who denied ever taking the bet, wouldn't pay up. I complained to Dodie that Uncle George was always picking fights, but she said Uncle George was only teasing and if Daddy didn't mind, why should I? Which provoked me to needle her inanely. "If Daddy doesn't mind, why should I?" I sang. But there was no point; Dodie wouldn't engage. I almost thought she didn't have the energy.

A few days later, Aunt Fanny came over after supper to play bridge. Virginia Carman stood in for Uncle George. Aunt Fanny's violin teacher, a recent widow, relished a good card game, and the chance to escape her small house, so crammed full of memories and dusty stacks of music, African violets and pictures of her husband Roy that the rooms didn't have spaces, they had aisles.

The four adults sat around the little table in the Playhouse. Dodie and I played canasta in the tent until it got too dark to see. Then she lay back on her cot and pulled air in through her nose. Goldenrod, the last flower of summer, had started to bloom.

"Are you OK?" I asked, regretting how I had resented her earlier defense of Uncle George.

She nodded without breaking the tide of oxygen that rose and fell in her chest.

It was a windless night and we could hear the shuffle of cards and the cheerful clink of glasses. In the tent my only sister labored for a deep breath. I monitored her carefully.

"Grand slam," hooted Virginia Carman's falsetto.

"Get Mom," whispered Dodie from her cot.

Urgent feet hastened down the dark path to the Playhouse.

My mother laid down her cards and came. She gave Dodie a

drink of water and settled the covers around her while the game continued three-handed.

Dodie's throat whistled; her chest expanded and contracted.

"Are you going to get the doctor?" I asked.

My mother waved me off with a distracted hand in my direction, sat down on the edge of Dodie's cot and told her to pay attention. She told her to use her imagination to picture the air going in, a big stream of air, flowing in, then flowing out. Nice and easy. In. Out.

Minutes ticked by. In, out, breath as ragged and insubstantial as the selvage edge of fabric.

"Should I get another glass of water?"

But my mother was focused only on Dodie, as if the strength of her concentration could open Dodie's lungs. Nice and easy, she insisted. In. Out. My mother inhaled each inhale, exhaled each exhale. I watched, appalled at myself for begrudging Dodie my mother's undiluted attention, and offered up a small prayer in the form of a self-serving bargain: I would practice extra every day if God would just restore my sister to normal. And turn some of my mother's attention toward me.

Gradually the hunch of Dodie's shoulders relaxed. Her breathing slowed to a regular, even rasp, then a smooth rise and fall, rise and fall. Clear. Or nearly so. And she went to sleep.

My mother tucked the blankets one last time and stood up.

"Mom?" I hoped she would come sit on my cot for a minute, too. I wished she would tell me a story like one of Uncle George's. Something about when she was a girl, perhaps. Or when I was little. Something that made me as much hers as Dodie was.

"What is it?" It was a bright, starry night, crisp with hints of fall.

"Nothing."

"Dodie will be all right now. Go to sleep." And she was gone.

I lay there and listened to the crickets. Trills as unbroken as night. Tried to convince myself they were only crickets, not radiation-soaked monster ants in a movie. The moon seared shadows of pitch pines onto the walls of the tent, menacing strokes like jagged antennae. I listened to each intake of Dodie's breath.

"We did it! That's the rubber!" Virginia Carman's soprano.

I sat up and drew my feet, wide as the blade of an oar, under me. I pushed the hair, stiff with salt, from my eyes. My face was too broad, my eyes too sunken, my legs too short. But in spite of all that, for a brief instant I wondered if my sister ever wished she were a Grainger, like me. In the dim light Dodie's foot had come uncovered, her sculpted, slender foot. With one forefinger, grown thick with callus from practicing, I reached down and touched the bubbled skin of her poison-ivy ankle. I felt the crusted calamine lotion where the poison had wept, and then I pressed that infectious finger to my ankle, that narrow intersection of bone and tendon and artery.

The Playhouse door opened. There were good-byes. Mrs. Carman's Studebaker drove up the driveway. The Playhouse door closed.

Then I reached under my cot for the Windward Antiques fan. Six ostrich plumes placed there for safekeeping. Six extravagant plumes that had purchased my silence. A dollar a feather. I spread it open, a shield against the shadows, and placed it on top of Dodie's covers. Raising no dust. And I willed my sister not to suffocate.

Work continued on the house. Mr. Gill began to nail sheets of plywood to the roof rafters. We were still a thousand dollars short, a number that hung over us, ominous as a missing persons list. Dodie's asthma staged ongoing minor attacks, but nothing that required another miraculous cure such as the one my mother effected that night and for which she took no credit. What I thought had been a general improvement in her mood turned out instead to be a retrenchment. She was merely conserving energy while her resentments put down roots. The question of Gloria, the issue on which my mother had chosen to make her stand—for Aunt Fanny's sake—went unaddressed. Daddy was spending all day every day typing in the woods. Mornings, my mother went to play the piano at Aunt Fanny's. When she got back she drew the curtains—finished now, twelve conscientious stitches to the inch—and took long naps in the Playhouse.

My parents had stopped fighting about money. They had stopped talking about it altogether.

11

STORM OR VIOLENT STORM

Beaufort Number 11
Wind Speed 64-72 MPH
widespread damage occurs

A year is a symmetrical measurement. Round as a pearl and knotted from the next by a birthday. Mine marked the close of summer. Or nearly the close, when chlorophyll-saturated foliage hung heavy and sunlight took on an amber tinge.

On the morning I turned twelve, I woke up early. Dodie was still asleep. A sprig of hair fell over her cheek across the tip of her burnt and peeling nose. Sun was creeping down the side of the tent and I could feel the humidity as it warmed the dew on the canvas.

This was to be my day.

I got up quickly and rowed over to Nicole's to deliver instructions to come at five. There was a beehive of activity at Bunker Hill. Gloria was down to help Uncle George clean the boat. She said she couldn't come to my party, she had work to do, and anyway Fanny needed "breathing room." But she and Uncle George wondered if I wanted to take a boat ride after supper. They were going anyway, she said, and needed some weight in the bow.

At five sharp Uncle George anchored his boat off our shore and Aunt Fanny drove his fat Buick down our driveway, slavishly braking over every hump and scraping bottom nonetheless.

We ate hamburgers and store-bought cake on the picnic table under the pine tree. Uncle George gave me a Pablo Casals record and said I could come any time and listen to it on his hifi. Digory gave me a rock collection with specimens of crystals in a little clear plastic box divided up into compartments. From Dodie and Nicole I received a Lilt home perm with a note saying they would "administer" it, which made it sound like a vaccination. My parents gave me a real Brownie camera and two rolls of film with admonishments not to waste them. And Aunt Fanny gave me a packet of seeds for a garden. Her confusion was great because she thought she had bought foxglove. Was sure she had picked foxglove. But when I unwrapped it, the envelope was clearly marked "phlox," complete with picture. I wouldn't have known the difference. To console Aunt Fanny my mother emphatically declared phlox a splendid choice. But when she did so, I noticed that Aunt Fanny was merely befuddled, whereas my mother was genuinely concerned.

Then Uncle George said we'd better get going if we were going to be back before dark. Possibly we'd go all the way to Monomoy, but first we had to pick up Gloria.

"Are you hurrying off?" Aunt Fanny fumbled with a button at her neck.

"George wants to take Lily before dark," said my mother. She moved closer to Aunt Fanny. "But I wanted to ask you about your mother. How is Agnes?"

Uncle George signaled me to head for the beach and gave my mother a grateful look, which she returned with an accusing one. For making her turn on Gloria, whom she liked. For making her use Gloria as a test of my father's loyalty. And here was Gloria, direct evidence that my father had not yet told Uncle George it was wrong to bring her here.

But all this was lost on Uncle George.

We waded in up to our hips and hoisted ourselves—simultaneously, opposing sides—into his outboard. Gloria was waiting on the far shore. She was decked out in necklaces, bracelets and earrings like a ship in full rigging and did a little barefoot hula as Uncle George threw her a line and cut the engine. She held tightly to his hand as she stepped into the boat and settled herself, knees to her chin, bangles coming to rest, in the seat next to his, ten poppy red toenails in a line on a navy cushion. At last year's talent show everyone said their soft-shoe looked practically professional and would have won easily, except that it was a show, not a contest.

I sat in the stern. Uncle George took the wheel, standing up to navigate the twisted eddies of the creek until it widened at the boys' camp; then he sat down and pressed the lever until the sound of the motor rose a step and we picked up speed. Sailboats dotted the bay.

Gloria leaned against Uncle George. She gave off a sense of contentment with her perfume. "Oh my gosh, I nearly forgot." She pulled a small box from among her skirts and held it out to me. "For you, Kiddo."

I came to the slow realization she was giving me a present.

"Take it," said the no-nonsense Gloria.

I obediently untied the gold silk ribbon and handed it to her. Inside was a silver pin in the shape of a lily, stamped "sterling silver" on the underside.

"Oh, Gloria," I stammered. Something so fine, from someone so….jazzy.

"Just say thank-you and be done," said Gloria, gruff as a matter of policy. "Never gush. It's unladylike."

I wasn't sure whether I was supposed to hug her or not, but before I had to make a decision she ran the pin smartly through my collar and said, "It was just lucky I had someone to give it to."

Her full attention was a dazzling thing.

Ten scarlet toes—belonging to feet that knew how to dance the rumba and do a perfect cartwheel—found a spot on the dashboard. Gloria leaned back to catch the warm evening sun on her face. Hair cropped so short it required a single drop of shampoo, she liked to brag. Dodie and I were drawn to her, iron filings to a magnet. When she visited us once in New Jersey on business with Uncle George, she tucked her plentiful skirts up into her waistband and showed us girls that she could still do a perfect back flip, even at her age. Over she went in the front yard no matter who was watching, necklaces pitched recklessly, thighs glamorously exposed. "Lily, if there's one thing I wish for you, it's that you grow up to be a character," she once told me. "None of this dull sameness. Have the gumption to stand out."

We headed south leisurely, toward Chatham. Simpson Island slid by on the left, then Hogg Island. Uncle George picked out the channel with quick, casual glances. *Red Right Returning*, he told me, pointing to the markers. I stretched out across the stern, lay my head against the gunwale and let my hand trail over the side of the boat. The water felt warm in the evening air. Gloria's skirts fluttered against my leg. In the quiet drone of the motor their voices rose and fell.

At first they talked business. Accounts and deadlines. The light turned more golden and the sailboats thinned. Still we continued. Gloria moved her feet from the dashboard to Uncle George's lap. He had one arm looped over the wheel. With the other hand he massaged her toes.

Aunt Fanny needs breathing room, Gloria had said. And now

my mother had made Gloria the lynchpin in her litany of complaints against Uncle George. One she expected my father to do something about.

And for some reason it struck me all at once. *He was massaging her foot.* I had always thought no one mentioned Gloria because her presence was so normal. It had never occurred to me no one mentioned her presence because it was *not.* I had never seen Uncle George massage Aunt Fanny's toes. Maybe she wished he would but couldn't ask. And that was what changed my mother's mind: Aunt Fanny couldn't stand up for herself. She wasn't strong enough to put up a fight. Not like my mother's fights: unintelligible, ineffective. And desperate.

"How do you think Fanny is doing?" Gloria asked.

"I don't know," Uncle George sighed.

There was a long pause. The engine hummed without missing a beat.

"What if you got her a new boat?" suggested Gloria. Aunt Fanny's sailboat, with which she would not part, was so unseaworthy everyone called it the Lusitania.

"She doesn't want another boat. Anyway, she could sail a drawer with a handkerchief and a couple of clothespins."

Gloria murmured something I couldn't hear.

"Lydia's good for her," Uncle George continued. "But they'll be back in New Jersey soon. No, if it keeps up...." His voice trailed off.

When Uncle George checked Aunt Fanny into the locked ward at Mass General, Digory and Nicole had to go live with Grammy Grainger for six months. No one ever said a word about it. To spare her the embarrassment.

"I don't know how she puts up with my brother." Uncle George's voice was just audible over the engine. They weren't bothered about me.

"Don't be silly. Wes has always been good to Fanny."

"Not Fanny."

"Lydia?" Gloria gave a small, knowing laugh. "You wish she had married you instead?"

Uncle George shrugged elaborately. "It never got to that point. Tucker liked me. But she liked Wes. Right from the start. Then after she and Wes were engaged, there was one night.... I was in my cups. She took it as an insult." There was a long pause. "Tucker's not going to give them money. BerthaMelrose will put a stop to that."

"I hope you're wrong."

How often bleak news began with BerthaMelrose, could be inferred from the orderliness of her china cabinets or the precisely needlepointed cushions of her chairs. Could be found in the tight wording of her letter: *The enclosed is for Lily. Would you see that she gets it?*

Please.

"Oh, I'm not wrong about *her*. I can tell you stories about BerthaMelrose. She makes me look like the Easter Bunny. Am I right, Lily?"

I thought he had forgotten I was there. I shifted in my seat, stiff with the effort of reinforcing that impression. Then he began a story I had never heard before. A story Tucker had told him because he knew he could trust Uncle George to keep it to himself. A story Tucker had to tell *someone*.

Tucker's office was two floors above Uncle George's in Stanhope Street. One night they played cards so late he missed the last train so he stayed with Uncle George and Aunt Fanny for the night. When he got home the next day he found BerthaMelrose home alone. Lydia couldn't have been more than nine or ten. She said Lydia had tracked mud in on the kitchen floor, so she locked her in the barn. She said Lydia could track mud in the barn all she wanted. She could stay there until she learned to wipe her feet. "*That's* BerthaMelrose for you," said Uncle George.

"How long was she...? What mother would...?" said Gloria.

"I know." He said things about BerthaMelrose. He talked about Tucker. He described the barn. I could see my mother, a girl of nine or ten.

I made the story mine.

I could see BerthaMelrose, could see her polished and laced black shoes, her opaque, flesh-colored stockings, the way she stood stooped with her bosom resting on her waist. I could hear her say she had other things to do than mop the kitchen floor all day long. I could see Tucker's barn, the largest barn in the county and it took four hundred gallons to paint the outside. I could see the cattle door with its heavy hardware. Once used for livestock, but Tucker drove only his car through it now. I saw the cavernous interior. Looking up I could see the rafters receding into the dust-filled distance. Unused stalls along each wall. Overhead, operated by a hydraulic lift, a housing to cover his car so that bat droppings wouldn't eat the paint. Tucker was proud of his bats. He insisted bats only roosted in a tight barn. My mother would have been afraid of bats. She would be scared that their bony wings would get tangled in her hair. It would be silent in the barn. She would be crouched in a stall, listening for the bats. "Lydia," Tucker must have crooned. "Lydia." But she would be afraid to answer. Afraid he was as mad at her as BerthaMelrose was. At last he must have heard her whimper, and found her hidden in a far corner under an old horse blanket. With nothing to eat or drink since the day before.

"Lydia," Tucker would have whispered, shocked. He would bend gently over her, try to lift her while she promised, "I'll never do it again, Daddy, I'll never do it again," over and over. He'd carry her to the house, but she would have cried and begged him to put her down. Then he would understand. She was dirty, uncombed, had soiled her pants and could not go inside that way. And the weight of her wet dirty underpants would be proof of how much she had to be ashamed of. And so Tucker would have stripped her bare and washed her in the

179

chilly stream of water from the old hand pump, and wrapped her in a blanket and carried her to bed.

Gloria moved; her bracelets jingled. Uncle George had stopped talking.

"As near as I know," said Uncle George, "BerthaMelrose never spoke of it. Tucker made sure he was never gone overnight again."

I tried to shake that picture from my mind. To fix the bats back in the barn and roll the green door shut. But I faltered over and over on this one stunned thought: My mother was once *nine*. Or *ten*.

"Why didn't he leave her?" Gloria said at last.

Uncle George didn't answer right away. "I don't know. Why didn't I leave Fanny?"

I waited to see if Uncle George would answer his own question, but he didn't say any more. Gloria was sitting with her arms wrapped around her knees. An ordinary and lovely pose. Uncle George's hand hung loosely on the wheel. He looked in my direction, a little startled to see I was still there, trying to remember if he had committed any serious indiscretions. Reassured by my scrupulously neutral expression. "What do you say? Shall we see if we can make Monomoy?" He opened the throttle. The engine rose in pitch. Gloria squinted at the sun, low on the western shoreline. "We might just make it."

The landscape slipped past us: taffy-colored beaches, deep green scrub pine, silver gray cottages here and there. We passed a trawler with its wake of screeching gulls on its way back to Chatham fish pier. The shore became sandier, lower, sparser, and finally on our left, only a long sand spit. We followed it its length, farther and farther, until Uncle George slowed. We were alone now on the water as we rounded the end of the point. Monomoy. The tip of the Lower Cape. The light had changed to a watery violet, and as we followed the buoys out past land's end the sun sank behind us. Uncle George cut the engine.

"There it is," he pointed. "Don't lose sight of it, Lily. That's the last buoy before Spain."

I looked in the direction he indicated. In the sudden stillness one rounded post rose and fell with the swells of the water. It was the only visible thing. Everything else blended together. Behind us no distinction between heaven and earth. In front the horizon had given way to a lavender-pink liquid, connecting sky and sea. No up or down, no parallel or plumb. Streaks of purples and golds shifted over what surely must have been water or what surely must have been cloud, but I could not distinguish either. The boat rolled gently this way and that, afloat in the center of a world as seamless and as rainbowed as a soap bubble.

Gloria's hand came to rest on my shoulder. "I've never seen it like this," was all she said.

"Me neither," said Uncle George.

We drifted. Nothing had shape or form. We rocked gently with the surface waves and heaved more slowly with the pendulous rhythm of deep ocean swells that began far out to sea and gathered toward us.

Then the light faded sharply.

"I'm afraid we're going to lose that buoy if we don't turn back now." Uncle George cranked the starter. Silence. He cranked it again.

"What is it, George?" An edge to Gloria's question.

"Oh, she'll start."

The buoy now lay some distance between Monomoy and us. I squinted to sharpen its outline. The engine coughed and died.

"What can I do, George?" Now there was alarm in her voice.

"Put out the anchor, Lily." Uncle George had his back to me.

I slid past him to the prow and dug to free the rope from the spare life preservers. I shouldered the heavy iron anchor and threw it as hard as I could in the direction of the buoy.

We all knew that the line was too short to do more than slow our drift a little.

"Gloria, check the fuel line when I bring the motor up. And Lily. Keep your eyes on that buoy." They bent over the stern.

I held the buoy tightly in my sight. It dipped and blurred. I blinked. It tried to disappear. I willed it back. It rose and fell in the stillness. I stared harder. It winked at me. Finally it slipped into the sea, leaving not a ripple where I knew it must have been.

I felt the boat lurch as Uncle George yanked the starter. Twice. Three times. I dared not break his concentration. I wondered if we were near the spot where the Andrea Doria went down. I rubbed my eyes and peered into the watery distance. And all at once the engine's throb severed the silence.

The buoy peeked at me from impossibly far away. It led us safely to the channel, and Monomoy's sandy arms folded us back into Pleasant Bay. Gloria came and sat next to me. She drew me to her, lifted a layer of her skirts and wrapped it around my shoulders. I nestled against her.

I was twelve years old now. Not yet smart enough to think that Tucker might have been partly to blame, too.

Black shadows lengthened as we slit the satin surface of the water. Red right returning.

Home.

12

HURRICANE

Beaufort Number 12-17
Wind Speed greater than 72 MPH
devastation occurs

*B*y the end of August the walls were up, the house framed in, the roof on, and the whole structure covered with tarpaper. Word came from Tucker that he'd like to help, really, but it just wouldn't work out. No explanation was typed on his letter-head stationary. Nickerson Lumber had dumped a load of roofing shingles in the driveway and small-craft warnings were up for Hurricane Carolyn. Harbormasters cautioned the fishing fleet to stay home and boat owners to secure their moorings.

Carolyn sideswiped the Jersey shore on a Saturday morning, pounding the boardwalk towns but doing little damage inland. All day my father followed reports on the car radio. Everyone hoped the storm would miss the Cape and blow itself out to sea. But just when we began to think we could relax, Carolyn veered. She sashayed up the Sound, practicing her pirouettes. She flirted with Long Island, flicked her skirts at Newport. Then she dropped all pretense and took a bead on Nantucket and the Outer Shore.

Uncle George said we were in for a doozy of a storm.

My father said we'd see. Weathermen had a way of building these things up to make themselves feel important. He brought the dinghy well up on shore, though, and nailed shutters in place over the three working Playhouse windows. The little keyhole window alongside the door was too small to pose a danger.

All day we watched the sky thicken. We ate early so that my mother could get the supper dishes out of the way. By eight o'clock it was black as pitch. The wind had come up and there was a good chop on the pond when we went to bed.

Dodie asked if we could sleep in the Playhouse, only this once, but my father said there just wasn't room. The tent was snug and safe. We had weathered storms before and this would be no different. He wouldn't be surprised if it passed us right by.

I held the tent flaps together while Dodie tied them shut. The center pole swayed. Wind blew the walls out, then whooshed them in, out and in, like an old-time squeezebox accordion. Dodie made a point of acting unconcerned, and I did likewise. Nonetheless, we moved our cots together. We changed into our nighties and climbed under the covers. I lay next to her and listened for her breathing, but tonight I could hear nothing over the wind.

Sometime later a furious racket waked me, a spitting wind, a barking rain. I felt for Dodie. She was sitting upright on her cot. Rain drove against the tent from the pond side, then whipped us suddenly from the rear.

"Dodie?" I said.

"Go to sleep."

"I can't."

184

"Yes you can."

I saw her face in a flash of lightning. "Dodie?"

The wind was coming stronger. It ripped against the tent, then left a sudden vacuum as it changed direction and snapped the canvas from the other side.

"It's all right," she said. "Give me your arm."

She reached over and took my arm in her lap and began lightly to scratch. The reassuring drag of her nails against my skin. She scratched without extracting a promise to scratch her in return.

The storm continued to build. It wrestled us for our little square of ground. It tricked us with unexpected lulls and then erupted with new strength. Wind tore through the trees, hissing and hacking. We squeezed together on Dodie's cot.

Near midnight a bolt of black fury howled at us from across the pond. It sucked all the air from the tent. The walls collapsed in toward us, then ballooned with a roaring noise and exploded into shreds. The center pole buckled, fell and buried us under a snarl of sodden, cold canvas. I groped for Dodie. Grasping hands clutched mine. She clawed her way out from under and pulled me free. We dashed for the Playhouse. Rain pelted our nighties. The door swung open. My father was there in the sudden lamplight.

"I was just coming to check on you girls. You're soaked! Here." He took the towel from its hook.

Two high-pitched voices vied to tell what happened. Two high-pitched voices vied for sympathy.

My mother helped us change into dry clothes. A nightgown for Dodie. Hers. A shirt for me. Daddy's. My father put on his trousers and slicker and braved the rain to pull my cello from the tent.

"The wind went through here like a freight train," he said when he got back and we were huddled on the bed. My cello was all right; we'd worry about the rest later. Dodie had a scrape on her leg and I a small cut on my arm, I was pleased to note. Wounds to make my parents regret they made us sleep in the tent while they stayed warm and dry behind shuttered windows. I begged for Band-Aids, which were duly applied. Then my mother tucked us into their bed and told us to go back to sleep.

Dodie fidgeted first with the pillow, then with her damp hair, which smelled sweetly of soap and honeysuckle. She closed compliant eyes. I was not sleepy.

Light from the kerosene lantern flickered against the walls. Our little Playhouse seemed to me as good as a fortress. My parents sat at the table and talked, comparing worries. They took out each stone from the individual collections they had been harboring, dried it off and placed it on a pile between them. The pile grew higher and higher. Did we have enough food in case the roads were blocked later? Were we under any trees that might go?

The largest stone went unspoken. There was to be no loan from Tucker. There was no margin of error.

At first they kept their voices low, a quiet rampart against the night. I rearranged my father's sweatshirt, which had bunched up under me. Lightning flashed and leaked in through the shutters and the tiny window by the door. There was the bureau with a bouquet of sea lavender. Flash. The popcorn bedspread, crocheted square-by-square, and laboriously stitched together. Flash, flash. Two silhouettes either side of the lamp, taut with worry.

My mother asked how we'd get through the rest of the summer without the tent.

My father said the tent had served longer than we had any right to expect. "What we've got to pray for now is the house."

There was a short prayer-length silence. A moment to brace for the destruction of all he had built. My father wasn't normally a praying man. Dodie shifted next to me.

"Lydia?"

My mother didn't reply. She was busy adding up troubles. Measuring the depth and breadth of all that had gone wrong.

"Can't you say something? Am I alone in this?"

Say something. Say something *hopeful*.

She found her tongue. "You don't want to hear it." Then she said it anyway. "All our savings down the drain."

A look of disbelief on his face. Surprise at the size of her pessimism. For he knew from experience, after months of convalescence on the sofa in Grammy's parlor he knew with absolute certainty: it was always possible to recover. "It's not down the drain yet."

More silence. A skeptical silence.

"Am I the only one who cares about the house? Lydia?"

I watched from the corner. *I* cared about the house. Out there in the dark, wind-gutted rooms blistered with rain. I cared how many times Daddy had hit his thumb helping Mr. Gill hammer two hundred pounds of nails, one by one. I cared about the raised hearth, every brick tuck-pointed and trim, where we would sit in front of a warm fire. Halfway between a picture window facing the pond and a kitchen window facing the hill.

"It's been nothing but trouble."

Try, I thought. Try.

"Is that so," said Daddy. "Is that so?" Twice.

"Look, Weston, it's no one's fault." Now that ruin was a gust of wind away, she could afford to be charitable.

My father feigned a look of enlightenment. "Oh, I see! Except that it's not no one's fault; it's *my* fault." He waited for her to react. Her eyes had wandered instead over to Dodie and me. He began to stack up the arguments on his side. "Because if you like living like this, you could have fooled me. Anyway, the girls couldn't sleep in the tent forever."

"You girls should be asleep," she said. She lowered her voice and started her own stack. "There are other places we could spend summers."

My father hesitated, taken aback by this new direction. "Meaning...?"

"Never mind," said my mother. She hadn't decided yet just how high to escalate.

"Say it."

"Nothing." Then she decided to make her argument anyway. To put forth, too late, one ill-conceived proposition. In optimistic tones. "We could spend the summer at home. In New Jersey." The worst option. The option that spelled failure. The option no one wanted.

We could sail the ocean blue.... A silly hornpipe lodged in my head.

"Ninety eight degrees and traffic jams? Be my guest." There was a new sarcasm in his voice. Rain scoured the roof, slithered over the shingles, peeked in cracks, probed for weakness.

A look of uncertainty crossed my mother's face. She shifted in her chair while she cast about for a reply. Then she let down her guard, suddenly earnest. Almost pleading. "Weston, you never asked me. I never had a say."

"Say what you mean, Lydia." He had taken on an alarming persistence.

"You know what I mean." Her hands went from the table to her lap, to the table again.

"Then say it."

Sail the ocean blue....on a glittering ocean liner. I made up a new verse, but couldn't make the words fit the tune.

"What? What do you want me to say?" Then she settled the question of escalation. She decided on what she had wanted to say from the start. Whatever the consequence. "You had to be near George. You had to outdo George." She got up from the table and backed against the dish cupboard, putting distance between them in the cramped space. "You never say a word about the way he treats you."

"How does he treat me, Lydia? Can I be the judge of that?"

My mother snorted. "We'll lose everything, but you'll have the satisfaction of knowing you got the better of *him*." Flashing eyes dared him to say it wasn't so.

"So we're back to George. As usual." A new note laced with bitterness. "You won't be happy until George is out of the picture. You won't stop at Gloria, will you? It's really George you're after." Wind clawed the shutters. Looking for teacups to shatter.

"No. You're wrong." Her voice went cold. "George didn't do this." Enunciating with exaggerated patience. One hand reached for the shelf to steady herself. "You got in over your head. All by yourself."

Now my father was quiet. The fingers of his right hand worked a rough spot on the corner of the table.

I sat up a little. *Silver*. That worked. *...on a silver ocean liner*.

We couldn't pay our bills, my mother said. Speaking quickly now. Flushed with the friction of words tumbling over words, released in a torrent. Other people had *electricity*. Other people could buy their daughter a *dress*. She had been saving all her words for this night.

"Is that what you want? Is that it? Money? Because I'm not going to fight with you about it. Here. Take it." He came to his feet and wrestled with the dresser drawer. He withdrew his wallet and smacked it down on the table in front of her. "Take it all. Buy whatever you want. Just buy it."

Snap went the guidelines. Whoosh went the water over the decks. Tilt went the list to starboard.

A smile played over my mother's lips, a dreadful little smile, because she had finally gotten him to say exactly what he did not mean. "Well, that'll solve everything."

"No. You know what would solve everything? I'll tell you something. George is a saint compared to your mother."

When metal met metal, when twelve and a half tons of steel pierced twenty-nine tons of steel, what lightning sparked between them? What choked sound did they make?

"She's a selfish...." He had her backed against the cabinet now.

"My mother?"

Dodie, who had been perfectly still, turned her back to me and brought the pillow over her ears. I had forgotten she was there.

"My *mother*? This is *your* doing," my mother continued. "Too late!" Her head was tipped back, every inch an accusation. "Now what are you going to do?"

"Damn it, Lydia, I don't *know* what we'll do."

But she had said *you*.

He wiped his face on his arm as if he'd been doused with spray. He roused himself to say a different thing. Searching to make a better point. The same point a better way. "Lydia. If she could only...."

Listing. Taking on water.

"Don't you try to...." One hand gripped the shelf. The other plied the air in front of her face. A gesture as if fending off beating wings. Wings equipped with sonar. Highly accurate.

"Well, isn't that what this is about? Isn't it?"

"It's not *my mother's* fault." She tried to shoulder past him.

"Lydia!" He grabbed her by the arm and pushed her back in the chair. "She won't even come visit you. Face it. She doesn't think of anyone but herself."

"Let go."

When the *Stockholm* prow ripped open the *Andrea Doria's* starboard side, how many minutes did they drift, tethered to each other, before the *Stockholm* let go?

"Why won't you get it? She doesn't care about you. She's never had one generous impulse in her life."

"Why should she? Why should she bail you out?" My mother stood up and tried to pull her arm away. He wouldn't let go. Steel on steel.

"Because you're her daughter. Because people do that. Regular people. *Nice* people. But not her." He took a breath. A bolt of oxygen to fuel his words. "She doesn't care about the girls. She can't stand *me*. And she's *never* cared about you. She never wanted children. She never wanted *you*."

My breath stopped. My mother's arm went rigid in my father's fist. My father let go of her, his startled face frozen at what he himself had said. Even BerthaMelrose would not have delivered a punch so mean.

My mother took her chance and shoved him away from her as hard as she could. He teetered and fell back against the table.

"Damn you," she said between clenched teeth, barely audible. "Damn you," she said, louder.

A clap of thunder shook the Playhouse. Reverberated across the Outer Shore.

"Mama." I got out of bed. Dodie tried to pull me back. I wrestled myself free and went to her side.

"Damn you," she said again, shouting now. Eyes like boils. She shoved the chair at him with her foot.

A teacup rattled. One blue cup upside down on its saucer. To keep the flies out. To keep the dust out. Delphinium blue.

"Lydia."

"Too late!" she shrieked. She opened the Playhouse door and rushed out into the rain. She slammed the door. Wind blew out the lamp. She opened the door and slammed it again. "Damn you," she yelled.

No lamp to extinguish this time. No additional darkness possible.

Daddy went out, took her by the arm and tried to hold her. I followed. Rain fell like sheet metal. Deep rivulets poured down the driveway. I seized her other arm. She shook me off. She struck at Daddy.

"Mama, stop!" I screamed.

She wrenched herself away and yanked at the door again. Dark inside. Teacups chinking inside. A board from the sash came away from the flimsy screen. She tore it free and smacked it against the ground. Lightning flashed. Her face was twisted and wet.

I didn't know her.

"Damn you," she screamed.

She raised it over her head and blindly struck the ground with all her force. I lunged for her and tried to pull her down. My foot caught on her nightgown. I staggered. She broke free. I fell. She lifted the board. I lay splayed on my back. She looked at me. I couldn't tell if she saw me. The board hovered, midair. Her face contorted. I made a movement, something between reaching for her and flopping to one side, arms awkward as flukes. She hesitated. Her hand wavered. She rotated slightly to the right. Then I heard the board hit the wet ground. I heard something split. Sand spit into my nose, neck, eyes. I felt my forehead open. It ran warm and wet and thick with salt.

———

When I opened my eyes, Uncle George's Buick was idling in the driveway with the lights on. Gloria was pulling on my arm.

"Can you get up?" I thought she said.

Rain fell steadily, but the wind seemed to have lessened. Lightning came in spasms.

Uncle George had his arm around my mother, some distance away. She pulled away from him and started toward the beach. He drew her back. She was crying.

Gloria pressed a towel to my head and led me to the car. "... to Dr. Poole's," she mouthed.

More lightning and I saw Daddy emerge from the Playhouse wearing a slicker, car keys in hand. He ran a lost hand through his wet hair. Dodie, blurred, peered from the little window. Rain slithered down the windowpane in stops and starts so that I couldn't say which were the window's teardrops and which, if any, were hers.

I turned to Gloria, whose lips formed the words, "to the doctor." I looked back as she drove me up the hill. I saw it all in the momentary flicker of lightning: Daddy limping to the car, Dodie standing damp and still, Uncle George leading my mother back to the Playhouse, havoc on all their faces. It's the sounds I can't remember. The rain, the motor, voices: it was as if I were watching a picture with no sound. Except that over the scene, laid on top, moving in its own time, was my mother's music. Piano music, played slowly, that moved upward, hesitated and moved again. Chords that reached for something. All I heard was the music.

13

CALM

Beaufort Number 0
Wind Speed less than 1 MPH
calm; smoke rises vertically

"Does it hurt?" Gloria bent over me the next morning. I turned my head on the pillow. I was in Nicole's bottom bunk. Apart from Gloria and me, the place was silent and deserted.

"Twelve stitches," she said. "That's a nasty cut." It was still raining, but the wind had died. "As soon as you can, you should get up. They need our help."

I did not know that this blackness that felt like drowning was grief. It was almost a relief to attach it to simple destruction. *The first good storm....* "It's the house, isn't it?" I finally asked. A loss that could be weighed and measured. Counted out in pennies. To put from my mind that a larger loss, sadness beyond size, could burgeon in the small spaces between drops of rain. "What happened to the house?"

"The house? Nothing. What made you think that?"

"The main beam. I thought it would split down the middle."

"No, Lily. Goodness no! The house is fine." Gloria impatiently dabbed my forehead with a cool washcloth. "It's Fanny. We can't find Aunt Fanny."

I listened to the rain. Just like that, a reprieve and a new worry. One danger exchanged for another, and a third cataclysm that manifested itself in a one-inch slice of my forehead. For the first time I became aware that my head throbbed.

Gloria noticed my hand feel for the point of pain at my hairline. "Come have breakfast. I've heard Pablo Casals has a scar in exactly the same spot. Let's get you fixed up, and then we'll see what we're supposed to do."

I took a seat on the couch with the cat. Thoreau opened one perturbed eye. Outdoors the rain had turned everything to burnished tin.

"Why would she take a boat out in that weather? Even if she was upset."

I didn't know, but Gloria wasn't really asking. My presence in the room seemed to grant her leave to carry on a conversation that didn't require the involvement of another person. She took a bowl from the cupboard, shook cereal from the box and set the box on the counter. "I just don't see why she would do something rash after all these years."

I stroked the cat; loose fur flurried for a moment in the air.

"None of this would have happened, you know, if it hadn't been for the storm. I only got as far as *Harwich*. How was I supposed to drive to Boston in a damn hurricane?" She took out the milk, held the spout to her nose, sniffed, poured some into the bowl and put it back, all the while checking the window repeatedly. She motioned me to take the bowl, remembered after the fact to find a spoon in the drawer and continued, "She must have tried to get to your parents'." I reached for the spoon, but she held it fast. "You're going to hear things, Lily. If anything happens to Fanny, people will say it's because of me. But I swear," she let go of the spoon and motioned for me to eat my breakfast, "your Uncle George was just saying goodnight. It was no more than that. Fanny could see that." She glanced from the window to the clock and back to the window again. "Someday you'll understand."

This was what I understood: Gloria's ramblings were like a trail of crumbs she hoped would lead to blamelessness. Uncle George loved Gloria although by rights he was supposed to love Aunt Fanny. And as long as she was sharing Uncle George with Aunt Fanny, Gloria didn't have to worry about which part of him was hers; she had agreed to a certain apportionment. But if Aunt Fanny was missing, then so was the equilibrium.

And this: everyone was too preoccupied with finding Aunt Fanny to notice how hard my mother wished BerthaMelrose loved her; and until we found out Aunt Fanny was all right, no one cared that my own mother had herself gone crazy last night.

I finished eating. Gloria rinsed the bowl and dried her hands, little ablutions to keep her from picturing all the unfortunate ways Aunt Fanny's disappearance could turn out. Without make-up Gloria lacked her customary crispness. As if sensing this herself, she reached for her purse, took out a lipstick, applied three swift, firm strokes to her lower lip. She pressed her lips together, scarlet pincers to trap any and all panic inside.

"There now," she said.

She walked me down the hill to the freshwater spring, Aunt Fanny's spring. I was surprised Gloria knew about it. The rain had let up. She sat down on the storm-soaked bank and motioned for me to sit beside her. She took my head across her lap and began to ladle sweet, cold water onto my forehead with her hand as if she believed in the magic Aunt Fanny and I knew was to be found there.

Twelve stitches. What a coincidence, same as my age, Gloria said. Just twelve stitches; it had been a glancing blow. An errant bounce when the board hit the wet ground. An accident. She stressed this with a look. Head wounds bled a lot; it made them appear worse than they really were. Good thing she and Uncle George got there when they did. They had come looking for Fanny. She paid no attention that the water wet her shorts, ran down her leg and soaked the straps of her sandals. In between glances toward the house and listening for a car, she was intent on providing a convincing dose of hocus-pocus to wounds she couldn't quite assess.

Cold water trickled over my ears, chilled my neck and made my shirt all soppy. And it took away the burning from my forehead. When my forehead was numb, she took me back up the hill and told me to curl up on the couch until she got back. She couldn't just sit there and do nothing.

I listened until the sound of her car was gone. Before I left, I gave Thoreau a pat. A deep, satisfied cat-rumble vibrated from his throat and chest all the way to his tail, which twitched against his will.

The Lusitania was nothing more than a dory. A two-person craft at most, equipped with a single mast and a pair of oars for getting out of tricky spots. It was yellow with pale aqua trim, Aunt Fanny's cheerful, "Monet's garden" color scheme. Many coats of paint had rounded every corner and edge. Recognizable even if it were broken to bits.

I kept my sneakers on and eased myself into the water from Uncle George's submerged wharf. Overnight the pond had outgrown its banks. Higher not by inches but by feet. It slurped up bayberry bushes and beach plums, it licked at the trunks of trees. At first I bushwhacked along the uneven ground of the new, unrecognizable perimeter. But I was having such difficulty that by the time I reached Dr. Poole's, in whose living room last night I had sat still while he sewed up my forehead by candlelight, I decided to wade deeper, up to my waist and chest where the footing was easier. The black water tensed its cat muscles. It leapt uninvited over Dr. Poole's front doorsill. Barnacles with shells like needles on Mrs. Withington's dock clawed my arms and legs as I shinnied through the pilings. I had the idea to drag the Clamshell along as I searched, but when I reached our beach it was gone.

I made my way to the mouth of the creek, now a gaping maw regurgitating the sea into our little pond. The water was so high, it was hard to judge the tide. I took a tentative step to test the current. I felt it pull against my legs, tug me towards the bay and beyond. Everything I knew told me not to leave the pond. Everything I knew made me doubt I could get back. I pushed aside a thicket of seaweed and stepped into the current. It ran deep. I started to make my way up the creek. Gradually my legs adjusted to the temperature of the water, my feet felt the contour of the bottom through my sneakers. The certainty of my mission supplied a surprising measure of assurance: I could cover miles of shoreline, and eventually I would find Aunt Fanny tied up somewhere, waiting out the storm. I would deliver Aunt Fanny safely to my mother and earn a pardon for all that had transpired last night: for the meanness of my father's declaration that BerthaMelrose never wanted my mother, the certainty that she still didn't. For the flailing devil that took hold of my mother. For me, whose interference had made everything worse.

Already cold and hungry, I scrambled over rocks, around boulders. Unseen things scuttled from under my feet. I scanned both sides of the creek, the woods, peered into the roiled water. I found the Clamshell, upright and full of water, wedged against the old millstone, its rope trailing over the side. The anchor was missing. I decided to leave it there for now and continued. A step at a time, as Daddy had often instructed. Every step took me a step farther from the pond, our child-ocean cupped in its protective tidal pocket. Too small to swallow Aunt Fanny.

The creek began to widen out and open into the bay, still without a sign of a yellow dory with aqua trim. Not an oar, not a handkerchief, not so much as a cotter pin.

A steady drizzle had started and even though the temperature was warm, I began to shiver. A squadron of geese flew so low that I heard the click and whir of their wings. Sailing felt like flying, Aunt Fanny had told me once. She was always trying to get my mother to learn to sail. Another way to make music together. The flutter of wind, the rush of water, racing the big white clouds for the horizon. Funny that sailboats, from a distance, looked so peaceful. A peace that was all motion and sweep. My mother would like sailing, said Aunt Fanny. She played the piano that way. When my parents were first married, my mother used to time soft-boiled eggs by playing the Minute Waltz three times in a row. In her hands the Minute Waltz— Aunt Fanny let me in on this little secret—actually took under sixty seconds. As far as I knew, I had never heard my mother play the Minute Waltz.

I pushed on.

At the boys' camp the broad, rumpled surface of the bay opened before me. I couldn't see the far shore in the mist and drizzle. I hadn't stopped to consider how big the bay was or how unfamiliar the shoreline. "I can do ten more steps," I told myself. And another ten, like slow practice when the job, taken as a whole, looked too disheartening. I was nearing Viking Point, counting my steps, when I heard a shout and saw two boys in a canoe out in the bay towing something toward the camp. They were having difficulty. The smaller boy shouted again, his voice a bit panicky. I fixed on the aqua keel of a small, capsized boat the color of daffodils. The broken mast was being dragged by the stays. The boys labored closer.

Floating alongside, tangled in the rigging, there was another indistinct form.

They struggled to bring in their load. Their weight shifted, the canoe tipped, and they half-swam, half-waded toward shore. The yellow boat rolled. The mast twisted in the water and the bundle next to it shifted. A glimpse of fabric, dull with sediment, but unmistakably a glimmer of periwinkles, Aunt Fanny's bathrobe.

I charged forward, fighting for breath. The tide dragged at my legs. I carved my way through water thick as lava, slogged to reach Aunt Fanny, bursting with belated good deeds, bent on clearing up whatever little misunderstanding had sent her out into the night, even while I knew I was too late. Aunt Fanny's housecoat billowed out as two irreverent boys, changed by the gravity of their discovery, guided her reverently into shore. She floated facedown. They had dragged the boat, the mast, the rigging, but they hadn't brought themselves to touch *her*. The smaller boy ran for help. The other boy, Nick—not yet bad enough to get packed off to his father's—waited, awkwardly unsure whether his part was done. With frightened, horror-frozen fingers I grasped her and brought her toward me. Her bloated skin felt like sponge. My teeth began to chatter and I could not make them stop.

Nick knelt in the wet, coarse sand to free her from the ropes. I sat in shallow water and eased her over, face up. Her mouth was shades of granite like the rain-pocked water. Her lips seemed on the verge of speaking, poised to conjugate a verb or to say something unexpected. Her fern-green eyes had turned milky, all misunderstandings boiled down to a concentrate and sealed over with paraffin. Sitting in water to my waist, unable to control the chattering of my chin, I cradled Aunt Fanny in my lap.

Summer leaked away.

The possibility of absolution leaked away.

Safe haven, sucked out on the rip tide.

I imagined the boom had hit Aunt Fanny on the head at about the same time my mother struck me with the board—an *accident,* said Gloria—and that Aunt Fanny's relief was as great as mine to sink in to a welcoming blackness. Then, in the silence that followed, I held my breath because I thought I could hear music. But Aunt Fanny had breathed deeply. Had she felt the cool liquid as it filled her lungs? Did she hear music as her heart used up the last of its oxygen? Did she go to sleep just as I woke up?

Nick huddled close. With one arm he helped hold Aunt Fanny. To look busy. Or unafraid. His other hand went around my shoulders and pressed me to him. To still the shaking. I felt his clumsy, warm breath on my neck, the same breath that had teased, "Any bites?" He said nothing. I realized I was crying. Behind us people scurried, shouts went back and forth, blankets were brought, a stretcher was carried down the hill. But on our little soaked square—half in the water, half out—we were quiet. The bay lapped innocently at our legs, deposited grit inside my shorts. Heavy clouds lumbered over the treetops as Hurricane Carolyn, weary of the dance, dragged her skirts across Cape Cod, making her tired way north and back out to sea. I hugged Aunt Fanny to me. Her fingernails were clipped and tidy, violin calluses whitened the tips of her water-wrinkled fingers. I let Nick stay there with us, even though we didn't need him.

Until Uncle George was summoned, until Nicole and Digory arrived, until the ambulance finally took her away, Aunt Fanny was mine.

———

"Why did you vanish like that? Why did you?" accused my mother when we all finally gathered at Uncle George's that night.

Nicole huddled on the couch, giving the cat her undivided attention. Digory had disappeared into the sleeping porch. Uncle George sat at the table staring at Aunt Fanny's Bible open in front of him. He was supposed to be looking for verses Aunt Fanny liked. His highball went untouched.

"But she's all right. That's the main thing," said my father. Aunt Fanny was at the undertaker's in Boston, but I was here, safe and sound.

My mother looked up from the onions she was chopping. Then looked again, closer, as if surprised to find the crosshatch of stitches in my forehead. Her head shifted back on her slender neck, a miniscule but perceptible retreat to put space between us while she searched her memory. As if so much had happened since last night, she had to disentangle what feelings the sight of me aroused. I waited for a sign that of all the things she might grieve or repent, I might be one. Her eyelids flickered with what she found in the thin air obliquely to her left. I saw her weigh, ponder, prioritize. One firm final blink and both eyes landed squarely back on me. Warned that our little woes would have to wait. We were there to comfort Uncle George. We were there because we needed a place to sleep now that the tent was ruined. We were there because in the presence of communal grief, fighting would not be allowed. A cautionary look to say she understood her job and intended to discharge it to the best of her ability. Tonight she knew she would not be permitted to blame my father for what happened to Aunt Fanny because he could have spoken to Uncle George, but didn't. Because he could have gotten Uncle George to give Gloria up, but didn't. For tonight she would have to put the matter of BerthaMelrose aside. Tonight her job had nothing to do with me. All this she could save for another time, when we weren't at Uncle George's cooking supper, washing dishes, making our best effort to disprove that when the two shells of an oyster are split apart, the oyster dies.

Dodie set the table, I filled the water glasses. Someone called Digory. Daddy served up my mother's goulash: minced hamburger mixed with onion, corn and canned tomatoes. No one put a record on the hi-fi.

I watched Nicole pick at her plate and move all the pieces of onion to one side. I got up, went to the kitchen and poured three glasses of milk, took out the jar of strawberry jam and put a generous spoonful into each glass. Then stirred. Observed the jam yield and melt into the vortex formed by the swirling spoon. Tasted. Marveled at how delicious it was, what good a blob of strawberry jam could do. I carried the glasses back to the table and gave one to Nicole and one to Dodie. Then had a moment of confusion when I realized I should perhaps have fixed a glass for Digory. But Digory's inhospitable face warned off any gestures of uncommon courtesy on my part. It was clear he wanted no sympathy, no special treatment, nothing that would confirm he was the victim of a tragedy.

My father watched Uncle George's untouched plate. "You should eat, George."

"I'll have to go into Boston tomorrow. They already want to know what Fanny should wear." This was the first thing Uncle George said all night. His face looked puffy and bruised. "They didn't want to let me see her. What did they think I was going to do? And I'd already seen her before they even got there." He turned to my mother. "I said I'd keep her company, damn it, or else have her moved to another funeral parlor." They let him stay a little while, but for once he took no pleasure in getting his way. "I kept thinking she'd wake up. I shouldn't have let them send me home. What if she woke up?"

My parents exchanged uncomfortable glances, each inquiring of the other if it was best to humor Uncle George. Just for the time being, to get him over the hump. Or if it was better to insist right from the start that Aunt Fanny was gone for good.

"I should never have let her keep that boat. I should have known."

"George. No ship was safe last night. It wasn't the boat."

But I could see in Uncle George's face that Daddy's words, meant to absolve, had the opposite effect, for if it wasn't the boat, then what was it? Gloria. Uncle George himself. Or all of us. My father's failure to intervene. My mother's failure to speak to Uncle George herself. How we all assumed Aunt Fanny was stronger than she looked.

"I should sell this place, is what I should do. I've had offers." Uncle George spoke the words as if they were detached from any action which might be necessary to make this happen. His hands rested in his lap and looked as if they couldn't stir themselves to so much as sign a piece of paper.

"Sell?" said my father. "*This* place?" He shook his head from side to side as if by doing so the foreign body of such a drastic idea might slip into the right sized slot. "You know what they say about hasty decisions."

Uncle George looked incapable of haste. He looked incapable of activity of any kind. "No. What." He asked this without a thimbleful of interest. His blue tailored shirt, the same one he was wearing when he stumbled from his Buick that morning and rained down on Aunt Fanny and me like shards of shattered glass, looked like it had never, ever been pressed.

My father let silence roll in as a fog bank would, a thicker silence because it had once been filled by Glen Miller, by fractured violin playing, by stupid little squabbles now imbued with retrospective happiness.

Uncle George pushed his plate away. "I'm supposed to meet with the undertaker tomorrow. I just...." His sentence petered out. Deep creases ran from either side of his nose to the corners of his mouth.

"They've done this a thousand times, George. They'll know what to do." My father studied his bowl. When he made goulash, he always added freshly shelled peas if they could be had. He looked up at Uncle George's strangely inert face. "I can go too if you want."

Uncle George toyed absently with his fork. "Flowers," he said as if testing out a word he didn't recognize. "Flowers." Uncle George, the cunning owner of an operation as complex and demanding as the printing business now stymied by the necessity of flowers, closed one eye. He rubbed it to eradicate any images that might have lodged there. "I don't know about flowers." He stopped to regain control of the quiver in his voice. "Fanny knew about flowers."

Aunt Fanny may have lacked any promise whatever on the violin, she may have been an indifferent cook, she wasn't especially good at math (although downright smitten with numbers in the abstract), she wasn't stylish or witty or even out-going. But there was no question she had a feel for plants. She tended the flora in her garden as if they were honored guests. She fine-tuned the care and feeding of each individual, gave them pet names, hummed snatches of Beethoven or Mozart for their amusement and—she was convinced—their well-being. She made a point of studying the healing properties of certain plants, recommended chamomile for colic, milkweed for warts, primrose for coughs. She had applications for cowslip, lavender, hollyhocks. From time to time—with no fanfare—she provided my father with a poultice of this or an infusion of that, things meant to strengthen a withered limb, increase circulation or to soothe overburdened muscles.

Uncle George pooh-poohed Aunt Fanny's remedies, thought any kind of garden an indulgence. But tacitly endorsed the small medicinals she quietly supplied to my father. After the polio, when my father was well enough to return to fifth grade, my grandparents couldn't afford a wheel-chair, and so little George—younger by two years—had to wheel Daddy to school in the only conveyance available: a baby carriage. Daddy, a fifth-grader, got pushed to school every day in a baby carriage. They both insisted it had been an expedient—a welcome!—solution to a bad situation. Humiliating for both. It was a story Uncle George told once and never referred to again. Strong, invincible Uncle George: strong enough to spare my father further reminders that, growing-up, Daddy had been—like Aunt Fanny later—an encumbrance.

No one knew what to do with this crippled Uncle George, how to bring back the dynamo, or if it was even desirable to do so. My father got up from the table and came back with a piece of paper and a pencil. "Let's make a list. We'll start at the beginning and make a list of everything that needs to get done."

"For God's sake, Wes." Uncle George reached across the table, took the sheet of paper and crumpled it into a ball. "Do you understand anything?"

My speechless father sat down without a word, hurt to the quick because he was only-trying-to-help. And because, as Uncle George was now a widower and clearly suffered the greater injury, Daddy had to nurse his hurt feelings in silence, thankful that Uncle George had at least vitality enough to quarrel.

Digory began rhythmically to kick the table leg. Nicole, the only one who had been eating anything at all, emptied her mouth onto her plate.

My mother knitted her eyebrows into a single furrowed frown. "I can do the flowers." She looked up, held Uncle George's eyes with as much concentration as if she were carrying a very full pot of stew. My mother would not expect Uncle George to have the decency to shoulder his share of guilt. She wouldn't expect him to have honest emotions. She would have expected him to make a performance of his grief. She was prepared to judge the quality and degree of his mourning, and to find it inferior. But Uncle George must have caught her, like me, off-guard: I was entirely unprepared for genuine despair. "I can choose the flowers. I know what Fanny likes."

Uncle George's eyes reddened. The skin hung from his cheekbones in loose garlands. A single glistening wet spot appeared at the base of one nostril.

"Fragrant things. Heliotrope, lavender, roses. We'll see what's freshest."

Dodie slept in Nicole's bottom bunk to keep her company. My parents slept in the guest room, Gloria's room. It didn't seem right to take Aunt Fanny's room and so I slept on the sofa. Before I turned out the light, Dodie came in and offered to scratch arms, allaying my fear that a mere twelve stitches might have failed to live up to her expectations. "Tomorrow you and I are going to sleep in the new house," she said. "Daddy says he doesn't know why he didn't think of it before, now that the roof is on."

I should have been excited, or at least relieved, but I found myself longing instead for the scent of morning dew on damp canvas again, longing for all things to be as they were before the storm. In my dash for the future I had assumed that all change was for the better. "Aren't you allergic to sawdust?"

"It's all swept out." She didn't even mention my forehead.

I smiled. It seemed to be what she was expecting. But the stitches made my face stiff and it felt more like a wince.

"Who was the boy who walked you back?"

I shrugged. "Nobody."

Nick had stayed with Aunt Fanny and me until Uncle George claimed her from my arms. When a counselor brought a blanket, Nick draped it across my shoulders. Nick sat with me in the mess cabin while I drank a cup of hot cider. After Uncle George told me to go to his place—that was where everyone was waiting—and left with the ambulance, Nick offered to walk me. He squared his slim shoulders, he helped me over a fallen tree, he whistled off and on, he made my legs less tired, he didn't dwell on the stitches that scored my forehead. Nick said little, but he had known all the right things to do.

"Mom didn't like it," said Dodie. "On top of everything else."

"Why not?"

"He was holding your hand."

"So?"

"I'm just saying."

After Dodie left, Thoreau curled up on the sofa at my feet. I lay in the dark and listened to the rain. Nick *had* held my hand, somewhat stiffly, all the way home. I let him; it would have seemed ungrateful not to. I didn't know if he felt obligated, or if it made him feel helpful, or if he just felt sorry for me.

I hoped my mother would come in to say goodnight, could banish the memory of how it felt when my fingers sank into the swollen pulp of Aunt Fanny's body. I wished she could answer the question: What use was finding Aunt Fanny if it was too late? I listened to water running in the bathroom. I heard the toilet flush. I heard the bathroom door open, foot-steps, the bedroom door close. She hadn't said a single word about what happened before everything went black, not a word about the deep-freeze of BerthaMelrose's heart, nor about what I had done to make her rampage like the angry wind.

———

The next morning Daddy drove into Boston with Uncle George. My mother stayed to answer the phone that began to ring as soon as it was light. Digory accepted the Norgeot boy's invitation to go deep-sea fishing for the day. Dodie became Nicole's self-appointed valet, and the sight of their tight twosome engrossed in a restorative game of cards made it clear they had no need of a third. Aunt Fanny's, without Aunt Fanny, was like a garden without blossoms.

I rowed to our side of the pond, dug our cots out from under the ruined tent, let them air-dry and then set them up in the new house. Our big new house with an upstairs and a downstairs and a chimney with a hearth and a picture window facing the pond, yet I crouched our cots together in the corner closest to the Playhouse.

I knew I should practice. The talent show was coming up in four days. That was, if I was still going to play in it. The funeral was to be on Wednesday and so technically I still could perform on Friday. But when I asked my mother that morning if we could rehearse, she had gaped at me, appalled, as if the question was an affront to Aunt Fanny's memory.

I went to the Playhouse, careful not to cut myself on the raw edge of the broken screen door. It was dark inside and so I got a hammer and pried up the nails that held the shutters in place. I stored the shutters in the crawl space under the Playhouse, returned the hammer to my father's toolbox in the outhouse. Inside, apart from an overturned chair and the unmade bed, things did not look amiss. Cups and saucers which had drummed a devil's trill during the storm sat serenely in their accustomed places. My cello leaned against the far corner, where my father had left it.

I set the chair upright in the center of the room, unpacked my cello, rosined the bow and tuned the open strings. I turned the smooth ebony pegs, felt them slip under the tension of the strings, find traction and hold. I started with a scale. D major because that was the key of my Capriccio. D major because I felt as solitary and exposed as the full moon and D major was a sunny key, one with the potential to calm the dry wind that blew through the hollows inside me. D, E, F# and so on, three octaves up, three octaves down. Listening for Mr. Metcalf's voice, listening for my father's voice, trying to invoke Mr.

Metcalf's cheery encouragement or my father's studied advice, something to reassure me that after all that had happened there was still this one thing I could do, one worthwhile thing: perform with my mother. But I heard only the dullness of the isolated notes following one after the other in succession, rising, falling, leading only to the next repetition.

I had held onto Aunt Fanny as tightly as if she had been my own mother, as tightly as I had wanted to hold my mother to me, to prevent her from spinning off into the clattering darkness. I remembered that when Uncle George found Aunt Fanny and me, when he disengaged her from my clutching hands, I heard a sound, a moan that grew into a brittle wail, hovered, then rent and splintered off into fissured crevasses, a foreign, inhuman sound with none of the beauty of the fabled elegies heard at Blackfish Creek. Nothing at all like the whales' luminous and ghostly good-bye. At first I thought it was Uncle George's cry. But it had come from me.

———

Two days later we drove to Boston for the funeral. The funeral parlor was brick on the outside and satin on the inside. It was the last place Aunt Fanny would see before they closed her casket. The lid that covered her legs was heaped with roses, foxglove, violets, lily-of-the-valley, lobelia, jasmine and wisteria, all seen to—on Uncle George's behalf—by my mother, who under no circumstances would have defected and bought an impersonal, hot-house "floral arrangement" knowing, as she did, that Aunt Fanny would have been just as happy with a few sprigs from her broom bush.

BerthaMelrose and Tucker were there. BerthaMelrose brought a handpicked bouquet from her garden, which, she was quick to point out, was not at its best in late summer. She was wearing a gabardine suit, which looked very hot, and a hat with a net that came down to the bridge of her nose. She was more hunched over than I remembered and carried a cane she used as much for punctuation as balance. Tucker hugged Uncle George, kept one hand on his shoulder as if to transmit a degree of steadiness. Digory, wearing a suit and tie, made an ill-at-ease stab at shaking the hands of the thirty or so strangers who came to offer their condolences. Dodie stuck by Nicole, who slumped in a chair and only spoke when spoken to.

While people were still arriving, I watched my mother lead Tucker outside. Standing on the sidewalk she seemed to plead with him. I heard only a few words from the doorway.

Tucker: "...a *lot* of money...."

My mother: "I know....But...."

Tucker: "...your mother....I'm sorry...."

I saw her unquiet hands open, close, clasp each other, fumble at her neck, twist, fiddle with her purse, accept Tucker's folded white handkerchief, wipe her nose and eyes. Unable to succeed where my father had failed. Discovering for herself the limits of Tucker's love. All our remaining hopes now pinned on my father's dissertation, his ticket to a raise. Tucker brought his head close to hers. He said things close to her ear, shook his head, opened his hands in a gesture of helplessness, frowned, consoled, concluded, put his arms around her. And they stood like that, my apologetic but faint-of-heart grandfather comforting my defeated mother, ashamed because she would far rather have done without than find herself in the position of asking and being turned down.

Everyone said how natural Aunt Fanny looked, as if she were sleeping. I thought she looked waxy. There was no evidence of the bruises which the medical examiner said indicated she probably had drowned in the pond immediately after she set out. Wind and current must have carried her to the spot where she was found.

Pretty soon the pastor walked to a podium and cleared his

throat. He said what a good wife and mother she had been. He said we might be tempted to view it as an untimely, tragic accident, but that was only because our vision was too limited to understand God's mercy and wisdom. He did not say the word suicide. No one did, because no one would ever know for sure.

There was a spinet piano in the back of the room and my mother played Claire de Lune by Claude Debussy. Claude Debussy was French and Aunt Fanny would have liked that. Heads turned when Gloria came in just after she began. She sat in the back and left just before we ended with the twenty-third psalm. After the service BerthaMelrose, standing on the steps, rapped the ground with her cane and declared to anyone within earshot, "She has her nerve." My father looked quickly to see if Uncle George had overheard, then murmured something to placate BerthaMelrose. To everyone's surprise my mother interrupted in a furious whisper, "Oh for heaven's sake, Mother, Gloria loved Fanny." The only angry words I had ever heard her direct at BerthaMelrose. Her color deepened, her chin quivered, her fuming eyes held BerthaMelrose's without blinking. Bertha-Melrose's obvious displeasure was surpassed only by my father's astonishment as he gaped first at my mother's flushed cheeks and then at BerthaMelrose, who began to sputter but settled for an audibly vicious exhale.

Before we left the room so the undertaker could close the lid, my mother stood at Aunt Fanny's casket for several minutes. She let a smidgeon of irritation show when she straightened Aunt Fanny's already-straight buttons. Irritation that Aunt Fanny, whatever she might have intended, and being the closest thing my mother had to a sister, had got herself drowned. My mother would have guided her to safety. Would have tried, at least. I saw her take from her pocket a small flask of Evening in Paris, identical to the one on Aunt Fanny's bureau, unstopper the bottle and place a drop behind each of Aunt Fanny's ears. Two small drops, one of reproach and one of forgiveness. It was like a prayer, but even the right prayer couldn't change the fact that after betraying Gloria, she still lost Aunt Fanny.

Aunt Fanny was buried in a cemetery on a hill next to her parents. Their headstone gave their names and dates and beckoned in block letters, L'INVITATION AU VOYAGE.

———

The next day Uncle George made an effort to start getting their house ready to close up. He and Digory took the boat out at the town landing and winched it up onto the trailer.

When he checked his mailbox, the duets Aunt Fanny had ordered were inside. Bach. "You keep them," he told me. "She meant them for you."

I took the music. It was brand new but the edges were discolored as if it had sat on a shelf a long time. The twelve pages weighed practically nothing and I felt a prickling, a premonition that whenever I played Bach, Aunt Fanny would be there.

My parents began to tinker at setting things to rights on our side of the pond. They had put the wreckage caused by the storm on hold: the broken door, all reference to finances or the stinginess of BerthaMelrose. They started slowly, as if trying to find their place in a book they had set temporarily aside. Whenever I searched my mother's face for clues to understanding what had happened between us, her eyes scuttled away, burrowed in, sought camouflage.

No one mentioned the talent show.

A dour Nicole came over to help us rake up the tarpaper and debris strewn around by Hurricane Carolyn. All that roofing would have to be redone, Daddy said. But fortunately the damage was superficial.

My stitches, which Nicole only now seemed to notice, prompted her to ask, "Geez, Lily, what'd they sew you up with, fishing line?" It was the first emergence of interest or curiosity since Aunt Fanny died.

Dodie gave her a look.

"Well look at her. She looks like...."

"Just never mind," said Dodie. She headed in the direction of Triple Tree. "You coming?"

It seemed a good idea, if we were to start again, or continue, or whatever it was you did after someone died, to begin at Triple Tree, my touchstone for what mattered. Nicole and I put off raking and followed Dodie up to the knoll. In the clearing where the tent had stood, the twisted heap of canvas still lay on the ground. Water had puddled in the stiff folds. I poked the pile with my toe. Then Dodie gripped my arm and gasped. I looked in the direction she pointed. The hurricane had savaged Triple Tree; Nicole's branch was snapped off low at the trunk, leaving a jagged, flesh-colored gash. Lying on the ground, the branch was itself the size of a tree. The leaves had already begun to curl. It changed not only my tree, but the whole view to the pond and beyond. I did not know how this could have happened without my knowing. Now I thought I could feel the splintering of wood, could hear the heavy thud the limb must have made when it hit the ground, leaves trembling with the impact.

Dodie climbed and we followed her up into the remaining two trunks. Our tree took us in; it made space for Nicole on Dodie's branch. It had rained again that morning and so I placed my feet carefully on the slippery, wet bark and held fast to a branch overhead. We'd be going back to New Jersey soon. Seventh grade would mean making all new friends. I peered through the branches, across our pond, past Aunt Fanny's; leaned out to get a better view and lost my grip on the branch I was holding, which snapped back and doused us with raindrops.

"Oh great, Fizzface," said Nicole. "Now I'm soaked. Shit."

Dodie wiped her face with her shirttail. Her prehensile toes took her to a higher limb. Then she reached for a branch and tugged on it. Sprinkled again.

"What …." said Nicole. Eyebrows that for three days had shut out sympathy now crooked with consternation.

Dodie jiggled the branch she was standing on. "Come on Fizzface yourself," she said and jumped harder. Using her shirttail to wipe her pale face with the weak eyes and a mouth—not unlike mine, I noted—on the verge of laughing. "Come on!"

I made one tentative bounce.

"Oh shit," said Nicole and she began to stomp her feet. The tree vibrated.

Dodie climbed to a fork in the trunk, grabbing branches and jostling them as she went. Triple Tree burst with exploding diamonds. Nicole stomped and, for added effect, wiggled her behind. I laughed out loud. I tilted my head back and caught the droplets full on my face. Nicole shimmied and bounced. Dodie was clutching branches and shaking them as if they were pompoms. And our tree joined in, added its own rolls and flamadiddles, like soft snare drums. Made us a quartet.

Finally we slowed. Our laughs became twitters and then contented moans. Dodie climbed down to me. We sank into the trunk and gripped the bark, wondering what had possessed us. Then another round of laughter. Wet. Out of breath.

Almost content.

"Oh, that was funny," I sighed. Dodie rested against the trunk and I leaned against her leg. My hair dripped. My shirt stuck to me. We grew quiet.

"I'm hungry," I said finally.

"Me too."

Nicole, as if remembering why laughter was wrong, went slack as a sail without a breath of wind. Her smile wobbled and faded. Then she shook herself. "Hey, that was great. Let's do it again." Enthusiasm a trifle forced.

Dodie wiped her glasses on her shirt and resettled them on her nose. "We're supposed to be helping."

"Just once more," said Nicole.

It had always been hard to imagine that anything bad could ever happen to Nicole, she was so insulated by her pretty curls, her nerve, and Uncle George's pocket money. It was unnerving how quickly Fortune had turned on her. "We better get back," I said. Daddy would be wondering where we were.

Nicole clung stubbornly to Dodie's shared branch. "Then don't. I don't care anyway."

"Aw, Nicole," Dodie coaxed, one foot feeling for a foothold.

"Anyway, I'm going to Spain," Nicole reported with an air of having regained the initiative. "Until Christmas. My father's not taking Gloria; he's taking me." Proof she could wrest Uncle George from Gloria. Proof he loved her best.

"Wow." Dodie found her foothold.

"Spain," I said.

She monitored our reaction for a sufficient level of excitement and determined we fell short. "And besides...." She made us wait until she was satisfied she had our full attention. "My father got an offer on our cottage. He's going to sell it and lend the money to your parents. He said otherwise you'd go under."

A well-timed trump card. "We would not," I said staunchly, slow to perceive the good news hidden in the insult.

"How do you know?" asked the ever-practical Dodie.

"Your father was talking to my father." She sounded sure of herself. "My father said the Pope would grow a tail before your father finished his dissertation." Perhaps this meant Uncle George was starting to feel better.

Just then I heard my mother call me. I saw her through the woods coming up the path. I felt for my footing on the wet branch.

"Lily?" she called again.

"Yes?" I felt Nicole's victorious eyes on me.

"Could you come here, please?"

I hesitated, then decided to let Nicole have her little triumph. I wasn't sure yet how much I had lost in the last days, but I knew Nicole had lost more.

I climbed down and met my mother on the knoll. The sun was trying to burn off a damp haze. Pockets of blue appeared, wisped away, appeared again. Her hair was clipped back in a barrette. One wave had escaped and faltered at the brink of her forehead. She had on her faded shorts and a touch of lipstick. In the gray morning light she looked like an old painting whose colors have dimmed under an accumulated varnish of age and neglect. I tried to guess how much was still wrong between us. The hurricane already seemed so long ago.

She looked momentarily confused. Her face folded into itself, and then opened partway.

"I need you," she said.

We had not been alone together since the night of the storm. I had been unable to tell if that had been by design. "Yes?" I said once more. I felt a blush of hope begin to rise.

"I have to measure you for the hem." She meant my dress.

"Oh."

Her eyes scanned my face, stopped momentarily on my stitches, stitches we had not yet discussed. She lifted her hand and brushed the wet hair from my cheek. I held still. "Did you get some breakfast?"

"Yes."

"What?"

"Cereal."

"Oh." She paused to digest my answer. Eyes interested in something over my right shoulder.

"Did you know that blood isn't red?" she said. "Not many people know that blood is actually blue. It only turns red when it's exposed to the oxygen in the air. Did you know that?"

"No. I didn't." It sounded made-up.

She couldn't look at my stitches. She looked everywhere but. Her eyes examined something in the woods behind me, over my head, on the ground. Then I finally realized: her restless eyes were a gum eraser, hard at work erasing what happened. Rubbing out, rubbing out, until at last even the stitches left no scar. That was how I knew she was sorry. Sorry not just that I got hurt. Gloria was only partly right: at the last instant my mother hadn't meant for the board to hit me. She was sorry for the moment *before* that, a long moment, when she hadn't been sure.

"It's true. Are you coming?"

I followed her to the Playhouse. Daddy was replacing the screen in the door. He had a mouthful of tacks, which he extracted one by one and tapped into place with his hammer. My mother stood me on a stool by the window, placed a handful of pins between her teeth and began to pin the hem evenly all around. Below the knee, now, because I was no longer a little girl. The organdy fell in soft folds.

Hold still, I thought she would say. Or *Stand up straight.* But her lips were clamped around the pins.

They worked silently, side by side. It was evident that an armistice had been declared. They could afford to be cordial to each other now that money no longer threatened to foment a war between them, now that Uncle George was quitting the pond for good, now that Tucker had proven he could not be relied on to provide sanctuary or even some small amount of aid. They only had each other. My father had told my mother BerthaMelrose never loved her; my mother had said *Damn you* to my father. But each was still glad the other hadn't died.

I stood up straight and looked out the window. I had come to want this dress. I had imagined that my mother would zip me into it and fret over tying the sash in a bow with big plump loops, that she would straighten the collar and smooth the skirt. Then she would stand back and gaze at me and I would see in her eyes that she was pleased and that I was growing up. Through the window I could see a boat in the pond tug at its mooring. I could hear the sound of tearing cloth and splintered metal when the tent collapsed. I could feel the sting of Dr. Poole's needle and how my head still throbbed even now. I could feel the weight of Aunt Fanny's body pressing on her heart and lungs. I wondered why my mother needed to finish my dress at this moment.

I obeyed the pressure of her hands, which turned me slowly in a circle.

When my mother and father were finished, when they had emptied their mouths of pins and tacks, they stood in the doorway looking at me, my father positioned solicitously at her side.

"It turned out nicely," she said.

"It turned out great," he said in the voice of this new deferential truce.

I looked from one to the other. I stood on the stool, weighted with the evenness of the hem, the three yards of material in the skirt alone, the mile and a half of thread sewn—was it the full twelve stitches to the inch? I stood there fingering the sash, putting a crease in the fabric, Murray's best cotton organdy, and wondered what had brought my parents so close together there in the doorway, and left me standing so alone on this stool.

"You look beautiful," my mother said then. "It was worth it. Don't you think so?" she said to my father.

"Every penny," said my father. "Here, I'll help you down."

———

Dr. Poole took the stitches out just in time for the talent show on Friday. The ground was still saturated, but the sun came out. A ripe, late-season sun. Beach plums were deep purple. Twelve jars of wax-sealed jelly were already packed in a cardboard box for the trip to New Jersey. Queen Anne's Lace had started to dry on the stalk. Wild rose petals were giving way to the rosehips underneath. Trainees at Quonset Point were furloughed for the long weekend. The guns over Target Ship were still.

My mother helped me into my dress. I stood on the daybed to look in Daddy's shaving mirror. I had to view myself in sections. Frothy skirt, shirred waist, darts shaping the bodice over the surprising beginnings of a bosom. Unironed, only basted in spots, the collar asymmetrical because of a last minute shortage of ribbon: it was still the most beautiful dress I had ever worn.

When we got to St. John's, the stage was set up and the piano in place. My father had put a folding music stand in the car in case I wanted to change my mind and use music. He had practiced bowing with me. I was supposed to slide one foot back and bend graciously at the waist. All I had been able to muster so far was something on the order of a dogged little stoop.

Chairs were set up on the lawn. A few people were seated already. My mother picked a row toward the front and sat down.

The Namequoit bus drove up and Nick got off with the other boys. A woman in one of the folding chairs turned around and waved at him. Hair, glossy as a beaver pelt and drawn back into a terse bun, gold earrings clipped hungrily to flaccid ear lobes, nylons with seams and high heels, for poking holes in the ground. She patted the arm of the man next to her and he lifted two fingers to Nick in recognition.

I found a spot off to one side where I could unpack my cello.

My uncertain fingers fiddled with the latches. We had not rehearsed in over a week. Nor had I been able to locate the compass of Mr. Metcalf's voice inside myself. One thought— music or no music—did a little jig in my head. I opened the case, tightened my bow and rosined it. I plucked the strings. Still in tune. Nothing to do but go sit by my mother.

The magician, wearing a cape this time, put the finishing touches on his table. The Namequoit boys filed into their seats, swatting each other with sailor caps, which were to be their costumes.

Uncle George drove up with Nicole, Daddy and Dodie, all soberly aware of their obligation to cheer us on.

We filled a whole row.

I played a few bars of Capriccio mentally to see if I could remember it. My mother fingered imaginary keys in her lap.

The chairs filled. Pretty soon the camp director stood up and welcomed everybody. He announced that the tap dancer had dropped out, but Lester Cobb had agreed to step in and do bird calls instead. "And so without further ado," he ended. That was the signal to start.

Music. No music.

I had played from memory at the dress rehearsal. But a dress rehearsal was like an air raid drill; everyone knew it was fake. I could bring the music up with me and still play from memory. That would be the thing to do. But what if I needed to look, and couldn't find my place? No, if I used music, then I had to use it from beginning to end.

Lester Cobb's birdcalls, I had to admit disloyally, sounded much more authentic than Mr. Metcalf's Ruby Throated Warbler. And he looked like a bird too. His overbite protruded beak-like. When he whistled, he developed hinges on his long neck that allowed him to hold his head at surprising angles. And he went unnaturally long without blinking.

I turned around to see if I could see Nick's reaction, but couldn't find him.

The men of the barbershop quartet all wore matching plaid bowties. They didn't have a piano accompaniment; they found their notes on a pitch pipe and hummed a chord before starting each song.

I decided to use my music. Even if it meant putting a wall between me and the audience, as Mr. Metcalf had warned. Even if a translator—Sight—stood between me and the language of music. Only a small betrayal, hardly worth agonizing over when I needed this to work out with my mother. Failure would mean far more than simple embarrassment.

The closer it got to my turn, fewer details of Capriccio came to mind. The magician had ironed out the kinks and his act went without a glitch. When applause broke out for the last scarf trick, I went over to get my cello.

Eeny meeny. Mr. Metcalf won. I re-decided: not to use music.

My mother seated herself at the piano and gave me an "A." I tested my strings. I could sense her mentally prepare the tempo, unburden herself of distractions, release the weight of whatever was on her mind. I sensed her folding herself into the music she was about to play. She watched for my signal and began.

I counted eight bars and entered a little unsteadily on a low note and climbed gradually through the middle register. I worked my way up, aiming for a high dissonant fermata—the question mark that was supposed to set up the whole rest of the piece. It followed a difficult leap up the neck of the cello. I had practiced it over and over, just as my father had prescribed. Again and again I had over-shot. Finally Mr. Metcalf had stopped me.

"Lily. Lily. You mustn't keep that up. You are practicing *in* the mistake. It's in your mind, not your muscles. You must think about it in another way. Hear the note before you leave the one

222

previous. Above all, you have more time than you imagine. Take your time."

If there were, say, fifty people in the audience, that meant there were one hundred ears altogether. Two belonging to my father. Two for Dodie. And so on down the rows. All waiting for my high note. I steeled myself for the shift. Was it sixth position or seventh? My right hand tightened on the bow. The tone immediately tensed and grew thin. What would Mr. Metcalf do?

I took a breath and exhaled. The piano chord changed—my cue—and I heard a richer harmony than I had ever noticed before. I felt my mother connect her part to mine. I gave a little extra vibrato on the note before the shift. My mother gave me that extra millisecond. I prepared the height of my arm. I found the note in my mind and made the leap. A slide, not really a leap, taking time, more time than I thought I had, and still I arrived together with my mother on the high note. The dissonant note. I leaned on it. *Savored* it, as Mr. Metcalf was fond of saying.

Without dissonance, music was nothing. A stew without seasoning.

We held the chord together and then ripped into the presto. I forgot about having no music and when I did, I felt like I was hearing it for the first time, hearing what it wanted to say. The music told my fingers what to do. It snatched us up and held us fast in the blur of the tempo my mother had set. The scales and flourishes fairly played themselves. My mother's solid accompaniment adjusted, lifted my line; I felt her pivot and delineate the arc of each new phrase while she punctuated my rhythms with staccato harmonies. Nothing held us back. And I knew for one clear crystal moment that music was made up of magic, not notes.

At my last lesson Mr. Metcalf had said, "You'll never be good enough, Lily," and I cringed, not wanting to hear the truth I had dreaded from the beginning. But he continued, "None of us is.

Not the greatest cellist. Music is bigger than that. It's bigger even than the men who compose it. Devote your life to it and you still won't do it justice by half. I know what you're thinking. Why try, then?"

Once again he had anticipated me.

"Why indeed." He pointed to a volume of Bach. "Just look at that. There's enough there to occupy your whole life. Study it for ten years and you'll get cocky and think you've nearly got it. Another ten and you'll discover you have barely scratched the surface. But it does us the honor of allowing us to try. *Glorious music.*"

We dashed off the last three chords, three exclamation points to say we were done. To say I had known all along I could do it. I got to my feet and executed the bow Daddy had taught me, which was easier to do while holding onto my cello.

Everyone clapped, including—I noticed—Nick, who grinned broadly and clapped in big wide sweeps. Uncle George whistled loudly through his curled tongue. And even while I wrapped myself in the astonishing sound of applause, I felt a hole open up where the music had been. And when the applause ended, another hole opened where the applause had been. Already I couldn't remember what it had felt like when the music had taken everything over.

The hit of the show, hands down, was *There is Nothing Like a Dame.* Nick put a lot into it. He knew all the gestures perfectly, mugged and embellished, let us know he didn't take any of it *too* seriously. A born performer. But his father wasn't there to see it.

I looked for him afterward and spotted him receiving a red lipstick kiss on his cheek from his mother. His other parent. One of two. The one who brought with her a new husband whose erect posture denoted someone who wanted to be called "sir."

Uncle George, trying hard to put forth his jovial self, clasped my mother's hand, the hand that had just stretched for the difficult octaves. She let him shake it, her debtor's hand. Still grasping the music she leaned in towards him, a partial hug for a man who didn't want pity.

Dodie shook my hand, bashful because she had never done it before. Nicole said it sounded hard, which—strictly speaking— wasn't a compliment since Mr. Metcalf said my job was to make it sound easy. But it pleased me anyway.

Daddy—all smiles—said, "See, all that practice paid off. Next time will be even better." And in that moment I had an inkling it was not Daddy's sheer number of hours but Mr. Metcalf's little mental gymnastics that had made the difference.

I spotted Nick hanging around at the edges of our family. "You were good," I said to him.

"So were you," he said.

"Are you coming back next summer?"

He nodded.

"Me too."

"I'll take you sailing," he offered. An alarming prospect, but a year was a long way away.

"We're going now," said my mother at my elbow. She regarded Nick with curious eyes and, without waiting for an answer, steered me away. But not before he slipped a piece of paper with his address into my hand. A surreptitious act a little bit, I suspected, like a kiss.

After the show we all went back to Uncle George's for cook-ies. Suitcases and boxes filled the living room. Uncle George passed out individual bottles of ginger ale because the glasses were packed, and everyone walked down to the pond to watch the stars come out. Everyone but Aunt Fanny, of course, and my mother, who hung back because the music she had ordered from Boston had finally arrived. She wanted to try a few notes.

I started down to the beach, but changed my mind and went back to the cabin. Without noticing me, she started to play. Simple music, like a music box waltz. But the left hand played in one meter while the right hand melody wandered in another. The music was out of sync with itself. She was absorbed.

I liked the music. It wasn't as sad as Claire de Lune, which I now linked with all that was sorrowful. After BerthaMelrose stormed out on Easter, I woke up in the middle of the night to the sound of my mother softly playing Debussy downstairs. Light of the Moon. I got up without a sound and watched her from behind the banister. Tears slipped from her chin to the keyboard. Her fingers pressed the keys quietly, tenderly, and the notes slipped away into the night like dazed little fishes, released into murky water.

Now her two hands played their separate melodies, and when she spoke, she took me by surprise, because she hadn't given any sign she knew I was there.

"Hear this note?" she said. "When you are grown up, if you ever wonder who I am, I'm this note." She paused on one note and then continued the line.

It was a little note, unimportant as a drop falling into a puddle, and as quickly gone. It wasn't the highest note, or the loudest note, not the peak of a phrase. I don't know why she chose it, really, but when she played it, something inside me ruptured. The note pressed into me like a dressing on a wound, a tourniquet to staunch the flow of tears.

When she came to the end she turned and looked at me, almost startled, as if she had forgotten I was still there.

"Which one are you?" she asked.

"What?"

"Which one are you? Which note do you want to be?"

"I don't know."

"Well here, I'll start again."

And she played again from the beginning. Her fingers moved over the keys. I wondered how to choose a note to be. I wanted to choose *her* note, but decided she might say that was against the rules. Finally I picked a high one, soft, near hers.

"There. That's the one I want."

"This one?" She played my note, emphasizing it.

"Yes."

"OK. You be that one. That's a good one. See how it helps the melody move up? See how it bridges the others?"

Her hands found the notes without looking. She swayed ever so slightly in time to the music. She played on.

ACKNOWLEDGMENTS

Music has been my constant teacher, especially Beethoven Piano Concerto No 4, Andante con Moto (Chapter 12) and Ravel Concerto in G for Piano, Adagio Assai (Chapter 13)

My grateful thanks to Sea Crow Press: publisher Mary Petiet, for giving my book a home and editors Eugenia Nordskog and Janet Edmonds.

Thom Middlebrook, for his kindness and brilliance and his splendid cover art.

I am indebted to The Minnesota State Arts Board, whose support provided the gift of time and courage. And thank you to Ragdale and Hambidge Center for invaluable residencies that made that time fruitful.

Thank you to Anne Garton for including an early version of the whales chapter in the anthology *A Sense of Place: Cape Women Writers*.

Thank you to the Loft Literary Center for support in many forms over many years, to my writing firmament: longtime writing buddies, early readers and cheerleaders: Elizabeth Jarett Andrew, Carolyn Crooke, Mark Powell, Terri Whitman Pat Cumbie, Carol Dines, Carla Hagen, Alison Morse, Julia Klatt

Singer, Paulette Bates Alden, whose early trusted wisdom and gentle guidance benefitted my vision for the book.

To Karla Ekdahl and Siobhan Cleary for their generous and unflagging encouragement.

To Katherine Peck and Diana Peck, who teach me every day that nothing may ever come between sisters.

To my daughter, Hadley, whose own writing and love of literature convinces me that everything is possible, and to my husband, Dave Kamminga, whose love and support and steady presence makes it possible to fret and anguish safely over language and stories. You are the bedrock of all that's good.

ABOUT THE AUTHOR

Marcia Peck's prize-winning short-short fiction has appeared in Chautauqua Journal, New Millenium Writers (first prize), Flashquake (first prize), and Gemini Magazine, and elsewhere. She was a Glimmer Train Award finalist for "The Flavor of Borscht" and received a Pushcart nomination for her short fiction "Long Distance."

She is the grateful recipient of Artist Fellowships from the Minnesota State Arts Board, Loft-McKnight, and the Jerome Foundation as well as residencies at Hambidge Center in Georgia and Ragdale in Illinois. A cellist with the Minnesota Orchestra for her entire musical career, she is inspired by the rhythms and sounds of music echoed in language.

Marcia's love for Cape Cod has been a strong and deep current throughout her life. She and her sisters still return to the house their father built in Orleans. She lives in Minnesota with her husband and two very naughty dogs.

ABOUT THE PRESS

Sea Crow Press is an independent publisher committed to amplifying voices. In a rapidly changing world, we believe the small press plays an essential part in contemporary arts as a community forum, a cultural reservoir, and an agent of change. We are international with a focus on our New England roots. We publish creative nonfiction, fiction, and poetry. Our books celebrate our connection to each other and to the natural world with a focus on positive change and great storytelling. We have been building a literary community since 2020.